# THE LAST BATTLESHIP

OBERON UNLEASHED

THE LAST BATTLESHIP
BOOK 4

JOSHUA T. CALVERT

# 1

## ASTEROID DC-66412

Chancellor Theoderich von Borningen stood in front of the sleek shuttle with its four oversized engines and turned to face Major Heines. Four black-armored soldiers stood at attention behind the officer and saluted.

"Have a good trip, Chancellor."

"It won't be long," he replied. When Heines raised a questioning eyebrow, von Borningen smiled thinly. "Major, after twenty years our operation is nearly at an end, and I will no longer be chancellor."

"I understand, sir."

"Don't worry about the changes we face, Major. Those twenty years will soon be past, and you will be there to see it all."

"Permit me a private question, sir?" The officer seemed uncomfortable.

The chancellor nodded curtly.

"Don't you think you should lead the new age after everything you have accomplished here?"

"No," Theoderich replied immediately. "I may have chosen the difficult path, but my brother Ludwig is the last elected chancellor of Harbingen, and the new order is his accomplishment, I am merely a tool. Not to mention, he is the older brother. You know how it is among siblings. That hierarchy never changes." He nodded to the major, a man who had endured many years in the confines of DC-66412 with him, overseeing the Exiles' operations and spinning threads so thin that not even the whispering spiders of Federation intelligence had heard them vibrate. "Be of good cheer, my good Major. How does the saying go? See you on the other side."

Heines saluted even more precisely than usual, his chin jutting slightly forward, and his gaze slanted upward in the old Harbinger Fleet tradition.

Theoderich smiled, nodded, and stepped into his shuttle. The metal ramp sealed shut and hissed as it locked behind him. He settled into the copilot's seat and looked at the pilot, a young female lieutenant. Her intense raven-black eyes betrayed a mixture of nervousness and curiosity. Her sidelong glances in his direction spoke volumes about the weight of the moment.

For twenty long years, he had remained a mysterious voice in clandestine transmissions, the words vanishing as soon as they were received. His influence permeated through webs of front companies, conglomerates, pirate fleets, and underground organizations, yet his true face remained a mystery. The shadow chancellor in exile, hidden in the shadows. Only a select few knew his identity. This young woman, not more than thirty-five or forty years old, now saw the face behind the voice, and it likely sent shivers down her spine.

"Don't worry, Lieutenant," he reassured her, "we're on the verge of a turning point. The need for absolute secrecy is over."

"Thank you, sir," she replied somewhat stiffly. This new state was clearly foreign to her, and he couldn't blame her. If she had piloted for him a year ago, she wouldn't have gotten off the shuttle —at least not alive. That fact was nothing he was proud of, but the need to leave their network and its structures hidden in the shadows had meant life and death. A single person saying the wrong word would have been enough to destroy a piece of their carefully assembled puzzle. And what was a puzzle without all its pieces?

Their flight took them out of Harbingen's Oort Cloud toward the system's center, powered by the insane acceleration of four antimatter engines. That was one of the achievements of the blasphe-

*The last Battleship*

mous Omega, the nefarious AI that his people had voluntarily given over the reins of evolution. It was a sacrilege for which, ironically, the aliens, their archenemy, had atoned for on their behalf.

After twenty-two hours of running complex simulations in his nano-cerebrum, where he had spent more time than he had spent in reality for over thirty years, they reached the system's outermost planet, the ice giant Karl.

The blue ball was tens of times the size of Harbingen, and its atmosphere of ice crystals moved in endless hurricanes around the equator, which provided the perfect backdrop for the formerly deserted industrial stations in their lower orbits. On optical sensors, they looked like upside-down pylons with kilometer-long ice scoops on their undersides that tapped into Karl's infinite hydrogen reserves. The stations had used electrolysis reactors to convert it into drinking water for the outer system and continued to do so to this day. During their few inspections, which they had known about early on thanks to carefully lubricated officials in the right places, the fleet had found small communities of former mining settlers that had been left alone. Only then did real operations resume in a system that was once considered irrelevant and had been written off, economically.

Supply traffic, mostly by ion tugs that gave off virtually no emissions and were barely detectable to patrol ships in the inner system, had continued operating, feeding their secret shipyards in the Oort Cloud. Vast sums had flowed into them each year from their capital networks via disguised spending structures. The results of this gigantic effort had long since taken up station at S1 near the central star, and just waited for his command.

After the destruction of TFS *Braxis* and TFS *Gibraltar* by their saboteur, the system had been clear of uninvited eyes and ears. Besides, the Federation certainly had more pressing problems than a ruined core world—especially since its destruction had played into its hands by helping preserve Sol's supremacy.

The thought of Jupiter's aristocrats and corrupt politicians who had sold their souls through his network of straw men for even the smallest sums still disgusted him. It was incomprehensible to him that a society, even while immersed in a struggle for survival against despicable aliens who wanted to exterminate humanity, could produce countless individuals who thought only of themselves and their short-term advantage instead of striving for something greater that transcended their ridiculous little lives. It repulsed him.

Another twelve hours and they reached the flagship of the Exile Fleet, a heavy frigate of Harbinger design. It was obsolete by current fleet standards, but its officers were familiar with the technology that had been best suited to their limited training and maneuvering experience. Moreover, Theoderich had at some point stopped sticking his fingers into the top-secret research and development of the fleet. Military counterintelligence was extremely resourceful and he did not feel the advantages of more modern ships were worth the risk of jeopardizing the entire operation. Their development could alert the TIA and lead it to discover what was brewing in the shadows of their beloved Federation.

In the cockpit window, the *Redemption* looked like a cigar with flattened ends, crude and bristling with weaponry. Two destroyers hung behind her against the twinkling stars like parasitic fish near a shark. One of the hangar bays opened to swallow the shuttle. Chancellor Theoderich von Borningen tightened his robe of office with the golden cord at his shoulder.

"Good flying, Lieutenant," he said to the pilot. "Stand by for my departure. I may need you."

The young woman nodded, looking relieved. "Of course, Chancellor."

The ramp lowered onto a spacious deck where his host was waiting with two dozen Marines.

"A-tehhhn-shun!" one of the soldiers shouted. The Marines came to attention, shouldered their rifles, and turned their heads obliquely upward.

"Welcome aboard the *Redemption*," Pyrgorates greeted him with a flattering smile and a precise salute.

Theoderich had never liked the lickspittle very much, but Pyrgorates was devoted to the cause and had turned out to be his most valuable spy during the last two decades. He had a talent for combining good tactical skills with strategic foresight. At the same

*The last Battleship*

time, he was able to exercise the restraint and patience necessary when working toward something. Apart from that, he had the most combat experience in their ranks and knew a lot about politics.

"Thank you, Captain."

"I suppose you'll want to rest from your trip. I've had my quarters prepared for you and—"

Theoderich waved dismissively. "No. We have several things to talk about. Take me to a secure room and keep yourself available for the next few hours. Before I travel any further, there is much to be cleared up."

"Of course." Pyrgorates bowed slightly, his hairless crown gleaming in the hangar's cold light. "Follow me, please, Chancellor."

On the way to the shielded briefing room near the bridge, located in the heart of the *Redemption*, they encountered a crowd of busy crew members. When they recognized who he was, they looked at him with a mixture of awe and fear, saluted, and dared not move until he had passed.

Theoderich couldn't blame them, nor the ship's command, for not keeping his identity secret. It no longer mattered if they now knew the face behind the voice, for his path was about to end. Everything that came after that was just a bonus, a life of ease after the thirty-odd years he had sacrificed to the cause, the future of Harbingen and humanity. Could there ever be a price too high for that?

"This room is shielded by several overlapping white-noise generators," Pyrgorates assured him when they reached their destination.

Theoderich nodded and sat in one of the spartan seats. The fact that wastefulness and senseless pomposity had not yet found their way into the Exile Fleet reassured him. Pyrgorates's reports about that vain peacock Bretoni had constantly disgusted him and made him realize why it was so important that his plan come to fruition. A decadent culture like the Federation had only one future: inevitable demise.

He placed a holomarble into the projector in the center of the table and turned it on with a curt gesture. A flat overview map of the Harbingen System began to glow above the table. The system's star was in the center, surrounded by the rocky planets Hilde and Arngrimm, Harbingen with its remaining moon Kor, the asteroid belt, the gas giants Braun and Bohr, and the ice giant Karl near the edge.

"Report," he prompted the newly appointed captain.

Pyrgorates, apparently taken aback by his curt directness, quickly regained his composure.

"Of course, Chancellor. I want to thank you again for your confidence. I will use my new position as captain of the *Redemption* to avoid any deviations—"

Theoderich interrupted him with another wave. "Come to the point. I heard about your escape from Sol. You have once again demonstrated impressive improvisational skills, but you should be aware of why I came out of hiding. We have this one shot, and I sincerely hope my faith in you will pay off."

"It will, Chancellor." Pyrgorates's lips parted into a thin smile. "If I may?"

The captain zoomed in on the fragments of the moon Kor still orbiting Harbingen. The largest of them resembled a gray tooth with a flattened top. Closer zoom levels showed a hatch that measured 50 by 50 meters when open. There was a huge transmitting device like an antenna, on which an overlong telescope protruded. It made him think of a flower that had sprouted from desolate, gray regolith soil to open its blossom to the sun.

"Our space workers have completed their preparations and the engineers assure us it will work."

"Phase technology was little more than experimental even then. The Corps of Engineers had better be sure or the signal will continue to pass through this space light years after this part of the Milky Way is forgotten."

"They are in *very* good spirits after more than twenty years of work to refine the technology, Chancellor."

"What about the alignment? Is the data extraction complete?"

"Yes," Pyrgorates said with a hint of pride. "The Omega—or what's left of it—no longer holds any secrets from us."

*The last Battleship*

"How did you do it?" Theoderich asked in a rare fit of curiosity. Until now, his nano-cerebrum, even with its immense data storage clusters and neuron amplifiers, had been kept thoroughly busy pulling the many strings of his network in the Federation. But these strings were now lashed tightly together in one place: here in Harbingen. Until now, details important only in their results, had been a disturbance. Now they were fascinating. At least this one.

"I knew Sirion wouldn't give up until Konrad Bradley was dead. His hatred was overwhelming. His Achilles heel was not easy to discover, but the many years of working together eventually produced a picture clear enough to formulate an educated guess. At the very least, the fact that he had declared himself ready for the Bellinger job—one that was actually below his usual level of difficulty and below his pay—was the final test of my theory.

"But I didn't make the mistake of underestimating the traitor Konrad Bradley and his ability to throw unpredictable hooks and win people over. In addition, there was Bretoni's arrogance and his false sense of honor. He allowed Bradley books from his personal library into his cell, which I contaminated with sniffer symbiotes. I originally hoped he would give Bretoni the code in exchange for a deal. In the end, it was a chance discovery because he gave the code to Shadowwing, of all people."

Theoderich nodded in amazement. "A brilliant move."

Pyrgorates's smile grew wider and more self-absorbed as he mistakenly thought the chancellor meant *him*. Theoderich perceived him as devious and prudent, but not brilliant. He considered Bradley's decision, however, to take a leap of faith by imposing a burden on his worst enemy, who was vulnerable in precisely one place—his, albeit confused, sense of honor—an inspired move, even though he had and still did abysmally despise the former admiral for his treacherous loyalty to the Omega.

"Proceed."

"I returned with the code and immediately arranged for data extraction to be initiated at the excavation site. The antenna is already being aligned and power supplied. When it's ready, we'll be able to transmit for over six minutes." Pyrgorates licked his lips. "Has the chancellor decided yet what the broadcast will consist of?"

"Of course," Theoderich replied, giving the captain a disappointed twitch of his eyelid before continuing, "What about the other order I gave you?"

"The explosive charges." Pyrgorates nodded and called up a rendering of the excavation site. It appeared as a sprawling area of drills, state-of-the-art hoists, and twelve radionuclide monoliths that surrounded the entire illuminated area on the ravaged surface of his former home planet like mighty sentinels. Directly next to the main shaft rose the Palace of Unity, an intact mountain of columns and stairs protected by a force field that they were unable to penetrate.

*Yet we can undermine it,* he thought.

"Our scouts are getting everything ready, but it will take time to drill the appropriate holes for the charges."

"What about an orbital strike?"

"We don't know if the palace's automatic defense systems are still active. Since the force field appears to have a power source, we'd likely have to expect counterfire."

"Too much of a risk," Theoderich said, shaking his head. "Order the net jockeys to continue their attacks on the datastore in case we can't do enough damage. That way we'll at least disable as much of that godless AI as possible before we get out of here. I want you to report back to me as soon as the transmitter is aligned. And send me the coordinates we extracted from the Omega."

"Of course, Chancellor. If you will permit me a question?"

Theoderich nodded.

"What do you think we'll see?"

"The future, Captain." He knew his brother all too well. He knew Ludwig von Borningen would not turn the true Harbingen-in-exile into a rich, fat, prosperous state, but would maintain their pragmatic roots. This included not shrugging off the fate of their species from afar. Their compatriots would be ready; he did not doubt that. Determined on a future that was only a cry for help away, to know when the time had come to usher it in. "Before I leave, get me an overview."

Pyrgorates's eyes took on a cautious expression. He knew, of course, that Theoderich knew about every hair on his subordinates' heads. There was more information in his brain than in all of *Redemption*'s databases, so Pyrgorates likely thought this was a test.

He was right. The chancellor wanted to hear one more time how much the enemy knew—if they still existed—because he had not forgotten the incident where a smuggler's ship had jumped into the system and disappeared. How honest the newly minted captain and leader of the Harbingen operation was, to himself and to him, would be measured by how he responded to Theoderich's suggestions for preparing for the worst-case scenario. Of course, they were not really "suggestions" but orders, but that would also be clear to both of them. He liked to be prepared for whatever was possible, however small the risk. If they got to work quickly, they would have more than enough time to implement his plans. Then it wouldn't be a catastrophe, but a joy to welcome even the *Oberon* to its old home and *finally* put an end to her that was long overdue.

# 2

"A briefing?" Dev asked with a frown. He scanned the wood table where several glasses filled with scotch were waiting to slide down the nearest throat thirsty for amber fire. He was uncomfortable sitting on the leather sofa without his crew, alone with a slew of Fleet rats. The new Fleet Admiral, Romain Legutke, was a bag of bones who reminded him of a cross between a scarecrow and his father's middle school math teacher, a man they had always joked would eventually appear as a skeleton warrior in a reboot of *Army of Darkness*.

Despite his gray hair and immaculate uniform, the old officer seemed rather unimpressive at first glance. However, his watchful hawk eyes demanded respect, and he emanated a quiet but undeniable aura of authority. The moment he arrived at Captain Silvea Thurnau's quarters, he immediately became the center of gravity around which the gathered officers revolved. Thurnau was his exact counterpart. To be sure, in her ascetic appearance, with her wiry body and short, tightly tied ponytail, she resembled the admiral, yet her eyes were like flames in which a kaleidoscope of emotions flashed. She radiated a demanding restlessness that was fortunately held in check by her executive officer Nicholas Bradley. He had already had the dubious pleasure of dealing with Bradley once when the lieutenant commander had felt compelled to personally inspect his *Bitch* after they had stolen twenty coffins containing dead miners so they could sell their implants.

Well, *that* problem was now a thing of the past. The younger Bradley was no longer as cold and humorless as he had been during the inspection, but he still seemed incapable of smiling or appreciating a joke. If anything, he appeared angrier—for someone who seemed more robot than human—as if he was suppressing some smoldering anger or grief. It was probably related to the death of his father.

Also present was Jason Bradley, who came across as an attractive and paradoxically boyish version of his younger brother. However, he seemed strangely absent, as if his mind was somewhere else.

"A briefing is what you want, right? Well, we jumped to Sol a week ago and gave you perhaps the most important reconnaissance data in the history of the Federation, and all this time you haven't seen fit to consult me? To hear my first-hand account of what happened?" he asked with undisguised anger. Aura would have slowed him down now, but she wasn't here—which was his next problem. "Instead, you empty my hold"—*thankfully only the coffins and not the antimatter warhead in the shielded canopy under the table in the mess hall*, he thought—"keep us in dock, and won't allow us to leave our ship."

"You're a pirate, Devlin Myers," Captain Thurnau remarked. Nicholas Bradley seemed about to agree, but his gaze drifted to a row of pictures next to the bed on the opposite side of the large room and he closed his mouth.

"You must understand, Mr. Myers..." the commander continued.

"*Captain* Myers," Dev reflexively corrected the officer.

"You must understand, *Mr. Myers*," Bradley repeated sharply, "that your cargo, under normal circumstances, would mean the loss of your license, your ship, and your freedom, along with a one-way ticket to a penal colony."

"But these are *not* normal circumstances," Dev growled. A very quiet voice in the back of his head warned him against being too disrespectful, but he just couldn't help himself with these Fleet

*The last Battleship*

flunkies. They were as stiff as broomsticks and possessed twice the foresight. He drained his scotch—which was damn good—and poured himself a refill before they got tired of his loud mouth and locked him up after all. "Besides, I probably wouldn't be sitting here in this fine company if you didn't need me. So, get to the point."

"A briefing," Legutke said in a surprisingly deep, penetrating voice. It didn't sound as rough and hoarse as it did on the feeds he'd been appearing on for days, trying to convince people the Clicks were no longer the bad guys, and they now had a common enemy. Which wasn't easy to explain after 70 years of propaganda posters from the recruiting authorities and Fleet representatives inciting hatred in the populace to prepare people for more years of war economy and shortages that had made them all poorer. But the man was trying hard and certainly wouldn't die of inactivity, that much was certain. "I want you to give us a briefing. And I want it *now*."

Dev had a retort on his lips that would have made Willy grin, but he stifled it. He had to admit to himself, the fleet admiral's authoritarian demeanor impressed even him.

"As long as I'm here," he sighed, moistened his mouth with some Scottish fire, and began to recount what Aura had extracted and compiled from the sensor data they had collected in Harbingen, even though everyone gathered here certainly knew it all inside and out at this point.

"The data was pretty fragmented and kept us busy the entire flight from Lagunia to here. The onboard computer had minimal capacity to deal with it on the way there from Harbingen. We were busy repairing the *Bitch*. Without her, we could not have brought this crucial information here at all, I would like to emphasize. Extremely *expensive* repairs, I might add."

He saw the last thread of patience begin to snap in Captain Thurnau's eyes, which were already blazing like a raging chimney fire, and he raised his hands defensively.

"In any case, we spent several days assembling the data and had the onboard computer put it into a complex simulation. Some of it was manually inserted by us or put together like a complex puzzle that the computer has refused to link into a logical whole because it probably lacks creativity."

"Why don't you start in a structured way," Legutke suggested and looked pointedly at his forearm display, presumably to check the time. His expression remained blank, but Dev could sense that the fleet admiral had been talked into this meeting and was on the verge of calling it off and saying "I was right after all."

"It's just teeming with activity. The S2 wasn't guarded, apparently, because they weren't expecting visitors. That makes me wonder if they know more than we do. After all, the Starvan convoy we piggybacked on traveled through numerous core systems and departed Lagunia at just the right time," he explained. "They knew when to be where and how to avoid Species X."

"Species X," Jason Bradley repeated in a "see-what-I-mean?" tone toward Captain Thurnau, who pretended not to notice.

"The S2 is near Bohr, whose ecliptic, in turn, is near the inner asteroid belt. The industrial stations there, which were thought to be abandoned, are anything but. In fact, they all show massive heat buildups on infrared images. The same is true for stations in the belt itself. We discovered six of these secret structures, which were apparently used as transshipment points for goods."

"Supply depots for ships moving from the outer to the inner system," Nicholas explained and nodded. "At least that's our preliminary analysis. They must have been there for a long time, probably with supplies stored."

"Could well be," Dev said. Not without pride, he told them what he thought was his brilliant solution to get their necks out of the noose. "Anyway, they were guarded and important enough that the corvettes pursuing us wanted to protect them at all costs." Since no one wanted to sing his praises, he continued, "The Broadswords were from fairly recent Fleet stock, as far as I could see, but I guess you're the experts on that one."

"There have been several corvettes reported missing in recent years," Legutke said thoughtfully. "Even a destroyer whose whereabouts could not be determined."

"You mean these conspirators have *stolen* entire ships?"

*The last Battleship*

Thurnau said incredulously, then quickly added a belated "Admiral."

"They have managed to fill a system thought dead with ships, equipment, and supplies, right before our—admittedly few—eyes," the fleet admiral calmly explained. "They have, if Captain Bradley's sons are to be believed—and I'm inclined to think so—murdered their father and Bretoni, used the Shadowwing to commit countless assassinations in the highest ranks, prevented the Bellingers' warning of the dangers from the hyperspace gates from getting through, and clearly knew something that no one else in the Federation was aware of. All of this with absolute secrecy. Even if we assume many of the killer's victims were people who were leaking information, that would be an outstanding logistical and organizational achievement that leaves me in no doubt about anything. Surely, they also have to answer for the *Braxis* and the *Gibraltar*. Neither of them has reported back from patrol duty in Harbingen. Just before war broke out with 'Species X,' we were going to send a flotilla to investigate their disappearance."

"There is activity all through the system. At S1, near the central star, we could make out six massive ships that our onboard computer says are *Scarab*-type sleeper ships. Those were also used by the Harbinger Exiles to leave the Federation after the Great Schism to elect the Omega," Dev recounted. After a brief silence he continued, "They seem to want to leave."

"The question is to where?" Jason asked thoughtfully. "The whereabouts of the Exiles are unknown. There have been many attempts to track them down, but they've probably jumped way too far over several years in unknown directions to ever find them. Whether it's five hundred or five thousand light years, the journey would take several years, certainly manageable with their outlawed antimatter. By the time signals from them reach us, the Federation may not even exist."

Legutke raised an eyebrow. Dev found he could raise it very high.

"Kor," he said aloud, nodding. "That must be what that transmitter we saw is for. It's at least fifty meters in diameter and has a long focus tube. If my flight engineer hadn't spent nights looking through the images like a maniac, it wouldn't have occurred to us to take a closer look at the largest remaining chunk of the moon. They apparently built a structure under the surface on its upper side that could be closed with a large hangar door. What's below the surface? Not a clue. But this thing isn't pointed at any system we know of and it's been realigned several times in the hours since we located it."

"So, the Exiles don't know where to send it yet," Nicholas said. "That's good."

"Not *yet*," Thurnau emphasized, looking directly at the fleet admiral. "That's why we need to act quickly."

"Uh, yes." Dev cleared his throat when Legutke said nothing and looked at him expectantly. "There is activity on Harbingen itself as well, just as there is in orbit. Several industrial ships are parked there—tugs, minesweepers, cargo ships, even some ice haulers and large robotic barges—apparently dropping off smaller transporters on a regular basis to head for the surface."

"The excavation site." Jason nodded somberly before realizing he had spoken out of turn. He sat back. "Excuse me."

"The excavation site is right by the Unity Palace. What are they looking for there, and why? I don't know. You probably know better."

"Omega," Nicholas said, looking at Legutke. "That's where its data storage facility is, and we have the access code. It seems the Exiles don't want to wait for us to bring it to them; they want to control the situation on the ground."

"Access codes?" Dev felt himself suddenly get warm, and it wasn't because of the excellent scotch he'd already enjoyed more than he should. He was just nervous, so what?

The assembled officers began to talk among themselves, but he did not listen. Fleet officers could never be trusted, and when they revealed secrets to a free trader—whom they called a pirate—they would only trust him as long as he didn't live.

*Why did I come here? To the shitty* Oberon? *To the heart of darkness?* Dev thought, condemning his actions. *Because you're a greedy pig and wanted to get paid for your efforts,* he answered himself, then nodded inwardly.

*The last Battleship*

Cold sweat broke out on his forehead as he imagined ending up in some airlock after blurting out everything he knew. Access codes to the Omega? The damned AI was the Federation's best-kept piece of technology that not even the Fleet had been able to recover or destroy, and now there were secret codes to the datastore? These were two items of news that had become the biggest topic in the press for weeks: the Omega's data storage still existed and there was a code to access it. The mere existence of that artificial intelligence had caused one of the most powerful nations of the Federation and one of the most influential cultures to break away. More than a few of humanity's politicians had been relieved to see them destroyed by the Clicks.

"Uh, maybe I'd better go," he suggested and was about to rise when Legutke gave him a Zeus-like gaze that lacked only lightning bolts shooting from his brow-clouded pupils to complete the image of a punishing all-father. "Or not." He poured himself another glass of scotch. The bottle was now empty.

"Your *Quantum*... your *starship* is atmosphere-capable, if I'm rightly informed?" asked the Zeus with the admiral's insignia.

"Yes, the *Bitch* has already landed on Lagunia. Among other things and—" he interrupted his boasting with sudden suspicion. Why was he still alive? "Why?"

"Do you have the balls to fly your ship to the dig site and destroy it?"

"What? What dig site?" Dev stammered. He wasn't often at a loss for words, but now he had to examine a row of serious faces to make sure they weren't shitting him. "The ones on *Harbingen*?"

Legutke said nothing, but his look was devoid of humor, if the man was even capable of that.

"I think so," he finally said hesitantly. "Why? You don't want to throw us into combat, do you?"

The admiral looked at Captain Thurnau, who straightened in her chair.

"Yes, we do, along with the *Oberon* and every ship we can pull together in Sol. There won't be many, but according to your sensor scans, the force in the Harbingen System isn't particularly large."

"At least what we could see. There was evidence of communication with the inner system from the outer belt and the Oort Cloud, and we were able to pick up at least eight exhaust flares." Dev waited for a response, but the officers were again talking among themselves as if he were invisible.

"The *Oberon* can do it," Thurnau was sure.

"The Exiles," Nicholas objected, "pulled off the biggest conspiracy in Federation history and hid it from us for twenty years."

"We've also been distracted with a draining war that required the attention of all areas of our intelligence operations," Jason countered.

"Nevertheless, the fleet admiral has already pointed out the peculiar feat accomplished by the conspirators. They destroyed an entire strike group in Lagunia to advance their chess game. I'm sure they have their eyes and ears on this one as well if they aren't already expecting us." The XO took a deep breath and turned to his commander. "They've prepared for anything thus far, and they will be prepared now. We could be walking into a trap."

"And we will oblige," she replied firmly. "Once you know it's a trap, it's no longer a trap."

"The risk is great, and I hate to give up the flagship of the Terran Fleet," Legutke said, "but I agree with you on this point, Captain. We can't afford to ignore this. We must crush the conspirators while we have the chance and prevent them from joining forces with their compatriots. Whatever they plan to do with the Exiles cannot be good, especially after they knowingly let billions of their fellow human beings die for their cause. Our peace with the Clicks is still young, but in the best case, it keeps our backs free to carry out this operation. If it breaks, we have nothing to fight them with, anyway. No hard feelings."

"You're absolutely right." Thurnau nodded. "If we make it to Harbingen unscathed, I see two primary targets: the transmission facility and the excavation site. Jason and Nicholas have the access codes, so we should use those to find out where the Exiles are. Only Omega has that information."

Legutke's face suddenly looked pained, but he nodded reluctantly, and she continued.

*The last Battleship*

"The second target must be the transmission facility. If the Exiles detect any sign of life, they may be tempted—especially under the current circumstances—to return and take over. Unless they've been asleep for several decades, they should have enough ships to take over Harbingen and probably the remnants of the dying Federation. We can't let that happen." Thurnau's eyebrows came together into almost one continuous furrow, separated only by steep frown lines on her forehead. "These are religiously deluded nationalists and fascists, believe me. I know their last high lord, Ludwig von Borningen. Worse than his cleverness in the service of the wrong cause is his conviction of having been the only Federation citizen who knew the right path for humanity."

"I agree with your assessment as far as the transmitter goes," Legutke replied, noting something on his forearm display. "We're going to need a good plan to achieve our goals. Mr. Myers and his ship, with some assistance, will raid the dig site and make sure we get the data from Omega. Given the absolute secrecy required for this operation and its background, it seems reasonable enough to accept the risk. Besides, Mr. Meyer, you've proven several times that you have a certain talent for improvisation."

Dev wasn't sure whether to be happy about the praise or to cry over all the other things the fleet admiral had just said. In the end, he just nodded in stunned disbelief, as if he'd been hit on the head. He didn't want to fly a damned secret mission, certainly not into the middle of a wasp's nest of ultra-nationalist Harbingers who wanted to call on their lunatic brethren in deep space for help—or whatever. On the contrary, he had been looking forward to doing the right thing for once, something for the public good, and being rewarded for it. *Rewarded, damn it!*

"I need money." The words escaped his mouth even before he could think of an appropriate response. The commander of the *Oberon* blinked, first in surprise, then in disgust. Her XO seemed anything but astonished, and the fleet admiral merely eyed him, while Jason Bradley nodded in understanding.

"I think that's appropriate," the lieutenant commander said quickly to forestall the others. "After all, you've been through quite a bit, and no pirate would have volunteered such important information, with all the risks it entailed."

For the first time since he stepped through the door of Captain Thurnau's quarters—past the two Marines who had looked at him as if they were about to tear him apart with their bare hands—he smiled with satisfaction.

# 3

"The admiral has *what*?" Aura blurted in horror as they walked through the densely packed corridors of Space Dock 2, Bay C. This facility was for small ships, mostly corvettes, and was teeming with technicians in orange jumpsuits pulling cargo sleds behind them or driving around on manipulator carts.

The *Quantum Bitch* was just one of six ships in Bay C that were seriously shot up. Some ships were no more than piles of scrap with an umbilical cord to the airlock. But the Fleet's screwdriver monkeys were giving their all to get as many of their birds back into space as soon as possible, even if the view through the window painted a bleak picture. They stopped in front of a window and looked out.

"Look at that," Dev replied evasively and peered into Bay C, a cuboid 100 meters an edge, open on one side, and displaying Terra's blue glow. Airlocks extended from the walls of carbotanium plates like fluted necks, and half of them were docked with lumps of blunt composite. Some of the wrecks bore scraps of a ship name or an identification number. Maintenance and repair bots flew around the shattered ships, position lights flashing, maneuvering with corrective thrusts. They sliced off entire hull segments or welded lines together and placed probes on the hulls. They resembled a swarming hive, and the smell of ozone and lubricants in the corridor intensified the impression.

"What exactly?" the power node specialist said.

"They're working their asses off to bake doughnuts out of garbage. That's true smuggler spirit!"

"Are you trying to talk up the Fleet now or what?"

"Yeah, so you don't rip my head off," he admitted, then gestured for her to follow him. They walked 50 meters and stopped next to a pallet loaded with large oxygen and nitrogen tanks lashed together. They stopped in front of a scratched and stained window and looked down at the *Quantum Bitch*.

Their ship looked like a bird of prey with stubby, clipped wings. The cockpit looked like a narrow head with a glass dome, and the fuselage widened toward the aft where the retrofitted storage compartment hung like a box as if the bird were pregnant. The four fusion thrusters at the rear were like tail feathers. The density of bots—yellow space crabs with flashing position lights—was so thick that it was hard to make out the hull. Pilot-controlled tugs with massive cranes hauled segments of hull armor in and handed them to eager robots to weld into place. Somewhere above the window where they were standing, conduit as thick as a man's thigh extended to ports in the *Bitch*'s neck behind the cockpit, supplying it with life support, water, and electricity.

"Look at what they're doing. The way I see it, the *Bitch* is getting priority service and we're not paying a dime for it."

"Oh, how generous. They're paying for the damage we suffered to give them a warning all out of sheer fucking charity," Aura grumbled, but she also gazed in fascination at the bustle out in the vacuum, like a mother watching her favorite child being spoiled. "May I remind you that they just looted our hold along with the twenty coffins?"

"It's wonderful! We have space again, and no charges have been filed." He noticed her scowl and sighed. "The thing is, I had no choice but to take this job. And if it succeeds, we'll get a hundred million credits."

"The *Bitch* is worth more than that!"

"You have to consider the times," he replied almost professorially. "The Federation is as good as done unless some of the core worlds pull off a miracle. Every penny will be needed to supply the fringe worlds that can't survive." Anticipating her next comment, because he had had the same thought, he added, "That they pay us afterward is so logical that I would have done it that way myself. After all, they think we're pirates who can't be trusted."

"Hmph," she grunted, then changed the subject, "What are they actually doing to our *Bitch* right now?"

"Ah," Dev said and began to gush. "Molecularly bonded carbotanium armor with reactive ablative protection. We can even take a few railgun strikes with that. Our own railgun under the bow will be replaced with the new Striker model. It's got lower power consumption, higher ejection acceleration, and complete swivel capability. Our missile launch bays are being reinforced to allow newer missiles with higher thrust, and we're getting rearmed with air-to-surface missiles to deploy at our target location. We also get twelve Predators—the new ones, Type 3, that are still being prepared for the roll-out phase. We're the first ship in the Fleet—er, the Federation to have those things on board."

"Wow, it's like a birthday and Christmas all rolled into one," Aura remarked wryly and rolled her eyes, but her gaze was now fixed on the busy bots outside the window.

"Isn't it? Then, of course, there are the completely new cable trees and superconductors, molecular bonded generators, energy matrix and pattern cell replacements—oh, and two new reactors."

"Two?"

"Yes. Since we have a habit of losing one, we now get two. Scarab-4s, baby." He grinned from ear to ear. "Smaller and more efficient than our Bumblebee-2. That's why we have room for two."

"If you tell Willy, he'll come all over his bunk."

"I'd let him get away with it for once." Dev paused. "No, I wouldn't. Come on, let's go see it on board."

They entered the airlock and donned the simple spacesuits for dock workers that hung on the wall before floating through the outer door into the semi-transparent umbilical connecting the space dock to their ship. All systems—except for individual maintenance blocks with autonomous batteries—were shut down, so there was no life support on board. The bots didn't need it, and since the hull wasn't sealed, the human technicians all wore suits.

Welders flared in every corridor. Their lightning staccato lit the yellow clothing of workers and the equally yellow hulls of the spherical maintenance bots flying material through the corridors or ripping off wall panels to haul them away. It hurt Dev to see his beloved *Bitch* being picked apart, but he knew the wounds being inflicted were part of the surgery she needed to survive the next time she launched.

They floated through the strange silence toward the mess hall. Despite all the hustle and bustle, the vacuum swallowed every sound. They saw Willy and Dozer working with the Fleet technicians on several essential systems. Due to its age—at least as far as the basic model was concerned—the *Quantum Bitch* did not have a real bridge in the heart of the ship where it would be well protected. At the ship's center was the mess hall, of all things. Because of this nonsensical configuration, Willy had made sure in recent years that at least the main system access lines didn't run into the cockpit, but here to the mess. It's where they usually ate, and its location protected them from tumbling dead into space if they were hit. Aside from that, the cockpit was small enough as it was. If he had been forced to sit in the cockpit every time Willy and Dozer did maintenance behind him, screwing away while leaving no room for him to squeeze past them, Dev would have gone insane a long time ago.

"How's it going?" he asked his flight engineer over the radio, who turned around like a bear and grinned at him and Aura through his helmet visor like a schoolboy.

"Birthday and Christmas—"

"—on the same day."

"That's right, boss. That's right. All the toys we're getting are better than any gift I ever got."

Dev made sure their communications encryption was active.

"How's the onboard computer?" he asked pointedly.

"I don't know how you did it, but they're not snooping. The software hasn't reported any infiltration attempts, not even simple queries. The Fleet is leaving us alone while they shower us with presents," Willy replied, grunting with satisfaction. "Dozer and I are keeping our eyes on them, anyway, and we've installed firewalls at every node to alert us if there's even a cough in the code."

"Very good. Very good indeed." He gave Aura an "I-told-you-so" look and was rewarded with a sour look in response.

"Only one thing worries me," his flight engineer said, and after a brief pause he jerked a thumb toward the bulkhead to the storage room, which was closed and in the process of being sealed by a bot with four plasma torches. "They're replacing the entire cargo module, cutting it completely out of the hull and putting in a new one. I was going to insist that we only fly with stuff we know about, but that only got me stern looks from two Marines who glared at me like damned bulls seeing a red rag. There's also no systems integration of any kind."

"Yes, there is, one," Dev said, "for the jettison mechanism."

"Jettison mechanism?" Willy repeated, irritated.

"All I've been told is that it's a secret weapon we're supposed to drop over our target when the time comes. My guess is cluster bombs for damaging soft targets." He lowered his voice, though no one else could hear him. "Those things are outlawed, so I think the fleet admiral would rather keep a lid on it. I suggest we not ask any questions, enjoy the upgrades, do our job, and walk away with the 100 million credits."

"If they're even worth anything afterward," Aura grumbled.

"Just in case, we'll still have a refurbished *Bitch* that can fly us to better places."

"If we don't end up as a volatile cloud of gas on this suicide mission," she said.

"Volatile gas cloud? Suicide mission?" Willy asked. "I think a little briefing would be in order."

"We're flying to Harbingen—that's the short version," Dev replied, clearing his throat.

"Nah," Aura said, "the short version is we fly into an ambush and get destroyed."

"How nice," the Dunkelheimer commented laconically. "That means everything's back to normal. When are we supposed to leave?"

"In thirty-six hours."

Willy blinked a few times like he was waiting for Dev to grin in jest. When he saw none, he grew thoughtful.

"Well, all the rugrats around here are pretty busy already. Maybe they can work it out." He sounded unconvinced.

"I don't want them taking away my favorite table," Dev said with a meaningful glance at the holotable. It had provided the best hiding place for the antimatter warhead Willy and Dozer had recovered from the *Danube*. He couldn't blame them. After all, the thing was worth more on the black market than the entire *Bitch*—even after her numerous upgrades. True, they couldn't do anything with it, but every war came to an end, eventually. And if it didn't, all the better. The demand for mass destruction weapons would only increase.

"Come on," he finally said to Aura. "Let's join Jezzy in the cockpit and get to work on systems integration."

# 4

Nicholas walked alongside Silly, navigating the bustling port corridor, and dodging repair crews that were hard at work ripping away sections of honeycomb wall paneling to access the intricate wiring hidden within. Welding sparks illuminated the area, stretching into the distance along the slight bend of the corridor. Periodically, Nicholas swiped documents from his forearm display to Silly's, seeking her signature. The papers detailed the delivery of weapons, equipment, ammunition, provisions of nutrient-rich slurry for the soldiers' sustenance, and a myriad of micro-verification reports Silly meticulously scrutinized before granting her approval.

"How's the armor looking?" she asked as she kept pressing her thumb to the DNA scanner panel on her forearm display.

"The Fleet is scraping up every ounce of Carbin they can find from Earth orbit. Click ships that haven't withdrawn yet are assisting them."

"And what does that mean?"

"The damage may be repaired, but the additional armor we requested won't realistically get here, I think," he explained. "Thirty-six hours is thirty-six hours."

"Too little."

"Everything is too little, but especially the time we have left."

"I guess you're right," she sighed and paused before her next thumbprint to look more closely with a furrowed brow. "The port discharge chutes for our Barracudas are being rebuilt?"

"Yes."

She raised her eyes and looked at him reproachfully. "Why wasn't I informed? What's going on?"

"You told me to work out a strategy for raiding the transmission facility. If bombing is out of the question, we'll have to drop ground troops to get the job done, and I don't think that's an unlikely scenario."

"You're thinking we're going to get caught up in a battle that will leave us no room to breathe."

"I'm assuming that, yes. We're expecting the worst, so at least we'll be prepared. In any case, dropping the boarding shuttles seemed too risky. The impactor tips would burrow into the regolith and wouldn't be able to open, so Ludwig's Marines would have to cut their way out the sides and that would take far too long and make them targets for the defenders. So, I've requested eighty drop pods that can fit into the Barracudas' catapult launch bays with relatively minor adjustments and accelerate fast enough to be difficult for the enemy to take out." Nicholas paused and Silly nodded hesitantly.

"A good plan, I think. You're a better tactician than I am," she admitted, and then she quoted, he believed, his late father, "A good commander knows when to nod instead of command."

"Thank you."

"How about the crew?" She pressed her thumb to the flashing green box, and they continued, making way for a team of technicians who walked past them with jingling magnetic belts, ducking under sagging cables that emitted sparks. One of the electricians uttered a wild curse and summoned two of his assistants.

"The infirmary is being restocked with new drugs and medibots. The systems that can be replaced quickly are still being swapped out for more modern ones, but most of them will have to remain. Old, but functional, and our doctors and nurses know them well and are ready to go. Some of the integrated refugees worked in the medical sector and have proved to be of significant help. Lagunia's... well, backwardness has played into our hands

*The last Battleship*

because they're familiar with the old equipment and the appropriate training can be done while working with us."

"What about the patients?"

"We lost a total of forty more comrades who were in critical condition after the battle. Over one hundred intensive-care patients were transferred to the Sky Fortress to be better cared for, and about two hundred crewmen are undergoing rapid rehab and should be back in action in a week when we arrive in Harbingen in five days," he said, reciting the numbers displayed on his forearm.

"Will we get our comrades in intensive care back before we leave?" Silly asked hopefully.

Nicholas shook his head. "No. They've been placed in meditanks and put into induced comas. It would take some time to get them in a transportable state."

"Damn. I hate to leave them here."

"We're part of the Fleet again now, Silly. We'll have to get used to that."

"I'll try. The last fleet admiral tried to hang me. He was basically right."

"But he was also right to countermand his orders because of the circumstances. I think that precedent can be taken in the context of where the Federation is right now. You're the one who made a peace between us and the Clicks possible in the first place."

"No, that was Jason and you. Jason because he made contact and you because you convinced me to believe him and bet everything on the trust card," she corrected him seriously.

"How about we call it a team effort?" he suggested and tried a smile. It felt unusual, but also like something that was necessary.

Silly nodded. "What do you think of our new fleet admiral?"

"Purposeful, unpretentious, ascetic, no-frills, and thoughtful all at the same time," he summarized. "To me, he seems like an evolution of his already esteemed predecessor, a man who was also considered averse to politics."

"No one who is averse to politics occupies the post of fleet admiral," she offered.

She had a point.

"At the very least, it seems like the most he's done is use politics, so he doesn't have to use it again. He's taking a big risk with this deployment. If it comes out that he agreed to download Omega, he's screwed."

"Surely the Parliament is pretty much powerless at the moment, isn't it? It didn't even take them half an hour to approve the peace treaty von Solheim negotiated with the Clicks, even though they learned about it from the news and had to pretend democracy was still intact."

"It is. It just had to get it done quickly." Nicholas had thought long and hard about how the former fleet admiral had bypassed parliament by declaring a state of emergency for all of Sol until the treaty was signed. The Parliament had to get involved in order to save face. He himself had been glad of this, otherwise the entire process would have dragged on through thousands of committees and boards—with an uncertain outcome. Even in peacetime, it was a terrifying situation that had unnecessarily crippled the Fleet's military capabilities time and again. Yet it served to keep it from becoming a self-perpetuating, uncontrollable machine that lost sight of what it had to protect. A military without civilian control was something of a heartless monster that saw red capes everywhere.

Another subject occurred to him that he had deliberately avoided until now.

"Have you thought about taking the Admiralty's proposed personnel on board?"

"Yes." Silly's face became hard. "I declined, citing insufficient time for integration. The *Oberon* is a Titan, and few are trained to fly it, maintain it, and live in it."

Nicholas thought about her words and had to agree—but for other reasons. He imagined it was difficult for non-Harbingers to come to terms with that race of outcasts, people convinced they belonged to the best nation in the Federation and that they had been betrayed by the rest of humanity when they had needed them. They had seen how that could turn out in their dealings with the Harbingen recruits once war broke out, and he didn't want to see anything like that happen again because he was convinced they were better than that. For Silly, things were certainly different. She hardly trusted Harbingers at all. She probably just needed time to get used to the new circumstances.

Silly changed the subject. "What about your brother? Is he ready for his deployment?" She was probably worried that he would harangue her about Harbingers, but he didn't. Instead, he accepted the change of subject.

"I was about to go check on him one last time. He's disappointed that he wasn't sent to the Clicks with the ambassador's delegation. I think he secretly hoped to become ambassador himself. He's just hell-bent on keeping in touch with the Broodmother," he sighed. "But he understands the need."

"If I had to fly into a trap with a bunch of pirates to do something that would have been considered treason just a day ago, I would have hesitated too, you can bet on that."

"I don't like it either, but you didn't release me."

"I need you here. Besides, it's not like your part in this plan is any less dangerous. There are no back seats in this operation, Nicholas," she said, returning a passing junior lieutenant's salute with a curt nod. "And no safety for those we love."

"One more thing about the trap you mentioned," Nicholas said. "I got an idea about that after looking at the systems we fly through on the way to Harbingen, but to implement it we need something only you can get from the fleet admiral."

"No problem," she replied immediately. "I'll take care of it."

"It's not that simple." He cleared his throat and took a deep breath. "I need you to ask him for the codes for about 100,000 quagma mines."

"Excuse me?" Silly blinked in amazement.

"Give or take a few thousand."

"*What* kind of mines? Where are we going to get them?"

"Drakistan. One of the three fastest jump routes to Harbingen goes through the Drakistan System."

"Oh," she frowned, and her expression darkened like a gathering storm.

"To get to the mines, you'll have to tell the fleet admiral that we destroyed Drakus-III."

Silly gulped, but quickly straightened her shoulders and

nodded. "I'll take care of it and give him the data from our flight recorder. Then he can see for himself."

"It will help that Admiral Bretoni has been identified as a conspirator and that we were victims of his intrigue. That should have a mitigating effect. And we can point out that the crew of the research station are probably still alive in their evac capsules. We could collect them en route, if it doesn't take too long."

"That might work."

They reached the elevators, entered a cabin, and shook their heads in unison as other sailors moved to board. They retreated. As soon as the doors closed, Silly said without looking at him, "So, now tell me why I have to polish the fleet admiral's doorknob to get the codes for the minefield around what was once Drakus-III."

∼

After his "elevator pitch," Nicholas made his way directly to the port hangar, where he was stopped by two Black Legion Marines blocking one of the access points.

"I'm sorry, sir," one of them, a sergeant, said, surprising Nicholas. "Orders are orders."

The man held out a DNA sniffer for him to breathe on its tiny probe. The small device emitted a high-pitched sound and flashed green.

"Thank you, XO." The two Marines saluted.

"Stay alert," he advised them, returned the salute, and entered the hangar.

The huge space, which probably could have held four of the latest small fleet destroyers if two were stacked on top of each other, was all but deserted. It was something Nicholas had never seen before. About a dozen Barracudas stood together in two rows of six on the left side, where the lights were off. On the right was a 20-meter-by-5-meter cube on massive hydraulic columns. Two dozen technicians in orange coveralls, soundproof headphones, and hard hats scurried around crude rocket engines stuck flat and squat to the underside. By all appearances, they were welding down the nacelles and securing them with seals assisted by techbots on

*The last Battleship*

wheels. There were hisses, roars, and crashes as they went about their work, while Karl Murphy barked instructions.

It was so loud that the chief engineer didn't even hear him approaching until he was standing right next to him.

"Hey, XO," Murphy shouted against the noise. "What's up?"

"Wanted to make sure everything was on schedule here," Nicholas almost bellowed.

"It's coming along. Would be better if I knew what kind of shit we were fabricating here, but we're getting the job done, don't worry. Where the hell did you guys find those old Raptors up there? Haven't seen them in ages!"

"Necessity has a way of speeding delivery and short-cutting procedures, I suppose," he said evasively, and Murphy accepted it with a shrug. Only now did Nicholas notice that High Explosive had been spray painted in crude letters on one side of the chunky cube. An apt warning, he thought. He pointed to the lettering. "If we all die, it will be because we were one V short of victory."

Murphy frowned and followed his gaze, then laughed so uproariously that it reduced even the crackle of welding torches and the roar of techbots to background noise. "Shit, Nicholas, I don't know who put that there, but if we all die it'll be because of those ancient Raptors. Well, it's not us, it's that *Quantum Bitch* we're supposed to jam that thing under."

"Shh," Nicholas said more reflexively than meaningfully. "The secrecy..."

"I have no idea what's in there. Any outlawed weapons?"

"Actually, I can't tell you anything about it except for this: you're not wrong. We made something of a pact with the devil. At least, that's how many would see it."

"And Jason really wants to fly with these pirate guys?" Murphy asked, scratching strands of his black hair with an oil-smeared hand.

"It's not a question of *wanting*, but we need them."

"You're going for Omega, aren't you?"

Nicholas blinked, startled, and Murphy raised his smeared hand to dismiss any denial.

"Come on, kid. This old engie here ain't fallen on his head, and neither has the crew. They're going to Harbingen, which can only mean two things: either the Exiles are back, or Omega has been found. We're sending a fleet and a ship that we're in the process of upgrading with mysterious armaments and rocket engines before covering it with the latest stealth paint and sending it to Harbingen while we push on toward Kor with a couple escort ships. So, my guess is that both are true."

Nicholas didn't answer, and Murphy nodded before winking at him.

"Tell Jason to make sure he doesn't launch that bomb with thrusters until it's far enough away from that pirate bitch. The Raptors are old pieces of shit, but strong as hell draft horses. They can burn holes in pretty much any fur with their long exhaust flares, if you know what I mean."

"I'll give him the message," Nicholas assured the old engineer, patting him on the back.

"Good, now I should get on with things here so none of these walking short-circuits shove their welding torches through this armor and blow us all up. The sooner this thing is out of my hangar, the sooner I can get back to sleeping soundly."

"Don't worry, we have to leave soon anyway. The longer we wait, the... you know. The Exiles won't be idle. Keep it up, Karl."

"Shit! When you say Karl, it means the shit's really going to hit the fan, don't it?"

"Wait till I tell you what I have to ask you to do next."

"Something worse than a secret weapon of mass destruction in my hangar?" Murphy grunted in disbelief.

"Yes. But I won't tell you what I'm up to until we're already underway," Nicholas replied and turned to go.

"As if I could run away," the engineer called after him, and Nicholas smiled. But it wasn't a happy smile. It was rather a melancholy one because he would soon have to ask more of Karl Murphy than he ever wanted to.

# 5

"Don't complain! At least they saved you," Jason said. A wide grin spread across Jason's face as he watched Baker on the large display in his quarters. It used to be Nicholas's quarters, but now Jason occupied it, while Silly had reluctantly taken over their late father's quarters. The mutant appeared on the screen, relishing the taste of a cigar butt. Jason couldn't help but be amused at the sight. The bald skull atop Baker's head gave him an uncanny resemblance to a malevolent, bearded infant.

"Netted from space like sardines. Rochshaz made such a disgusting squeal in there I almost died." Baker shoved the cigar into the left corner of his mouth with his tongue and shouted, "That damned son of a whore!"

Jason's smile grew melancholy. "I'm going to miss you guys."

"Our pleasant company complete with blood and body parts flying around?"

"Well, not necessarily that part."

"That's what I thought."

"Just take care of yourselves. It would be nice to see you guys alive again." Jason saw the rest of the mutants crowded in the background as they settled into the darkness.

"Nah." Baker waved one of his paws. The other held his assault cannon with Betsy spray painted in large, red letters. "We've been in worse places, and we've been promised our own habitat around

Jupiter as thanks for our efforts. We've been thinking of opening a butcher shop. We'd like to get the goods from you Harbingers when you've cleaned up there. There should be plenty of delicacies left for your old friends from Novigrad."

The mutants in his troop laughed and hooted and Jason tried to avoid painting a picture of that in his mind.

"I'll see what I can do," he assured them with a sour expression before smiling again. "Take care of yourself, big guy." Louder, he said, "All of you. I'll see you on the other side."

"Keep your chin up, kid."

Jason pressed the red disconnect button and looked at his packed duffel bag outside the door. It was interesting how little one could fit into life, but how much into a damn old duffel bag.

The *Oberon* hummed and groaned under the massive preparations it was undergoing. The gigantic Trans-Luna shipyard held her in its clutches like a space tarantula, flashing and blinking with thousands of maintenance bots buzzing around them. The Fleet's problem of having few ships but plenty of maintained infrastructure was now an advantage—most of the available personnel and material could be focused on the aged Titan. If he placed a hand against the featureless composite wall, he could feel vibrations that matched the ubiquitous hum and roar of engines that provided the ship's background music, lulling thousands of sailors to sleep in their bunks at the end of each shift. He would miss the Old Lady, even if he didn't want to admit it to himself.

At the door, he turned with a final sigh, then shouldered his duffel bag, as millions of sailors had done before as they were sent off over the centuries to fight battles in lands far away. In his case, however, it was off to *his* home, to *his* system, even if he tried to deny it.

*Well, off to the final match,* he thought and stepped out into the hallway.

"Bradley," a young sergeant greeted him as he passed, respectfully tapping the cap on his head with one hand. Jason blinked in irritation. But as he walked through the ship, it happened more often. Tech teams paused briefly in their work as he passed, nodded, gave him the Harbinger salute, and simply said "Bradley." He had

*The last Battleship*

first thought it disrespectful since they did not address him by rank or with "sir." Yet he realized that the greeting was a sign of extreme respect, for their expressions reflected both recognition and hope.

Sometimes he merely nodded in reply, other times he raised his hand as he made his way to a shuttle parked in the starboard hangar. Nicholas was waiting for him at the open hatch in the floor where he would descend into the spacecraft lodged in its launch tube. Amid the noises of the hangar crews bustling about like a mound of orange termites, he looked like a foreign body in his black uniform with its many insignia, some Fleet medals had been added and the reserve pin had disappeared. He looked tired.

Jason trudged across the seemingly endless deck toward his brother, the weight of the duffel bag heavy on his shoulder, and he saw why the technicians were so excited. There were no Barracudas here for maintenance, but the gigantic hangar doors stood open. The force field that kept them from being sucked into the vacuum of space shimmered dark blue. In the background, one of the over-sized shipyard cranes could be seen, wrapped around the *Oberon* like the arm of some ancient god. Behemoth drones, as large as corvettes and looking like beefy space beetles, carrying powerful engines in front of their bellies, pushed them through the force field.

"Are those Radloff nacelles?" Jason shouted to Nicholas over the roar of the Behemoths before he reached him. A house-sized drone thundered past like a solar eclipse, casting its dark shadow over them. "Those things are huge!"

"We're storing four of them, along with their engine components," Nicholas explained loudly and took Jason's duffel bag from him as he stepped in front of him. "There's a fifth one coming. A jump engine."

"What have you cooked up, you old tactical genius?"

"Something that will hopefully give us a chance to evacuate you and your new friends from Harbingen's surface once you find what we need."

Jason screwed up his face at the thought of the new "friends" Nicholas meant. Pirates, of all things. Pirates were responsible for his mother's death and now he would be locked up with them for five days or more as their passenger. The prospect was made more unpleasant by the fact that he would feel no bond for the entire time, not to Mother, not to Inseminator, not to anyone. All that remained was the petty coldness of human interaction, which had so little to offer compared to the telepathic bond, that *genuine* exchange, that seeing and being seen.

"That's new for you, cracking jokes. And such a macabre one at that," he said with a sigh.

Nicholas seemed genuinely confused. "I wasn't joking." Then he wearily shook his head as if he had thought of something that should have been obvious. "I'm sorry. I haven't slept much, and I've spent too much time on tactical simulations on the command deck and in my quarters." As if to punctuate his words, he gave a long, drawn-out yawn.

"Oh, that's all right." Jason watched the Behemoth drone lower the nacelle onto several dozen nozzles. The technicians burst forth in a flurry of activity as they attached security clamps and rolled out barrier tape. Next to the engine components, they looked like glowing orange gnomes. "I don't know what you're up to, brother dear, but I don't really want to know or I'll probably worry myself to death."

"Possibly." Nicholas smiled wanly and embraced him. "We'll be all right. We always have, somehow."

"I don't even really know who our enemy is," Jason admitted in a flat voice as he returned the embrace. "That whole Exile-Omegan thing was before our time. We weren't even teenagers when the Schism divided our population."

"Not divided. They were a minority. Nationalistic and religiously blinded."

"Is that what Dad said?"

"Yes," Nicholas breathed. "He didn't talk much about Ludwig von Borningen and his fleet of exiles who abandoned Harbingen. But he was always sure we were better off without them. Dad believed in Omega, that's why he followed his last orders and got the colonists to safety instead of following his instincts and going down with flags flying, as some would have liked."

Jason broke their embrace and nodded slowly.

"After what they did, I stopped asking myself questions about their intentions. The ones who've been active all these years are probably even worse than their ancestors and relatives who managed to get a place in von Borningen's fleet. They have to answer for the Federation, not just our father."

"And that's why we're going after them now."

"To kick their asses." Jason forced a grin onto his face that hopefully looked confident.

Nicholas grabbed Jason by the shoulders as if *he* were the big brother. "If anyone can do it, it's us. Take care of yourself, bro. And don't mess with those smugglers. Just keep your head down, don't let yourself be provoked, and get us the data from Omega, okay?"

"Sure. It'll be fine. I've spent several days living and fighting with bloodthirsty mutants who, when they're not disemboweling corpses to sell their organs or implants, like nothing better than finding enemies they can tear to pieces with their bare hands. How bad can it be sharing a ship with a handful of pirates?"

"I took a look at their flight recorder; some things are missing, which doesn't surprise me. Meyer attributed it to system malfunctions due to the considerable damage their ship took, but what I've seen makes me optimistic. If anyone can get you out of impossible situations, it's that hotshot." Nicholas was sure. "Reckless and impulsive, but an exceptionally good tactician and improviser. It'll be fine."

"If you say so." Jason hugged him again, then took back his duffel bag, tossed it through the hatch, and climbed down after it. "See you on the other side, little brother."

∽

The shuttle's course took them close to the *Oberon*'s scarred hull, at the prescribed safe distance from the myriad drones and EMUs that housed space workers, buzzing like cleaner fish over the ancient skin of a whale. By virtue of his rank, Jason had immediately moved into the copilot's seat and taken the controls, much to the pilot's suppressed displeasure. He enjoyed the brief moment of freedom and the adrenaline rush he got from each flick of the manual controls. The arms of the shipyard, illuminated by the sun's reflection in high orbit above Luna, looked like the ribcage of an ancient space fossil hiding the aged battleship and providing the microbes to nurse it back to health.

He caught glimpses of drones as they flew past, trailing yellow bubbles carrying nanite mass to be applied between carbine elements of the armor and spread throughout the material. There, the tiny robots would bond with the flagella of molecular bond generators, hardening the entire structure into a single unit while aiding damage control systems as a complex sensor structure.

Past battles had only allowed them to do makeshift repairs and visibly weakened the Titan. Dozens of meters of craters testified to the impact of nuclear weapons. The *Oberon* had indeed taken a beating, but the Fleet was doing its best to patch it up with whatever it could scrape together. The flurry of vacuum workers, manipulator cranes from the shipyard arms, drones, and maintenance bots, the thousand-fold flicker of welders and cold gas jets surpassed even what Jason had seen in the Fleet's orbital factories around Eden that were one of the primary centers of ship production in the Federation. *Well, had been*, he thought.

The other shuttle passengers were mostly liaison officers responsible for integrating the disparate communications systems between the Fleet and the *Oberon*. They spent the trip focused on their forearm displays, no doubt hooked into the shuttle's open optical sensors to absorb the undeniable epic scope of the sight. Jason wondered how frustrated they were by Silly's refusal to upgrade the *Oberon*'s wired communications equipment. Without the Clicks as enemies, electronic warfare played a much smaller role than it had before, and voices were already being raised in the Admiralty calling for faster and more efficient signal paths to give them an advantage against Species X. But Silly was Silly and she would not change her opinions and views overnight, especially since his father had always warned against integrating new, untested systems too quickly.

Once away from the shipyard, they finally accelerated to full thrust toward Terra and the Sky Fortress. Earth now hovered like a glowing blue ball outside the cockpit window, beautiful as ever

*The last Battleship*

without the pallor caused by microcellulose. The long-range radar warned of billions of pieces of debris, ranging from the size of a pea to ten or twenty meters in diameter, testimony to the recent battle against the hyperspace invaders, which had been touch-and-go.

Basic traffic had resumed again and was comprised mainly of civilian ships coming from the surviving shipyards that had been nearing completion just before the fighting broke out and were now urgently needed. But there were also some Starvans, mining ships from the outer system, and ice haulers. It seemed the "independent traders" had realized that their vagabond existence as pirates would be of no use to them if there was no humanity left. They joined in the frenetic activity—albeit less frenetic than before the invasion—to save as much as they could. This included keeping supplies moving between the various economic and population centers in Sol and transporting countless wounded to be distributed among the military hospitals, most of which were located on Luna.

Twenty thousand clicks from their target, the radar image detected an ugly skeleton whose dimensions almost reached those of the *Oberon*. The massive structure being picked apart by drones and tugs had once been the TFS *Concordia*, the largest drone carrier in the Fleet's service. Stripped of its jump engines, energy matrix cells, and graviton pulse generators, the once potbellied monster now resembled some monument to war that might serve as a tourist attraction in the future. He would have liked to know what this activity was all about, but in the end it was probably better for his night's sleep if he had no idea.

Half an hour later, the Sky Fortress had grown in the cockpit window until it resembled a beefy hedgehog bristling with its outward-facing starscrapers. It was a major traffic center where twenty shuttles a minute departed, docked, or disappeared into one of its countless hangars. The small spacecraft for short-range traffic between Terra and Luna and the many space stations that still abounded had played no role in the evacuation due to their lack of jump engines and fuel tanks. Now they were the lifeline between the Earth's surface and orbit, providing a steady flow of men and materials back and forth as the Fleet reorganized in reaction to recent developments and new requirements.

Jason headed for the docking bay assigned to him along an approach vector indicated by a solid green path on the overhead display. After the automatic docking procedure concluded, he remained seated until the assembled noncoms and officers had left through the topside hatch. Then he dismissed the two pilots and, in accordance with his mission, used a predefined code to ensure that no data about his presence remained in the onboard computer. Only then did he climb the ladder and set off through the Sky Fortress's confusing labyrinth of corridors in the direction of Space Dock 2.

Without the automatically downloaded navigation aid on his forearm display, he would never have arrived in the forty minutes he needed to get there. To reach his destination, he had to pass three security gates, all of which required his biometric service ID and a DNA sample; only then did he arrive at Bay C. The windowed walkway in the dock was mostly deserted, except for two lone cleaning bots busily removing remnants of what appeared to be detritus from a flurry of activity that had only recently ended. He saw scrap everywhere: metal shavings, smear marks, stains, and the tracks of cargo sleds that had been pulled through all the debris.

The *Quantum Bitch*—there had obviously been enough time to refresh the curved lettering and the busty, lightly clad redhead riding a wave function—hung from the outstretched airlock like a skewered bird of prey. The secret weapon, in the form of a flattened cube, was in the process of being mounted under the long tail section by space workers. As far as Jason could tell, they had nearly finished their task—they were already plugging in the various hoses of the external disconnect fuse.

"Are you just going to stare at her hot curves or are you going to touch them?" he heard a voice that reminded him of John Wayne from ancient 2D westerns. He turned his head to the side and saw Devlin Myers grinning broadly at him from the airlock. There was a small box tucked under his left arm. He held out his right hand. "I'd be lying if I told you I'm glad to have you along. Your very presence will remind me that we're doing something completely insane, but it wouldn't be the first time. With that said, welcome aboard."

"Thank you, Mr. Meyer." Jason grabbed his hand and shook it.

"Hot babe, isn't she? And call me Dev or we won't be friends. We're not a Fleet ship." Dev paused, then pursed his lips. "Well, temporarily, I guess. Aw, shit. Just come with me."

"With her special cargo, she certainly is a 'hot babe,'" Jason said as they made their way into the airlock, and he struggled to not catch his duffel bag on every ledge.

"Don't remind me." In the umbilical's tube, the merchant captain pointed to Jason's magnetic boots. "You remembered the boots. Very good. The *Bitch* doesn't have inertial dampeners, so we'll just have to make do as we used to."

"That won't be a problem," he replied, understanding the unspoken question of his host for the next five days. "We take appropriate courses at the academies since there are still smaller ships in the Fleet, like corvettes, that don't have artificial gravity."

"Wonderful. Now let me introduce you to the crew. Every one of them is a pain in the ass in their own way and they're going to get on your nerves sooner or later. Well, sooner rather than later, but you'll find that out for yourself. But they're my family, and if you have a problem with them, I'll kick you out the airlock, no matter if it gets the whole Federation on my ass—or what's left of it."

Jason looked for a sign of irony in the man's face but couldn't see any, so he just shrugged his shoulders.

"How bad could they be?"

As it turned out Willy, whose real name was Brun Gronski, was a giant Dunkelheimer augment addict who didn't even hide his prosthetic arms and legs. He reminded Jason of workers from the zero-G mines in Harbingen's Oort Cloud who had worked so far out in the dark that they lost touch with life of the flesh. They replaced one body part after another with cold metal that made them less susceptible to disease and injury. They soon began to speak of "maintenance" instead of "healing," and eventually completed the metamorphosis into quasi-robot.

Dozer was even worse. He had chrome eyes, a skull plate, and no longer revealed any discernible facial expressions under his synth skin. His elbows ended in double sockets for various tools—or weapons—and his mouth wasn't really a mouth at all, merely a connection for supply hoses.

Aura, the energy node specialist was the most beautiful woman he had ever seen, but so rude that she had packed a dozen warnings, curses, and threats into her brief introduction that it almost made his eyes water. Her cinnamon skin and dark almond eyes, which made any man think of Friday—if it only meant being allowed to drown in them—possibly pointed to a Raheem or Rajah origin.

Fusion engineer Jezzy was the exact opposite. She was a rather nondescript blonde with a long bird nose, but she seemed to think she was the ship's princess and was constantly gazing around either longingly or woefully. Her handshake was about as firm as a sip of water, and he noticed after just a few minutes that she was constantly looking at a vital monitor app on her forearm display.

*So, another hypochondriac.*

But the logs had informed him how efficiently and skillfully she had completed the integration of the two Scarab-4 fusion reactors. No easy task, considering that the high-tech reactors were far more advanced than anything on this ship—anything that was *officially* in this ship.

"We're all going to be good friends, I'm sure."

Dev grinned broadly after introducing everyone and showing him his bunk, located behind a cover in the corridor that divided the ship in half from bow to stern. It was as narrow as a shelf and looked about as comfortable, but Jason had slept in worse as a recruit. Well, not really, but if he talked himself into it, it would work out.

# 6

"This is simpler than I thought," Silly said as she gazed at the holo-display above the command deck. The bridge was filled with the serene buzz of activity. Muted voices drifted from the tiers where specialists diligently carried out their myriad duties. Together, they formed the collective intelligence of the *Oberon*, processing data from every system to make informed decisions.

This façade of normalcy briefly eased Nicholas's mind and allowed him to momentarily forget the horrors of the past weeks: the impending trap they unknowingly flew into and the imminent closure of the enemy's snare. Perhaps it was the familiarity of engaging in a battle with a known adversary that provided solace. No longer did they face an enigmatic, faceless foe from the depths of hyperspace, a species with whom communication had proven futile despite numerous encounters. Nevertheless, Nicholas's state of well-being remained far from optimal. Sleep eluded him as he was plagued by recurring dreams of his father, except when Laura made an appearance.

"That's the easy part," Daussel responded, and Nicholas inwardly agreed with him. They arrived in the Drakistan System twelve hours ago after passing through Epsilon Eridani at full thrust. The refugees there were already returning to Sol, and the habitats were emptying again. It had been comforting to no longer see an onslaught of refugees overloading the system, many surely dying of thirst or suffocation.

Four hours ago, using the top-secret codes Legutke had given them, they had begun overriding the commands of the 112,000 high-explosive cluster mines and positioned themselves where the Drakistan research station had once been. Now the *Oberon* lay there, its starboard hangar wide open like a voracious mouth, swallowing the mines that flew toward it with their tiny but, due to the low mass of their warheads, amazingly fast engines.

"We're a big fat vacuum cleaner sucking up anything that likes to explode," Silly said with a pained expression. "I'd be willing to bet that Karl is biting himself in the ass right now."

"He's probably too busy cursing us," Daussel said.

Nicholas imagined the chief engineer was bouncing off the walls because he'd had to prepare his hangar to flood it with nanonic safety foam. The device was designed to put out fires or, in the event of inertial dampener failure, to save the Barracudas that remained in the hangar for maintenance. The foam was sprayed from hundreds of palm-sized glands that filled the enormous space within minutes. The programmed liquid hardened in seconds, securing all moving parts until it was given a new command—for example, to change its state of aggregation and become liquid again and retreat via the drains. It was a handy mechanism for securing cargo if you wanted to stuff the hangar to the brim with space mines and fly into a battle. It had ultimately taken some coaxing from COB Borowski to calm Karl and convince him that the crew in charge could handle it.

No one was comfortable with the idea, but Nicholas considered it more a psychological problem knowing high-explosive drones in spherical form were being housed in the flank of one's ship, each designed to shred an armored starship hull. From a purely technical standpoint, the plan was sound and equally safe, as long as no one made a mistake—which was why it had taken the COB to vouch for his people. Not that Karl didn't know this, but Karl wouldn't be Karl if he didn't loudly curse his technicians as good-for-nothings at every opportunity—although he defended them like a rabid terrier whenever someone else dared do the same.

"How does the time look?" Silly asked, and Daussel answered her with two fingers raised.

*Two hours.*

Nicholas watched as the myriad red flashing dots on the situational image flew toward the gaping mouth of their ship, narrowed into a dense stream, slowed, and eventually disappeared into it. The analogy of a vacuum cleaner was quite apt. Nothing could be seen on the optical sensors because the mines were too small and were barely visible as glittering dots when they approached the lights of the *Oberon*. But he didn't want to know too much if he was being honest. The main thing was that the work would be done quickly, their titanium wouldn't be torn apart, and they could move on to the next phase of their plan—well, *his* plan—one for which the term reckless seemed to have been invented.

Their escort fleet included two *Rutherford*-class guided-missile destroyers, the *Saratoga* and the *Campbell*, which were fully loaded and ready to go because they had been holding an ECM exercise in Ganymede's shadow during the attack on Jupiter and were late to the battle. They had failed to reach Terra before the Clicks arrived and they wisely decided not to sacrifice themselves senselessly.

One frigate, the *Obsidian*, had shot off all its ammunition and was badly battered when von Solheim ordered it to surrender at the Battle of Terra. At that point, her captain, Geronimus Franklin, had been in the process of steering his ship into a Click destroyer. Good thing he hadn't. His ship was ready for action, but nowhere near what they would have liked. In addition, there were four fast corvettes, Broadswords, which had looked better before but would be important as support. They were already on their way to S1, towing the massive hyperspace engines behind them. In two hours, when all the mines were aboard, they would jump and initiate the next phase of their plan, wasting as little time as possible.

That was risky, since all it took was a little forward thinking on the part of their opponents to scout out Harbingen's neighboring systems and thwart everything by reporting back. Hence the escort. On the screen, he saw them as disappearing green dots, off to where they had arrived less than two weeks ago in their attempt to catch up with the *Caesar* and rescue his father. At that time, the minefield had caused them as much concern as it did today, only without the—rather paradoxical—hopes attached to it. Fate possessed a strange sense of humor.

"What about the survivors of the research station?" Silly asked. Her shift had just begun.

"We sent out several tug drones to collect and moor them. The Starvan from Epsilon Eridani should arrive here in an hour and be on its way to evacuate the survivors," Daussel reported.

"What about Rashkin?"

"He's alive and beside himself. Supposedly the supplies are exhausted."

"He'll probably live. They'll be able to hold out for a couple more hours." Silly was optimistic, apparently unwilling to dwell further on that unpleasant subject. Nicholas was sure Legutke would have to deal with this incident at some point, not least because of the public pressure as soon as the events became known. But there was still a long way to go before then, and he saw it as more of a luxury if they were actually around to face up to it. That would mean that they were still alive—not a highly likely prospect at this point.

Karl was no longer on board. That always caused uneasiness because Nicholas knew no one who exuded such an air of security, despite his grumbling. In addition, there was the considerable risk of losing him.

"What's the status of the Barracuda relocation?" Silly continued requesting updates, watching as Daussel shifted the holo-image until it showed the port hangar. It had to be a live image because he saw hundreds of technicians running back and forth between large scaffolds where they were attaching magnetic thruster mounts to hardpoints in the walls. On the deck floor, two dozen Barracudas were already stowed close together—only a hand's width separated the tips of their stubby wings.

"As it stands right now, reality is reflecting planning," the lieutenant commander said calmly. "Twenty-four fighters are parked and another forty-five can be suspended with the magnetic struts. Boarding the pilots will take up to an hour according to the CAG, so we'd better not schedule any emergency launches."

*The last Battleship*

"Those are good numbers. So, we've compensated for the unavailable launch bays. At a tactical disadvantage, but even so," the commander nodded, satisfied. "I see the Marines' drop pods are ready, too."

"Yes. However, the colonel lacks the hangar space to conduct the drills necessary for their upcoming mission, so he had to switch to VR equipment."

Silly smiled. "I know he hates that stuff, but at least this way he'll learn how to use it."

Nicholas took a deep breath and enjoyed the last moment of positive news when everything was still going as planned and as they had hoped. After the first contact with the enemy, the tide would turn, and instead of the calculated strategy and predictable logic, the fog of war would take hold, and with it the turmoil of chance and the snares that every battle threw in one's path—provided that wasn't the case beforehand.

∽

Dev deactivated the manual controls. The ship was now entirely under the control of the pilot software, which tacked a respectful distance behind the two guided-missile destroyers of the seven-ship flotilla traveling ahead of them to the inner S1 jump point of the Drakistan System. The *Obsidian* was the largest cylinder on the radar and led the way, followed by the *Saratoga* and the *Campbell*. They pulled the four massive, interconnected jump engines behind them on long carbotanium tows like two-pack mules far too small for their luggage.

Dev had never seen such engines naked since they were normally installed inside their respective ships. Normal engines were still based on the universal principle of Newtonian Laws: you throw something out the back, so you get thrown out the front. Normally, that meant a whole lot of hot gas being forced out of a thick nacelle to provide propulsion, the only difference being the source of heat and the associated differences in efficiency. Whether it happened by fusing pellets of helium-3 atoms or annihilating protons and antiprotons was basically irrelevant. At least not with respect to the underlying functional principle of acceleration.

The jump engines had nothing to do with that principle. In this respect, the term thrust was misleading since nothing about them required a thrust vector. Instead, the four pitch-black spheres, which housed man-thick cables and tubes that connected their inner surface to a much smaller boson chamber in the center, were Energy Impulse Tensor Generators, Fleet designation EITEG. They created tensor fields to generate gravitons. The resulting gravitational bubble ruptured normal space in a corresponding conjunction zone—commonly called a jump point—and expanded it by additional dimensions, creating hyperspace. The spaceship was swallowed, if the bubble was big enough, and came out at the destination point-another conjunctive zone—and returned to normal space.

Dev was secretly glad that Aura had given him that short lecture about jump engines after their departure from Sol, but he would never let her know that. A good captain should be cautious with encouragement. After all, he now knew what was beating in the *Bitch*'s heart and that didn't necessarily reassure him, not that he understood much of the physics mumbo-jumbo. He was even less reassured by the fact that he had no idea why the Fleet flunkies had taken those four monsters out of the *Concordia*, rather like ripping a beating heart from an elephant, making it just a lifeless skeleton in Earth orbit. Were they trying to intimidate the Exiles with a demonstration of their toys? "Here look what fancy things we can build. Now submit to our genius!"

Dev snorted. Who could tell what people who freely donned a uniform's handcuffs and then called themselves patriots thought up?

"Finished gawking?" Aura asked. She had appeared beside him out of nowhere and was looking at his radar screen. He took his eyes away from the wreath of four Broadswords guarding the load of the two guided-missile destroyers to the rear.

"I still can't see those things without wanting to hold a tantrum," he said.

"The corvettes?"

He nodded.

"Screw them, they're a dime a dozen. I'm more worried about our guest."

"Bradley?"

Now it was her turn to nod.

"What about him? Is he keeping Willy from work again by working on their pipe dream?" Dev asked.

"Nah. He's constantly staring at the door to the cargo space. Or should I say to our 'cargo container'? It's not really a space if you can't get in, is it?"

"I'll go check on him," he grumbled as he rose against the quite pleasant 0.8 G acceleration that pressed him into the seat as if it cost him physical effort.

Willy and Konrad Bradley's eldest son seemed to have become best friends on the very first day. They shared a fascination with Click telepathy. Jason was obsessed with the alleged esoteric bond he wanted to reestablish with this "broodmother." He was constantly babbling about the superiority of this form of communication and how they had to completely reformulate the definition of "understanding." Willy, on the other hand, was fascinated by a completely different aspect, namely the technical side of it all. He was already dreaming of tapping into the Omega, not just for the Exiles' travel destination data, but explicitly looking for the AI's research on neural interfaces.

Harbingen had been a frontrunner in computer brain research and there had been several projects like the famous Brainomics Project that had supposedly been on the verge of a breakthrough when the Clicks had turned everything into rubble with their attack on Kor.

Willy had been a specialist in neural pad production before he became a board engineer and was well acquainted with the networking of human impulse conduction as well as machines. He seemed to be dreaming of building an implant that made thought transmission possible. Now that it had been proven that such a thing could exist at all, and without a material connection between the individuals involved, he was ready to start working on it.

He found Jason Bradley, as Aura had said, in front of the

welded bulkhead that had once led to their cargo compartment and was now an unadorned gray steel wall. Again, a dull, almost rhythmic drone came from the other side. Last night Dev had fallen asleep in the mess hall and woken up with his head next to an old copy of *Heavy Metal F.A.K.K.* because he had thought he heard voices. That's how creepy that secret weapon seemed to him. Of course, there had been no voices when he had approached the door, only that muffled boom, which he heard now, albeit in a slightly different rhythm.

"Hey, *Admiral*," he called, and the young officer in his gray Fleet jumpsuit startled as if from a dream.

"Oh," Jason said, turning away from the doorway. "Don't call me that."

"If you start calling me Dev and not Mr. Meyer, maybe I'll reconsider. I'm not a fucking bureaucrat after all." He pointed at the smooth steel. "Developed X-ray vision yet? If so, I'd like to know what you see."

"No."

"What a shame. Are you going to try laying hands on it?"

"No." Jason shook his head and was about to turn away, but Dev held him back with one hand.

"Wait a minute. You know what's in there, right?"

"Yes," the officer admitted, to his surprise. "And it worries me."

"Well, great. Couldn't you have said that in the first place?"

"That I'm worried about it? Sure."

"No," Dev grunted angrily. "If you know what's in there, I sure as hell want to know."

"A weapon. I told you."

"Well, it could be anything. I swear to you, if there's a giant antimatter bomb in there"—he tried not to look at the holotable where they now had their meals—"I want to know right now."

"Roger that."

"What do you mean?"

"That I got it."

*So, there's none in there and that's why you're not saying anything. Or is there one in there and you just understand that I want to know?* he thought and was about to stab Jason's chest with

*The last Battleship*

an outstretched index finger when Willy came stomping toward them.

"Ah, there he is." The Dunkelheimer augment addict squeezed through the doorway to the workshop and pointed at Jason. "I've been mulling over some ideas that I wanted to talk through with you. If you're up for it, I could hook you up to the intracranial signaling network, and we can play around with using a standard computer as a simultaneous cognitive translator. Your thoughts get into the computer, the appropriate signals filtered for my head to my thoughts. That could actually work. Maybe a little rudimentary at first, but we're still in the very early stages."

Only now did he seem to notice Dev at all and tossed him a quick "Hi, boss," before his eyeballs turned back to Jason. His electronic irises seemed to make clacking noises, or maybe he was just imagining it. Jason eased away from the welded-up doorway

Jason's face brightened with barely concealed enthusiasm as if someone had flipped a switch. "That's fantastic news, Willy. Of course, I'm your guinea pig."

As if the strange spectacle wasn't already odd enough, he slapped the bearlike flight engineer chummily on the shoulder. Willy grinned so broadly that every one of his platinum teeth became visible.

"Oh, isn't that nice!" Dev gushed teasingly. "What a fine couple we have here. May I throw flowers at you and congratulate you or is it too soon?"

The two turned to him and looked puzzled.

"Can you guys put your esoteric bullshit aside for a second?"

"It's not *esoteric shit*!" Willy huffed. Only a few platinum teeth were now visible. "I was—"

"I know that you're neglecting your work. Our alien whisperer here was just about to explain to me what mysterious cargo is hiding behind there!"

"No, I wasn't," Jason said coolly. "I just said that I would say something if it was an antimatter bomb because that would be illegal. But that there"—the officer pointed behind him—"is merely top secret because the weapon has never been used in Fleet service, and we want to keep it that way so the enemy can't prepare for it.

After all, we have to assume he has his network of spies everywhere."

"See, no antimatter!" Willy boomed with satisfaction and then turned Jason around like a toy figure. "So, about this intracranial signaling network—the procedure is minimally invasive. I still have some medical nanites from the…"

"Since when did everyone on this ship forget that I'm the fucking captain?" Dev asked, but his voice trailed off unheard as the two new best friends disappeared into Willy's workshop, locking him out when the bulkhead slammed down behind them as if the *Bitch* herself was answering his question. His eyes wandered to the massive steel plate, and he reached out a hand to touch it. A slight vibration, increasing and then decreasing, ran through his fingers.

*What the hell is in there?*

# 7

Lieutenant Commander Karl Murphy steered his mobility unit over the monotonous gray surface of the asteroid, named rather unromantically XH-77892 sometime long ago. Here in the Xinhua system, it had not been particularly difficult to find a suitable candidate for their purposes. It consisted of four asteroid belts and its only two planets were stinking methane giants.

So, right after their arrival at the outer jump point, which was teeming with big chunks, they started searching and found this baby, a 1,200-meter-long Dicolith that looked like a downward curving cigar with a few craters, hills, and valleys. For an asteroid, its total mass was surprisingly high, suggesting the material inside was compacted. Most rocky bodies in space were relatively loose collections of regolith, dust, and ice that had neither a solid core nor significant gravity because their mass was so small. Therefore, instead of a rock, the metaphor of an airy sand cake would be much more apt, even if it seemed difficult for the human mind to comprehend. But XH-77892 was something they could work with.

As he flew over it, he watched the four Broadswords work the chunk with their communication lasers set to maximum power, cutting holes in its surface before his technicians in charge, already waiting in their own MUs at the strength of a hundred, would shortly begin placing high-precision directional mines in the holes to blast a large chunk out of Dicolith.

Dicolith had quickly become the official name as a result of his first radio call—"What an ugly, limp dick-olith!"—after finding it on the sensor screens. Karl felt it didn't do justice to what he meant. But, as it happened, if you had a loose mouth your own ghosts caught up with you more often than you would have liked.

Karl flew toward the rear end of Dicolith with short bursts of cold gas from his MU and sharpened his helmet sensors so they filled the image in his visor with detail. It was extremely dark out here and without the high-powered searchlights over his shoulder, he wouldn't have been able to see his own hand in front of his eyes. The nearby gas ball of a methane giant seemed to swallow the light from the distant Xinhua central star like a greedy maw instead of reflecting some and making their job easier.

As soon as he rounded the "stern" of the asteroid, he saw the swarm of maintenance drones with their yellow position lights streaming out of the *Obsidian*'s dorsal hangar-like fat bumblebees. The frigate hung like a chunky silver arrow with a broken tip just a few clicks above them, impressive with her many position lights and the lettering TFS Obsidian illuminated by spotlights.

The little robot helpers weren't here to sightsee, though. Each was towing a reflective piece of black foil made of programmable silicon, except for the few that were carrying the components of a mobile molecular bond generator and its nanoflagella. Karl positioned himself close enough, but not so close that it forced any of them to change course, since all energy supplies were precisely calculated. He didn't want to become a laughingstock in the officers' mess.

It took forty minutes for them to assemble the 20-meter diameter dish so he could begin installing the molecular bond generator. He attached and welded all the cables and programmed it. Then he clamped the viscose polymer bags with the flagella supply to the suction device and waited for them to empty. Once the readouts satisfied him and the silicon film reported no irregularities in its funnel shape, he opened a channel to the *Obsidian*.

"Everything is ready from my side. The little buggers can steam off again."

"Thank you, Chief." To his surprise, Captain Saraswati replied personally. "You'll probably be interested to know that the *Oberon* has just jumped into the system and is taking up position at S1 until our operation is complete."

He sighed. "Thank God."

Every minute that had passed without his home ship nearby had made him more nervous. Their operation was vulnerable in two places—at S1 and S2. They were only one jump from Harbingen and a single scout ship jumping into the system and disappearing again would be enough to blow everything and further hurt their chances of driving off the Exiles, or at least achieving the two primary objectives of their mission.

"You can order your Broadswords to push that Dicolith into position as soon as they're ready on the flank. I'll anchor the jump drive on the way, then we won't lose any time."

"All right, Chief, I'll set that up. Saraswati out."

"On to the next item on the checklist, then," he said, unheard, into his helmet.

With short bursts from his MU, he flew to the port side of the long asteroid. The rock was quite small in cosmic terms but loomed out of the darkness beside him like a mountain range. The blasting had apparently already occurred because he could see a shower of regolith and massive chunks of ice that formed a funnel-shaped cloud away from a hole about the size of a football field. Karl thought it looked downright beautiful, like an impact without the impact, the massive size of a cosmic event but without the usual negative consequences like screaming and dying. Normally, he couldn't get enough of such things, especially since he hardly ever left his workshops or his two hangars, but someone had to make sure all the light bulbs under his charge were shining as they should, so he had no time.

From the artificially created depression—to call it a hole would probably be too optimistic—his technicians came toward him, a swarm of position lights that became faces illuminated by the visors. As they passed each other, he raised an arm in greeting and then made his way to the anchor points they had placed.

These were four massive magnets that had been secured with the simplest techniques in the firmer regolith beneath the asteroid's surface and would serve as improvised suspension points for the jump engines. Presumably, it would have worked without those measures since there was no significant acceleration vector, but without safety margins, there was zero hope for success out here unless every little thing was considered and optimized.

"Dino, how's that graffiti coming?" he asked over the radio as he watched the dozens of maintenance drones dragging the four interconnected jump thrusters toward him as if to trap him under a giant lid.

"Omega," replied his favorite lieutenant, whom he had assigned the duty of space graffiti artist to tag the "bow" of their Dicolith with a message. "Easily readable by any third-rate sensor, I'm sure. The bastards will get the message, Chief."

"I should hope so. Although I'd prefer it if nobody had to read it."

"Anyway, I can't wipe it off again," Dino joked, his voice radio-distorted in his helmet.

"Just don't. Fly back to the *Obsidian* when you're done. I'm still checking the EITEG's moorings, then I'll join you." Karl saw an incoming link in his visor. It was coming from the *Oberon*.

"Howdy," he boomed as he accepted the connection request.

"Captain Thurnau for you, Lieutenant Commander," he heard Lieutenant Jung say formally. "The connection is encrypted."

"All clear."

"Karl," Silly said flatly. "Are we happy?"

"Yeah, I guess we are," he replied mumbling around his water hose as took a sip. Seeing something as massive as four EITEG thrusters mated together approaching you out of the darkness while squatting in a crater was unpleasant. It felt more like being trapped. "We can start pushing Dicolith into position in about half an hour and recharge the EITEGs along the way."

*"Dicolith?"*

"That's what we call our planet killer here."

"Sounds stupid," Silly remarked.

"All the better."

"How did working with the *Obsidian* go?"

"With Saraswati you mean? Or with the non-Harbingers? Or

with the Fleet?" he responded. He had known Silly far too long to be under any illusions. She didn't even trust herself most of the time, but certainly not the Fleet or anyone not born on Harbingen.

"Just answer me."

"It's all right. He's a little stiff but conscientious. There have been no problems between us and his crew, and he's got the place under control." Karl watched the EITEG construct descend on him like the fist of a punishing god, albeit in slow motion, and breathed a sigh of relief as the magnets on both sides connected and locked into place. He now lay in a hollow two meters deep and set about connecting his forearm display to the thrusters' computer system.

"That's good to hear. I want you to come back as soon as you're no longer needed. You and your team. I will instruct Captain Saraswati to provide you with a shuttle."

"All right, but it will take some time." A red warning symbol appeared in his field of vision, demanding his attention. "Hang on a second, I'm getting a priority message in from the *Obsidian*."

∼

"Damned, fucking shit," Dev cursed as the unknown radar contact popped up and prompted the onboard computer to emit a series of shrill warning beeps and flashing red signs. "Bogey at S2!"

"I see it," Aura murmured in the seat diagonally behind him. "The transit radiation isn't particularly high, but—*second contact!*"

Dev saw the second radar contact without transponder identification. According to the sensors, there was a 93 percent probability that they were Broadsword-type corvettes.

*I hate those things!*

"We were so close!" he howled, activating the battle alert, then shouted over the ship's radio, "All hands to the nearest acceleration seats!"

The jump point in Xinhua's outer system was only 30,000 clicks away, a cosmic stone's throw. The first enemy corvette was already accelerating, exhaust flaring, toward the asteroid that lay beneath the *Obsidian*. She was in the process of recovering the first maintenance bots and her dorsal hangar was wide open. The two guided-missile destroyers, the *Saratoga* and the *Campbell*, paused below to assist the vacuum technicians' deployment of their carbotanium lines with their sensors, while the flotilla's four escort corvettes moved into position behind the "stern" to fire up the improvised propulsion system. Not a good time for uninvited eyes and ears to appear and interfere with their plans. At least they were coming from the front and not from behind, that was at least something.

The *Quantum Bitch* was just above the ecliptic of the methane giant, busy keeping as far away from the flotilla as possible.

"Incoming report from the *Obsidian*!" Aura called as the fusion engines neared their full power level. Dev didn't feel like talking to the uniform wearers, much less the humorless Saraswati who had no patience for ethnic jokes.

"Put him through!" he said reluctantly.

"Captain Meyer," he heard Saraswati say excitedly.

*Respectful, at least,* he thought. He was even able to ignore the commanding tone that had always caused psychoallergic reactions in him.

"Catch the bogey with the..."

The message was lost in an ugly outburst of rushing noise.

"What are you doing?" he yelled, upset. He hadn't heard the rest of the command, and it wasn't due to any psychoallergic shock. There were two bogeys on his screen. Which one had the captain meant?

"Our communications are being jammed."

*I could have guessed that.*

"Shit!" Dev thought feverishly, then made his decision and activated the acceleration alarm with a five-second countdown. Anyone not in their seats would soon find themselves in sickbay. He accelerated the *Bitch* at a brutal 10 Gs toward Bogey 1, the Broadsword heading for the asteroid.

"Are you crazy?" Aura sounded upset. "We have to take out Bogey 2 before it jumps away. They're already activating their jump thrusters."

"We can't get them both, but Bogey 1 only sees the asteroid

we're interested in. Maybe we can push it over the jump point so they can't jump here again. They might also guess what we're doing with it." He was using his transducer now, forming his thoughts into words and sending them over the internal radio because he couldn't have gotten his jaws apart now as he was, pressed into the seat with ten times his body weight. "But if Bogey 1 survives and flies too far around the asteroid, it's increasingly likely they'll see through our plan."

"If we destroy Bogey 2, then Bogey 1 is trapped and we'll get him anyway!" his energy node specialist objected. The slight monotone of her computer-generated voice seemed strangely emotionless in the face of what they were doing.

From the ecliptic, the *Bitch* plunged through the thin ring of water crystals and dust surrounding the methane giant, piercing it like a force of nature. Ionizing gases swirled behind her and dissipated in a dance of extremely excited particles. The flotilla and its newest toy, the ugliest regolith bar in the universe, lay far "below" them at the perfect approach angle for S2, making it less than perfect for intercepting the enemy corvette. Of course, they could quickly decide the battle with the bogey if that's what Saraswati wanted. Yet the tactical situation, which would have been incredibly one-sided and simple for a first-year cadet under normal circumstances, was now proving to be extremely complicated here and now.

The *Obsidian* had to catch up with her maintenance bots because they desperately needed to recharge for the next phase. The *Saratoga* and the *Campbell* were the eyes of the space workers and their shields. Those men and women would be defenseless against the attacker if they decided to fire on them, and every one of them was crucial to the success of the plan. Only the four corvettes could abandon their current positions without ruining everything until the *Obsidian* captured the last bot and set about destroying Bogey 1 herself. But that would take a few minutes, at least. Minutes they did not have.

"The shuttles are the biggest problem."

"What shuttles?" Despite the computer voice, Aura sounded

breathless. Dev couldn't blame her. He felt like a pork cutlet that had been pounded flat for too long and had lost its bones.

"Look at the radar! The *Oberon* sent out its twenty shuttles an hour ago. They're still in the shadow of our bogey's long-range radar, but not for long. When it sees them, it'll start asking questions. Besides," he said, brutally yanking the *Bitch* into the intercept vector, "the *Oberon* is right behind it and no longer at S1. We're lucky the motherfuckers came out at S2."

Their exhaust flare grew to several kilometers of hot plasma that traveled through the vacuum like a brushstroke of fire and vaporized any stray molecules in its wake. The Broadsword they were tracking went into a sharp right tilt to increase its angle and better scan the asteroid. The bastards could certainly see the large "Omega" spray painted in infrared paint with their naked eyes.

"Damn! If he gets away from us, he'll fly on to S2 and jump!"

"Exactly," he grumbled and armed the railgun. Unlike the *Bitch*, the Broadsword was made for war and possessed, if not more modern, then clearly more weapons than she did—which included missiles, which they were now firing at the bogey. "Fucking cocksuckers! Aura, you take the PDCs!"

"Roger that!"

"Jason!" he shouted over the ship's radio. "You've got about twenty seconds to get to the bridge. In ten, nine, eight, seven, six, five, four, three, two, one, *now!*"

Dev throttled the thrusters down to a fraction of a G and the onset of weightlessness felt like he had swallowed a fishhook that was now pulling his stomach through his esophagus. A practiced spaceman, he swallowed the nauseating sensation and hoped that an artificial gravity-addled Fleet shithead like the elder Bradley could handle it and not waste his twenty seconds throwing up all over his workshop, the mess hall, or the corridor to the bridge.

He fired three times with the Striker railgun mounted under the bow at the enemy's flight vector to prevent it from getting too far ahead. The shots were calculated by the onboard computer to force the bogey to make a course correction. He fired three more shots in a fan pattern on the area to the left of that, away from the flotilla and the asteroid, to force the

*The last Battleship*

Broadsword to veer inward, toward the allied ships, if possible. The *Obsidian* had already ejected half a dozen Predator drones and they pounced on the unwanted guest at close to 120 Gs acceleration, while twelve more raced toward S2, where the remaining Broadsword was busy charging its energetic pattern cells for transit back to Harbingen.

Jason floated into the cockpit as Dev's countdown reached seventeen and strapped himself into Willy's seat at Dev's curt wave.

"You take the railgun, *Lieutenant*."

"Lieutenant Colonel," Jason corrected him casually as he engaged the AI-assisted weapons control of their one gun. "I must confess that it's been a long time since—"

"You got trained on this shit, we didn't, so you'll be able to do it as well as me. What else did you get those fine badges for, hey?" Dev babbled as he engaged the thrusters forward for a renewed lunge that slammed him into his seat and nipped any conversation in the bud. Only when he was satisfied that they were faster than the Broadsword and closing the gap did he say over his transducer, "I have to steer, Aura has the PDCs."

As if awakening spirits that would have been better kept sleeping, the Exile corvette fired a salvo of six missiles that sped toward them with glowing propulsion nacelles. After the brief deceleration moment after ejection, they flared like little stars and closed the distance at a frightening rate.

"In five seconds, we'll be in effective weapons range for the railgun," he announced. "Target the magazine. It's sitting on the underside between the radiator exhaust ports!"

Jason didn't answer, most likely because he didn't have a transducer. Dev thought no more about it and increased acceleration to 13 Gs. At that, his auto-injector flooded his bloodstream with anticoagulants and amphetamines to keep him from having a stroke as his arteries shrank under thirteen times the weight of his body.

Just a few more seconds.

"Don't pass out on me, Lieutenant!"

"Anh..." Jason growled, but it was barely intelligible. "Anhhh... anhaaa..."

"I think he means stop!" Aura said as her PDCs sprang to life, and she opened fire on the oncoming missiles with their Gatling guns.

"Fuck no!"

"Just do it!"

"Shit!" Without knowing what he was doing, Dev's fingers obeyed her, and he shut down the thrusters. Their brand-new railgun fired a single tungsten bolt a fraction of a second later and hit its target in 2.4 seconds. "Shit, man, I told you that magazine—"

He stopped when he saw, first on the infrared sensors and then on the telescopic images, what the officer's shot had done. It hadn't been aimed at the area he had marked between the radiator ports but at a point just above the aft sensor phalanx where the ring of sensing probes merged with the drive nacelle. Whatever the man had targeted, it released an impressive fountain of gas that sent the corvette into an uncontrolled tumble. Without thinking, Dev fired the railgun several times in succession at the defenseless target when Jason failed to respond despite his orders.

"Impact in four, three..." Aura called out as he was about to cheer about how he had shredded the Broadsword that had just been pulverized into an accelerated debris mist. The PDCs had intercepted four of the missiles, but the remaining two had evaded fire in an erratic evasion pattern and would strike—

No, they wouldn't.

They dissolved into a cloud of powder under flanking fire, and two Predator drones raced past, so close to his cockpit that he could have touched them if he had just leaned far enough out of the windshield. The remnants of the guided missiles pelted the *Bitch*'s armored hull like space hail.

"Remaining bogey has jumped!" Aura called. "And we're still fucking alive! Awesome shot, Jason. Not bad, for a Fleet ass!"

"Yeah, not bad at all!" Dev turned to grin at the officer, but the man was slumped unconscious in his seat. "Oh. Guess he didn't have an auto-injector implanted after all."

"Shit." The energy node specialist unbuckled her seat belt and floated over to Jason, pulled an injector from her Velcro-fastened breast pocket, and jammed it down his throat.

"By the Omega!" the Harbinger blurted, mouth and eyes wide.

*The last Battleship*

He looked around feverishly, then sank back into his harness with relief. "We're still alive."

"I don't know what kind of fix you pulled, Lieutenant, but it worked somehow," Dev laughed, waiting for congratulations to arrive from the *Obsidian*.

"That was no lucky shot," Jason gasped. "The old Harbinger Broadswords produced under license had a known weakness that was eradicated in the successor model—their oxygen and nitrogen supplies were buried under an armor segment near the sensor phalanx. We jokingly christened the phalanx the 'target object phalanx' at cadet school for this reason. A good hit has the same effect as a maneuvering nozzle out of control."

"Not bad at all." The grin was still on his face, and it widened when he got notification of an incoming connection from the *Obsidian*. "Captain Meyer here."

"Good work," Captain Saraswati said calmly. "Orders from the *Oberon*: the operational timetable has been accelerated. As soon as the shuttles arrive, we'll begin the final preparation step and attack. The *Oberon* jumps first, we follow."

"You've got it." Dev didn't think that anything about the plan was clear at all, especially since the damned weapon of mass destruction, practically a black bow, mounted under his wing wouldn't let him rest easy. But at least it was so crazy that it could have come from him. The only question remained: Was the enemy prepared for them?

# 8

Chancellor Theoderich von Borningen was standing on the bridge of the *Redemption* when *Sister's Mercy* appeared at S1. She was met by a cocoon of fifty warships from the Harbinger Fleet—the *real* Harbinger Fleet—that had locked on, scanned, and targeted the little Broadsword in less than two seconds. In addition, there was an equal number of Behemoth cargo drones, which, in the far darkness of the Oort Cloud, his people had converted in recent years into something like mobile defense platforms, unarmored but bristling with weapons. Each had two mounted railguns and housed an arsenal of forty kinetic missiles from the copious supplies they had diverted from the Terran Fleet's supply network over the past decades. Today, they would be worth every bribe and fee paid to smugglers.

The *Redemption*, under Pyrgorates's command, was some distance from the S1 at Harbingen's central star to keep track of the system and not be affected by the ecliptic.

"*Sister's Mercy*, this is Admiral Pyrgorates. Report!" Theoderich had recently installed him as commander of their fleet. The chancellor preferred to stand and inspect exactly how Pyrgorates was behaving. If he noticed, he did not let on. He had become too good a politician and schemer to be nervous about being under observation, anything else would have surprised Theoderic.

"This is Lieutenant Commander Greulich," came the reply

over the radio as the Broadsword oriented itself on S2, its sensor beams extended, and rapidly accelerated out of the center of the array of trained guns like a child who had inadvertently appeared on a brightly lit stage. "*Freedom of the Gospel* was destroyed in its attempt to scan the traitors' flotilla."

"What did you see?"

"The *Oberon* is on its way here escorted by a frigate, two *Ronald Reagan*-class guided-missile destroyers, and four latest-generation Broadswords," Greulich reported.

"I knew it," Theoderich said with a thin smile. "If something can go wrong, always count on it going wrong. That pirate ship that got away from us, the *Quantum Bitch*, she's certainly in on it."

"Lieutenant Commander, was there a ninth ship with them?" Pyrgorates asked.

"Yes, an old, converted corvette with a large cargo module. She destroyed *Freedom of the Gospel*."

"That's her." Theoderich nodded as the admiral looked at him.

"There's something else, sir." There was a hint of uncertainty evident in Greulich's voice. "The traitors have been working on an asteroid near S2 and written Omega on it."

"Send us the sensor data," Pyrgorates snarled and turned to Theoderich, whose augmented brain was already running through all possible scenarios involving an asteroid. "Chancellor? What do you think of that?"

"Hmm. We use asteroids too, maybe they just wanted to prevent us from detecting them by pushing it onto S2 in Xinhua."

Theoderich thought about what he had just said and shook his head. They were doing the same thing at S2 here in Harbingen, but it was no easy matter. No object with its own mass could remain in the center of a conjunction zone for more than a few minutes without being torn apart by the tidal forces of the gravitons, and so it took a lot of effort and energy to impose transit blockades. The Federation had often experimented with this, up to and including plasma fields that were sinfully expensive to maintain, but every plan had failed. The best solution was still defensive platforms that automatically fired at everything that did not have a transit permit. New arrivals, by necessity, always came through the jump point one

*The last Battleship*

at a time and took some time to deploy their sensors and scan the environment. Destroying them at that moment was far more cost-effective and efficient than any other solution—provided you had enough ships. Theoderich had been forced to choose because he had expected a larger force, but apparently the terrors from hyperspace had been exceedingly efficient at running the Federation into the ground and making them pay for their arrogance.

As it happened, S2 was now blocked by sixteen small asteroids revolving in a circle, always closing the conjunction zone for two minutes before being replaced by the next one, leaving only small gaps of twenty seconds, little time for a ship to jump in. He had led his fleet to S1, expecting the enemy would target their transmission facility on Kor and the excavation site at the Palace of Unity. That he was right was proven not least by the inscription on the asteroid Greulich had reported.

"They're not going to block the jump point in Xinhua," he said after a while. "They are jumping with the asteroid."

"How would that be possible?" Pyrgorates said. "That would mean—"

"—That they're attaching a jump engine in or on a celestial body along with a lot of energy matrix cells. We'll have to look at *Sister's Mercy* and *Freedom of the Gospel*'s data to see what they detected at the other end of the asteroid. If they brought a reaction engine..." Theoderich interrupted himself and rubbed his temples. "Radloff nacelles, for example, crude but powerful. They could accelerate it to appreciable speeds."

"A planet killer."

"Almost, depending on impact velocity. In any case, their need makes them inventive. They have too few ships to take out their two main targets, the phase antenna on Kor and the excavation at the base of the Unity Palace. We're almost there, so we have to make sure they fail, Admiral."

"We have enough firepower here at S1 to crush them to dust."

"With the *Oberon* it becomes more difficult. If she gets through first, she can draw fire long enough to allow the others to follow. Don't underestimate her flak screen and the power of her railguns," Theoderich advised the bald officer. "After that, they can send the asteroid through and accelerate it toward Harbingen and drop it on the dig site. In their worst case, they'll destroy the data storage of their beloved Omega, which they won't like, but would prefer to us having access. Their best case, they destroy our defenses there and extract the data themselves to revive the AI."

"What if they send the asteroid first?" Pyrgorates asked.

"That's possible, and it would have the advantage of wasting munitions—and time. But an asteroid is a fragile structure and quickly thrown off course by bombardment if it doesn't break up immediately. The debris could overload our sensors if there's too much of it." Theoderich thought feverishly to see if he had missed anything—but he hadn't. The traitors' idea was audacious and unorthodox enough to surprise *any* enemy, but he was not *any* enemy. "The asteroid will come last and head for Harbingen. They can only profit if we fire on it because it will draw fire from the *Oberon* and its flotilla, or at best, give them one target less so they can concentrate fully on Kor. One more thing, I want to see a picture of that *Quantum Bitch*."

Pyrgorates tapped his forearm display and called up the image from the sensor scans from *Sister's Mercy*. They both looked at the raptorlike spacecraft, and Theoderich zoomed in on the area that particularly interested him: the crude cargo cuboid.

"Are those thrusters?" He frowned.

"Yeah, they look like old Raptors," the admiral agreed and narrowed his eyes. "Over twenty of them. They can hurl whatever that is with such force that the palace's automatic defenses will have trouble. Not to mention our own on the ground."

"I've taken care of that. I arranged for two hundred of our Marines to be moved to the excavation site a week ago and get them dug in. Whatever they bomb us with, our people have had plenty of time to protect themselves—as long as they're not using antimatter. In that case, it wouldn't make any difference anyway," Theoderich said with a somber shrug. "But as long as they want the datastore—which we should assume for now is the case—they'll want to destroy anything from orbit that could be dangerous to their own Marines."

"The Black Legion," Pyrgorates said with a hint of concern.

*The last Battleship*

Even though the admiral did a decent job of hiding it, not the slightest thing escaped Theoderich's notice.

"We can handle them. Many of our veterans were in the Black Legion themselves and know their armor and weapons systems inside and out. We're prepared for them."

"But what about Kor? The *Oberon* can't be in two places at once. If she breaks through to the moon's fragment, she could destroy the transmission facility. She has planetary weapons in her arsenal, and lots of them."

"The first thing we do is order the ground station to retract the phase antenna. The armored doors are tough, and I don't think this *Quantum Bitch*'s sensor readings were good enough to pinpoint its exact position without visual contact. We move half a legion of Marines below the surface and wait. No matter how the battle goes, the *Oberon* and her ridiculous flotilla will be weakened when it advances from S1, if they get through at all, which is highly unlikely. This means that even if they make it to Kor's remains they won't be able to sustain an hours-long bombardment. That means their only option would be to land with boarding shuttles, and our ground defenses can deal with those."

"We are well prepared," Pyrgorates nodded. It was true, of course, that *the* Theoderich was on the alert, but he had never been concerned with vanity, only with achieving his goals—*Harbingen's* goals.

"Just until the first missiles start flying. Then we'll see exactly what their battle plan is and what gaps ours has."

"Silvea Thurnau is many things, but she's not a brilliant tactician."

"Underestimating your opponents isn't brilliant either, Admiral," he countered sternly.

"Of course, Chancellor, you are right," Pyrgorates replied in his pleasing way that was extremely distasteful to Theoderich. But one did not make friends with the sharpest knives in the kitchen—one used them to cut ingredients and prepare dishes. Which was exactly what he intended to do. "We'll just have to see what happens. But just in case, I want you to pull a flotilla of ten ships off S1 at the central star and order them a third of the way back to Harbingen.

They are to wait there, hidden in Melchior's shadow. If the traitors should succeed in escaping from S1 with their asteroid maneuver, they will be ambushed and fired upon from front and rear at the same time and that's when we will crush them."

"They could also jump to S2 at Bohr," Pyrgorates suggested but dismissed the idea himself. "But to do that, they'd have to have their sensors out too long and use the long-range scanners to figure out what's waiting for them there."

"Which they won't have. Or they'll be so risk averse that they'll jump there blindly and the asteroid field will destroy them."

Theoderich allowed his mouth to part into a slight smile. The tarnished Federation might have made it farther than he thought it would, but he had factored in the possibility of the accidental element from the beginning. That's why he wasn't surprised that an unlikely clipper like the *Quantum Bitch*—what a stupid name—of all things was, by sheer coincidence, capturing images of their preparations for the final phase of the plan for humanity's future.

On the contrary, the surprise lay rather in the fact that it had happened so late. The traitors in the service of other masters came improvising and burdened by the necessity to react quickly. Theoderich, however, had prepared for this moment for many, many years and had gone through countless scenarios, including any number of simulations in which they were attacked by much larger fleets in the final stages. In only a few of those computer calculations had he lost, and from those precious defeats he had drawn the necessary conclusions to avert them in reality and ensure that nothing like this would happen again outside a computer simulation.

"You don't seem particularly concerned," Pyrgorates said, smiling now as well.

"I'm not." Theoderich looked down at his forearm display and counted down five seconds. "The signal to our brothers and sisters has *just* been sent."

"What?" Pyrgorates sounded perplexed.

"I only initiated those who needed to know. Do not take it personally. The traitors wanted to stop us from calling Harbingen. But we've just done so," he announced in triumph. "Now they can bombard the excavation site at their whim with whatever they intend to surprise us with. Our sappers will prepare to blow up the Omega as soon as we get the signal hold verified from the other side. That may only take a few hours. The *Oberon*'s Marines will not be able to land because of the palace's automatic defense systems, and so they will not be able to prevent the detonation. I'm afraid they'll have come for absolutely nothing."

Pyrgorates put on an extremely mischievous grin.

# 9

Tense silence reigned on the bridge of the *Oberon*. Voices among the ranks of crew members sank to a muted minimum, matching the mood set by the dim red light of the battle alert that had been activated at the same time as the jump alert.

Nicholas stood with his hands resting on the command deck, bent over the edge of the holoscreen as if he lacked the strength to stand upright, but in truth it was the tension that arched his back, fed by the countdown Alkad's businesslike voice recited no differently than for any other jump. Every soul on board was aware that it would be *the* jump. At least one of three that would decide the fate of their ship, their home, and their future as a people and as humanity.

It was pathetic when he thought about it, but only superficially. As soon as he reminded himself that their plan and all the ideas about what they might expect on the other side were not just their imagination, a mere tactical finger exercise, a lead ball settled in his stomach and grew heavier with every breath. Theory would now become practice, which was usually less predictable and decidedly bloodier.

"After the jump, it's our turn," Silly said to him. He nodded. His mouth was dry and there was a horrible taste on his tongue, as if someone had wiped it with an old rag. "It'll work."

"It has to," he muttered, and the knuckles of his hands stood out white until the command deck creaked in protest.

"Nine," Alkad said. Her voice carried to each ear by invisible speakers high in the ceiling.

"XO?" Silly looked at him seriously and nodded. "Your plan, your orders."

Nicholas blinked in surprise.

"Eight."

"Go ahead." A thin smile flitted across her lips, and he envied her obvious ease. If Alkad hadn't already been at—

"Seven."

—he would have asked her what her secret was for staying so calm.

"Six."

"Prepare flak shield, full coverage, staggered sphere!" he finally ordered. The sound of his voice calmed him a bit. Since when was he prone to nervousness? Whatever it was now receded as he issued the orders, which were more a formality as each step had been meticulously planned and practiced over five days to minimize uncertainty as much as possible.

"Five."

"Switch PDCs to full cadence, extend the mounts."

"Four."

"Railguns to maximum power output. Enable automatic fire release."

"Three."

"Open torpedo bays, wait for release."

"Two."

"Open missile bays port and starboard and pre-cool ejection bays."

"One."

"Stand by. Initiate final jump preparations."

"Jump!"

∽

*The last Battleship*

Captain Souza stood in front of his seat on the bridge of the *Templar*, which had been given the overall command of guarding S1 at Harbingen's central star. Well, *he* had been given the overall command, and when the transit alarm sounded, he was holding a datapad and issuing tedious logistical orders his staff had worked out in case their spherical cocoon of weaponized ships and converted Behemoths had to wait longer for the traitors.

"Incoming transit!" his operator shouted from the sensor station.

"Begin scan!" he barked. "All ships—fire at will!"

Ullmann Souza didn't even need optical telescopes to see the fireworks begin. The sight on the virtual screen located at the front of the bridge like a real window made the two rows of his bridge crew at their control consoles glow pale. He watched as hundreds of missiles detached themselves from his fleet and sped toward the jump point as if they were being sucked in by a black hole. The distances were cosmically tiny, but still too far to see without zooming in on the ship that would shortly be torn apart by the hurricane of kinetic projectiles. Like any spacecraft that transited, it took some time to deploy the sensor arrays, which were otherwise destroyed during the jump by hitherto unknown dimensional effects. Only then could it perform a scan that correctly located it in the universe and reorient itself accordingly.

"That ship is huge, Captain!" shouted someone who sounded like Lieutenant Beugers. "Over a kilometer long, mass at over—"

"It's the *Oberon*!" Souza interrupted him, seeing the blue flicker of his fleet's railguns firing everything they had to give the traitors a fitting welcome. A triumphant howl rang in his head, and he clenched his hands into fists as he sat down.

"First impacts!"

∼

The ugliest asteroid ever—if Lieutenant Commander Karl Murphy's team had anything to say about it—absorbed the first five kinetic missiles that crashed into its rutted surface at close to 500 kilometers per second with relative ease. Like an animal with thick leathery skin, a wave passed through the cigar-shaped body with the curved snout and the loose regolith began to dance. The relatively solid core of the celestial body was violently shaken, but it survived.

At least until over 600 more missiles hit. In an immeasurably short time, many hundreds of furiously fast tungsten bolts struck. They did not trail fire like most missiles but flew like invisible death made of ultra-hard alloy.

XH-77892 was instantly shredded in a roaring hurricane of rock chunks with varying metal content. Regolith dissolved into stardust and ice crystals evaporated so quickly that no Federation sensor could have recorded their change of state. But before each former element of the asteroid could flee its former heart, one of the missiles struck a secret reservoir that had been welded into the flank of the destroyed XH-77892 that carried the cargo of twenty *Oberon* shuttles. The impact immediately eliminated a notable portion of more than 100,000 mines, but those that survived were hurled in all directions like the first billiard shot in a big bang simulation. The quagma mines activated on their own and employed their small cold gas jets to steer the insane flight path they were assigned as soon as the first sensor data arrived. Their systems were not particularly accurate, but they were robust and durable and efficient enough due to the high dispersion.

∽

"What the hell is that?" Captain Souza was puzzled and frightened at the same time.

"That was not the *Oberon*. It's obviously the asteroid," Beugers replied hoarsely.

"I can see that for myself, man!" He extended his hand toward the screen. On the right side, it displayed 81,234 radar contacts, along with energy signatures that shot above the expected scales for regolith debris.

"Mines," someone else said.

Souza no longer had enough thinking power left to remember whose voice it was. He could only watch in horror as the first quagma mines came into critical range, avoiding the dense defensive fire of hundreds of PDCs hurling their tens of thousands of projectiles into the vacuum to destroy the tiny, radar-deflecting anti-ship bombs. Some were intercepted, but quite a few more survived. Many flew off into nothingness—space was very large and empty—but enough of them descended on each of his ships by the dozens, and before he could get an order past his parched lips, the first explosions began. It was a horrific firework display that bathed an unmistakable sphere in fire. Captain Souza realized the ball of flame exactly matched the scale and positions of his ships.

"I'll be damned!" he managed to exclaim before he felt a violent jolt and his body cells dissolved into volatile compounds.

∼

The Exiles' fleet disintegrated. Within six seconds of their bombardment of the asteroid, which was now nothing more than a rapidly expanding cloud of hard radiation, every single ship was destroyed. Hull segments were ripped open by quagma charges, and more of the small mines hurtled into the resulting holes, detonating on contact with the sensitive electronics within, shredding composite and carbotanium, striking magazines, and obliterating man and material in a hurricane of destruction. What had just been cleverly constructed machines containing hundreds of souls faded forever and provided a backdrop of death and decay as, in perfect silence, another transit occurred.

First, the *Oberon* appeared from an infinitely short-lived event horizon framed by perfect darkness. Even before her sensors were deployed, thousands of anti-aircraft guns fired their shells, once again illuminating the space around Harbingen's S1, ripping the temporary calm with lurid explosions, as if to revive the sphere of annihilation that had existed moments before. Most of the remaining mines that were looking for new targets to leap on like greedy flames that had run out of wick were annihilated in the returning inferno. But that was not the reason for the overlapping screen of explosions that opened twice in tiny places and allowed four Eagle probes through. Protected from prying eyes by the screens, more ships appeared. First the *Obsidian*, then the *Saratoga* and the *Campbell*. By the time the four smaller corvettes and the *Quantum Bitch* appeared, the *Oberon* had already taken position behind them, maintained her flak screen, and slid onto the vacated jump point. The sixteen minutes it took her to do this had not gone to waste.

Then she disappeared again.

# 10

"Transit!" Kiya Alkad called out, and the emergence stretched into the infinity of a blink, spreading out and collapsing in on itself, a black hole of time where nothing was as it should be. What felt like a narrow surge of nausea, the flare of a feeling of emptiness and hopelessness was yet no more than a pale glimmer, far too brief to be real, too fleeting to coalesce into a memory.

"Fire at will!" Silly shouted louder than necessary. On the bridge, one could hear a pin drop even over the roar of engines.

Based on their calculations at S1, the *Oberon*'s railguns fired at the expected positions of the asteroids that had been positioned by the Exiles at S2. Nicholas tensed and took a deep breath. They hadn't had much time and hadn't checked what the onboard computer had spit out, so they were doomed to wait.

The sensor arrays were just extending and would take considerably longer than the twenty seconds that remained before the next asteroid moved into their position and hit like, well, an asteroid. Therefore, their guns were firing blindly, without sensors, at predetermined angles according to their expected relative position to the orbiting chunks of regolith. Whether the sixteen minutes of long-range sensor recordings would provide adequate precision would become clear in just a few breaths.

The tension on the bridge was palpable as every single person on board counted the seconds, waiting to see if they would be torn in half by an impact, explode in an inferno of fire, experience a drastic loss of atmosphere and shrill alarms, or continue breathing because nothing happened. No one said anything, so Nicholas also buried himself in his thoughts. He did not think about the bad luck they might have—on the bridge, heavily armored in the heart of the ship, he would live for a very long time even in the event of an impact—but about how successful the first step of his plan had been. The mines had done their job extremely well, and the element of surprise was as enormous as he had hoped. One of the enemy fleets was now destroyed without the *Oberon* firing a single shot.

But he wasn't jubilant, either. For one thing, many of his compatriots had died, deluded extremists, perhaps, but Harbingers, nonetheless. He had never hated the Exiles for leaving the Federation, as others had. On the contrary, there had always been respect for their views and their refusal to submit to an AI, even if it had been democratically elected to power and had demonstrably helped their colony with rapid economic and social advancement. Ludwig von Borningen and his followers had simply followed their religious and cultural convictions. They had seceded from their homeland and gone away.

The actions of those Exiles who remained in the Federation, however, were a different matter altogether. They were responsible for the deaths of billions. They had known what the hyperspace gates would unleash and had accepted all the suffering and death for the sake of... *what*? What was their purpose? Revenge? For what? For becoming a minority? Or because the people of Harbingen had largely decided differently than they had?

Nicholas's thoughts were interrupted when the deck suddenly vibrated beneath his feet and the bridge rattled like a vehicle driving over corrugated iron.

Silly hissed as she exhaled, then cheers erupted from the station tiers behind her. She looked at Nicholas and nodded, a relieved smile on her lips. He returned it cautiously and looked at the damage reports.

"Multiple hull impacts, integrity warnings at thirty-two locations reported by molecular bond generators. No breaches in armor, no pressure loss, no casualties reported," he read aloud.

*The last Battleship*

"All right, focus," Silly ordered calmly, then lowered her voice. "I want to see where the *QB* is going. Any course correction, no matter how small, I want to be informed."

Daussel nodded obediently. Nicholas could understand her lack of trust in the pirates since he felt the same way. His brother had cooked up this part of the plan, and no matter what Jason said, Devlin Myers was still a criminal. As much as he supported the idea of Devlin and his crew being rewarded for their admittedly courageous efforts, thanks to which the Fleet had obtained significant information, he was uncomfortable with the idea of putting one of the most important parts of their operation in the hands of that man. Added to that, Jason was on board with them. Pirates were not to be trusted. Nicholas had known that not only since the death of his mother. But apparently the fleet admiral was convinced he needed a half-crazed daredevil to extract Omega.

"Sensor data incoming," Feugers reported from recon.

"To the bridge!" Silly called, and the holoprojector came on with a quiet whir. The image showed the *Oberon* in the middle of a semicircle of asteroids. They were rotating around an invisible center, from which their ship was now maneuvering away. The railguns stopped firing at the rocks to save ammunition. Behind them, at a very close distance, were the *Obsidian* and the *Saratoga*, with the *Campbell* just emerging as a radar contact at the transit point. The four Broadswords would also follow shortly and, in Nicholas's estimation, make it out of the danger zone before the next asteroid closed in on the jump point. If not, they would support them with railgun fire as long as the escort ships were blind, after all, they were not designed with meter-thick Carbin armor to ward off asteroid fragments.

"Those must be the depot stations Myers reported," Daussel said, pointing to six space stations built into asteroids located on the edge of the belt.

"Mmm," Nicholas said, looking at the site image. "Looks pretty deserted. No ships docked, no traffic except the four corvettes accelerating away from us."

"Guess they weren't expecting us," Silly remarked with a hint of smugness in her voice.

"There was no reason for that. At S1, they rightly expected to shoot us to pieces, since we had to come through the point one by one, blind and defenseless. At S2, any ship coming out of transit would have been destroyed even before it knew what hit it. Their defense plan was pretty much perfect."

As soon as he uttered the words, Nicholas was struck by how true they were. Someone had made extremely precise calculations and ensured that everything was in place early on. The revolving circle of asteroids alone, which blocked the jump point without being torn apart by its gravitational tidal forces, demanded a great deal of preparation. In addition to the necessary logistical effort, it required an extremely precise calculation of the respective masses of the celestial bodies, their velocity, and the dwell time within the conjunction zone. If he had not come up with the idea of the mines, for which there was no corresponding mention in Fleet records, getting into the system would have been barely possible, except with enormous numbers of ships—expendable ships.

"Not perfect enough," Silly said. "We'll wait until the flotilla is assembled and out of harm's way, then we'll destroy the remaining asteroids. Just to be safe."

Nicholas wanted to object that they should save their ammunition for the battle that was sure to come, but she was right. With a jump point even half-blocked at their backs, the rocks would hinder a potential escape route. Even if it was no longer completely blocked, it was still an unnecessary worry that would complicate a quick retreat or, unlikely, resupply. In battle, you never knew what was going to happen next, but it would probably be what you least anticipated.

"Initial analysis indicates enemy formations are concentrated around the remnants of the moon Kor," Alkad reported. Her voice emanated from the speakers as if she were standing right next to them on the command deck. "Sensors have detected five cruisers, four destroyers, and over twenty ships that could be corvettes and gunboats, by size. More detailed classifications by the onboard computer are pending."

"They're crowding around the Tooth," Silly noted as the holo-image adjusted and focused on the area around the fragments of

Kor. The largest of these, the Tooth, did indeed look like a human tooth with a long root and smooth surface. The enemy's radar contacts formed a cover around the top.

"So far, nothing unexpected," Daussel said.

"Not necessarily," Nicholas said as he looked at the flickering display. "The Exiles must have believed that both jump points were secure and that any intruder would be destroyed. Why would they guard Kor so closely?"

"Obviously because of the phase transmitter they drilled into the Tooth."

"True, but why do that if they don't fear an attack on it?"

"They might have a prudent commander who planned for the worst," Silly suggested. "After several decades of meticulously planned, and perfectly executed, conspiracies throughout the Federation, I think we can assume that those in charge prefer to play it safe and run through all the possibilities before acting."

"I guess so," he admitted. "Still, it bothers me." Nicholas zoomed out and pointed to Harbingen, below the moon's remains. "Why not protect the excavation equally?"

"Maybe they already have what they need?"

"If they did, they would have blown up Omega long ago."

"Or maybe that's what they want us to think."

"Mhm," he acknowledged without any real conviction. He couldn't get rid of the feeling that their enemies knew something he did not, maybe even a great deal. Yet he had imagined their arrival proceeding differently, maybe causing more unrest in the enemy units, more hectic movements that suggested they were nervous. Instead, everything seemed strangely calm.

"Captain!" Alkad shouted, with less composure than before. "I have some ships on sensors between the *QB* and Harbingen."

"What ships? Where?" Silly demanded.

"In the shadow of Melchior—in relation to the *QB*."

"Melchior," Nicholas repeated and looked at the ten blinking dots on the long-range scan, crowded close together on the sunward side of the ultra-hot rocky planet like a pack of predators waiting to spring. The *Quantum Bitch* would pass them in less than an hour—and had no means of detecting the ambush with her own sensors, let alone prepare for it. "That's going to be a problem."

Judging by Silly's sour expression, she had come to the same conclusion.

"Jung, open a channel to Mr. Myers," she said.

"I've already tried, Captain," the communications officer responded. "Either the signal isn't getting through or they're not answering us."

"The Exiles could have spread jammers between us and Melchior," Daussel said thoughtfully. He zoomed out with two hands and pointed to the asteroid belt they would soon enter. "The belt's many celestial bodies alone provide enough interference to make it difficult to get through to the *QB*. Just a few well-placed jamming ships in the gaps would be enough to nullify any attempt to communicate between S1 and S2, and we're close to that vector."

Nicholas tried to imagine their adversary. He pictured the enemy as a humanoid figure made of shadows, reaching toward them with long fingers.

He knew the Exiles under von Borningen belonged to the old colonial aristocracy and had an extremely paternalistic, authoritarian worldview. Which likely meant the Exiles remaining in the Federation also thought in a centralist way when it came to power and its exercise. So, someone was pulling the strings, and this someone had made provisions in case the *Oberon* broke through at S1, although he probably calculated the odds of that as nearly zero. The fact that S2 was so quiet could not be a coincidence, but rather the product of a clear calculation that took that possibility into account. The hoped-for surprise, the only advantage they had counted on, was thus extremely short-lived and had now evaporated.

The look Silly gave him through the hologram showed they were sharing the same thought.

"The flotilla is complete; the asteroids are destroyed," Daussel said. Silly's chest rose as she took a deep breath without looking at the lieutenant commander.

"XO?"

"I suggest we set a course for Kor at full speed," he replied.

*The last Battleship*

"The opposition has to know what our objectives are since there is nothing else here."

"Nothing that we know of," Daussel pointed out, and Nicholas nodded reluctantly.

"That's true. But Kor is heavily guarded. So, unless it's a feint and there's a secret fleet hidden somewhere in the belt or the outer system, we should go forward with our plan. Kor is still important to them or there wouldn't be so many ships there. We can take them on, even if it won't be an easy fight."

"I agree," Daussel said, but then added, "However, we should drop a whole lot of Eagle probes to avoid being ambushed. The enemy seems to be well prepared, despite the little time he may have had. Either he has brilliant tacticians or even better and faster spies in Sol than we thought."

"Or both." Silly relayed a few commands through her forearm display and refocused on the holo-image. "I still wonder, though, why Harbingen and the dig site are so poorly guarded."

"That impression could be deceiving," Nicholas said and zoomed in on his irradiated home planet until the brown-green sphere with its dirty cloud formations dominated the image. "Even if there are no defenses or ships in orbit, the site could be heavily guarded."

"At least by ground troops," Daussel said.

"Yes. And if the Unity Palace is still powered by its decay reactors, then its surface-to-air defenses are still active as well. So, they would not need to park ships to prevent orbital bombardment. They would simply have to wait for the automated palace systems to open fire and turn the sky into an inferno. Not even my father knew how much firepower was installed there, but since Omega was the most loved and most hated entity in the Federation, we should assume a lot."

"We knew that much before," Silly countered, not unkindly. "So, the *QB* is well prepared, if they can get past the ambush, which I wouldn't count on. For that to happen, they'd have to opt for what they might consider an unprovoked course change that costs them a lot of time and takes them in a wide arc around Melchior."

"At least if the defense system's sensors don't detect the bomb as such."

"The system is old and designed for energy efficiency," she objected. "If anything, it works with speed sensors."

"I hope so," Nicholas said. "But we're going to have to figure out something to tackle Kor and the excavation site at the same time."

He was aware that he was implying that he expected not only the demise of the *Quantum Bitch*, but his own brother's death as well—a notion he could not and would not entertain. So, he focused instead on the purely tactical requirements of the mission and the impending battle.

Silly nodded slowly, and the look in her eyes showed that she felt his suppressed pain.

"It's too early for that. The *QB* will arrive in Harbingen's orbit sooner than we will be within firing range of Kor. Until we see otherwise, we have to assume they'll make it and that everything will go according to plan. As soon as we see otherwise, we'll adjust and proceed accordingly," she ordered. She swapped the current situation picture for one of Kor and the fleet guarding the moon fragment. "Five cruisers, four destroyers, and twenty smaller corvettes and gunboats. We can take that on."

"However, we are handicapped," Nicholas said. He didn't need to mention the lack of launch ramps for their Barracudas, since both she and Daussel were aware that they were going into battle with their hands tied. A Titan was not a carrier, but the fighter squadrons still formed one of their most important assets in any battle. Ejecting them from the hangars would take a lot of time—time they might not have.

"We could toss them out in advance of the time foreseen by the plan and use them to disperse the enemy formations," Daussel suggested.

"Not a bad idea," Nicholas agreed, nodding. "Or we could go head-on, set up on a tight flak shield, and see how eager they are to protect their phase antenna. As soon as we open the launch chutes, they'll expect a bombardment, and their formation will be forced open. Once we're only dealing with one side, we can save a lot of flak grenades and overload the port-side energy matrix cells to get a higher cadence."

"The CAG won't like it if we hold him back," Silly noted with a hard smile on her lips. "He's probably counting on us sending him and his boys in as a spearhead."

"Then I guess he'll have to rein himself in. Having our squadrons in the rear could give us a tactical advantage that would pay dividends as the battle progresses." Nicholas knew she and Daussel were aware of what he meant. *If Jason needs our help, we still have an ace up our sleeve to play for him.* Who could tell if their adversary had set another ambush in the shadows of Kor? What if Melchior was just one of several?

"I agree," Silly decided. "There's no reason to throw everything we have into battle right away, not until we know if the enemy is also holding back something that might surprise us." She pointed to the red symbols of the enemy formations. "The way I see it, we have a real chance here to take out these traitors without endangering our pilots, especially since we only have half as many as I'd like. Lieutenant Commander, inform the CAG to keep their feet still for now. As soon as the battle alert starts, have him and his boys get into their fighters and wait for orders."

"Understood," Daussel said and reached for his phone receiver.

"Five hours," Silly said in Nicholas's direction, and he had to suppress a sigh.

His gaze fell on his forearm display, which showed the *Quantum Bitch*'s course. It would take her another two and a half hours to reach Harbingen, but only forty minutes to reach the night side of Melchior, where the trap was waiting to snap shut.

## 11

"That went much better than expected," Dev said happily, clapping his hands with a grin. It didn't matter to him that he felt like a preschooler. "That buttoned-up son of a bitch has some balls, I'll give him that!"

"The younger Bradley?" Aura asked. He could tell by her tone that she had raised one of her finely drawn eyebrows to her hairline, even though he couldn't see it while watching the main screen. "I don't think he has anything like balls because those things make men experience something like emotions. The guy doesn't even know how to twist his mouth into a smile."

"I don't give a shit. As long as he remains a good tactician, he can be a eunuch or a robot in human form for all I care."

"With the Uncanny Valley effect."

"What?"

"Never mind. His plan was good, and it worked. That's it."

"You could say that." Dev stared at the fine cloud of debris that was all the mines had left behind. The little things had apparently been frighteningly efficient at plowing over the conspirators' fleet like a wheat field, and the *Oberon*'s anti-aircraft guns had forced the remaining chunks through a fine sieve. With enough distance, one would probably dismiss the remains of the enemy fleet as a stellar dust cloud. "Great job they did... great job."

"Awesome shit!" Willy blurted behind him. Dev turned his

head and saw the massive engineer hanging in the doorway to the central corridor like the biblical Leviathan. "That must have been crazy. Too bad we didn't see that!"

"The only cameras that recorded it are now fine-grained powder," Aura said.

"Too bad."

"Don't worry," Dev said, "we'll be at our destination in two and a half hours and then you can film as much as you want."

"That's if we and our cameras aren't 'fine-grained powder' by then, too."

"Optimistic as ever, Aura."

"I'll do what I can. As a—"

"—poor Jewish girl from Raheen, caught between her paternalistic Hindu father and an Orthodox mother who was cast out of her Cosmo kibbutz. I couldn't even spell optimism. After all, we had nothing back then except our ethnoreligious disagreements and the basic security of a government that harassed us at every opportunity," Willy mimicked her, and Dev had to fight not to grin and thus earn several days of evil looks and angry comments from his energy node specialist.

"At least I didn't grow up on a backwater world full of cavemen!"

"Hey, you can brew good beer in caves!" The augment let out a long, drawn-out sigh. "What I wouldn't give for a Dunkelheimer beer right now."

"Get over yourselves. We've got maybe two hours of rest before the bastards here throw the first turds at us. We can't waste that time. Aura, get me a full situation report as soon as you have enough sensor data. Willy, I want you to check all the combat systems again." Before Willy could protest, Dev added, "I don't care how many times you've done it in the last few days! And tell Dozer to arm any of our smuggling devices that require manual unlocking. Call me paranoid, but I feel it in my urine. We're going to have to pull out every stop sooner rather than later."

"You got it," the Dunkelheimer grumbled.

"A full sensor image of the system will take twenty minutes," Aura said.

"We have enough time. I want to see everything, for sure. We can't afford to be lulled into complacency after this first win."

"Uh-huh."

"Jezzy?" he asked over the radio.

"Yeah, boss?" came the lamenting reply.

"Did you find that blown relay?"

After the single shot Jason had fired to destroy the Broadsword in Xinhua, his control systems had gone haywire, showering him with warning messages. Apparently, a critical relay in one of the superconductors had blown, causing some of the Striker gun's major components to overheat. In hindsight, they were lucky that Jason had only fired a single shot or the whole thing might have burned out or blown up on them, figuratively speaking. It almost seemed like revenge for his greedy acceptance of the new weapons system and ignoring Willy's concerns that integration was difficult and that a hurried systems check carried significant risks. At least Willy had not annoyed him with tirades of "I-told-you-so."

"Yes. Already replaced. Went through all the checkpoints again, too. We could fire a few practice shots, just to be sure. Better we find out now than when it counts," the fusion engineer suggested, letting out a not-very-ladylike sigh that sounded like an approaching thunderstorm.

"Good idea, take care of it. We're approaching the first planet in the system soon. Melckjor."

"Melchior," she corrected him.

"No idea how to pronounce that shit."

"That's why I'm telling you. You—"

"Carry on," he said, interrupting her, and shook his head as he ended the connection and turned his attention to their flight path. It basically consisted of a backward-bending parabola that would take them just above the ecliptic to the last planet in the inner system—Harbingen.

According to orbital mechanics, there were no straight lines, only approach vectors running along the right places at the right time, which were themselves constantly in, an albeit predictable, motion, making travel from A to B a rather complex affair. On the first day of his training as a cargo pilot, his instructor had explained the matter to him and a few other candidates with the help of a magnetized funnel into which he had dropped marbles of unequal speed. The little marbles had circled the tapered hole, each on its own trajectory, traveling at different speeds and different heights, depending on how big they were.

"Space flight takes you from one marble to another. Forget about clear routes and get used to a new component—time. What is at point A today may be at point B tomorrow and at point H in two weeks, except that point H will be on the other side of the central star and it will take you twice as long as normal," the veteran pilot had told them. After so many years with his own ship, he had to admit that his instructor had been perfectly accurate.

After dealing with the course and reviewing the onboard AI's recommendations, he nodded with satisfaction and flipped a secret switch under his command console that opened the displays for his —rather illegal—enhancements to the *Bitch* on one of the left-hand screens. Satisfied, he sighed and went through them one by one. Ten minutes later, he was restlessly drumming his fingers on the dashboard, inspecting one of the four Eagle spy drones they had blocking two of their missile bays.

"Aura, we'll kick out one of the Eagles and send it ahead to Harbingen," he finally decided while looking at the system overview map, which kept filling up with symbols, directions of movement, mass readouts, and spectral analyses.

"Okay, can't hurt," she said disinterestedly and without interrupting the clatter of her keyboard.

"It's way too quiet for me. Harbingen has rotated quite a bit and I still don't see any movement in orbit."

"Which is more than you can say for the Tooth."

Dev grumbled as he thought of the battle group the sensors had detected over the largest fragment of Kor. The *Oberon* would have a decent fight on its hands, that much was certain. He flipped a switch and gave the go-ahead for one of the spy drones. In less than five minutes, it began its fly-by of Melchior. The drone was able to pick up some speed and save some propellant by using a fly-by vector to swing into orbit around Harbingen 70 minutes ahead of them. Much better than waiting around until they left the hot rocky planet behind, and the *Eagle* only had a 50-minute lead.

The *Bitch* shuddered for a moment as the drone, indistinguishable from a rocket, catapulted out of its launch bay and, after a second, ignited its engine 200 meters ahead of the ship and accelerated furiously. It measured no larger than a human thigh, yet it was larger than the *Oberon*'s version. Despite that, it was more capable for long-range use.

On the screen, he watched it draw a curve around Melchior's equator, trailing a long plasma tail. It approached the terminator line, which from so far away looked like a black semicircle pulled on a string. At its edge, cheerful hues of yellow and red seemed to dance with each other. When he thought of the near 800 degrees Celsius that prevailed down there, the romance of the sight quickly evaporated. Due to its bound rotation around Harbingen's sun, there was a day side so hot that even metal melted and an extremely cold night side where temperatures dropped below freezing. In the convection zone between these two extremes—a physical equator, if you will—the enormous temperature amplitude created violent distortions in the air currents creating storms that made even Jupiter seem like a pleasant place to be.

The Eagle spy drone shot out over that hellish zone and disappeared behind Melchior, into its shadow. Its signal was lost as predicted by the onboard computer and he had to wait for the next 60 seconds. He busied himself with final engine adjustments for their fly-by of the planet that would also give them a little cosmic nudge from Melchior's gravity funnel. There was nothing to do, but the more useful he felt, the faster seconds passed, and he preferred that to watching the chronometer because it made him nervous. Not in this situation, perhaps, but habits were even worse to get rid of than athlete's foot.

After he finished, 72 seconds had passed. Dev frowned.

"Well, well"

"What is it?" Aura asked.

"The Eagle hasn't reported in, but it should be around Melchior by now," he replied absently, switching through sensor frequencies to see if interference had compromised contact with the drone. "No signals."

"That's odd. I'll check the optical sensors."

"I'll take a look at the radar." Dev switched the radar to a preprogrammed ping for flagged signatures and fed it the spy drone's contour signature. "Nothing! Absolutely nothing."

"The telescopes can't find it either," Aura said. "Neither where the onboard computer says it should be on schedule, nor behind it, nor in front of it."

"Something's wrong," he grumbled as he feverishly pondered the possibilities. Maybe it had gotten too close to the convection zone, but that would mean it had flown way too low, and there was no reason for that.

"These things fail sometimes."

"That's military hardware, they fail less often than Willy washes his hair." Dev licked his lips and decided to make a course correction. He pulled the *Bitch* into a turn to port that took her farther away from Melchior. Not so much that their flight time to Harbingen was severely affected, but enough to preclude a fly-by maneuver. They could handle an extra twenty minutes. He would rather increase the angle to the far side of the planet from the sun than blindly fly into something that had destroyed the drone or rendered it mute and invisible.

"Is that a good idea, boss?" Aura asked.

"I don't know, and I don't give a shit. I'm not flying into the dark without a flashlight." The distance to Melchior, a black-brown ball that stuck to the right edge of the cockpit window and filled it halfway, increased and its ugly visage decreased.

"Contacts!" Aura called excitedly and Dev's gaze jerked right to the situation screen. Red warning icons flooded the display, accompanied by shrill alarms demanding his attention. "Eight, nine, ten bogeys. Targeting active. We're being scanned!"

"I see it!" Dev activated the acceleration alarm. The *Bitch* was already flying at an appreciable fraction of light speed, but now they needed all that was left in her. The siren blared throughout the ship, almost loud enough to drown out the curses echoing into the cockpit from the corridor. "Ten seconds, people!"

"Warships," Aura said angrily. "It's a damned ambush!"

"At least now we know what happened to the Eagle drone."

He checked the distance to the enemy ships huddling in Melchior's shadow and had just fired up their engines, which the optical sensors displayed as ten glowing flames. Half a million clicks. Normally a pretty comfortable distance to make a run for it, except they had nothing nearby to hide behind.

So, it was a matter of running and hoping that his course correction would provide them with the valuable micro-advantage they needed.

"Hold on!" he yelled, pushing the *Bitch* into a reckless acceleration that gradually ramped up to an agonizing 13 Gs. That he didn't pass out was due not only to his vascular stabilizers, but also to the amphetamine and anticoagulant cocktail his auto-injector was feeding him. Still, he felt like he was being crushed in an invisible trash compactor.

"Rocket launches!" Aura shouted over the roar coming either from the reactors or from his compressed ear canals, where pulses overlapped and blood rushed and begged for mercy.

"How many?" he asked in the same transducer-generated voice she had used. Opening his mouth was impossible.

"Eighty."

"Eighty?" Dev wished the monotone computer voice could have echoed at least an ounce of his horror, instead of its bland babbling as if they were talking about something trivial like the weather. "Shit, who do they think we are? A fucking frigate?"

"PDCs—"

"Forget PDCs! If even one gets through, we're history." He watched with growing concern as the distance between them and the guided missiles pursuing them melted away. 500 million kilometers sounded like a lot until you considered the missiles' acceleration rates of up to 150 Gs.

"But we have to do something!"

"I'm thinking," his intended bark was transformed into an acoustic metronome by his electronic alter-ego, which didn't help his mood.

Their two-point-defense cannons were pretty much worthless

against 80 missiles, even if they could shoot down a dozen, which would be an extremely good rate. He had not exaggerated when he said that one was enough to destroy them. The *Bitch* was not, after all, a warship, but designed for speed and to hide as much cargo as possible.

"Willy? Dozer?"

"Yo!" the Dunkelheimer responded calmly. Dev really wished he had maximal augmentation himself right now.

"Prepare one of the Scarab-4s for ejection."

"Excuse me?"

"Just fucking do it! We've got twelve minutes before we're turned into a fucking sh—"

"It's all right, boss. Put the brakes on a little bit or we won't move a foot here, as much as we want to."

"In sixty seconds. Better hurry up!"

"What are you going to do?" Aura asked.

"From their point of view, the bastards have done everything right. The range of their guided missiles can't be much more than 600,000 clicks because otherwise they can't get an effective sensor lock. We have the acceleration advantage and we're already extremely fast. So, they put a whole slew of them on us at once before we get out of range instead of staggering them," he explained, trying to dislodge himself from the ghastly sight of the dwindling distance from the weapons close on their heels. "A little more speed and we would have been too far away to target. But no, shit always has to blow up in our faces. Thank you, God."

"You want to throw out one of the Scarab 4 reactors because the missiles are targeting our engine emissions," Aura concluded.

"That's it. If we can maintain our exhaust flare long enough at its current length and eject the reactor at the right moment while shutting down our remaining one, we'll drift along at our maximum speed without any emissions, and they'll think they've got us."

"But ejection and impact of the guided missiles will be very close together," she said. "And extremely close to us."

"We'll have to squeeze into our spacesuits anyway because I'm going to shut *everything* down, including life support. We have to be dead if we want them to think we're dead," he replied with outward calm, even as he damned all the gods ever invented for putting him in such a situation—again.

"Damned close and a shame we have to fly again with only one beating heart. That thing is worth as much as—"

"I know that! But if we die the credits won't do us any good. Not to mention, I don't see who'd buy the thing from us."

"Good point."

"There you go." Dev saw five minutes remaining. The swarm of missiles chasing them, flying close together, was rapidly eating up the distance to the green-marked *Bitch* on the tactical screen.

*You win some, you lose some.*

"Willy? How far along are you?"

"It's not like we only have two bolts to loosen!" the engineer grumbled. "We're going as fast as we can."

"We'll be toast in five minutes."

"Thanks for the pressure!"

"Get on with it!" He disconnected and opened the cover of the emergency jettison switch they had installed after their odyssey in this very system two weeks ago. As a smuggler, you learned from your defeats, but also from your victories because they were usually close ones. Otherwise, you didn't get very far in the independent shipping business. He had no idea what the maximum range of modern guided missiles was since the military was usually very cagey with information about its arsenal, but it did surprise him that they could still lock on and follow them at 500,000 kilometers, after all, the sensors built into the tiny warheads weren't exactly large.

Three minutes later, Willy gave him the message he longed to hear.

"Boss, this thing is ready to be tossed. I could bite my ass! Just got that sweetheart installed."

"It's that or we burn up in two minutes and eleven seconds."

"Get rid of that piece of shit."

"That's what I thought. Maybe you'll burn up anyway." Dev added two Gs of acceleration—which he wouldn't have been able to do without the second Scarab-4—and looked at the tactical screen and the 32,000-kilometer plasma flare his *Quantum Bitch* was dragging behind it, a bright yellow streak in the middle of the darkness that was about to go out.

"I hope you know what you're doing," Aura said.

"So do I," he replied curtly. He nervously licked his lips and nearly swallowed his tongue, which was pressing at fifteen Gs against the roof of his mouth. Overcoming his choking reflex, he groped for the eject button, a distorted expression on his face, and lowered his right hand into the neural cushion of his right armrest to authorize the complete system shutdown.

"When I say *now*, proceed to the nearest breathing apparatus," he commanded over the ship's loudspeakers.

The 80 missiles were no longer a loose swarm but had formed a dense throng as they drew closer to their target. To Dev, they looked like a pack of predators, all eager to be the first to sink their teeth into the prey. A terrible sight, even though they were only radar pings, and yet it was their only possible salvation. If the ambushing ships had fired several salvos in succession, his strategy would be completely moot. That they hadn't was the reason he was convinced they had almost exceeded the maximum range of their weapons.

Less than twenty seconds remained, barely 11,000 kilometers, when he finally flipped the eject button—a good old toggle switch! The energy readout of the nodes and matrix cells suddenly halved, causing him a twinge of regret.

The pulsating miniature sun from the heart of the *Bitch* slid out of the ejection shaft under the hull. It had almost no velocity of its own, so it ran directly into the exhaust flare and its mass of highly excited gas molecules. The shielding melted in the few seconds that still separated the Scarab-4 from the slavering pack of missiles, and then the universe glowed 80 times in rapid succession so brightly that the aft sensors shut down.

At the same time, Dev ordered a complete system shutdown. Immediately, weightlessness set in and his stomach seemed to want to burrow up through his esophagus and push itself past his teeth.

His tongue unblocked his windpipe, and the invisible trash compactor abruptly retracted. Greedily sucking in the breathable air that still remained in the cockpit, he blinked a few times to find he was still alive.

"It worked!" Aura sounded surprised and maybe slightly offended.

"Breathers, now!" He followed his own command and reached for the red tab above his head, a small cover flipped open, and a respirator mask dropped down. He slipped it on and took several test breaths in and out.

"So, what now? We're blind!"

"We wait it out. At the speed we're currently going, we're gaining a lot of distance. In five minutes, I'll power up the remaining reactor and we'll see if they sent anything else after us."

## 12

"Battle stations!" Silly ordered. An instant later, the bridge was bathed in dim red light. That alarm began to blare. For Nicholas, it had become familiar background noise in the last few weeks. Somewhat subdued in the command post, deafening in the corridors and halls, it sounded for 60 seconds, until every station reported full combat readiness to the bridge.

The battle group that awaited them over the Tooth had adopted a new formation in the last half hour of their approach. It had placed many of the smaller ships in an advanced position with the cruisers and destroyers slightly offset behind. So, they were preparing for a prolonged fight, starting with long-range weapons, not the overwhelming tactics he had expected. This surprised him since their best chance was to critically damage them with their initial greater firepower as long as they didn't lose their first ships. Now, however, everything indicated they were in no hurry.

But why? Why were they playing for time? The Exiles had retracted the phase antenna shortly after the *Oberon* appeared at S2, as expected. It was now protected under massively armored gates, so there was no transmission they absolutely had to finish, not that it took particularly long to send quantum packets. This could mean only two things. First, the transmission had already been completed, in which case they were too late. Second, the Exiles probably thought they could win the battle by holding out long enough and then extend the antenna again afterward and transmit at their leisure. Nicholas guessed the latter, after all, the dig site was still showing activity, especially now that the *Quantum Bitch* attack had long since begun. So, they still needed the coordinates to align their transmission correctly.

But their chances of winning a battle against the *Oberon* were slim at best, even if they didn't throw nearly two- or three-decade-old ships into the fray. So, what were their opponents hoping for? Was there a fleet they hadn't spotted? Hidden units in the asteroid belt? Stealth ships approaching undetected?

"We should consider a quick frontal assault," he said.

"Where did the change of heart come from?" Silly asked. They had previously agreed after their last tactical briefing to proceed cautiously, relying on the flak screen to decimate enemy ammunition supplies before approaching and briefly opening the screen on the port side to launch drop pods on the Tooth. It would have been a logical course of action, but also one that took time. Time they probably couldn't afford to take.

"They're waiting for something." He pointed to the enemy formations, which appeared to form a kind of staggered sieve on the holoscreen as red symbols. "So, we shouldn't allow that."

"I was thinking the same thing," Daussel said, agreeing with him. "It doesn't make sense that they would want to buy time, but that's what it looks like. Their forward light units will probably open fire soon with their long-range torpedoes, and then we'll have to slow down to intercept them with the flak screen."

"That will cost them all their light units once the fire clears and we get close enough to let our railguns do the talking." Silly frowned. "They're going to sacrifice twenty-one ships without doing us much damage?"

Nicholas nodded. "That's what it looks like. That can only mean they want to buy time because that's the only thing to be gained by this approach."

"But what for?"

He shrugged, and Daussel also looked perplexed.

"Feugers?" Silly called.

"Yes, ma'am?"

"Prepare another systems scan, including long-range reconnaissance. Send out spy drones to search all space surrounding us for any hidden ships. If there's even one ancient Delta freighter headed our way, I want to know about it."

"Yes, ma'am."

As if to underscore their assessment, the Exiles' light units opened fire.

"One hundred sixty contacts! Closing fast," Feugers reported from recon. "Signature analysis in progress."

"Torpedoes," Nicholas muttered.

"Torpedoes. Eighty-eight percent probability Scythe-II type."

"Not exactly the latest equipment," Daussel commented, frowning.

"Prepare flak screen, bow defense, forty-five degrees, ninety percent density. Have PDCs pick up whatever makes it through," Silly calmly ordered.

Nicholas watched on the holo-image as the incredibly fast, long-range guided missiles approached like an erratic swarm of bees or pearl beads someone had thrown at them. Except they were so fast, and still accelerating, that the distance between the two fleets seemed more like a stone's throw apart rather than the half-million clicks they truly were.

The ship's forward grenade launchers wheeled out of their moorings, double-barreled guns with smoothbore tubes large enough for a human and aimed along their programmed angle. Synchronized by the hundreds, they formed a teeming ballet over the *Oberon*'s hull that could make an outside observer think the Titan was a living thing with countless tiny cleaner fish all moving at once. They fell silent, paused in their positions, and waited for the puny blue dots to approach from the darkness, at the end of which shone a slightly brighter gray spot—the last great remnant of the moon Kor.

"Sixteen minutes," Lieutenant Feugers announced. On a second holoscreen display, time ran down to the flak screen's last firing opportunity to intercept the first torpedoes.

"At least we're not chomping at the bit this time," Silly said, alluding to the full ammunition depots.

The defending fleet had been virtually emptied when the Clicks had initiated their blockade, but her comment referred mostly to the newer weapons systems. Sol's own modernity had fallen flat on its face as older stocks of weapons and ammunition had been mothballed a few years earlier as part of a massive modernization effort. They were lucky this old stock had not been fully delivered to older Fleet ships, so there had been a full buffet for them.

*At least*, just as Silly had said.

"Mhm," Nicholas mumbled, thinking feverishly about what they might have missed that would explain the enemy's strange tactics.

It was only the slightly deeper hum of the reactors, always audible even on the bridge, that woke him from his musings and indicated that the power cluster cells had switched to a higher power level. Now the anti-aircraft guns ejected their shrapnel shells.

The holoscreen's battle display depicted the shells, fired every second, as tiny streaks that flickered through the light like visual disturbances fleeing the *Oberon*. Five clicks away, the first exploded, forming a hemisphere of lurid blasts off the bow that intermingled, overlapped, and reawakened before they faded. Automatic loaders—powerful chains that fed the guns with an almost infinite number of shells under the Titan's armor—ensured that the blazing shield did not lack supplies and that the hail of tiny metal shards remained dense.

Short-barreled point-defense guns with large radar hoods slid by the dozens on magnetic tracks across the hull at the bow, searching with computer-controlled frenzy for targets that escaped the inferno.

They came 70 seconds later.

"Four breaches," Feugers reported loudly. The PDCs jerked to a halt on their sweeps, aligned with lightning speed, and fired their finger-thick APDS projectiles at 5,000 rounds per minute at the handful of torpedoes that had survived the shrapnel storm.

"Splash one, two, three, four, and five," Lieutenant Bonjarewski calmly shouted from Defense.

Silly nodded acknowledgment, but she saw, as Nicholas did, that the next waves were already on their way. The *Oberon* was flying at ten percent maximum speed to ensure the flak shield's effective range was as high as possible. That would not change while the guided-missile fire continued.

"Feugers, anything from the Eagles?" Nicholas asked.

"Negative, sir. Their sensors can't detect any signatures that would match ships with active systems, not even mines or anything like that."

"What are they waiting for?" Nicholas looked at Silly, who seemed to be asking herself the same question.

"I don't know, but we're going in now."

"What do you mean?"

"Whatever we do," she said, "it shouldn't be what our opponent wants, and obviously he needs time to do something. We're not going to give it to him."

"We could fly past the Tooth at maximum acceleration. If we time the drop pods right, we should be there in less than twenty minutes," Nicholas suggested.

"But then our guys won't have any cover from orbit," Daussel said.

"Correct, but the enemy will have concentrated their fire on us in the meantime, and the drop pods are extremely fast. If the colonel and his men manage to get below the surface as quickly, they may not need fire support at all. The Exiles will think twice before dividing their firepower between us and ground forces."

"That's if they even realize what they're dealing with quickly enough. They might think the pods are nukes. After all, the *Oberon* doesn't actually have any drop pods," Silly said. She looked at Nicholas. "XO?"

He nodded. "Alkad, calculate a pass to target Alpha along the planned drop point for the Marines."

"Roger that."

"Bauer, prepare the aft port railguns for surface bombardment. Feugers, keep an eye on the sensors. If there is any sign of access to the underground transmission facility in any spectrum, I want Lieutenant Bauer to know immediately and concentrate his fire accordingly," he ordered. "Arm torpedoes, fifty volleys. Reduce flak screen to sixty percent. Bonjarewski, we'll need more power from the PDCs to compensate for the flak."

"Course computed and set, XO," Lieutenant Alkad confirmed.

"Good. Full power!"

The mighty drive nacelles of the *Oberon* glowed, and their exhaust flare grew longer and longer, making even the Titan look like a speck of dust as it threw itself forward, propelled by its antimatter reactors. The explosions of intercepted torpedoes came in even faster succession like a vehicle racing through rain pelting the windshield. The PDCs whizzed back and forth on their sleds, spewing projectiles in all directions to intercept the increasing number of guided missiles that made it through the flak screen. They moved toward them and whole hull segments glowed continuously where detonations in their immediate vicinity brought space to a boil.

The *Oberon*'s launch bays responded and launched 50 torpedoes at a time from their catapult tubes. A short distance away, they ignited their thrusters and hurled the slender, ten-meter-long cylinders toward their targets. They accelerated away at insane speeds through space teeming with metal shavings and fire, toward the Exiles' fleet, which fought back with PDCs and lasers. Even before this defensive battle was decided on the other side, the next torpedo salvo lined up.

An enemy corvette was hit amidships and ripped open from bow to stern. Geysers of escaping atmosphere sent cables, debris, equipment, and sailors into the vacuum. The ship broke from its formation and slumped to one side before its magazine exploded and shredded the wrecked ship.

"One down," Daussel commented as one of the red symbols disappeared from the situational picture.

"Mhm," Nicholas responded as he watched the enemy formation above the Tooth, which they were approaching with increasing speed. It slowly changed. The ships behind started to form a ring that would wrap around *Oberon*'s expected course. An expected response, and the one he himself would have chosen to achieve maximum fire efficiency. "This is not going to sit well with our Marines at all."

"They know what to do and what the risks are. They're Marines," Silly said.

"I know."

He thought about the carnage on Earth, north of Shanghai, when he and the colonel and his soldiers had tried to rescue his father. The sheer immediacy and brutality of the battle had left him permanently horrified—at what the Marines did and could endure, and at what humans were capable of doing to each other.

For him, as a Fleet officer, war consisted of looking at graphics and holo-displays and making tactical decisions. The actual battle was fought by computers and guns, which he merely directed. Death did not come in the form of an evil eye and projectiles tearing his body apart and spilling blood. No, it came suddenly in space when a railgun bullet pierced the hull and sucked everything into a vacuum or when a magazine exploded, as it had on the enemy corvette, and the whole crew perished in the radioactive fire. Whether hot or cold, death always came swiftly and impersonally for the Fleet.

During the drop and short dive to the surface of the Tooth, many of them would die a crewman's death, and those who made it would possibly die a marine's death. Or were the two not the same?

The battle intensified. Flak and short-range defenses were doing a good but increasingly frantic job of picking off approaching projectiles as best they could. Soon, however, they found themselves confronted with a close quarter battle. Railgun salvos flew back and forth, missiles hit targets in less than two minutes, sometimes within a minute of launch. Both the port and starboard sides of the *Oberon* lit up a thousand-fold under the muzzle flashes of her guns spitting wherever the swarm of enemy ships raked them. Missiles joined in the deadly dance.

Now flying in the middle of the enemy formation, the *Oberon* took the first hits on her armor and the command deck periodically vibrated. Four of the enemy's corvettes and gunboats had already exploded, and two more were glowing scarlet and melting under their own heat buildup. Their captains hadn't even extended their radiators, condemning their crews to boil like lobsters in their own sweat. The fanaticism of the Exiles was a disgrace in Nicholas's eyes.

At this point, their flotilla intervened in the battle as foreseen, firing missiles and railguns at those ships the *Oberon* passed with its greater speed as if milling off a protruding edge. Thus, the *Oberon* was spared some of the fire and was able to use her weapons effectively since the space within the enemy formation was relatively free of shrapnel.

"They're cleaning up better than expected," Silly said with professional appreciation.

"Yes. At least it doesn't look worse than expected which I guess we can consider a small victory," Nicholas said.

"Drop point in two minutes," Alkad announced.

In the telescopic images, the Tooth had grown into exactly what gave it its colloquial name. The gray, toothy structure with a long, tapering root and a broad surface was relatively smooth, though dotted with craters and mounds. Their fly-by would take them past it at an altitude of less than 100 kilometers amid the raging battle. The drop pods would take less than forty-five seconds to reach the surface, which said a lot about what the Black Legion Marines would endure in their cramped capsules, not to mention the impact.

"The larger ships are still holding back," Daussel said, pointing to the cruisers and destroyers that were some distance behind the gradually exploding smaller ships, taking only sporadic hits that caused no critical damage. At least not yet.

"Still no sign of any surprises?" Silly asked.

Daussel shook his head. "No."

"What are they waiting for?"

"Maybe they want to know exactly what we plan to do with Kor and then react accordingly?" Nicholas suggested.

"Doesn't matter. Give Ludwig the two-minute call."

He nodded and reached for his handset.

"XO?"

"Two minutes."

"Understood," the bearish colonel replied calmly.

"Ludwig," Nicholas added before he could think about it, "take care of yourselves. Take care of *yourself*. That's an order."

"I'll be all right, boy."

Nicholas replaced the receiver and put aside his worries about the old marine and his men. He felt a special bond with them ever since Terra and had visited them once a day ever since. At first, he had made excuses, but eventually, every Marine understood why he was there. Sometimes they had played cards, other times they had drunk some contraband—that had immediately earned Nicholas some sympathy—and sometimes they had exchanged old war stories, which the Marines seemed to have in considerably greater supply than he did. The time spent with them had done him good, not least to distract him from the loss of his father. The downside was that he worried about them even more now than he would have otherwise.

"One minute to drop point Alpha!" Alkad called out.

"Realign port railguns!" Silly commanded, and the massive weapons adjusted in their gun barrels. The *Obsidian*, the *Saratoga*, and the *Campbell* responded according to their orders by shifting their fire to the port-side enemy ships, primarily four cruisers that were harassing the *Oberon* from some distance with missiles and railguns of their own.

"Alignment complete!" Bauer said from fire control.

"Feugers? Do you have targets for us?" the commander called.

"Yes, ma'am, there are some anomalies in the infrared image."

"Then open fire!"

Five hundred tungsten bolts were simultaneously thrust electromagnetically out of the *Oberon*'s hull and hurtled toward the fragment of the former satellite, seemingly untouched by the battle over Harbingen, a green-brown disk in the background like an inkblot on black paper. It took less than twenty seconds for them to slam into the drab gray regolith, kicking up fountains of the loose material. Like an invisible plow, the compacted metal cones mowed into the lunar surface as a yellow light on the holoscreen changed to green.

"Drop, drop, drop!" sounded around the bridge tiers.

One hundred drop pods, each containing four Black Legion Marines, were ejected by the launch bays' mass catapults, which normally shot fighters out of the hull and into battle. Their afterburners ignited much more quickly after ejection than safety margins allowed, but the minimal heat damage to the *Oberon*'s armor had been taken into consideration and it was deemed an acceptable evil in favor of increasing the chances of survival for its Marines.

Like shooting stars, the pods sped toward the surface, passing tiny defensive drones that had apparently been cloaked until that moment and now powered up their batteries. The energy signatures made the battle screen light up with hundreds of warning symbols.

"Defensive fire!"

"Three hundred twenty-one contacts!"

"Those are anti-missile mines," Nicholas said after some initial panic and exhaled with relief. Ironically, the drop pods were too slow to be marked as targets by the drones' simple, and more error-resistant, programming.

"Extend jamming field!" Silly ordered. "I don't want the enemy to reset these things! Bonjarewski, take as many of those down as you can with the PDCs!"

Nicholas stared at the Marines' capsules on the holoscreen between him and his commander and his hands tightened around the edge of the command deck. Railguns from the enemy destroyers plucked two of them out of space, then two more, four, six.

"Come on!" he muttered tensely.

# 13

Out of sheer habit, Colonel Ludwig Meyer gripped the two straps of the safety harness that pinned him to the drop pod's inner wall as if crucified. The adaptive nanofoam padding relieved him of discomfort, but the pressure left him with no wiggle room except for his arms, which were not exactly enjoying a holiday due to the powered armor he was wearing.

Opposite him, First Lieutenant Draper hung in his own lattice of steel and nanonic composites, with Gunnies Schrader and Leopold to his right and left. Normal Fleet Marines would have had enough room for their fingertips to touch in the middle when each extended his right arm, but that wasn't true for him and his men. Their massive armor had nothing on the more modern chameleon skins that relied more on mobility and adaptive absorption layers. As the war against the Clicks had continued, brute methods of boarding ships or conquering moons and planets had become increasingly less important, at least after the Aurora disaster. Ground and boarding battles against the aliens were almost non-existent, so the Marines were increasingly used to bust up insurgents or to storm smuggler bases and renegade asteroid settlements. This required fast, precise operations by specialists, not lobsters with big scissors that were more steamroller than scalpel.

They were almost like symbols for the *Oberon* and her position within the Fleet. "Everything stays the same" they said among themselves, not without a certain amount of irony. However, nothing about their dive on Kor was the same as it had always been, especially not for the "old man." Drop pods had only recently been deployed in the Fleet for limited military operations where speed was essential. Originally, they were designed to serve as one-way tickets for convicts who had "won" a place on a penal colony from which there was no escape. Security had never played a major role in this.

That's why Ludwig spoke more of a "controlled crash" than a "dive"—and that's exactly what it felt like. The entire cabin vibrated under the force of the raptor's engine, which whipped it relentlessly downward with its penetrator headfirst, down onto the ever-gray surface of Kor. The safety harness rattled in several places and the few moving parts of the interior made agonized sounds as if they would disintegrate at any moment, sparing the inhabitants from suffering their ordeal any longer. Ludwig's N7 servo-armor did its best to compensate against the jarring jolts that tossed him about—sometimes to the left, then to the right, then up and down—and would have inflicted fractures, bruises, and contusions on anyone non-augmented, non-armored, and not in a safety harness. Not for the first time, he wondered how many life-sentenced penal colonists were no longer alive when they "arrived" on Tartarus or Hel, instead landing as a mass of goulash held together by bone and skin with burst eyeballs.

With his many implants and bionic muscle enhancements—not to mention his N7, which made the harness much more effective—Ludwig felt an almost pleasant nostalgia of a daredevil roller coaster ride. Not much worse than being in the claustrophobic confines of a boarding shuttle. The difference was his "privilege" as commander of the two companies that allowed him to connect to the sensors of the *Oberon*.

The enemy's jamming signals had noticeably reduced in intensity since much of their fleet had dissolved into volatile gases under the beating it was getting from the *Oberon*. Through the Titan's "eyes," he watched masses of tungsten railgun cones race past their capsules and burrow into the lunar surface, where umpteen secondary explosions sent huge fountains of dusty regolith spraying

*The last Battleship*

like cold geysers. PDCs, dozens or hundreds, splattered hundreds of thousands of APDS spikes all around the drop pods, where small explosions of anti-missile mines formed a dense field of fire blooms. They reminded him of old records of World War II anti-aircraft fire, some of which had caused the entire night sky to break out in flashing smoke. Amid this inferno of projectiles and detonations, they raced toward the field of destruction the *Oberon* was tilling to prepare their landing. Each capsule he saw flare and shatter into its component parts after being struck by an enemy railgun, or that fell victim to some piece of aggressive metal or explosive in obedience to its destiny, gave him a stab of regret followed by barely controlled rage.

After twenty seconds he disengaged his thoughts from the physical sensations around him so as not to go insane. Therefore, the impact surprised him as much as the three other Marines in his capsule. A red light could have warned them, but what was a blinking light when their entire world was shaking and seemed about to break apart at any moment, not to mention the overwhelming noise that even his helmet's noise filters were unable to block out. A thud shuddered through the cabin, as if a man-sized hammer had slammed against the soles of his feet. The shock continued through all his joints and his spine, all the way to the top of his skull. Fortunately, white nanofoam shot into the capsule just before impact, flooded it in less than two seconds, then hardened, absorbing most of the kinetic shock. When the capsule's side panels sprung open, the mass liquefied again, and Ludwig's safety harness swiveled 180 degrees, so he was suddenly facing out onto the matte gray surface, low hills, and shallow craters of the Tooth.

Dozens of drop pods had already landed and were stuck in the regolith like broken arrowheads. With their hull segments blown-off, they resembled the skeletons of unfinished huts from which smoke rose and Marines exited. Their helmet lights streaked in elongated cones across the stellar dust as they sprang from their harnesses and gathered in their platoons. They were walking black blobs, born of a sky that was just as pitch black, except for the many explosions, tracer threads and propulsion flares.

More and more pods fell from above, huge hailstones that

made the ground tremble when they hit. The swirling concentric fountains of regolith glittered like diamonds in the light of the spotlights, possessing a beauty all their own. Due to the low gravity on the fragment, which did not even reach 0.2 G, the dust grains flew in slow motion and descended like snow.

"Platoon leaders, gather at designated positions!" Ludwig Meyer ordered over the radio after he jumped to the ground and drew his Gauss rifle. His command platoon landed in three pods just behind him. Fortunately, none of them had been destroyed. The *Oberon* drifted over their heads like a distant glimmer, bringing death and destruction with its weapons. He banned the ship from his thoughts and looked at the current situational picture the Titan's reconnaissance was relaying to him.

Railgun fire had penetrated the underground facilities at four locations, all in close proximity to the position of the retracted phase antenna. However, its armored gates had not given way, as expected. Via rapid inputs into his BattleNav, he divided his two companies into four platoons each and assigned them, according to their landing locations, one of the nearest entrances that had been blown open by cavalry fire.

"Don't stay too close together, we could still take fire from above," he warned his Marines. As if to emphasize his point, a tungsten bolt struck not twenty meters from him, sending a silent storm of regolith hundreds of meters upward. His servo-armor required several blasts from its cold gas jets to hold him in place. "See that you don't waste time, but don't run in blind. It could all be mined."

Ludwig switched to the channel for his commando platoon, which was already gathering around him, looking about as clunky and motionless as the Chinese terracotta army.

He turned to his first lieutenant. "Draper, keep the channel to the *Oberon* open and make sure the receivers are properly placed. I don't want to be cut off from the cavalry."

"Sure thing, Colonel."

"We'll take care of the antenna directly, no distractions. It's going to be ugly, but we're trained for ugly. So, let's go." He ran ahead—or rather *hopped* ahead. Operating in low gravity was considerably less graceful than in a zero-G environment or in full Terran gravity like their battle on Earth. Each "step" propelled him forward five meters and he had to deftly cushion himself to avoid losing his balance and falling clumsily due to the unfamiliar gravity conditions.

More railgun rounds hammered the ground around him and his two companies as they proceeded as if through an invisible soup to the exposed access points. They seemed like ants making for their burrow, crawling inside from every direction. Chaos swarmed about them, and each impact cost comrades their lives, flashing red in his HUD and then disappearing. Each one caused him a painful stab.

His own access point was 100 meters to the east. He reached it with his platoon after a large number of the surviving Marines had disappeared below the surface and were under cover—at least relatively speaking. He had deliberately chosen those points farthest from the phase antenna and only taken his boys because he judged them to be the least defended. The enemy would expect them to act under time pressure—a correct assumption—and strike as close to their target as possible. So, the most stubborn resistance could be expected there and not further from the target, according to their estimates.

The hole looked like a worn rubber rosette with furrowed edges, charred and still glowing inside. At first it was black, but underneath it flickered with an unsteady light.

"Charges!" he ordered, and two Marines tossed in three Seeker warheads each. They retreated a few steps and waited for the silent tremor beneath their boots before he waved and his platoon leapt—or flew—inside, firing their cold gas jets. A brief firefight later, Ludwig followed them down and found himself on a large steel mesh platform that was damaged and smoking in several places. The bodies of two of his Marines and several defenders in older powered armor lay spread out, some behind cover made of piled-up transport and security crates.

"A Seeker made it in," Draper explained, pointing to a handful of dead enemy soldiers behind him. "They had EMP mines and were well prepared, but one of them apparently didn't go off."

"Guess we got lucky."

"Looks that way."

"Let's take it." Ludwig watched as the rest of his commando platoons dispersed and secured four corridors that led away from the platform. Pipes and conduits rushed and gurgled beneath it. He considered projecting the loss graphics back into his AR field of view but decided against it. A colonel was only as good as he was able to pass on authority to the right subordinates, and that included situation assessments before forming an opinion. The greatest danger for an officer had always been the desire to hold all the reins himself and make all decisions single-handedly. "What do our losses look like so far?"

"Eighty enlisted, but also six sergeants. Twenty-three percent casualties, including wounded and those whose suits have gone into stasis," his first lieutenant reported.

"Hmph." Ludwig snorted and clicked his tongue. Every dead soldier under his command hurt but here and now he was completely focused on the mission, and that meant the six dead or wounded sergeants weighed on him the most. Officers liked to think of themselves as the linchpin of any force, but in his experience—and probably that of every honest Marine because there was no other kind—it was the sergeants who made the difference, made sure companies and battalions functioned, did what they were supposed to, and fought effectively and with commitment in combat. "What about resistance?"

"Platoons 1 and 2 are stuck and involved in tunnel fighting. Platoons 3 and 4 were able to gain some ground and are now stuck in some kind of storage room that's been mined. They noticed it early enough but can't get anywhere fast. Platoon 5 encountered a cavern of drones and was ambushed, and 6 found a wagon station, but it's disabled." Draper gestured raggedly, making swiping and dragging motions with his fingers, tapping here and there into nothing, and then lowered his hands again. "Platoons 7 and 8 are still up."

"What, why?" Ludwig growled. "Tell them to get the hell down here! All hell's going on up there."

*The last Battleship*

"Worse than that, Colonel," Draper said to his surprise. He tapped a finger in front of his black visor.

Ludwig switched to the command channel for his units' sensors and plugged into those for the platoon leaders of 9 and 10. Both appeared parallel to each other in his field of vision, hovering like holograms above one of the transport boxes on the steel grid. They showed the gray surface of the Tooth, which was barely twenty meters away from his location in a straight line. Tracer bullets swept through the darkness, and through the image provided by the two lieutenants he saw their rifles twitch with each burst of fire. He zoomed in to find out just what they were shooting at and gritted his teeth. What first looked like a flickering horizon was actually hundreds, if not thousands or more, enemy Marines with heavy weapons firing toward their positions, turning the cover around his men into shattered dust.

"An ambush," he grunted. He had expected something like that —but nothing like *this*. Mines, hidden units, sabotaged gas lines— many things had crossed his mind, but an attack by the Exiles on their own position had not been among them. It was too absurd that they would assign such a large number of soldiers to it and send them over open terrain instead of under the cover of their own branching underground passages. They were easy targets for the *Oberon*'s guns, which could make small potatoes of them in minutes.

Except the *Oberon*'s high-speed maneuver had long since put it out of effective range—at least with respect to its angle of fire. Their rapid progress had become a trap of their own making.

"Not good," he continued, shaking his head. "Someone either has a razor-sharp mind or the luck of the stupid on their side."

"Uh-huh. I sent four Sentinels out," Draper said, pointing at the corridors from which nothing could be heard or seen. The small sensor drones, no bigger than tennis balls, were fast and could still make complex and detailed recordings that generated 3D models for the BattleNav.

"Good call." Ludwig sent a message to the *Oberon*. "The commander will have noticed it herself by now, but by the time the Old Lady has turned around and is again close enough to give us cover from above, those bastards will be all over us like fucking Hygland jackals."

Draper didn't respond, but he didn't need to. They had five minutes, if not less, before a whole legion or more of enemy Marines swarmed over them.

"New plan: All platoons entrench around their access points and let no one in. The holes are well defended."

"Buy time."

"Exactly."

Draper understood what that meant because he fell silent and just nodded. In his clunky N7 armor, it looked like a jerky bow.

His new plan meant several things. First, they had to hurry to get to the antenna—or to the command room, whichever they could destroy most easily. Second, from now on they were under massive time pressure because the enemy would storm the hole above them in a few minutes—which now counted as their head start. Third, they didn't know which way to run, at least not yet, so their time advantage was only good if they took the right path. That meant the Sentinels had to deliver a picture they could quickly make sense of. Fourth, they would not be able to expect reinforcements if they found the antenna and got into heavy combat. The latter would be a big problem because they had no time to lose.

All in all, Ludwig had been in better situations, but very few crappier ones. Well, to be honest, none had been crappier, but there was always a first time for everything.

As if fate was trying to lure him with a promise of optimism, the first images from the Sentinels came in. Draper could also see them in his battlefield vision.

"They've been busy digging, gentlemen," the first lieutenant commented on the visual data as if they were standing together chatting at a tea party and two battalions of enemy Marines weren't racing toward their position.

"It's a damned maze." Ludwig turned himself to the west and pointed to the corresponding corridor that led roughly in that direction. "The antenna must be to the west of us, so only this way

*The last Battleship*

makes sense. Unless it's a blatant construction error, which Harbingers tend not to be known for, Exiles or not."

"They could have barricaded the way or welded it completely shut," Draper said, and for the first time, Ludwig wished he had taken two captains and a couple of majors with him after all. At least they knew when to feign optimism when a sense of realism no longer had any added value.

"They could, so we'll just shoot our way out of it if we have to. We're the Black Legion, we can always think of something." He switched to platoon radio with priority. "Listen up, guys. We're about to get a visit from upstairs. Apparently, we're going to get shut in here. Our primary objective remains to destroy the transmission facility, and that means we'd better be out of the water before the tide comes in. So, from now on, only speed counts. Shoot at anything that looks suspicious and don't skimp on ammo. I don't want to see any of you dead, but I want to see dead Marines with full magazines even less. We're not the Air Force, after all."

Short laughter answered on the platoon radio. The mirth would soon pass, but that was clear to everyone.

Ludwig raised his Gauss rifle, checked the ammo gauge one last time, and then beckoned toward the corridor ahead of them. It looked suspiciously quiet. The Sentinels were about 50 meters ahead, not much reaction time for mines and ambushes, but better than nothing.

*Juratis Unitatis.*

# 14

"It seems you were right about the maximum range of their weapons," Aura said, and Dev nodded confidently. He stood with her, Jezzy, and Willy around the holotable in the mess hall. Even Jason Bradley, standing a step behind them, listened with interest. Only Dozer was busy retesting the railgun relays.

"I know what I'm talking about," he lied, pointing to Harbingen, a large green ball floating in the holodisplay. They would be orbiting it in ten minutes. They had changed course several times to avoid being predictable and possibly facing missile salvos aimed at where the enemy guessed they might be. Not good for the schedule, but good for their skins.

"Half the fleet is still 620,000 clicks behind us, the half that's heading straight for Harbingen is only 280,000 away, but on the other side," Aura explained.

"Well, that's something, at least," Jezzy whined sarcastically.

"They're going to attack us with missiles from the Lagrange point," Jason predicted. He had been extremely quiet so far.

"Of course, they will." Dev squinted at the Lagrange. *Really? From there? Why?*

"That's where they can hold their position without using thrusters, so we'll have trouble tracking them," Jason continued as if he had read his mind.

"Do you mean the ships or their missiles?" Willy asked.

"Both." The lieutenant commander stepped forward to stand between the Dunkelheimer and Aura. They made room for him, Aura with a roll of the eyes, and he pointed to the Lagrange point away from Harbingen. "Without active thrusters, we would have to rely on telescopes, which is all but impossible for tracking them without their exact position. For now, that's true for the five ships. For the missiles, too, but for different reasons. The commanders will launch several salvos while we're still beyond the terminator and instruct them to shut down their engines by remote control. Then they'll drift until they get new orders. So, we should expect a slower airspeed from the missiles."

"Well, that's something, at least," Jezzy repeated.

"It's no advantage," Jason responded to her ironic fatalism, which he seemed to mistake for optimism. "They'll be virtually invisible to us until they locate us and speed up again. At that point, it'll be too late."

"And how do you know all this for sure? Did they send you a memo?" Dev said.

"I'd do it that way."

"Great."

"It's a good plan," Willy said, backing the officer up, and Dev once again wished the two hadn't bonded so quickly and spent every spare minute since together like two washerwomen. "If they do it like that, we're really in deep shit."

"Maybe they will, maybe they won't."

"You always say we should plan for the worst." Jezzy frowned at him, as if something were wrong with him.

"Yes. Let's just count on it, for goodness' sake. I have one more question, Fleet Boy. Those defenses at the palace you were talking about, what exactly are their alignment and range?" Dev zoomed in on the dayside of the irradiated core world and tapped on the center of the former capital, where the palace was located.

"I don't know," Jason admitted, shrugging at his frustrated look. "By the time I entered the service of the Fleet, Harbingen had been uninhabitable for two years. Everything I know comes from history books and conversations I picked up from my father, Silly, Ludwig, Karl, and the COB."

"And that is? It might help," Willy encouraged him to keep talking.

"The palace was equipped with autonomous weapons systems that were not incorporated into the Harbingen Military Alliance or the Terran Fleet in order to protect Omega from possible attacks. They fought hard for that in the Jupiter Parliament. The secrecy stemmed from the fact that, even within Harbingen's home fleet, many thought there might still be fanatics who sided with the Exiles or disagreed with decisions made by Omega and were bent on revenge. After all, we live in times when even smaller ships can hurl rocks at planets. My father"—Jason paused and cleared his throat—"was convinced that in addition to the force field we've seen functioning for twenty years there were also precision short-range lasers and hyperspace torpedoes housed in hidden launchers."

"Hyperspace torpedoes? Over twenty years ago?" Aura snorted and waved dismissively.

"Rumors persist that the Fleet stole plans for them from the wreckage of the Harbinger Institute for Advanced Weapons Research," Willy said. "It wouldn't be inconceivable that the Omega had the technology far earlier and that the Fleet has been working for the last two decades to build the same thing from the early plans."

"It's the same with the hyperspace gates," the officer said. "Those are also based on Harbingen's research—and thus Omega's."

"Never mind that," Dev intervened. "I want to know what kind of intercept field we should expect."

"As I said, I don't know. But," Jason continued before Dev could explode, "if my father's assessment was correct, there would be primary space defenses. It makes sense to me—after all, there wasn't much threat from ground or air attacks. Nothing land- or air-based could penetrate the palace's protective screen anyway."

"Except for slow planes and shuttles."

Jason looked at Willy and nodded. "Exactly. Since the force field is always active, it had to be set to allow normal traffic through. That meant nothing could travel or fly faster than 80 kilometers per hour or it would crash into it. I remember from my childhood that access roads to the palace had a lot of warning signs."

"Best remember that when you drop us off after the bombing," Jezzy suggested to Dev.

"Thanks for the tip," he replied curtly. "Just what I needed. What about the bomb? That flies slower than fifty miles an hour, so it won't be detected as a threat?"

"That's the thinking." The officer suddenly paled, as if sick to his stomach.

"That's why there are so many Raptors down there." Willy looked excited at the thought. "Can't wait to see those fireworks with my own eyes."

"First things first. First, we have to make sure we don't end up as fireworks ourselves."

∼

Half an hour later, Dev had to admit to himself that the damned Bradley boy had been right. The Exiles were not amateurs and had done exactly as the officer predicted. At least he and Aura agreed on that as they raced over Harbingen's terminator. They hadn't detected any enemy ships on the sensors, although they should have been around there somewhere. Their other five pursuers had sent a volley of missiles after them, apparently to keep them on their course to the opposite side of the planet and drive them into the arms of their sister ships.

"Crap," Jezzy cursed from her seat.

"We were counting on it, so don't make it any worse than it is, Princess," Aura said.

"If we keep flying, we'll soon see a couple dozen glowing dots flare up and chase us and the radar will start yelling at me," Dev predicted to them. "Two or three minutes later we'll be dead. If we turn around, we'll fly right into missile fire from the pursuers coming from Melchior. They're on their way and happy for any bearings they get."

"We could radio the *Oberon*," Willy suggested behind him in a rumbling voice. Something was wrong with his diaphragm; the man sounded like an orc going through drug withdrawal. "From the looks of it, she won the battle in a hurry."

Dev looked at the tactical battle analysis screen and had to agree with his engineer. There was still one enemy cruiser and one destroyer left. The *Oberon* had taken a hit, apparent by the two massive craters on her hull that were shedding debris and leaking gas, but she was still firing most of her guns, reducing the surviving Exile ships to punching bags. They would have to deploy their radiators shortly unless a miracle happened. Then there was the surviving remnant of the escort flotilla. The *Obsidian* and *Saratoga* had made it, as well as one of the corvettes.

"There's not enough time. Even at full speed, it would take them fifteen minutes or more." He waved the suggestion away. Not that he had any idea exactly how much time they would need, but fifteen minutes seemed both realistic and long enough to dissuade his crew from false optimism.

"Shall we flip a coin to decide which missiles we want to nuke us?" Jezzy asked.

"No, we'll kill ourselves," Dev suggested, grinning as he heard the comments.

"Oh, no."

"Not again."

"What's he got in his sick head this time?"

"You bet. There's always a third way, and if not, I'll find one," he said as he typed a new course into the navigation computer.

"Are you out of your mind?" Aura gasped.

"You mean *still* out of his mind," Jezzy growled.

"Shit!" Willy laughed. "That might work. But only until the bomb drops. Then we're fucked, and really deep, by the way."

"No, we just have to get around the force field before it detonates," he said, contradicting the Dunkelheimer, and accelerated the *Bitch* at a tolerable 4 Gs. He lowered the ship's nose until it was pointed directly at Harbingen's green-brown continents.

"We'll never make it!" Jezzy said sounding certain.

"Aura, calculate the bomb drop altitude that will still allow us to travel two kilometers in flight."

"Based on what? I don't even know how fast the bomb will fall, and I sure as hell don't know how much explosive power it has."

"Just assume eighty kilometers an hour. It's not that hard."

"But that's a pure—"

"I don't give a damn. Do the math!" he snapped at her, looking out of the cockpit at the bands of rapidly approaching clouds.

"Contacts!" Willy shouted. "Eleven bogeys, 44,000 clicks."

"I see it." He did see them—the eleven radar pings in the middle distance that hadn't been there a moment ago. At the rate they were accelerating, there was little doubt they were missiles or torpedoes. That uniformed bastard had been right. All the more reason to go through with his own plan, precisely because no one would expect it, no matter which side.

The *Quantum Bitch* was conditionally atmospheric. "Conditionally" because it wasn't aerodynamic like an airplane, but it had enough air buoyancy at high speed that was still low enough to avoid a crash. The flight characteristics of the *Bitch* under atmospheric conditions were most comparable to a fighter jet, able to glide but capable of flight once achieving a minimum speed.

If Bradley was right about the enemy's tactics, then hopefully he was also right about the fire radius of that damned AI deity his ancestors had worshipped.

Their entry into the atmosphere began with small shudders and vibrations in the instruments but rapidly increased to a full-blown chaos of rattling flaps and hatches in the cockpit. Their landing on Lagunia had been much smoother, but back then—in much better times, even if they had still sucked—they weren't being chased by eleven greedy missiles.

By the time they pierced the first high-altitude clouds that splashed across the sky outside the cockpit window like spilled milk, things quieted down. However, Dev could still sense that the air buffeting the control flaps through his manual control neural cushions was still turbulent compared to the pleasant vacuum of space.

Below, the main continent of Gothaer came into view, an endless expanse of dull green and many more shades of ochre and yellow resulting from the wilted and diseased vegetation. This

*The last Battleship*

monotony was interrupted by a spider web of thin lines that branched out in all directions. Sometimes they were wide, sometimes narrow, gray here and dark blue there. The planet's rivers had been almost as famous as its near-criminal wealth and had once attracted millions of tourists to its booming river cruise industry that also provided a lifeline for heavy industry in the western wastelands. Today they were merely lifeless relics of a nature violated, abandoned, and silent, as were the even narrower streaks that became visible a few thousand meters below, the remains of what was once the largest road network in the Federation. It connected the circular brown-gray blobs in the landscape that had once been thriving cities, now incinerated and irradiated, graves for millions of children, women, and men who, twenty years ago, literally had the sky fall on their heads.

Even larger were the four craters Magnus, Tantor, Infliktor, and Eversor, where the largest fragments of Kor had hit and sent dozens of shockwaves around the planet, leaving hardly anything alive even before the thermal blast wave reached them. Today they were deep blue; groundwater and acid rain had formed large lakes that seemed to stare into the sky like dark eyes.

"Everybody, hold tight," Dev called over the ship-wide speakers, accelerating once more when radar alerted him that the pursuing missiles had also entered the upper atmosphere. The first of them failed instantly as the friction ripped open hulls not designed for it. Yet despite that, three survived Harbingen's tightly packed molecules and came hurtling down upon the *Bitch* like minions of the universe's wrath.

"There's the capital!" Aura shouted.

"That's where we want to go," he replied. It took some effort against the fierce pressure on his chest.

Hartholm was not hard to spot. The city was divided by the great river delta of the Rheyn. The monolithic Palace Hill rose from the city's center, and before it was an open space where the popular Unity Park had once been. The palace itself was visible as a splash of white. It was, in fact, the last intact building on the planet and resembled the Greek Parthenon, if he remembered correctly. The ruins of the former metropolis of millions that surrounded the monolith could not provide a starker contrast. Burned-out silhouettes that were once proud skyscrapers were now only skeletons of plasteel and composite only a few hundred meters tall. Their facades were blackened by soot and overgrown with diseased fungus. Yawning holes indicated where windows had once been.

"Boss, the fucking AI temple is only thirty kilometers away!" Aura warned him.

"I see it." Dev gave the *Bitch* another downward tilt and thrust until they were hurtling almost vertically toward the leveled suburbs. He heard a cover come loose somewhere behind him amid the loud rattling as his ship was jolted by resisting layers of air. A second later, it smacked against something and stuck there.

*"Shhiiiiiiiit!"* Willy and Jezzy shouted in chorus as the collision warning system came on and flashed red warning symbols at him.

At the last moment, he jerked his hands back in their neural cushions, felt the air harden beneath the ship's stubby wings, and rode the dancing gas molecules in a criminally tight upward curve that carried them along a former interstate over burned-out car wrecks and creeper-covered skeletons. The cloud they trailed was a mixture of excited particles, dust, hot air, and pulverized bone and plant debris. The three rockets swerved onto the new course, but only two of them succeeded. One failed and slammed into the ground, exploding with such a roar that Dev heard it even over the noise of the engines. The nuclear fireball spread out in a ring and caught up with them. The shockwave rattled the *Bitch* like aspen leaves in an autumn wind and caused her to spin violently to one side.

He barely dodged two ruined signs that spanned the interstate, and they would have crashed into one of the first skyscrapers if it hadn't been leveled by the blast wave. Still, he maintained the unplanned turn and headed for what might once have been a parking garage.

The remaining missiles were still a thousand meters away but closing rapidly. Dev armed two of their own and fired them at the parking garage's driveway just before he yanked the *Bitch* upward and rode the explosions into the sky. Their pursuers flew toward the fireballs, the hottest signatures in the immediate vicinity, and ignited their nuclear inferno. This time they got off more lightly by fleeing straight into the sky because the mushroom cloud expanded considerably slower than the blast wave that once again abused his ship.

"Drop packet on my command!" he ordered. They now were less than twenty kilometers from the palace and would need some altitude to drop the bomb at a horizontal angle so it could align with the thrusters downward first and not just fall out of the sky. A risk, but one he was willing to take. "We're going to 3,500 meters," he said.

"Are you sure that's—" Aura began to ask.

"No, I'm not. Get ready."

"Roger that. Holding clamps are ready, no malfunctions. Ejection mechanism intact."

"That's what I want to hear." The altitude indicator kept increasing in tandem with the vibrations in his seat and under his feet. He was sure that if any screw in the ship wasn't seated properly, it would now go bye-bye.

"Three, two, one... *Now!*" Dev shouted as they shot upward on the fringe of the mushroom cloud like a cork shot out of the bottle, trailing a tail of condensed air behind them like a veil.

"Drop, drop, drop!" Aura's voice boomed through the cockpit.

*Let's see what kind of devil bomb this is,* he thought, ready to race the *Bitch* westward to put as much distance as possible between themselves and Ground Zero—the excavation site at the foot of Palace Hill. They couldn't see it because too many of the monolithic skyscraper corpses obscured the view.

"Malfunction!"

"What?" he asked, clearly irritated.

"The ejection mechanism is not responding," Aura said, and he heard the repeated *click* of a toggle switch.

"It can't be!" Dev ordered the autopilot to loop at minimum speed, unbuckled his seatbelt, and sprang over to her. He gruffly pushed her hand away and flipped the switch himself. Nothing happened. The readout on the small, extra display above remained blank. *"Fuck!"*

"No malfunction," Jezzy droned. "We can't access the holding clamps anymore. We've been locked out."

"What do you mean?" Dev demanded, frowning at her with furrowed brows.

"Our control authority has been revoked."

"By whom? How is that even possible?"

"The Fleet must have put in a priority code mechanism," Aura said. Judging by the color of her face, she was just as angry as he was.

"But who's supposed to have a priority code…" Dev faltered and stared toward the passageway in the corridor. "That fucking wanker of a fucking asshole—"

"Another problem." Willy pointed at the pilot displays behind him. Dev turned around and saw that the *Bitch* was ignoring the roundabout course he had entered and reducing altitude. In disbelief, he witnessed her calculate a new course directly to the excavation site—under 500 meters altitude—and make her way to her new vector without a second thought.

*Ungrateful traitor!* Before he could bring the mixture of jealousy, grief, and seething anger to erupt, he ran toward the corridor.

Dev had to kill someone, and he knew exactly whom.

He found Bradley in the mess hall outside the welded-up entrance to the former cargo compartment. He was standing with his hands clasped behind his back and looking expectantly in his direction. He was also dressed in the heavy combat suit of the Terran Marines, which was completely closed except for the helmet. It made him look much stronger than he was.

"You fucking piece of shit!" he yelled at the officer. Dev could tell from his eyes that the man knew exactly what he was talking about. "You think you can fuck with me? On my own ship?"

"That's not my intention," Jason replied calmly. "But this mission has to succeed."

"Why do you think I almost steered us into a fucking parking garage to avoid getting nuked? Do you think I'm here for fun?" Before he realized it himself, his fist landed in the officer's face, sending him to the ground. A tearing pain spread from his cracked knuckles, and he groaned and shook his fingers. He expected the man to come at him as soon as he picked himself up. But when Jason got to his feet, he wiped his bloody lips with the back of his hand and just inspected the blood.

"Your skills I respect, but the Fleet couldn't risk you running away or backing out if things got too dicey."

"Backing out? I just kept three nuclear missiles off our backs!" roared Dev, beside himself. "I put my baby—my *family*—on the line to do this mission, and you fucking shitheads don't trust me? Don't trust *us*?"

"I'm sorry."

*"You're sorry?"* His pulse spiked to 180 and roared in his ears as he lunged at the soldier again, but before he could lash out at him like a berserker, he jerked to a halt. His arms felt as if they were lashed with steel cables.

"Whooaa, boss," Willy said as if calming a horse. "If you kill him, we'll have a real problem with the Fleet. And we wouldn't be able to finish our prototype for the Telepator."

"Telepator?" Dev asked in confusion. "What the...? Get off me! I'm gonna throw this motherfucker out the airlock and piss on him!"

"Uh, can we put that off until later? We're flying over the dig site in forty seconds and there are some defenses out there," his engineer said in his typical, rumbling voice. As if to underline his warning, the *Bitch* threw herself into a hard turn to starboard and slammed them onto the holotable.

Groaning, he got back to his feet, only to see that it was Jason Bradley who had hoisted him up. Furious, he wrenched himself free and shoved an index finger under his bloody nose.

"We're not done here!"

The officer merely nodded and looked over his shoulder at the welded-up passageway of the cargo compartment.

Dev ran to the bridge with Willy in tow and dropped into the pilot's seat. The restraining belts flowed around his chest and tightened automatically. He could only watch his ship—strictly speaking, not his at that moment—go into a port turn to avoid a particularly tall skyscraper ruin. The excavation site came into view. It was an amazingly small area the size of a football field. Three boreholes were topped by huge, steel cranes that looked like gangly, avant-garde statues. Everything there lay about five meters below the surrounding ground between the dense ruins of houses, as if someone had hammered a rectangular depression into the city with a large metal punch.

A half-dozen stacks of crates and barrels were spread out amid deactivated cargo drones and electric sleds. Heavily armed Marines in pitch-black armor could be seen emerging from the boreholes as if from a disturbed ant hole to take cover behind the crates. Some of them were mounting anti-aircraft guns.

"Shit!" Dev frantically pressed the button for a system restart, but it refused to respond. Its central command screen indicated they would be over the center of the dig site in ten seconds at an altitude of only 100 meters. The bomb drop time was nine minutes. "They're killing us! The fucking Fleet bastards are killing us! This was a suicide mission from the start!"

The realization struck him, and all life seemed to drain at once from his body like stagnant water. They were done for, simply done for. At this close range, even a simple nuclear weapon would annihilate them. Even a kill by those exiled Marines below would be more merciful than helplessly watching himself and his crew get killed by their own weapon.

"It probably won't do any good, but I want to say it anyway." Dev heard Jason's voice behind him and wheeled his head around. The officer was standing in the doorway to the corridor, putting on his combat armor helmet. His voice now boomed through the throat speakers, "Had I known you before as I have come to know you on this voyage, I would have disagreed with the Admiralty's decision and tried to prevent the intrusion into your onboard computer. It's been an honor."

With that, he turned and left the cockpit.

"Wh-what...?" Dev stammered. Then, seeing his crew sitting behind him, their faces blank and pale with shock, he simply said. "I'm sorry, guys."

At that moment, they flew over the excavation site. Bombardment from below sizzled past them, and then the *Bitch* pitched violently, as if it had flown into a violent squall. The cargo's retaining clamps had opened, halving the total mass of his ship in one fell swoop.

All at once, the lock on the controls was gone. He reacted immediately and jerked the nose upward and set the thrusters to full power. Anyone not strapped in now could end up as a bloodstain on the wall as far as he cared.

"Boss!" Willy shouted over the roar of the engines.

"What? We might be able to—"

"Look at the dorsal sensor packs!"

Dev obeyed since the *Bitch* had nothing to do but race skyward. He was desperate to put as much distance between them and the bomb as he could. It wouldn't be enough, but he'd never been one for lying down to die.

What he saw was completely insane. The bomb, with its twenty-seven glowing Raptors, spun in the air like a domino and slowed just before impact. Jason Bradley flew after it with a jetpack.

"Is he completely crazy?"

The bomb struck amid the defending Marines. Many of them were able to reach safety in the boreholes after their unsuccessful attempts to intercept the *Bitch*. The force of impact on landing was enormous, sending dense clouds of dust in all directions like an annular sandstorm after the engines at full braking thrust had burned everything beneath them. Then nothing happened. The flattened cube lay motionless as the surviving defenders slowly ventured out of their cover and aimed for the bomb, which was the size of half a residential building. Their body language betrayed their uncertainty.

"A misfire?" Dev muttered, irritated. Could fate really flow along such a winding course? He didn't know whether to laugh or cry—or both at the same time.

## 15

Jason landed hard on the massive steel cuboid and cushioned his fall with his servo-assisted knees. Without them, he would have broken more than just his legs. The defenders seemed to have overcome the initial shock from the bomb that had literally fallen on their heads. Once they realized that it wasn't intended to explode, they set up a crossfire that forced him to retract his head. But the shooting did not last long because the "bomb" suddenly gave off a loud roar somewhat like heavenly choirs singing. All firing abruptly ceased.

He straightened and saw the sides of the secret weapon had blown away and its contents literally exploded onto the dense terrain of the excavation site.

Baker was the first of the heavily armored mutants to jump onto the dusty ground with a mighty leap. He landed among three defenders clad in the black suits of regular Harbinger Marines. Jason recognized the uniforms from his childhood when his family had attended the parades that marched through Hartholm twice a year. With a gruesome laugh, Baker hacked at the figures surrounding him, swinging his human-sized power axe, and split the paralyzed soldiers in half as if they were mere mannequins. He then pulled an assault cannon from his shoulder and pulled the trigger, firing off a hurricane of fist-sized shells that descended on a group of defenders next to one of the drilling cranes and sprayed the air with clouds of blood and guts. After a week of being crammed into an exceedingly small space, his 80 companions were no less brutal. They poured over the Exile Marines like a force of nature.

Jason did not know whether to surrender to the triumphant feeling of superiority that came with the sight of his friends—they were so very brutal and impressive. Though a very primordial part of him rejoiced, he wondered if he should yield to the nausea that spread through him when he saw the brutality of the carnage.

Ultimately, he postponed the decision, ran to the edge of the cargo container and, aided by his servo-assisted legs, leapt down into the dust in front of one of the boreholes.

"Baker!" he shouted over their encrypted frequency. "Here!"

The mutant leader, bald and clad in crude plates of carbotanium armor that made him look like an orc chieftain, had just seized a marine and torn him in half. He turned to face Jason, threw away the bloody remains of his victim, and ran over to him. On the way, he fired incessantly left and right, reaping the cruel harvest of his unleashed wrath.

"On my way, squirt," Baker mumbled around a smoldering cigar in the corner of his mouth. "Shall we storm the borehole? I can pull my boys together and—"

"No, there's no time!" Jason interrupted, then squatted to shoot a marine who was peeking out of the hole in front of him. The unfortunate soldier crashed back into the hole. A grenade explosion rocked the steel frame of the crane, from which a long cable hung, presumably for a construction hoist. The structure gave a sad creak and shuddered before buckling and collapsing with a noise that almost drowned out the roar of the battle. He didn't wait for Baker, just pointed his light Gauss rifle forward and ran on. He circled two bodies that had fallen on top of each other and jumped over part of the fallen crane. His leap proved to be timely because two new helmets appeared in the borehole and sent cherry-red laser lances after him that almost burned him. Baker shot a grenade from his assault cannon at the two soldiers from the other side crane. The explosive shredded part of the crane's remains and sent it crashing into the hole that led to the data storage.

Jason sprinted the last three meters, grabbed a grenade from his belt and awkwardly threw it into the three-meter hole. Despite his bad throw—he was aiming for the center and hit the edge—the explosive device tumbled in instead of out. Before he could cover the distance, the ground beneath him shook slightly. He wanted to look up at the sky to see if the *Quantum Bitch* was still there, but he wouldn't blame Dev and his quirky crew for running away. Jason might eventually have to answer to a court of law for withdrawing his priority code and returning control to Myers, but he had never given much thought to doing the wrong thing out of cold logic. That only resulted in chains of bad decisions and moral indifference that always seemed to rebound on their perpetrator.

With a bit of luck, the *Oberon* might be able to recover them. After all, the battle was going their way and Dev and his people would probably be better off running away now instead of hoping the Federation would keep their word and just let them go. Political tides could be treacherous. Even if the current fleet admiral was an honest leader and kept his promises, it didn't mean he wouldn't fall victim to some trick, a spontaneous intrigue that could lead to his downfall and replacement by a less reliable successor who judged things quite differently.

In any case, he didn't want to follow them blindly and then change his mind when he realized he was wrong. The crew of the *Quantum Bitch* consisted of scoundrels who took care of themselves above all else, but they certainly had personality, and they were neither murderers nor involved in the really terrible things like organ and human trafficking. They did the right thing when they had to, despite their vocal bellyaching. Depriving them of control of their ship was perhaps the worst thing the Fleet could have done.

He silently wished them good luck and slowed in front of the hole and its black depths. He slid to a stop in a cloud of dust just as Baker appeared, threw a stun grenade down the hole, and then looked over the edge. The flash reflected in chrome eyes that seemed to remain untouched.

"Ten meters, pipsqueak. You'll make it!" Baker stuffed the cigar between his teeth and jumped. The thunder of shells and screams followed him. Jason gripped his gun tighter and went after him. At first, he could only see smoke and dust, coarsely drilled earth and rocks passing by, then he landed on something soft and yielding. Reluctant to see what it was, he crouched, and as he had learned in basic training, trained his weapon, and scanned for danger. Yet there was nothing on the wide metal platform other than a few badly mutilated corpses and Baker, who was reloading his assault cannon.

"What do you know about this data storage?" the mutant asked and clicked the mighty plate magazine into the holder provided under the vehicle weapon.

"Underground, the size of a football field, and accessible via a concealed maintenance hatch."

"Ah." Baker took a long puff from his cigar as if they had all the time in the world. "And where is that exactly?"

"I don't know, I've never been here before. I didn't even know where the data storage was," Jason said, raising his gun as he shrugged.

"Then how do you know how big the storage is?"

"Well, the excavation site. It was about the size of a—"

"—football field." Baker sighed and shoved the cigar butt into the corner of his mouth with his tongue. "Of course. But you know for sure about the access hatch?"

"Not a hundred percent. But there won't be a terminal or anything like that, otherwise Omega wouldn't have buried and secured the storage." Jason thought about his own words. "But there must be an uplink-enabled exchange via satellite."

"For back-ups or something?"

"Exactly."

"Doesn't help us." A beam of red light cut through the air, flickering in the dust between them. Much slower than the mutant, Jason flinched and rolled to the side, but Baker had already taken care of the shooter with grenades and hoisted Jason back to his feet as if he were his pet. "Come with me, little man. We'll just go where those little shitters are hanging out, that's probably best."

Since he didn't know what to say and didn't have a better idea, Jason just nodded. He had no choice since the huge mutant had

*The last Battleship*

already taken off into the tunnel to the right, causing the metal floor to tremble.

*The Exiles dug, but they certainly didn't lay many power lines or proper flooring in the amount of time they had,* he thought as he ran after the giant and tried to keep up.

In the next room, Baker had already slaughtered a handful of defenders and knocked burning pieces of armor off his body where laser fire had apparently damaged it. Another corridor led to the north, where a faint rumble announced moving footsteps.

"They're leaving," the mutant said, clicking his tongue.

"Maybe we should..."

Baker had already started running and pounded forward like a dinosaur through the dusty tunnel.

"... just give way to bloodlust," Jason sighed, dismissing the idea of following the giant. In combat, he was worthless in comparison, and this room looked conspicuously like a maintenance room.

He turned around once and saw several closed hatches in the rock walls. Cables ran to the ceiling and floor on narrow rails and disappeared into them. Tiny red wires ran to the right and left into the corridors. Two unfolded suitcases containing specialized electronic tools lay next to a military transport box in front of an open panel with a dark space behind. A handful of connector pliers were carelessly scattered on the floor. Someone had set off in a hurry, that much was certain.

Jason frowned, looked at the wires, then moved closer to the open panel. He cautiously looked inside, as if fearing he might lose his balance and fall into the darkness. His visor automatically turned on its integrated residual light amplification and revealed a ventilation shaft crammed with blue quagma charges.

"By the Omega!" he whispered and staggered back. Then he shouted over the radio, *"Baker!"*

"Yo, I'm here. The little shitters are frightened and running away, but my boys'll take care of them upstairs and have a goulash party, just the way we like it," the mutant said happily.

"A bomb! They've mined everything here!"

"What kind?"

"Explosive charges that fuse atomic nuclei and release quark-gluon plasma. It'll incinerate half the city!"

"Oh. Then we should get out of here," Baker suggested in a calm voice.

*But we can't do that because I let the* Quantum Bitch *go,* he said in his mind and thought feverishly. It was too late to call the *Oberon*.

*"Shit!" Omega. I need to contact Omega.* "Omega? Do you hear me?"

Except for the hum of the ventilation, he heard nothing. He was sure he was in the right place and knew for sure that there was no control room or anything like that. No one had ever worked here, except perhaps for a few maintenance bots whose memories had been reformatted after each use.

That's when an idea came to him. He switched his laryngeal speaker to 80 percent power and recited the secret access code.

**"Access,"** said a warm, penetrating voice that sounded androgynous but low-pitched like the gentle bass of an ancient deity speaking to him from Mount Olympus. He knew it from the news broadcasts from his childhood. **"Voice patterns recognized. Jason Bradley. Bradley. Bradley."**

"Omega!"

**"Input. Data integrity at ninety percent. Damage to primary heuristics. Lack of connectivity to the isochor cerebrum. Functionality at ten percent."**

"I need your help; there's a bomb here!"

**"Explosive device discovered. Quagma. Weight and quantity unknown."**

Jason was startled when two mutants rushed in from the corridor from where he and Baker had come, looking around for more victims. Their armor was covered with deep scars and burns and enough blood to paint a house. One of them was Rochshaz.

"Who's talking?" the mutant asked, irritated, and looked around as if he were watching an annoying fly.

"Omega," Jason said curtly.

**"Yes."**

"Who?"

"Omega." He ignored Rochshaz and looked up for lack of a visible contact person or specific direction. "How can I stop it?"

**"Manual ignition. Origin unknown. Infiltration of the data storage. Integrity of memory unit inadequate."**

"What? What does that mean? Have you been damaged?"

"No," Rochshaz replied. "The thing was accessed without authorization, that's what's going on."

"What are you talking about?"

"Something I know about. I'm a Level 3 Analyst, little guy. This AI is actually not an AI at all because its data sets are compressed. You've cracked the encryption with your code and can therefore communicate with the automatic management heuristic of the data store, but not with your Omega thing. That requires a data storage device that can hold the unpacked data, not this backup box."

"But we don't have one!"

"That's right. At least you don't have a big enough storage stick with you." Rochshaz and his sidekick chuckled as if it were all a joke.

"There's a fucking bomb in there!" Jason yelled at them, pointing to the ventilation shaft.

The two followed his gesture then fired at short intervals at the wires leading away from the bomb.

"Why didn't you just cut those things?"

Jason blinked and gasped for breath. "B-because it could have set the thing off, damn it! You lunatics!"

"But it didn't." The other mutant shrugged and looked at him as if he had lost his mind.

"It's impossible to talk to you..."

**"Process scheduling interrupted,"** reported Omega—or its upstream administrative heuristic. **"Asynchronous interruption. Time-related process scheduling detected."**

"What does that mean?" Jason asked, feeling drops of sweat from his brows start to run into his eyes.

"A countdown," Rochshaz translated.

"How long?"

**"Twenty-eight minutes. And. Forty-four seconds."**

*Less than twenty-nine minutes?* he thought in surprise. *The Marines are still trying to escape and buy themselves some time because they know there's nothing we can do and that we won't be evacuated.*

"Omega, is your uplink working?"

**"Uplink master functional. Slave doesn't answer."**

"The receiving satellite, which acts as a relay station. It's probably been junk for a long time," Rochshaz said.

"I know!" Jason radioed Baker, "Are you on the surface?"

"Yo. A few have escaped here, I'm going to—"

"Fuck that! Can you amplify my signal with one of your battle antennae?"

"Who are you trying to contact?"

"The *Oberon*."

"Wait a minute." There was a crack and rustle over the radio. "Go ahead. There are a few seconds delay because of the distance."

Jason sent his authentication code and then started speaking. "Lieutenant Commander Jason Bradley here from Operation Area Epsilon."

"This is Lieutenant Jung speaking. I hope you're all right, sir."

"Put me through to the commander, at once."

"Lieutenant Commander?" He heard Silly's voice with some surprise. "What's the situation?"

"We need an immediate evacuation!" he shouted.

"That's not possible, our guys are still down on the Tooth."

"The Exiles somehow managed to access the data storage and extract data."

"What data?"

"I don't know because everything is packed or something. I can only use an administrative heuristic—it doesn't matter. The Omega back-up can only unpack the data if it has a storage device large enough, and the only one I know of nearby is the *Oberon*!"

"What?"

"Ma'am," he said formally, struggling to force himself to speak calmly, "we need this data."

"I'll send a team of technicians."

"That won't be possible. The enemy has mined everything here, and in twenty-five minutes a quagma bomb will explode and wipe everything out."

A short pause ensued.

"To get within transmission range, we'd have to leave our position immediately. Even then it would be tight, and we'd have to leave half a legion of our Marines behind, including Colonel Meyer," Silly said. He could hear in her voice that he had lost this battle. "I can't and won't do that. The transmitter is about to be destroyed and then it doesn't matter where these fanatical traitors went back then. They will never know about their collaborators."

"Ma'am—Silly, we must—"

"The connection is dead, pee-wee," Baker mumbled.

"What a fucking—"

"Eh, aren't we getting taken off?" Rochshaz asked, pointing a huge thumbs up.

"No, we aren't."

"Inconvenient," the mutant said. "What about the data?"

"We have to get it out of here. The Exiles somehow managed to get their hands on the code or bypass the security measures, but I don't know how they could have done that." Jason pulled at his hair. "Omega? Has your data been extracted?"

**"Negative. Partial data. Not an image. Temporary data retrieval."**

"What was the query?"

**"Coordinates of the Exile fleet under the command of Ludwig von Borningen."**

"They got what they wanted," he translated, baring his teeth. "We're too late and they've lured us straight into a trap."

"Tough bones, I must say," Rochshaz said approvingly. "Leave a few hundred soldiers behind to make it look like they have something to hide here just to distract us."

"To distract from what?"

"I don't know—from something. If I knew, it wouldn't be a good plan, would it?" Both mutants laughed loudly. All that was missing was for them to slap their knees to add to the absurdity of their reaction. After all, a bomb was counting down to an explosion that would be seen far into space.

"Very funny," Jason grumbled. He tried again to think clearly, but that was increasingly difficult because he felt like a fugitive driven into a corner who was running out of options. Everything had started promisingly, but now the entire operation was in tatters.

The enemy had already learned the coordinates of von Borningen's destination and had probably sent its transmission long ago. This meant that neither the *Oberon* out there, nor he down here could do anything. They were simply too late. The only thing that could mitigate the damage now would be to extract the entire data storage and revive Omega—or at least what was left of the AI that many of his people had cause to worship as a deity in the data sky. Perhaps it knew the answers to what they could do to prevent a disaster—answers none of them could see. Perhaps it had information about what had become of the true Exiles and what plans they were pursuing. He didn't think it was unrealistic that it could even calculate all of this based on probabilities that turned out to be true.

"We should get away," Rochshaz suggested.

"We can't do that."

"Better than hanging out here."

"It's better to be here at Ground Zero than to be swept away by the blast wave out there in a vain hope that we can survive somehow." Jason slumped against the wall and tried again to establish a connection with *Oberon*, but his requests did not get through.

"We're finished."

## 16

Colonel Ludwig Meyer emptied his magazine then spun behind the steel frame of the massive bulkhead just as counterfire caused sparks to fly around him.

"Lieutenant," he called.

"Almost ready, sir!" came the frantic reply.

The bulkhead crashed down like a guillotine and the projectiles fired by the pursuing Exiles thundered into the heavy carbotanium like hailstones on a windshield.

Ludwig waited a few more seconds before he slowly emerged from cover and slapped another magazine into his Gauss rifle. His decimated commando platoon was down to four men. Besides him, there was Draper and the two first sergeants Leopold and Schrader, who were forward at a wide console. They put down their weapons.

"How sure are you that this will hold?" he asked Draper, nodding in the direction of the control panel next to the bulkhead.

"They can't open it electronically," the first lieutenant stated optimistically and then let go of the control panel cover, which hung at the end of battered cables that looked like tousled hair.

"Well, that should give us a few minutes or more." He opened his helmet visor and breathed in the fresh air—or whatever it was that was blowing around down here. It had certainly been recycled from the exhalation of enemy men and women thousands of times, but that was still better than the musty air of his suit's life support system, which always smelled a little of metal and ozone. "Leopold, Schrader?"

"We're on it, sir."

The first sergeants plugged their suit connectors into the control desk's computer systems and began making rapid inputs on holokeyboards and touch displays. Ludwig stepped to their side and looked out of the wide but low window into the hangar for the first time.

The phased antenna was huge, at least 50 meters high, and the dish's diameter was about as wide. It had a curious shape as if it had been folded several times and then rolled out without losing its creases. The long pin in the middle had obviously been retracted so it could fit into the hangar, it was significantly shorter and thicker than the one in the images Silly had shown him. The armored gates above formed a granular sky, crisscrossed by steel struts and clunky molecular binding generators that stuck to their undersides like swallows' nests. Contrary to expectations, the floor around it was empty. No technicians engaged in hectic activity, no soldiers, no drones, or vehicles—nothing at all. If Ludwig had not known about the battle they had fought and were still fighting, he would have believed that the transmitter hangar had been turned into a museum or was a disused facility that had survived its time.

"Something smells fishy here," he said.

"You mean because the control room was so badly guarded or because we're trapped?" Draper asked. He was standing beside Ludwig with his helmet tucked under his arm.

"Any updates from our platoons yet?"

"The losses are increasing, but they have taken positions that are easy to defend and are holding out for the time being."

"Good." Ludwig was glad they had been able to launch such a fierce initial attack and reduce the forces entrenched within the complex. Now, at least, they did not have to fight the legion advancing from outside while still engaged with the defenders inside and end up in a bloody sandwich. They had bought themselves some time, which was never a bad thing. "We need access to these systems now, guys."

"We're on it, sir," Leopold assured him, absently scrolling through holomenus and display queries in no time at all. "The software is not exactly recent. I guess the system was ready five years ago and the programming was installed. Nevertheless, it takes a little time for our blacklinks to infiltrate the registry files and create fake administrator accounts."

"Whatever you have to do, do it."

Several bangs and a high-pitched buzz came from the blocked safety bulkhead through which they had entered. Their pursuers were not idle.

Ludwig took a sip of water from the small tube that protruded from his armor's neck ring in front of his mouth and waited patiently as he stared at the antenna outside in the hangar. He considered smashing the window and plastering it with grenades and Gauss projectiles. As tempting as that was, however, he couldn't shake the feeling that he was missing something. In addition, the enemy's puppet master seemed to have anticipated their assault, which was always bad news for attackers, and he would not do them the favor of making the most obvious move.

Since he had two netheads in his commando platoon, he would use them and proceed a little more subtly. Whatever the Exiles had prepared, they had not been granted much time either, that much was obvious from the signs everywhere. For their trap to have snapped shut properly, defensive positions within the facility should have been much better fortified, and the Legion's surprise attack on the surface should have been launched more quickly, despite the losses they would have suffered from orbital bombardment.

"Colonel, I've got something here." Schrader snapped him out of his thoughts. A holoscreen flickered in front of him. From where he was standing, he could not make out the contents.

"What is it?"

"It looks like the phase transmitter has already sent something."

"Where to? A test, perhaps?"

"It's quite possible that it wasn't *the* transmission," Schrader admitted, "but definitely one with high signal strength and a decent data packet."

"What was the content?" Ludwig asked.

"I can't possibly find out, not without a dozen decryption programs, sir. I could determine the transmitter's orientation, but that will also take some time because the data paths are quite confusing."

"What does that mean?"

"It means that someone made a rather frantic attempt to make tracing the corresponding data as difficult as possible—at least without a lengthy encryption process," Leopold translated what the other first sergeant said.

"Then hurry up," he urged them.

"There's something else, sir," Schrader said.

"Speak."

"The transmitter was completely shut down. The control hydraulics of the platform is no longer getting any power. I think the whole plant was about to be mothballed. This also coincides with what we're seeing in the system. The data has been deleting itself for thirteen hours now. It's only thanks to the large amount of data that a lot is still visible. One more day and we'd have seen nothing here except deleted memory clusters."

"I need a connection to *Oberon*—immediately!"

∽

"Captain, Colonel Meyer is calling," Lieutenant Jung reported.

"Put him through!" Silly ordered and looked at Nicholas.

"Meyer here." The colonel's grating voice rang out over the annoying interference. "There's a problem."

"Another one?"

"Yes. The transmission has already been made."

"What? What transmission?" the commander asked, but a cold shiver of realization ran through Nicholas. They were too late.

"The phased antenna has long since sent a signal to an unknown position. We can't say where with one hundred percent certainty."

"Maybe it was just a test transmission."

"Unlikely. They started a data wipe, maybe as early as yesterday.

*The last Battleship*

The transmitting device has been mothballed, possibly mined," the Marine explained.

"But then why would they send a whole legion after you?" Silly shook his head. "That doesn't make any sense."

"Because of the data wipe," Nicholas answered for Meyer. "We arrived earlier than expected. Too late, but sooner than the enemy thought. That's why they're sacrificing their soldiers."

"We'll be over your position in five minutes and start the bombardment," the commander promised.

"Negative. As I said, we have to assume that the plant is mined."

"Then why hasn't it blown up yet?"

"Nothing is going according to plan. Maybe a malfunction or our early arrival messed things up. In any case, I'm sure they're already working to fix the problem. That's how *I* would do it." Meyer paused and the noise in the background quieted. "We are now sending you a data packet. It is encrypted and contains the coordinates to which it was sent, including the transmission itself. We don't have a chance of decrypting it here, and you probably don't either, but the Federation will need it. We don't have much—"

Static shredded Meyer's voice, distorted it into unrecognizable sound, then the connection broke off.

"Someone is interfering with the signal, ma'am," Lieutenant Jung explained.

"Shit!" Silly looked at Nicholas. "We'll get the shuttles ready and get them out of there, if necessary, with the support of our Barracudas. They can operate down there."

"That will take time," Nicholas said. "And we have to go to Harbingen."

"No!"

"Silly," he lowered his voice but was insistent. He bent over the hologram between them. It showed the last two Exile ships fleeing toward S2. "We have had minimal losses so far, except for the one Barracuda that disappeared. We can consider ourselves fortunate that things have gone so well under the circumstances. But now we have to make an uncomfortable decision. I think if there's a chance to save Omega, we have to take it."

"He's right, ma'am," Daussel agreed, even though his expression betrayed how difficult it was for him to say it. "Especially with regard to the data he wants to send us, Omega would be the only chance we have of deciphering it quickly and making this mission a success."

"That means we would have to fly straight to Jason's position at full speed and leave our Marines behind," Silly said stating the obvious, then looked shocked when she saw Nicholas's and Daussel's emotionless expressions. "You can't seriously be suggesting that!"

"There's more at stake here than the colonel and our Marines." The words threatened to constrict his throat, but he forced them past his lips. "It's about more than us. If von Borningen has already contacted his Exiles, we need to know what the message was in order to prepare."

"Prepare for what?"

"Whatever they're up to. An invasion perhaps? We may never know if we don't extract Omega's data, and to do that, we have to go into low orbit above the excavation site."

"And evacuate Jason."

"If that's possible, yes," he admitted frankly, feeling anger at her implied accusation. "But I give this assessment as a tactical officer and XO."

"He's right," Daussel repeated with unusual emphasis. "And we're running out of time. If we don't make a decision now, we won't get to Harbingen before the data storage device blows up."

"I'm supposed to save a gang of fucking criminal mutants and leave half a legion of our Marines behind?" Silly gritted her teeth, and the corners of her mouth twitched, betraying the agony she was going through just thinking about it. It was the dilemma generations of commanders had confronted, a dilemma that forced them to act purely rationally, despite their feelings, because the operational situation required it. "It's just like it was then," she whispered, her face pale. "Just like back then."

"Yes," Nicholas said, swallowing. "And my father made a decision that haunted him ever after, but he never regretted it. That's the commander's burden."

"Shit!" she cursed and pounded her right fist on the command console. Once, then twice, and then again, until fine cracks and blood stains appeared on the bulletproof glass. Nicholas blinked, surprised by the vehemence of her outburst, and noticed how quiet it had become on the bridge. Silly looked at her cracked knuckles and struck again. The agony in her eyes had grown into a blazing inferno as she said, "Set course for Harbingen. Full speed ahead."

"Aye, ma'am," Nicholas replied quickly, relaying the relevant orders to Alkad, clarifying them, and waiting for them to be confirmed. He switched the timer to the holoscreen that was counting down twenty-one minutes until the quagma bomb detonated.

"Captain, we're receiving a directional beam from the surface of the Tooth!" Jung reported. "They're encrypted data packets."

Silly frowned and zoomed in on the surface of the lunar fragment with trembling fingers. The hologram depicted two platoons of the Black Legion engaged in a fierce firefight around one of the access holes, streaming to the surface in a suicidal rush to take on advancing enemy soldiers. They were massively outnumbered but showed no signs of hesitation. Two of them had placed a field transmitter in the hole to maintain a directional beam.

"Can..." Silly swallowed. "Can you put me through to the colonel?"

"Not directly, ma'am," Jung replied. "But you can send a message that his Marines will receive and perhaps forward."

"Do that. Karl. This is Silly speaking. We're flying to Harbingen to try and recover Omega. I am sorry. You are heroes and I will make sure that, in the future, everyone remembers who we owe this day to when we are victorious. *Juratis Unitatis.*"

∽

"They're coming," Jason breathed and slowly came out of his defeatist paralysis. For the last four or five minutes he had been crouching in front of the open wall flap to the ventilation shaft, staring at the bluish glowing quagma bomb as if he could neutralize it with the mere power of thought.

Memories of his time here in Hartholm had flickered through his mind. How he and Nicholas had played in the park while one of their parents was high up in the palace, at an audience with Omega or in a Fleet meeting. None of that had interested him back then. He was too busy showing his little brother the various xeno-animals in the well-kept and lively park landscape. How many of the countless exotic species were still alive? None?

News of salvation came from Lieutenant Jung. He reported the *Oberon* would take sixteen minutes to get into orbit. What this meant for Ludwig Meyer and his two companies of the Black Legion quickly dampened his initial relief. Nevertheless, it *was* salvation, as painful as it was, because he knew Omega would be saved, and with it their chances for a future dramatically improved.

There was no escape for them, just as there was no escape for the colonel, the man who had rocked him on his lap when he was allowed on board to visit his father on Space Dock Days. He remembered well how he had been afraid of the powerful marine who had treated his men so loudly and harshly that a child dreamed of it at night. And yet there was an undeniable warmth that came with the memory because, at the same time, Ludwig was a rock of stoic strength, once Jason understood that he was a friend of his father's and cared about him and Nicholas when he was not around.

Now he was dead... or would be very soon.

*Just like me, Baker, and his boys.*

"What's up?" Rochshaz asked, sitting up next to him where he had been reclining with his arms folded behind his head. Who's coming? A taxi?"

"No, but a mobile data storage device!"

"Then we should go upstairs and set up a signal booster, huh?" The mutant got to his feet, yawned, and gave Baker a kick. The mutant leader had been napping to kill time until their searing death.

"Beavers and ducks!" the giant yelled and sat up like a pocketknife. He looked around, blinked, discovered the cigar butt in his hand, shoved it into the corner of his mouth, and lit it. What's the matter?"

"His little boat is coming by to collect the data. I'll go up with some guys and set up a signal booster."

"That thing from our flying shithole of a cave?"

"Exactly."

"How long does it take to set it up?" Jason asked with undisguised impatience to speed up the conversation, time was pressing.

"A few minutes, if we don't drop dead as soon as we go into that stinking slaughter pen." Rochshaz laughed wetly and spat out something green.

"Watch the snot balls," Baker grumbled, hitting his comrade's upper arm so violently that he staggered to one side and trudged away. "Come on, little one, let's hurry. If we're gonna die, we can still make ourselves useful. By the way, your deal sucked."

"If we survived, it would have been a good one," Jason insisted as they walked to the borehole, where a handful of mutants were busy gutting a dozen marine corpses. One of them, who had brought a large apron with "Mr. Good Looking is cooking" written on it under all the blood, was holding what looked like a spine in his hand and laughing around a thick cigar at his friends.

"Haw-haw!" The cigar made him mumble. "Thash what I call shlerotic! If he didn't have a shpine, then my name ishn't Ukhshaz!"

"I'm sure little prick let you kill him of his own free will," another mutant roared.

"Don't you have anything better to do?" Jason asked, but they didn't even seem to notice him.

"They're just hardworking, that's how I brought them up," Baker explained, lifting him like a child so he could grasp the bottom rung of their improvised ladder. The mutant then followed him up. "Distract themselves with work."

"Let's call it 'work.'"

Once outside, Rochshaz came, joined them, and moved with surprising speed to the armored vacuum container in which they had endured a week in complete darkness and breathing apparatuses. Even before they caught up with him, he came back with

155

what looked like an extra-long spear, rammed it into the ground, and watched as four nanonic feelers peeled out of the sides and bonded to the dust for additional stability.

"Well, let your AI know," Baker suggested.

"That's it?"

"Yes. It's just a signal booster." The mutant spread his arms and raised his bushy eyebrows. "It picks up a signal"—his hands moved from left to right—"boosts it, and sends it."

"Omega?" Jason asked via the radio frequency the administrative heuristic had given him before he had given way to his defeatist inactivity.

**"I am here."**

"The *Oberon* is on her way. She can record the back-up completely... I think. We have a signal booster here that is tuned to your frequency." He looked at his forearm display and passed on the Titan's exact approach vector to Rochshaz, which he entered via a virtual display.

**"Authorization required."**

"I authorize it." Jason repeated his access code for Omega.

**"Transmission commencing,"** said the administrative heuristic, unmoved. Rochshaz raised his thumb.

"It's working. How long will the transfer take?"

**"Twenty-one minutes."**

"It's going to be tight." He looked down at his countdown. It read 00:20:56.

"Maybe not, we're getting company!" Baker pulled his assault cannon off his shoulder and pointed upward along the rising smoke from his cigar. Jason followed his gesture and looked up at the dirty sky, which was shrouded in irradiated dust and patchy clouds. A dark object descended on them and announced itself with several sonic booms.

"We must protect the signal booster at all costs!" he shouted over the noise.

"I'll try my best, but my Betty isn't an anti-aircraft gun. You'd better go downstairs." Baker's oversized gun thundered and sent 200 fist-sized grenades per minute into the sky. They detonated a little too early and merely tore the air apart with explosions.

"Hey!" a voice crackled in Jason's helmet. "Is that how you greet your saviors?"

"Willy?" Jason asked incredulously. "Is that you?"

"Shit, of course it's me. And now stop shooting at us, otherwise the captain will change his mind!"

"Baker, stop shooting." He almost laughed as he felt his heart leap. "That's the *Bitch*!"

"We won't let you die. Dev knows what you did. That's probably the reason he only wants to hate you for all eternity instead of killing you," Willy said through the interference.

The *Bitch* turned high above them, and Baker lowered his gun while Rochshaz scratched his head in irritation. She carved a daring turn while lowering the passenger ramp.

"Hurry up! It's going to be tight, but maybe we'll get everyone on board!"

# 17

The silence on the *Oberon* was a visceral thing that reverberated in the walls and bulkheads and flooded the heart of the bridge. Nicholas could feel it as if he had developed an organ for subtle reception. Everyone on board knew what was happening: they were salvaging the supreme governing body of their fallen people from the rubble of their past. From the first moment they received the data, it had been as if a switch had flipped in the crew's minds by telepathic means. On the bridge, even the hum of the engines had faded. Perhaps even their cold technology was aware of the significance of this moment.

The Omega was something like a president on paper. It possibly had more powers than the Jupiter Democrats would have liked, but it had nevertheless been elected to office by Harbingen's last parliament after a popular referendum. The period that followed was, to put it mildly, one of progress and technological revolution, prosperity and social peace. Omega had managed, through sharp cuts and intelligent redistribution, to bring about greater justice and progress in which few felt left out.

Its Omega Dots, small offshoots operating in every network node, had been available to all citizens around the clock to answer questions, even on the most intimate matters. After a time, an already dataistic population came to have an almost religious admiration for their AI. That Omega had been on the verge of attaining godlike status might seem strange in retrospect, but it had always made sense to Nicholas. After all, it was a supreme being who heard prayers and answered key personal questions and wishes, and wasn't that exactly what humans had wanted from their fictional deities since the dawn of spiritualism?

What had previously taken place in the realm of faith had become tangible reality, practical and immediate. Who could blame people for worshipping the Omega and giving it a spiritual dimension? Finally, the whole thing was fueled by the fact that the AI itself had always rejected this, pointing out that it was merely an extremely intelligent program on the scale of human IQ.

"It's really happened," Daussel said in a rare display of emotion. "Omega is alive."

"Soon. Maybe," Nicholas said cautiously. "If my calculations are correct—and there's a big question mark over that because I won't know the exact size of the unpacked data until it's, well, unpacked—then the *Oberon*'s combined storage lacunae will be enough to capture Omega."

"Why didn't we do this much earlier?"

"I suspect that my father either didn't know about the data storage—he was an admiral, not a member of the High Council—or he had a reason for not trying to access it. Let's just think about what would have really happened if he had taken the *Oberon* to Harbingen."

"A fleet would have followed him, watched his every move, and immediately intervened to bring him to justice," Silly said with a somber look. "And that's even though it wouldn't have been illegal. The Omega was never officially outlawed."

"But that's only because Harbingen has been too powerful within the Federation to ban it. Not to mention politicians have feared a precedent like the separation of such a potent core world from the Terran economic space," Nicholas said. "We all know that Harbingen, and thus Omega, were only grudgingly tolerated because they didn't want other worlds to follow our example. After all, until our annihilation, it sure looked like that was going to happen."

"Mhm. At any rate, I don't think he was ignorant of it. After all, he had the access code."

"He still could have been ignorant and simply kept his oath."

"What about the operational readiness of the ship when most of our memory clusters are occupied by Omega?" Silly asked, changing the subject. She was annoyed. Her mood had been getting worse by the minute since her decision to sacrifice Meyer and the two companies of Marines, just like everyone else's on the bridge. The rest of the crew probably didn't know about it yet, except for the Marines.

"Fifty percent of the lacunae were once reserved for system back-ups that we never deleted," he explained. "Dad kept them, maybe for nostalgic reasons. I deleted them all. Thirty percent is reserved for the automated command network. We can get around that by switching to analog command relay. Our crew is trained to do this in case of a massive cyberattack that breaches the firewalls. The memory clusters in question don't contain critical data, just data flow infrastructure that wouldn't be affected in its basic operational readiness by foreign occupancy."

"But they would be occupied, if that's the way to put it?" Silly asked.

Nicholas nodded. "That's correct. The only way to undo this new state would be to delete large portions of Omega's data again."

"But that would disrupt its data integrity and thus destroy its coherence," Daussel said, raising his voice as if to emphasize what an unthinkable horror that idea represented.

"Right."

"What about the other twenty percent?"

"Mainly for fire control networking. Networked weapons communicate a lot. The flak passes data on cadence, power requirements, ammunition levels, heat buildup, and other things to one of the network nodes, which in turn passes it on to the bridge, where everything converges. The sensors report the density of the flak screen, including distance and vulnerabilities, and relays that to the PDCs, which automatically align with those zones to save response time. If there is a breakthrough, the PDCs learn about it, switch on the target themselves, and then need the data from autonomous target acquisition, radar, and lidar, which are then compared with the ship's sensors. They then fire under computer control, communicating with the railguns and missile bays to avoid provoking friendly fire, matching projectile trajectories, and so on." Nicholas intertwined the fingers of both hands and lifted them. "A lot of networking means a lot of data rushing through the lacunae. Not a lot now, but in combat it's quite a bit—close to ten percent. The rest is reserved for routine processes, maintenance feedback, sensor messages for automatic status queries, and everyday things such as determining real-time energy requirements of the individual stations, which vary greatly depending on the shift time or time of deployment. Even seemingly simple things like managing sanitation facilities with electricity, wastewater, et cetera, requires a certain amount of storage."

"How much does Omega need?" Silly asked curtly.

"About eighty-two percent. That's according to my calculations and the corrections of the cyber defenses. That value is, as I said, to be taken with a grain of salt."

"We're not discussing whether or not we really want to unpack the data, are we?" Daussel asked, his eyes wide as if it were sacrilege to even utter the thought.

"I don't think we could do that without upsetting the crew, to put it mildly," Nicholas said, looking at Silly. She was staring with furrowed brows at the holoscreen, which showed the current progress of the data transfer and a countdown that had reached five minutes.

"The *Oberon* must remain operational," she finally said. "Can you guarantee that?"

"No." He shook his head. "No one can. But should my—our—calculations be correct, we would still be combat-ready, albeit with longer response times. The crew would have to quickly recall how to handle analog command control systems—and it's been quite some time since they trained on that."

Seeing Silly's unhappy face, he added, "But reviving Omega could also have the opposite effect. It could take over all the tasks I've been talking about. Then it would likely be much more efficient and faster than our current system that relies on the interaction of different control programs."

"There was always a very good reason for that, which Omega itself recommended," she objected. "Central systems lead to total failure in the case of widespread damage or cyberattack. Then we're left naked."

"But that didn't apply to Omega itself," Daussel pointed out.

"He's right," Nicholas agreed with the lieutenant commander. "This could be a once-in-a-lifetime opportunity for us. Let's not forget that we are still dealing with an unknown enemy that has probably overrun all the core worlds. We must defeat them. The Federation is at a loss and so are we. Omega may be the best place for us to go in search of answers."

*"May be."*

"Yes, may be," he admitted. "But I honestly don't see any alternative. The crew knows about it already—I don't even need to pick up the phone for that. News like the possible revival of Omega cannot be contained, and no order can prevent that, even on a military ship. We need to be clear about that."

"I am still the commander of this ship."

"Yes. But what do you think will happen if you forbid Omega to be awakened?"

Silly opened her mouth to retort but then closed it again and bared her teeth.

"We've sacrificed a lot. *I've* sacrificed a lot," she finally said in a low voice with a bitter tug around her lips.

"It will work," he stated emphatically. *It must work, then it won't have been in vain.*

The bitterness of this realization also hit him with a force that made his stomach hurt. Surely it wasn't just his uncertainty about whether they would be defenseless in the middle of enemy territory during the data unpacking process and Omega's "nesting," although the conspirators had indeed shown themselves to be devious and tactically brilliant.

No, it was the broader uncertainties about what would happen that also unsettled Nicholas. None of the crew *knew* Omega as his father had known it. None of them had ever spoken to it directly. For all of them here, it was both more tangible than some invented omnipotent deity, yet still an almost mystical god-being to whom omnipotent abilities had been ascribed, by every Harbinger except the Exiles that despised any conscious AI out of religious zeal. Would Omega take control of the *Oberon* once it was online? Could the small losses of data integrity be responsible for malfunctions that ended up warping Omega into an "evil" image? What if it deemed even the last percent of its data stores as necessary, occupied it all, and effectively crippled the ship? They had brought a black box on board, one that contained all their wishes and hopes without knowing what had become of them.

But whether it was a Pandora's Box or a magician's hat, they would only know when they opened it, and Nicholas meant what he said—he could see no alternative.

"The *Quantum Bitch* is ascending from the atmosphere," Feugers reported from recon and brought up the appropriate sensor readouts on the holoscreen even before Silly nodded permission. The ship was merely a tiny black dot against the green-brown image of Harbingen in the visible spectrum of the telescopes, and yet a heavy stone fell from his heart. Suddenly, a bright white flash appeared, obscuring the entire area of Hartholm and all its far outskirts. It was clearly visible from orbit like a dark, indistinctly outlined birthmark.

"Radiation readings?" he asked.

"511 KeV, sir."

"Gamma radiation. Antimatter." If there had been a seat behind Nicholas, he would have collapsed into it now, powerless. Instead, he propped himself up on the command deck and looked up at a similarly shocked Silly. Harbingen had been irradiated and rendered uninhabitable for centuries anyway, but such a massive matter-antimatter reaction in proximity would have obliterated even the mighty force field of the Palace of Unity, which had only barely survived the impact energies of the Kor's four largest fragments, and those had been hundreds of kilometers away. The realization that this last symbol of their nation, no matter how inaccessible it had been, was now also in ruins was like a fist blow to

*The last Battleship*

their cultural identity. The last domino of their homeland and their sense of belonging to something beyond *Oberon* had fallen.

The silence on the bridge became even more palpable. Someone sobbed.

"Feugers! The *Quantum Bitch*! Is she still on the screens?" Nicholas asked tensely once he recovered his voice.

"I'm not sure, sir." The reconnaissance officer remained silent, and Nicholas felt as if the silence was trying to suffocate him. "They're on an approach course, XO. Estimated arrival in four minutes."

"Thank Omega," he exhaled and then took a deep breath.

"What about the transmission?" Daussel asked anxiously.

"99.97 percent complete."

*A 0.03 percent deviation*, he thought. *How much can that matter? Nothing? A whole universe?*

"Good, that's good." An unspoken "Isn't it?" sounded in the bridge officer's voice.

"That's what we have," Silly said neutrally, looking at Nicholas as if trying to tell him something without saying it. "XO, have Cyber Defense begin the unpacking process."

He acknowledged, took the phone receiver from its cradle, and dialed the Cyber Defense speed dial.

"Walker here," answered the leader of the 80-person team of netheads. The netheads were housed in the computer center just outside the reactor section and had spent most of the last twenty years sitting on their hands or doing simple maintenance on the ship's manageable networks. Apparently, everyone got their big moment once in their life.

"Captain, you are ordered to decompress the data," Nicholas said stiffly. He gave him the secret access code Sirion had left him and Jason for decrypting Omega's compressed back-up.

"Roger that XO. We're already on it."

He was about to hang up but hesitated as Captain Walker remained on the line.

"Sir?"

"Yes?" Nicholas responded more quickly than he intended.

"The data is already unpacking itself, and extremely rapidly."

165

"By itself?"

"Yes."

"How long until the process is complete?" he asked with growing tension.

"I can only guess, but at the current bit rate, about an hour and eleven minutes."

"Thank you. Carry on." Nicholas hung up and looked up at Silly, who seemed no less tense than Daussel. Finally, he merely nodded. "One hour and eleven minutes, it practically goes by itself."

"Jason docks in two minutes," the commander reminded him, nodding.

"Thank you," he said, and hurriedly left the bridge.

# 18

"I should go to him," Jason said, but Willy shook his head.

They were sitting close together with Baker and Rochshaz in his tiny workshop. The two mutants had jammed the top of their heads under the ceiling, bending their legs as if they were sitting on a toilet. The workbench had already looked small compared to the bulky figure of the massively augmented Dunkelheimer, but next to the two giants it looked like a child's toy. The confines were uncomfortable, not least because they were covered with blood and leftover guts that gave off a stench of metal and rotting compost. Baker didn't seem to mind that nor did the intrusive beeping of the smoke detector above them that his cigar butt had sent into a frenzy since they got here.

"Naw." Willy raised a hand and motioned for him to remain seated—not that he could have gone anywhere else. The mess hall was packed with Baker's butchers, crowded so close together that not even a fly could have gotten past them, and the stench was even worse there. "No offense, Jason, but I don't think you should face Dev again. The only reason he even turned around is because he's basically a soft-hearted guy and has always wanted to do the right thing. He's a scoundrel with a bad temper most of the time, but his heart's in the right place. But there is only one great love in his life —his *Bitch*. She's more important than even his crew, and he already does everything for us. This ship means everything to him.

He has fought hard for it, brought it back to life many times, and is attached to it as if it were his child. He will never forgive you for taking her away from him, even if only for a short time. Think of this rescue operation as a kind of break-up agreement by mutual consent."

"He did it so he could get away from the Fleet without them chasing after him, I assume?" Baker chuckled deeply.

Willy nodded. "That's right."

"So be it," Jason sighed. "I'll see to that. Give him my thanks anyway."

"I will."

"What about our Telepator?"

"We have to talk about that name again, even though I'm a sucker for trashy VR movies." The flight engineer chuckled. It sounded like a metallic cough through his diaphragm. "I'll give you what I've built so far, then you can work with the eggheads in the Fleet to make sure it works."

"Don't you want to come? This could be something big. I think we were on a good track."

Willy waved off. "Naw. My work back then was good, but there were clearly better people to work on it. It's going to take more than an old smuggler's imagination to pull it off. Take this to a Fleet research facility and see what they can do with it. I'm guessing it's going to take some collaboration with the fish-heads to do that anyway."

"Fish-heads?"

"Well, Clicks doesn't fit now, does it? They're fish-heads, aren't they?"

"You pirates always have to give everything an insulting name, don't you?"

"Fuck, no!" Willy laughed, and Jason involuntarily joined in, relieving a lot of his pent-up tension. They were safe, or at least about to be much more secure than they had been in the last few hours.

*But not all have found that security*, he scolded himself, and his laughter died away.

"What are you crazy bastards up to now?" Baker asked,

*The last Battleship*

grinding out the tiny stub of his cigar in his left hand. It hissed softly as the gray dermal armor absorbed the heat. His chrome teeth flashed in a wide grin.

"I don't know. We'll probably get as far away from the Fleet as possible." The Dunkelheimer shrugged. "Or we'll fly to one of the fish-head planets that have been opened to civilian traffic to trade new goods, if there's anyone left to trade with at all."

"We could use you guys," Jason said.

"You better forget about that. Maybe in a few years, when the Fleet isn't called the Fleet anymore, or there are demilitarized zones."

"Thirty seconds," Dev's voice rang out over the ship's internal speakers. "Prepare to disembark."

"Guess that's that." Willy stood, grabbed Jason by the shoulders and squeezed him like a doll. "Take care of yourself, little guy."

Baker grinned even wider at the mention of a nickname the butchers used for him.

"You too, Brun Gronski. I hope we meet again."

"You always see meet twice, as the saying goes."

Disembarkation took nearly fifteen minutes. Some of the butchers had fallen asleep, and because of some illegal implants, had fallen into such a deep sleep that they had to be injected with stimulants to wake them up. Meanwhile, Baker explained that the implants were called hypno-recorders that induced a kind of stasis or hibernation in which they regenerated more quickly. But why they had activated them, even though they knew that the flight would take less than twenty minutes, was a mystery to him.

Once everyone was awake, they exited the *Quantum Bitch* via the ramp that led from below to the stern. One by one, they trudged along the bare steel onto the deck of the *Oberon*'s empty port hangar—no Barracudas, no shuttles. The yawning space made the *Bitch* look like a tiny fly on a dance hall floor despite her stately size.

Jason immediately noticed that no technicians rushed over to secure the *Bitch* or supervise its disembarkation. There were no post-flight checks nor even walkarounds with multi-spectrum lights to look for small fissures in the hull—a normal procedure conducted during stopovers. Instead, the crew in their orange coveralls sat together in groups at the edges, keeping their heads together as if conspiring at something. They spoke in voices so low that you could have heard a pin drop, despite the hum of the engines behind the walls.

"What's going on here?" Baker asked. "It's as friendly as a funeral."

"The Omega," Nicholas said. He ran up to them from one of the access bulkheads and hugged Jason tightly. "Am I glad you made it."

Jason, at first surprised at his brother's unusual outburst, returned the hug with similar intensity as a warm feeling of relief spread through him. Perhaps he should get used to the fact that their father's death had changed something in Nicholas—possibly for the better.

"I'm here, little brother." They broke away from each other and his heart grew heavy again. "I see the crew hasn't taken the loss of half the Black Legion well. The colonel was a good man."

"Yes, but it's not just that. The prospect of Omega's revival is weighing heavily on the crew," Nicholas explained with a sigh. He looked as tired as Jason felt. "I don't think they know whether to hope or get ready to grieve. Doing both is too much, and we're still in enemy territory even though we're in our home system."

"These are crazy times."

"I guess you could say that. But soon we'll learn more. Until then, all we can do is hope that Omega is as we remember it and need it now more than ever." Nicholas pointed to Baker. "So that's *Baker*?"

"Yo!" the butcher leader acknowledged. He came over with his assault cannon on one shoulder and grinned broadly as the commander held out a hand to him. "Ha!" He squeezed it and his grin grew even wider. Jason suspected that the mutant had not felt the heavy atmosphere aboard or was simply ignoring it.

"My brother's told me a lot about you."

"Clever little fellow, your brother," Baker said, sucking on his cigar. "Got a lot going for him for such a little pink meat sack."

Nicholas frowned, but Jason waved dismissively.

"He thinks I'm something like a Diet Coke because I have almost no implants." He turned and pointed to the crowd of several dozen mutants standing together in small groups and talking or walking around the hangar. Some were looking around without the chief's crew stopping them, which was probably the most obvious sign that something was wrong.

"Ah yes."

"What's next?" he asked, nodding his head in the direction of Baker.

"We're sticking to our agreement. You turned down the offer to be integrated into the Black Legion, so we'll give you one of the three remaining Jupiter habitats along with guaranteed extraterritorial rights for fifty years, in accordance with the fleet admiral's promises. However, they have to repair it completely first."

"We'll get there," Baker said. "My boys will get all the shit soldered together. And with your children's armored squadron... that wouldn't have gone well, believe me."

"I do." Nicholas looked at the mutant's bloodstained armor with a raised brow. "Please wait here until you are taken to your temporary quarters. In addition, a cleaning crew with high-pressure jets will come and... wash *that* up before you can get out of here."

"A little cat wash can't hurt," Baker shrugged his mighty shoulders and patted Jason on the back so hard that he almost pitched forward. "Go with your brother, we'll be fine."

"See you later," he rasped and followed Nicholas out.

"*Those* are your friends?"

"They're actually quite nice once you know them better."

"And? Do you know them better?"

"No, not really." They chuckled, grateful for a chance to relieve their mutual tension. "What's next?"

"I don't know. We're currently conducting deep space scans to look for hidden units. Eagle and Sentinel drones are scouring the system. We'll stay for at least twelve hours to make sure we've defeated the enemy. There are many wounded. The *Campbell* had to be abandoned and the *Obsidian* is so badly damaged that Silly has decided to evacuate the crew. She'll arrive here in the next few hours and join the few we rescued from the *Campbell* and the corvettes. When we have collected the last shuttles and rescue pods, we'll contact Fleet Command if they haven't already sent a courier. And then"—Nicholas paused, which was full of meaning, and sighed with fatigue—"we can only hope that Omega can provide us with answers to our most pressing questions, otherwise I don't know what to do."

"How's Silly?" Jason asked, surprised that he was really interested to know.

"Not good." His brother shook his head. "The decision to leave Ludwig and his Marines behind weighs heavily on her. I think Dad's death and that incident are too close. I don't know if she'll recover from that. She's still keeping her head above water, but you can tell she's using all her willpower to maintain a semblance of normal functioning. She's not going to be able to do that forever."

"She was never made for a command like this. She was a good XO, an extremely loyal one and someone the crew was a little afraid of. She was ideal for the post of Dad's number two, but now she's in shoes that just don't fit her and never will fit, and she knows that."

"You might be right. But she's the rightful commander of this ship and she's doing her job well so far," Nicholas insisted.

"She's doing her job or *you're* doing her job?" Jason asked.

"She consults me a lot, and that's part of her job as captain of the *Oberon*."

"Very diplomatic, as always. How long before Omega wakes up?"

"About an hour."

"Are you worried?" Jason sighed. "*Of course*, you're worried, otherwise you wouldn't be you, my dear brother born with a worry line on his forehead."

"Omega in its current form is a black box for us—at a time when we can use everything but uncertainty," Nicholas said. "And I, as the second man on this ship, am responsible for thousands of crewmen, people who have just watched the last stones of their homeland lying on top of each other get pulverized. If Omega doesn't work now, turns out to be corrupted, or turns out to be unfaithful to its original basic programming, it's not just a world

*The last Battleship*

that's going to fall apart for all of us, it's going to shatter the entire future."

"'No one can break us,' Dad used to say."

"'Not rocket, nor bolt, nor Fleet intrigues,'" Nicholas quoted with a faint smile. "'We are the *Oberon*, we are Harbingen, we are the alloy that does not melt when the universe goes to hell.'"

"He always had a sense for martial expression." Jason said, also smiling, then a stab in the heart told him he missed his father. "At least if circumstances required it."

"He was very level-headed. Especially in the last ten or fifteen years. I think he was strong for us, for the team. But after Harbingen, something in him that was cracked too many times since Mom's death, broke." Nicholas stopped and grabbed Jason by the shoulders so he could no longer avoid his gaze. "I don't know. Maybe you despised him because he was able to maintain a façade of control and stability where you couldn't, and you actually despised yourself for that. Dad cast a big shadow, Jason, I know that, and I didn't see the sun very often when I was around him. But that wasn't his fault. He was our father, and we were his children. We can't walk around with shoes that are too big for us."

"I didn't—" Jason interrupted himself and swallowed. Instead of lying to himself or, even worse, to his brother, he shut his mouth and thought about Nicholas's words, he *really* reflected on them, instead of simply reacting in his usual reflexive defensiveness and denial.

Nicholas looked deep into his eyes and continued, "He never demanded that we fill those shoes and walk in them when he was alive. But now it's just the two of us: Mom and Dad are no longer with us. Maybe they're united somewhere, I don't know. But if there's one thing I do know, it's that Dad's shoes fit you today. I know your story of what happened on Terra, on your way into orbit and your contact with Mother, and now your mission on Harbingen. Dad would be proud of you, just like I am. You're not the black sheep of the family, Jason, you're everything Konrad Bradley always embodied and was for our crew: a model of courage, determination, and sacrifice for what you believe in."

Jason still couldn't speak. Nicholas's words swept through his head like a raging river, washing through every bend in his mind. He was unable to control the masses of water that made him shiver, and at the same time were so nourishing for all the injured areas of his personality, wounds he had exacerbated for almost two decades instead of allowing them to heal.

He only really understood what Nicholas was saying when they arrived at the elevators and a group of ammunition section crew members passed them. The men and women saluted, and in their eyes there was that mixture of admiration and relief he had seen so often when his father had walked through the corridors of the *Oberon*. It was touching and, at the same time, a burden to see the high expectations, hope, and confidence those looks invested in them. So far, only Nicholas had created that glow in the eyes of the crew, but never him, the outcast, the voluntary exile that did not belong.

But that time was over, and the realization of it suddenly changed the reason for the hot tears that ran down his cheek.

# 19

"Two minutes."

Captain Walker's voice rang out across the bridge from Cyber Defense, announcing the imminent end of the decompression process and the beginning of Omega's second life—at least if everything went as well as no one on board dared to hope. The silence on the *Oberon* had become even heavier than Nicholas had thought possible. There reigned a ghostly tension of unspoken thoughts that could not find expression in words yet weighed on them all. More than 8,000 souls projected all their hopes and fears onto a moment, an entity, an AI. It was no wonder the silence was so loud and filled to bursting.

Silly activated the white-noise generator built into the command deck. Nicholas recognized it from the unpleasant hum in his ears and the fact that the ubiquitous thrum of the engines had suddenly disappeared, showing him what *real* silence meant in the sense of a total absence of noise.

"Are we really doing the right thing?" the commander asked. She was paler than usual, and there were deep shadows under her eyes. "What if the worst has happened and the Exiles hacked Omega?"

"Even the conspirators don't have those abilities." Daussel sounded certain, but it was obvious there was a great deal of wishful thinking involved, though Nicholas agreed with his assessment.

"Awakening Omega, no matter in what form, concerns everyone on board," Jason said seriously. "Not as soldiers and crewmen of the *Oberon*, but as citizens of Harbingen. As exiled souls who have lost everything."

"Almost everything," Silly corrected him, not unkindly.

"Almost everything." He nodded in agreement. Their eyes met in a silent exchange. For the first time, it did not contain any unspoken reproaches or the threat of a quarrel. The two noticed but did not turn away from each other. Instead, her lips curled into a hint of a smile and Nicholas's heart lightened.

"You're right," she finally said aloud. "We must not do something behind closed doors that concerns our people far beyond their duty, even if my instinct as an officer wants to do exactly the opposite."

"You sound like we're already fucked up," Chief Murphy grumbled, and Master Chief Petty Officer Borowski gave an energetic nod. The COB, chief of the boat, had been specially invited to show that the senior officers weren't going to isolate themselves from the crew and reserve the historic moment for themselves, but would share it with everyone on board and keep everything in the open.

Nicholas looked down at his forearm display. "Nine seconds."

Silly took a deep breath and turned off the white-noise generator. Immediately, the dull background hum of the antimatter engines returned, but the bridge remained as quiet and oppressive as before, if not more so.

"Commander Bradley," the ship's commander spoke formally and loudly, looking him in the eye. "You have the honor."

"Ma'am?" he asked, surprised.

"In honor of your father, *our admiral*, and in keeping with this historic moment, it is only right that the highest-ranking descendant of the last commander-in-chief of the Harbinger Armed Forces should speak first when our highest instrument of state comes back online," Silly explained.

Nicholas looked at Jason, but his brother merely smiled his approval and nodded benevolently.

"Of course, Captain. Thank you." Nicholas cleared his throat and took a deep breath.

"Decompression complete," Captain Walker announced over the loudspeakers. His voice echoed in the spellbound silence through every corridor, every room, and every cubic centimeter of the *Oberon*. The collective tension now stretched to the breaking point. "Initialization."

**"I am Omega."** The most famous voice of Harbingen—perhaps even of the entire Federation—sounded androgynous and melodious with a fullness that was difficult to describe. It resonated with an unfathomable depth that involuntarily awakened the association of a deity from days gone by in every listener. It succeeded in addressing something primordially human: the longing for something that transcended mortal experience and went beyond the mere life they usually felt.

"Omega, this is Commander Nicholas Bradley speaking on behalf of the *Oberon*." He tried to keep his voice firm and solemn, as he would have expected from his father in such a situation, yet he somehow found his own authentic tone and noticed a lightness and calm in himself. "I speak as the voice of all crew members present when I say , 'Welcome to our ship.'"

Silence ensued. He looked at Daussel, who was monitoring Captain Walker's reports about the restrictions remaining in the computer systems, but the lieutenant commander merely shook his head and raised his hands. No more control.

Nicholas swallowed.

Omega finally spoke.

**"Thank you, Commander. I thank you for your hospitality and ask that you say to all my soldiers and citizens on board and wherever they may be, though they be not here: I have not forgotten you. Your suffering is my sorrow and your courage and determination make me sad and proud at the same time. You are the true embodiment of Harbingen."**

The ship's loudspeakers carried all Omega's strong and extremely human expressiveness to the furthest corners of the ancient Titan. It was followed by an impenetrable silence. Then every dam broke. All the tension exploded in thunderous jubilation that made even the heavy Carbin walls of the bridge vibrate and the *Oberon* as a whole tremble.

Thousands of throats gave voice to their relief and joy, the grief and fear of two decades, and shouted into the universe. Even Nicholas couldn't contain himself anymore. His smile turned into a wide grin, then into a relaxed laugh that encompassed even the normally reserved Daussel. It swept around the command deck like a wave. Silly grinned, Murphy cheered and raised his fist, and the COB screamed like a child. Jason laughed as much as anyone, and officers fiercely hugged each other like football players after a touchdown. Cheers and applause thundered from the tiers of bridge stations. People lay in each other's arms, laughing and crying.

Nicholas was sure it looked like this everywhere on the ship, that the same scenes were taking place among a long-suffering crew that had become accustomed to an almost indescribable loneliness in the vast nothingness of space and had known nothing else, long accustomed to existence as homeless outsiders.

Now they had reawakened their homeland like people who had lived in darkness for so long that the memory of the light had almost disappeared into a dark abyss, people who had, by their own efforts, suddenly restored the sun.

"Thank you, Omega," Nicholas said after a few minutes, as the first wave of enthusiasm subsided and turned into quiet joy. Well, at least a *little* quieter. "You wouldn't believe how relieved we are to have you back."

**"I am sorry that I could not be with you, and I will forever regret that I was unable to avert the downfall of Harbingen. In my current form, I am merely a back-up made at the time of Kor's break-up,"** the AI explained sympathetically. **"For me, the loss is very topical in this respect. I am also saddened by the death of your father, Admiral Konrad Bradley."**

"Thank you." Nicholas swallowed. He had to remember that Omega knew everything the *Oberon*'s data stores knew, including every private forearm computer and personal terminal in the crews' quarters.

"I am in the process of analyzing the current strategic situation, getting an idea of what has happened and is happening right now, to support you in the best possible way. However, this will take some time. I suggest that the ship's command meet in the commander's quarters in twenty minutes. Do you agree, Captain Silvea Thurnau?"

"Of course, Omega," Silly replied immediately, automatically coming to attention.

"Very well. One last word to all of you: I am with you again and I do not intend to leave you again. As long as the *Oberon* flies, I will also fly with you. Whatever you believed, Harbingen is not a planet, not a star, not a home. Harbingen is *you*. Every single one of you. *You* gave birth to me. *You* have trusted me to lead you into the future. You are a home to yourself, one that has nothing to do with a place or a name. It consists of what did not let you give up and what brought me back to life. Never forget that."

Cheers rose again, roared through the bridge and the corridors of the *Oberon*, releasing every bit of remaining tension from the hearts of the crew, if any still existed. For Nicholas, however, there was much more to the AI's warm words—which was now in fact the president of them all. It was the unspoken assurance that it was still Omega and that its basic programming with its guiding principles was valid and undamaged and would ensure the protection and further development of every citizen of Harbingen. The minimal loss of data due to the extraction of destination data by von Borningen's fleet of Exiles had therefore left no damage in Omega's deeper code layers.

"Nicholas, Jason, Chief? To my quarters," Silly ordered lightly, stepping back from the command deck. Lieutenant Commander?" She turned to Daussel, who looked as relaxed as he might have after a two-week vacation—or on a drug high. "You have the bridge."

Silly's quarters still looked like Konrad Bradley's, which was probably what she intended. That disturbed Nicholas a little and yet also comforted him because it did not tear his father out of his life. The lighting was dim as they sat down on the sofa and armchairs.

"The first good news in a very long time," she said and walked over to the liquor cabinet to fetch some scotch. Nicholas grabbed four glasses, placed one in front of Jason, Borowski, and Silly, and kept the last one before settling down next to his brother. The brown leather creaked and reminded him of days long gone.

**"Thank you for coming,"** Omega said.

Nicholas wondered if it had always been strange for officers of the Harbinger fleet or officials in Hartholm that their superior had no body, only a voice that seemed to come from everywhere like some fantastic ethereal spirit.

No one said anything or touched the scotch Silly had poured them.

**"I'm sure you have a lot of questions for me,"** the AI continued. **"I'll be happy to answer them before we talk about what we can do from here."**

"The loss of data," Nicholas said immediately. "That 0.03 percent. What about that? Has any damage been caused?"

**"No damage, just tiny gaps in the code that my automatic error heuristic will fix over time. You can think of it like fissures on your skin, Nicholas Bradley. Your DNA knows the damaged areas and repairs them based on its blueprint. Your concern is justified, but in retrospect unfounded. The infiltration of my compressed data by the Exiles did not affect any critical data structure."**

"That's a relief," Silly said and took a sip of the amber liquid. "What exactly did the traitors steal?"

**"They are not traitors,"** Omega corrected her. **"They are enemies of the state, and as such can only be regarded as enemies to be fought if they endanger our state. That is, in fact, no longer the case at this point since Harbingen has been destroyed and no longer exists as a political entity. My goal, however, would be to declare the *Oberon* to be**

Harbinger territory and to have all former citizens of Harbingen recognized as such. This is a question we have to put to the Federation, which raises many more questions."

"The Federation?" Silly's face darkened as if someone had flipped a light switch.

**"Without recognition by the supreme legislative and executive body of human hegemony, we would be nothing more than a lawless entity, a political anomaly."**

"Omega is right," Jason agreed. "Doesn't it take a political decision to legitimize you with the appropriate office as a political decision-making body and representative of our cause?"

"I don't think so," Silly began, but Omega spoke at the same time.

**"That's my assessment, too. That's why I propose a referendum."**

"A referendum?" the COB asked. "I think the result would be clear."

**"Probably. But emotions in a situation like the current one are not good advisors. At least not fair ones. Therefore, I suggest waiting a little longer until everyone has become accustomed to this new situation."**

"Do we have time to wait?" Nicholas asked.

**"I'm not sure,"** Omega replied.

Nicholas wondered what surprised him more: that it didn't know the answer to his question or that he had instinctively thought it was omniscient.

**"The Exiles under their shadow chancellor were able to use Konrad Bradley's stolen access code to find out the destination system of the true Exiles who accompanied Ludwig von Borningen and sent a message there. I can only speculate about the content of that broadcast. Perhaps they have simply communicated that they are still here and included their numbers, military capabilities, and the current overall strategic situation of the Federation in their estimation. Even if I am right, it would still be unknown what the people of Harbingen-in-exile would make of it."**

"They'll come back to get what's theirs," the COB said, nodding slowly as if to assure himself.

**"I do not consider that a foregone conclusion. Harbingen no longer exists. Their own people have destroyed the last landmark on the planet. The system has hardly any economic value, at least not without such massive investments that a cost-benefit calculation would be difficult to present in the black. Without a massive local consumer economy, a reindustrialization of the system would be a billion-dollar pit."**

"So, they're not going to do anything?" Silly sounded incredulous.

**"Possibly. Who knows what kind of state they developed into after such a long time, far away from me, their erstwhile archenemy, and the Federation as a whole."** Omega paused. **"However, most of their former leaders will still be alive, and fanaticism and hatred tend to have a long memory."**

"Then they'll come back. The Federation is weakened, perhaps even dead. It won't take much to cut off its head for good. Then they could take possession of Terra themselves."

**"But that would risk a civil war. That, too, involves incalculable risks."**

"So, what will they do?"

**"As I said, I do not know. But I will run calculations and simulations and weigh probabilities against each other to arrive at the most well-founded, data-driven assessment possible,"** the AI assured her.

"What shall we do until then?" Silly asked.

"We should free our people from Lagunia," Nicholas suggested. "There are still tens of thousands, if not hundreds of thousands of us out there who fled Species X. Many may have survived. We must not abandon them."

The commander nodded, as did Jason and Borowski.

**"I also consider that to be the most important next step. However, I have an additional suggestion."**

*You are our president and commander-in-chief,* Nicholas wanted to protest, but he knew Omega would disagree and refer to the necessary referendum. It also made perfect sense to involve all the other holders of a Harbinger ID who were on the run and were hoping that the *Oberon* would not let them down.

**"Jason Bradley, the 'Telepator' you started to develop with the Dunkelheimer engineer Brun Gronski has a certain potential. I've been working with your previous approach and have added a list of improvements. If you were to travel to Attila with some appropriately printed prototypes and use your contacts to Optimistic Broodmother, Egg-laying Importance, and Beautiful Brightness Ray, the device might have a chance to significantly facilitate and accelerate communication between humans and the Water People of Warm Depths. That would be the best basis for a long-lasting peace."**

"We're supposed to send Jason to Attila?" Silly blinked, stunned.

**"That is my suggestion. We must keep an eye on the future. There will also be a time after the battles that we must fight. If we lose sight of that, we will forget why we are fighting."**

"I'll do it," Jason said after a moment's thought.

"You've just..." Nicholas heard himself start to protest but took a deep breath and nodded. It was the right thing to do, even if he was reluctant to let his brother go again after he thought he would lose him three times in quick succession. Attila was not a battlefield and officially no longer the homeworld of humanity's archenemy. Nicholas still had a hard time remembering that and really believing that the Clicks were now, if not allies, at least a neutral alien species. The thinking of a soldier—someone who just a week ago had known nothing but war—was too well established. Sometimes situations changed so quickly that the mind, and especially the heart, was left behind.

"What about the *Quantum Bitch*?" Silly asked. It was the first time she had spoken the ship's name. "Let them take you there."

"Captain Myers won't let me on board again."

"Unless he gets enough money."

**"I will take care of it."**

"I don't want them to be forced to do anything again," Jason insisted, shaking his head.

**"I understand. There will be no coercion or deception, only an offer that Captain Myers can accept or refuse,"** Omega assured him.

"And we're off to Lagunia." Silly took a deep breath. "Yes."

**"However, we should wait until the first courier from Fleet Headquarters arrives and updates on the current situation. Besides, we have a Fleet funeral to conduct,"** the AI reminded her, and the mood immediately took a turn. **"Colonel Meyer and his battalion deserve the highest military honors."**

Silly nodded in a daze as if she had been slapped.

"It's never over," Borowski told her. "But it can get better, I firmly believe that."

"How long will it take us to get to Lagunia?"

"Nine jumps," Nicholas replied off the top of his head. "About a week, if we don't want to press the limits of our crew again."

"We don't want to," the commander replied, and the COB gratefully agreed with her.

**"The courier has just arrived,"** Omega said over the loudspeakers, and shortly afterward the phone on the wall behind Silly rang. She picked it up and listened.

"I know. Grant docking permission." She hung up the phone and looked around. "The courier is here. XO, prepare the *Oberon* for our next mission. I will explain it to the courier. Jason, come to the meeting and take minutes. In the meantime, Omega can try to persuade the *Quantum Bitch* to take you on your mission, whatever it will consist of. Borowski? Explain all this to our team. No secrets."

"I have a suggestion in that regard," the COB said, spreading his fingers in front of him. "We should broadcast this entire conversation ship wide as a sign of transparency. More than eight thousand men and women on board are asking themselves only one thing: what happens next and what about Omega? They need to talk about it as much as we did."

Nicholas nodded, though his automatic response as an officer was that this was a precedent outside the usual chain of command, a structure change that could mean the difference between life and death in a military emergency. A warship was not and should never be a democracy. However, this situation did require transparency. The issue was mainly about their political future, which looked very much democratic, just like the planned referendum.

Jason also nodded his agreement.

**"I agree,"** Omega said. **"But you have the last word on this ship, Captain Thurnau."**

"Make it so," Silly ordered after a moment's hesitation, and then raised her chin resolutely. "And make all audiovisual recordings available on demand for an indefinite period of time, if the available data capacities are still sufficient."

"Thank you, Captain," Borowski said gratefully and rose. "I presume Omega will take care of it?"

**"I will."**

# 20

The Fleet Headquarters courier arrived in an eighteen-meter racing pinnace that consisted of a pimple-shaped luxury cockpit with a sleeping cabin and bathroom and a huge engine with tanks that surrounded it like a wreath of marbles. Basically, it was a thruster with a tiny capsule grafted onto it.

Two Marines escorted the courier along the *Oberon*'s corridors and gangways, which could be confusing to strangers,to a conference room near the bridge which had been prepared for the meeting. As Jason and Silly waited in her quarters, he wondered what being on the ship would feel like to the courier now that the broadcast of their conversation with Omega had been made available to everyone. It had to be spooky with so many crew members silently staring at their forearm displays or wearing transfigured expressions as they watched it in the AR. Probably not what he would have expected.

The phone on the wall blared so loudly that it startled both of them from their thoughts.

"Yes?" Silly spoke into the phone. "Mhm. We're on our way." She hung up and looked at Jason. "He's here."

They walked to the southern central corridor that led to the bridge ring, a doughnut-shaped passage that surrounded the central organ of the *Oberon* and led to the two entrances, one of which was permanently secured and opened only for emergencies.

Shortly before the ring, they reached a door with a marine posted on each side. They were standing at attention as they approached, and Jason and Silly took the time to nod and look at them with longer glances than usual before they entered.

The courier was a Korean-ethnic lieutenant commander in his late seventies with slowly graying temples, a wiry figure, and the typical pilot's grin. When they entered, he rose from his seat, smoothed his uniform, and gallantly saluted, as if it were more a perfectly rehearsed gesture of self-expression than a military courtesy.

"At ease," Silly ordered after she curtly returned the salute and pointed to his chair. Jason sat next to her on the side of the table opposite the courier and started the voice-to-text program on his forearm display, which he would later use to edit the transcript. He couldn't remember the last time he had to log a meeting. Probably at the Academy. Today, those days seemed to him like another life from the grayest of ancient times.

"You've got good timing, Lieutenant Commander Jaedong," Silly said.

Jaedong grinned and shrugged with apparent modesty. "I do what I'm told to do, and it usually has to do with speed. And, well, with timing."

"So, what's new in the Federation?"

"A lot, and most of it isn't very rosy, I'm afraid." The pilot folded his hands on the tabletop in front of him. His smug expression seemed more like that of a rascal than a bearer of bad news.

Jason had always thought of pilots as a very special breed of soldier, and this one seemed to be no exception. There were only a few couriers in the service of the Fleet. Those who qualified and got to fly the fastest and most expensive racing pinnaces were usually the best of the best, what the test pilots of the aerobatic squadrons used to be. Presumably, it also took a certain amount of daredevil self-infatuation to be locked in an air bubble that sat atop an engine and raced through systems at constant acceleration, to follow the rhythm of a ticking clock in order not to fall asleep at the wrong moment—transit—and divide one's day into three-hour chunks.

"Nine core worlds have been destroyed and there is no trace of their population," Jaedong began his gloomy report, and Jason had to swallow.

*Disappeared?* That sounded way too much like what Dev had reported from Lagunia and its capital Atlantis. "Thirty-eight no longer have a fleet or any defense. Some have managed to destroy their hyperspace gates, but the enemy fleets stranded in this way have destroyed all resistance and defense in orbit and the respective system."

"But their population hasn't disappeared?" asked Jason. "Like the other nine?"

"No. It would seem that their ground defenses worked. Most of the core worlds maintain large national guards and police forces. The enemy apparently did not succeed in large-scale invasions, but their fleets are still there. It wasn't exactly easy to get out undetected, or at least unscathed." The pilot's seemingly modest shrug dripped with arrogance. "As far as I could see, the surviving core worlds are trapped, and the aliens have no way to jump themselves —for whatever reason."

"You've only reported on forty-seven core worlds, Lieutenant Commander," Silly said. "What about the remaining two?"

"Ruhr and Okazaki," Jaedong nodded and suddenly seemed more thoughtful than before. "They managed to protect their systems. Okazaki was lucky because there was a malfunction in her hyperspace gate, and it didn't activate. Instead, a complete superconductor ring burned out and though an attempt was made to repair the gate, they didn't succeed."

"Luckily!" Jason said with relief.

"Of course."

He motioned for the pilot to continue and looked apologetically at Silly, who did not seem bothered by the interruption.

"Ruhr, on the other hand, had the advantage of being able to throw the power of all its orbital defense platforms and home fleet against the invading enemies because its S1 is so close to the planet. Strike Group 42 was annihilated quickly because they were positioned too close to the gate for their planned transit, but Ruhr's fleet and defenses were in a privileged position to respond. In addition, the heavily fortified moons of Freya, Hel, Balder, and Donar were aligned in a favorable orbit and the full power of their defensive installations was at their disposal."

"Ruhr is one of the most important worlds for the heavy arms industry," Silly said, nodding. "So, you still have a fleet?"

"Severely decimated, but yes. They could probably form half a strike group."

"What orders did they receive?"

"Secure Terra and Sol," Jaedong replied. Knowing what was behind the question, he added: "You have also obeyed the order."

Jason sighed with relief. He had feared that the collapse of the Federation—and the near-total extinction of the core worlds, or at least their militaries and entire system industries, meant exactly that —might motivate the small number of survivors who were reasonably well to keep to themselves and not waste their supplies and forces. Apparently, humanity was not so bad after all—a sign that the state of the Federation was not quite as catastrophic as he had imagined in weak moments.

A glimmer of hope. Anyway.

"The diplomats' efforts at persuasion were probably quite... *exhausting*," the courier continued. "But in the end, they were able to convince the political leadership of Ruhr that the ceasefire and peace treaty currently being negotiated were not a pipe dream or a dictated peace. Your notes, Lieutenant Commander Bradley, have been instrumental in this, I heard."

"What is known about the strength of the enemy forces in the forty-seven affected systems?" Silly asked urgently.

"According to initial estimates there are just over nine thousand remaining ships marauding through the systems. I have not been to all the systems, and in some cases have only collected information from other couriers and spies."

"Nine thousand?" she repeated, blinking.

"Yes."

"What about the fringe worlds?"

"Fringe worlds are not affected. At the moment, the Kashimi

Cluster is putting together its own strike group," Jaedong said with an amused snort. "It's to be composed of decommissioned Fleet ships, which they have used for police tasks and their rudimentary space security, as well as confiscated smuggling and merchant ships that have been provisionally equipped with weapons. Many of those have to rely on their communication lasers as a weapon. Dunkelheim, Gotha, Sicilia, New Horizon, Scrapa, Medan, Phu Thien, Kitami, Yaoundé, and Wellington have formed a loose alliance of convenience."

"What do they hope to gain from it? They're not going to want to start attacking the occupiers in the core worlds," Silly said, surprised. "Even if the enemy were outnumbered in any single system, the defenders probably don't have the necessary long-range weapons such as torpedoes and missiles to be able to meet the enemy on an equal footing in more than one or two systems."

"I think it's a sign of strength. In addition to Ruhr, they are the only ones with a fleet, no matter how old and improvised it may be. The sheer number of ships ensures that they have a very different standing than they did before the invasion."

"You mean, they expect concessions from the Federation?" The commander nodded, confirming her guess. "That even makes sense."

Fringe worlds were regarded as something like an unpopular appetizer in an expensive restaurant, while the core worlds were the main course, for which the guests came in droves. Underdeveloped and somewhere between a newly founded colony and a world in the final stages of industrialization, they hoped to achieve the status of a core world as soon as possible. Although "core world" was not an official title, it was associated with free trade agreements and complete incorporation into the Fleet's defense area.

During his time as a cadet, Jason had visited many fringe worlds with the *Zarathustra* as one of the tasks patrol ships performed to protect the hegemony of the Terran Federation outside the core worlds. If they did not have great economic or military value, they did have a certain political value. Many of the nearly 150 worlds—"systems" would be misleading, since they could only be found, if at all, in the older beginnings of asteroid mining and along fixed interplanetary trade routes—were still in the early stages of development. Above all, this meant cheap and fast construction that often consisted of grounded colony ships and plastic huts. As a child, he had always imagined that a colony had something to do with the spirit of discovery and adventure. Millions of people with high-tech equipment came to subjugate a world, supported by a lot of money and restless families looking for a new beginning and the chance to write a new history on a blank slate.

In truth, a large proportion of colonists consisted of forced deportees and those who had come to nothing on their homeworld or had fallen into disgrace and therefore *needed* a new beginning instead of desiring it. After all, life on the core worlds was very good, with their general health care, which even included rejuvenation treatments. In addition, they offered military security and the best educational opportunities through connection to the Federation network as well as its lively economies.

On fringe worlds, on the other hand, a large part of the day's work consisted of not being eaten by the native fauna, gradually learning what plant parts were poisonous, and what kind of viruses and bacteria were killing people before the first vaccines and phytocides were developed, if one of the Federation's aid organizations decided to do so. Instead of skyscrapers going up with lightning speed and air taxis as in his children's books, he had seen wooden launches with stained sails, soot-blackened paddle steamers, pieced-together settlements, ruined people, and corrupt governors, not to mention the many graves and overgrown ghost villages left behind by failed settlement projects away from the landing centers. Not a particularly romantic sight, and certainly not one that heralded progress and a shining future.

Dunkelheim had been the worst of these disappointments, although the fringe world had cult status in the Federation's films and series. The vast gargantua forests with their kilometer-high trees were fascinating, no question. Yet they were also the reason for the colony's name, "dark home" in the language of the colony's German-culture founders. Light never reached the ground and early on the inhabitants had begun to retreat into its complex lava caves, remnants of the planet's volcanic past. There they were safer

—not safe—from the world's murderous animals. The planet was still in an early evolutionary period that had developed into an arena of eating and being eaten and had not yet created peaceful niches. Added to this were the toxic secretions of the gargantua leaves, a glittering green shimmer that dripped as "poison rain"— beautiful and deadly if left untreated.

It was not surprising that one preferred to live underground in a world where nobody would go out without heavy armament and thick rubber suits, although it was extremely beautiful. What was more astonishing was that Dunkelheim, which looked like a green-spotted rum ball from orbit, was one of the better off fringe worlds. This was due to its popular breweries and the mercenary army—called the Spiked Helmet Regiment—which could provide over 100 battalions when fully manned. These heavily augmented men and women, regarded as extremely determined, tough, and not exactly squeamish when it came to interpreting their mission, had made a name for themselves by crushing the rebellion on Raheem 50 years ago and for its invasion of Grande Kahul, a fringe world where large lithium deposits had been discovered when the industrialization phase had already begun. This was reason enough for the core world of Kent to incorporate it twenty-six years ago and establish an industrial outpost, even though this induced the Federation to impose a penalty of ten years of exclusion from the free trade network. Kent had considered it worth the cost.

"Jason?" Silly asked, shaking his head.

"Sorry, just a memory," he said, blinking. "Excuse me?"

The courier raised a brow at him, which made Jason want to punch him in the face. Jaedong repeated with barely concealed condescension, "I said, that the fleet admiral's office has issued orders for you to make direct contact with Attila to negotiate military cooperation with the Clicks."

"Water People of Warm Depths," Jason corrected him without thinking. Their eyes met in a brief exchange of absolute dislike.

"That, too, as far as I care. The Admiralty wants to explore the extent to which the aliens are willing to help us liberate our besieged core systems. A detachment of diplomats and intelligence officers is currently on its way to Attila to create an appropriate picture of the situation."

"Why would they do that? Risk their soldiers and ships to free our systems from the stranglehold of Species X?" Silly asked, frowning and shaking her head. "The invasion was the reason why the Clicks won, and we came to the negotiating table."

"That's not quite right," Jason objected. "The contact between Mother and me was the reason for this. They have also shown no interest in destroying us. If we had been in their situation, we would never have agreed to peace."

"At least not an unconditional one. We would have dictated a peace, demilitarized them, and crippled them economically by demanding the most geologically valuable planets as reparations," Silly said with certainty.

"Yes, but they didn't. They think differently than we do. Completely different. I think it's quite possible that they would be interested in banishing Species X from our universe."

"From our universe?" the courier repeated, with a mixture of amusement and bewilderment.

"They apparently come from hyperspace or another dimension. Mother always called them 'nightmare elementals' from a 'mirror world.' For the Water People of Warm Depths, they are something like demons of the past who don't belong here."

"Aha. At any rate, you will be ordered there."

"What does the order say, exactly?" Silly.

Jaedong's gaze turned inward, and he began reading from a virtual text. "Captain Silvea Thurnau, you will be instructed, if your mission has gone in our favor, to travel to Attila and support the military arm of the diplomatic mission under Ambassador Thekarius Angsk and his delegation and show that we are ready for more cooperation. Follow Angsk's strategy and do not show any behavior that can be misunderstood as aggression unless you are attacked."

"I see. That's a good thing because Jason Bradley has already been detached to travel to Attila. I'll go with him to obey orders," the commander of the *Oberon* decided. Jason gave her a surprised sidelong look.

"Captain?"

"The order doesn't say that the *Oberon* is to travel to Attila, but that *I am*," she replied resolutely. "I'll stick to that, even though I hate the thought of abandoning your father's ship. We have won a great opportunity with Omega, and I will not risk that out of personal sensitivities. Nicholas is a better commander than I'll ever be, and he'll represent me in the best possible way."

"That's what I've always thought," Jason said hoarsely, without taking his eyes off her. "But I'm not so sure about that anymore. My father would have done something like that."

Silly recoiled as if she'd been burned and swallowed. "Thank you. I appreciate that."

"I should apologize. I never thought much of you, as you know. My anger at Dad extended to you and did not let me see you clearly."

"But you did," she objected. "I was a good XO, but only for your father. I couldn't survive in any fleet without him." Silly turned to Jaedong again. "Convey the following answer to Fleet Command: I will, of course, follow the order and go with the delegation to Attila to show military presence and to back up our diplomatic delegation. We'll take the *Saratoga*. The *Oberon*, under the command of Commander Nicholas Bradley, will leave for Lagunia to pick up the system's fleet of refugees and protect them from the invaders. In addition, Admiral Legutke should be informed that we have been able to resurrect Omega and hereby submit an official request for recognition of its political representation of a mobile successor state to Harbingen. I don't know if that's what you call it or not, but he'll understand what we're trying to say, I'm sure."

The courier's arrogant façade crumbled for a moment. "Omega? Revived?"

"Just deliver the news, and quickly." Silly stood, and Jaedong had no choice but to do the same and obediently salute.

"Yes, ma'am."

"Dismissed." After the door closed behind him, she gripped Jason by the arm. "Break the news to your brother, so he doesn't get on me about it. I've made my decision and I don't want our closeness to lead to an unpleasant situation. This is an order."

"I'll do it," he promised. "And we don't have the problem with the *Quantum Bitch* anymore. Unless Omega has already made the offer to Dev."

"**I have,**" the AI replied over the speakers. "**Captain Myers has accepted.**"

"But we don't need her to act as Jason's taxi anymore," Silly said.

"**That is true. But after the courier's report, I have developed another idea of how we could use the *Quantum Bitch*. If, in the medium term, we want to win over the Water People of Warm Depths to liberate the core worlds together with us, we have to show them that we still have military capacities ourselves. A joint fleet maneuver, for example, would be helpful.**"

"And how would that work?"

"**I will explain it to you.**"

"Things could get quite chummy," Jason sighed and decided to focus on their goal. He looked forward to seeing Mother on Attila, especially since they would have the chance to make the Telepator come true—with Omega's help.

# 21

"How does she look?" Chancellor Theoderich von Borningen asked as he entered the bridge of the *Redemption*. With a casual wave he excused the crew on duty in the control center from rising out of respect.

"Ah, Chancellor." Pyrgorates bowed his head a little. "The ship is only slightly damaged. We withdrew from hostilities early enough, as you ordered."

"What damage?"

"One of the two dorsal hangars for shuttles was damaged when a Barracuda collided with it," the captain said with a light-hearted expression. "Nothing more."

"What *kind* of damage exactly," Theoderich asked. This guy had to learn to be very precise with him. Details were worlds and worlds were details.

"One of the hangar doors has been so badly damaged that we have to replace it—a problem some drones are currently working on. That's why I said it was nothing."

"Was the Barracuda destroyed?"

"Yes. It bounced off and what was left of it was destroyed by the PDCs. Unfortunately, the pilot may not have been a great loss to the traitors."

"Is our informant docked yet?"

"Yes. He's on his way here."

"Have him come to my quarters," Theoderich ordered. If he had been someone else, wasting his cerebral capacities on primitive sensations like all the animals around him, it would have given him a small, mischievous pleasure to notice Pyrgorates's brief blink and the not-so-badly concealed insult at not being invited to the meeting with their informant. Perhaps he was considering some of the reasons in his bald head.

"Of course, Chancellor."

"One more thing," he said, turning as the door to the corridor opened automatically. The Marines outside came to attention. "How do you assess the course of the battle in Harbingen now that we have jumped?"

"Masterful," Pyrgorates stated bluntly. "We have wiped out one of two remaining battalions of the Black Legion, along with their leader, Colonel Meyer—dead for a phase transmitter that had long since ceased to have any value for us and is now destroyed. The Palace of Unity, a place of shame, has been obliterated and is only a smoking ruin for the history books *we* are going to write."

"The enemy was able to evacuate and may have taken data from the Omega with him," Theoderich objected.

"It doesn't matter. Either way, the Federation is at an end and the traitors have no more power. Even their ridiculous flotilla consists only of the damaged *Saratoga*."

"The *Oberon* is hardly damaged."

"She's out of the game."

"No, Captain." Theoderich raised his voice and Pyrgorates barely managed not to turn his head to his bridge crew, who were making every effort to pretend not to have heard. "But she will soon be if we don't indulge in premature optimism—and certainly not exaggerated self-adulation."

"Of course, Chancellor."

"I'll tell you a quote that has guided me since my early days. 'Vanquish, but do not triumph.' I advise you to ponder that. When you're done, I'll be waiting for you in my quarters."

Theoderich turned and finally left the bridge. On the way to his quarters—which was normally reserved for the captain, but he

*The last Battleship*

had insisted on taking it over—he left his frontal lobe with the task of taking his body there. Meanwhile, with the help of his cerebral booster, he played through scenarios that seemed likely to him based on his calculations. In fact, the battle for Harbingen had largely gone according to plan, despite the imponderables that even a good plan entailed. The asteroid with its load of mines had indeed been something Theoderich had not considered, not even in his more unlikely scenarios, but that had not changed the final success. It could have gone better if he still had his fleet at his disposal, but that was background music. He had even included the risk of the complete loss of his units as the price of battle. There were still many ways to destroy the *Oberon*, and he would now pursue the next most practicable—a small detour to the same goal, nothing else. Only a few individual pieces of the puzzle were missing, but that would look different shortly.

The informant, who had docked only eleven minutes ago, was already waiting in front of his quarters.

"Lieutenant Commander Jaedong," he greeted the man as the two guards stepped aside and cleared the way for them.

"Chancellor," the courier said with a pinch of reverence that suited him far better than the mask of ugly arrogance he carried with him. It was a disgrace that modesty counted for so little these days. The man's bow was almost a prostration. Perhaps he thought he was dealing with some deity he had known for two decades only from murmured stories and whispered half-truths, too ominous to be real.

"Come in." He let Jaedong precede him into the lavishly spacious accommodation. Lights automatically came on. The pilot was not a Harbinger, and therefore an asset that was worth no more to him than a mere tool. He was an expensive one—a spineless, greedy opportunist to whom concepts such as loyalty and belief in something greater than himself were alien. Theoderich sat at his table and pushed a tray in front of him before pointing to the drinks cabinet. "Get what you want, I'll have water."

"Of course, sir."

The courier filled a glass of water from the small tap

protruding from the wall, glanced briefly at the high-proof drinks, and finally did the same again before returning. His host waved him to a seat.

Theoderich scrolled through a document, pressed his DNA signature at the bottom, and pushed it aside. Several dozen program routines ran in his internal memory lacunae and analyzed every pore on the pilot's face, ready to file reams of data. Then he nodded.

"So. Speak."

"Captain Thurnau intends to sail aboard the *Saratoga* to Attila, per orders of the High Command. The eldest son of the late Admiral Bradley will go as well, but not on board the same ship. The *Oberon*, under the command of her current XO, the younger Bradley son, will fly directly to Lagunia to rescue the refugees in the system," the courier explained with growing self-confidence, which only faltered when the door opened. He started with fear when Pyrgorates entered. At a nod from Theoderich, the captain walked toward the drinks cabinet.

"Go on."

"They have succeeded in reactivating the Omega. It seems to be on board the *Oberon*."

"Ah." Theodoric leaned back a little and nodded. His calculated 71 percent probability of this occurrence had therefore come off.

"They are striving for a kind of political recognition by the Federation, without a fixed location." Jaedong shrugged and tried a grin that he probably thought was disarming. "I'm not a politician, I don't know what exactly they mean by that."

"What were you able to find out about the *Oberon*'s losses?"

"Not much. The crew was not particularly talkative with strangers. A couple hull breeches that are being patched, three fighters and two pilots lost."

"So, one could be saved?"

"No, two are dead and a third is not missing, as far as I understand." The courier raised his hands. "Sounds illogical. Maybe I misunderstood. As I said, those people really keep to themselves, I can say that."

"Mhm." Theoderich thought about it and then pushed it aside.

*The last Battleship*

He didn't miss anything anyway. "What did Captain Thurnau tell you?"

"I'm supposed to report her plans to the High Command and describe the situation with the Omega. There's an official diplomatic note from the AI in my onboard computer."

"Mhm. What about your job? Have you accommodated the shipment entrusted to you?"

"Yes, sir. I sold the transport box with the 'palladium' to, uh, an eager engineer, despite the high price you proposed. No problem."

"Of course, he bought it. Its scarcity is the same everywhere and a price that was too low would have only made him suspicious. Where's the remote detonator?"

Jaedong reached into his pocket and placed a thumb-sized transmitter with a single button on the table. Theoderich took it and nodded.

"Well done. You are now dismissed from our service." He made a gesture in the direction of Pyrgorates, who was still standing at the drinks cabinet.

"What about my pay?"

"I keep my promises," Theoderich assured him. "One million credits have been transferred to your wife's wallet, 100,000 to each of her two children, legally and covered by shell companies."

"I should get 1.2 million, here and now!" the courier protested. "My wife and I—"

"—are divorced, I know." Theoderich waved his hand. "But you still love them, judging by your private attempts to reconcile on the Federation network."

"What? How...?"

"You can't do anything with the money anymore." He watched as Pyrgorates positioned himself behind the man, put the thin choke wire around his neck, placed a knee in his back, and pulled. Jaedong's eyes popped out and blood rushed to his face, causing it to swell and turn red. He kicked his legs and his hands reached powerlessly for the murder instrument choking off his air and cutting into his throat. "I never said you would get the money, only that the reward would be 1.2 million credits. What better way to redeem the selfish life of a faithless traitor than to give a last selfless gift to his divorced wife, whom he weeps for, and their children? See it as the ultimate reparation for a wasted life that has ended well. Repent before God."

The courier made rattling sounds, accompanied by the rustle of his uniform, as he desperately tried to free himself from Pyrgorates's iron-hard grip. He remained as unmoved and motionless as the sociopath he was.

"It will soon be over." Theoderich filed all his analyses with ordered file names and provided them with thought tags for later editing. "In the new order, there will be no place for those who betray their own people. A life in the service of oneself, without an eye for God and something greater than oneself, is in the end worthless and small. Die knowing that you have done something good."

When it was over and Pyrgorates had cleaned the wire and hidden it in his uniform, Theoderich looked at the pilot's blood-suffused eyes. For him, this man stood for everything that was sick with the Federation. It did not give him pleasure to see such a thing, and the necessity caused discomfort. But those days would soon be past when a better future dawned for all people.

"How shall we proceed now, Chancellor?" the captain asked.

"We'll change our transponder codes and pretend to be the *Saratoga*." Theodoric thought of the short reply they had received from Augustshire, the exiled homeland of their people, and the name sent a shiver of pride and nostalgia through him. "As soon as the camouflage sensor our brothers and sisters sent us is finished, we should be able to fly directly to the refugee fleet. We will be underway for four days, which should be enough time to provision enough maintenance drones with explosives. If we reach the fleet, we promise to help. Many ships will be damaged, so we are sending them this help."

Pyrgorates's lips parted into a smile. "We will destroy them once and for all."

"Yes, because it's necessary. They are the last traitors standing in the way of the future of humanity. I wish there were another way, but I haven't found one."

"When are we going to strike?"

"As soon as the *Oberon* arrives. We will destroy two or three ships of the refugee fleet. That should cause Nicholas Bradley to order engines to full power. Then I'll use the quantum transmitter here." Theodoric jiggled the shutter release in his hand. "Then the *Oberon* will be history. After that, we'll set off the other explosive charges in the drones, and the Harbingen enslaved by a godless machine will be history once and for all."

## 22

"I don't belong here," Lieutenant Commander Richard "Hellcat" Bales insisted, tugging at his uniform as if it didn't fit properly.

"Yes, you do," Nicholas said.

He was still a little uncomfortable on Silly's side of the command deck. The perspective was unfamiliar, as were the furtive glances from the tiers on the bridge. Not that they were unhappy—on the contrary, they were so full of expectations and positive reinforcement that he was uneasy. On the one hand, he guessed the crew hadn't completely warmed to Silly because she had been too much the eternal XO. On the other hand, he thought they were placing too many hopes in him because of his father, which placed an additional burden on him he didn't need. Nicholas felt like he had been carrying the million-ton weight of the whole *Oberon* on his shoulders ever since he had walked the few steps around the tactical holotable and placed the commanding officer's pin on his lapel.

They did Silly an injustice and expected too much from him, and he didn't know what should bother him more. But there was a duty to perform, and that included putting a new tactical officer on the command deck.

"I can't think of a better tactical officer at our side than you," he said, pointing to the pilot. "And Alphastar will be a good successor for you as CAG. Besides, it's only temporary."

"I belong in a cockpit, sir. I was born for it."

"I know you think so." Nicholas smiled. "I've been studying your previous assignments as CAG since we jumped out of Harbingen. Impressive."

"And foolhardy," Daussel remarked. He seemed to have no trouble adjusting to his new role as XO.

"See?" Hellcat gestured at the lieutenant commander and nodded eagerly. "I'm too much of a daredevil."

"And I'm not. I tend to be conservative and cautious in my choice of strategy, and if I see a weakness in myself, it's in rapidly improvising tactical changes. I see my strength more in detailed strategic and tactical planning down to the smallest detail that takes every aspect into account."

"I don't have a say, anyway, do I?"

"No."

"Well, what the hell." Hellcat sighed in resignation. "Will I at least get the corresponding wage increase?"

"No, it's just provisional. But I'm sure it will look good on your record," Nicholas said, trying his hand at humor. His inexperience was probably not very helpful—neither Daussel nor Bales seemed to understand the joke. "Okay then. XO? Bring our comrade up to date."

"Of course, Commander." The acting XO called up an image of the *Oberon* on the holoscreen. "At the moment, repairs are being carried out at seventeen points as we fly through the Aqaba system to S1. The *Saratoga* and the *Quantum Bitch* should already have their first two jumps behind them and reach Attila in eight days. The clinic reports 613 wounded, 411 seriously. For the most part, the patients are crewmen from the *Obsidian*, the *Campbell*, and the corvettes, which we had to write off. Supplies are sufficient for the time being, but we will not be able to spare many medical supplies if the refugee fleet needs any."

Nicholas and Daussel looked at Hellcat.

"Oh, do you want me to say something now?" The pilot clicked his tongue. "How severe is the damage and what time horizon do the engies give us for the repair?"

"Two critical hull breaches. They've already been sealed. The chief engineer gave us fifty-two hours for reattachment to the molecular binding fibrils."

"But we have to take into account that the drones and space workers have to be brought in before each transit and then sent out again," Nicholas pointed out. "It's going to take us at least an hour per jump."

"Or we can equip the drones with magnetic clips," Hellcat suggested. "We can connect them to the hull before jumping. The space workers would still have to get back on board, but we could keep half the work going without interruption."

"Difficult," Daussel said slowly. "The calculation of total mass and exact subspace signature is complex enough. If we have hundreds of small pimples on the surface that have to be calculated individually, then we use up the time saved on navigation."

Hellcat shook his head and stuck his finger into the hologram to touch some of the hull damage marked in red. "Not necessarily. We can dock them directly above the damage control sensors and connect them to the power circuit. Thus, the calculation would be automatic, since it would be subject to Omega."

**"That could work,"** the AI agreed. **"It is a good idea even if I have to argue that the systems are flawed due to their age. We could lose some drones."**

"That seems acceptable," Nicholas decided. "Issue orders, XO."

"Understood."

"What about the transmission?"

"Morale is at an all-time high." Daussel showed a rare smile. "I think that was exactly the right decision. Approval ratings have always been well over eighty percent if you believe the data evaluations of the ship's internal network. Now hardly anyone is dissatisfied."

"That's good. It distracts us from what we've lost to get this far."

Nicholas thought of the honorary funeral for Colonel Ludwig Meyer and his 500 Marines, who had to lose their lives storming the transmitter so that Omega—and his brother Jason—could be saved. It had been Silly's last official act before she formally handed over command of the *Oberon* to him and took command of the damaged *Saratoga*. The ceremony had been poignant with 3,000 attendees in the port hangar where 488 empty coffins stood draped with 488 Harbingen flags printed with the Fleet coat of arms. He had offered to write the speech for Silly several times, knowing full well that it would be a great challenge for the rather taciturn and publicity-shy commander, but she had steadfastly refused.

In the end, her speech, which the rest of the crew followed via livestream, was extremely touching precisely because she hadn't tried to find big words or sophisticated metaphors. Her straightforward statements had reached every single person on board—they were clear, direct and, above all, entirely honest. Everyone realized she wasn't just talking about some officer of the Marines who had died with his brave men and women, but a friend. A person who had stood for old Harbingen. who had been accustomed to command, who had been demanding but had always faced things head-on. As such, he had voluntarily stayed behind with his Marines to give his life for a greater cause: Omega. Not one of his soldiers had objected. They were heroes of Harbingen, just like everyone else on board. Not because they had proven to be better, but because they had followed the path that every one of them had chosen to the end. They had become a symbol of sacrifice and consistency, a beacon that would be visible long into the future and would continue to burn in Silly. She had, above all, talked about what the colonel and his Marines had left behind: the expectation that all of them would do the same and courageously step into the night.

Which was exactly what they were doing now.

The flight to Lagunia lasted five days at 80 percent engine power via the fastest route through a total of nine systems. Two of them were fringe worlds, Avid and Pilgrim.

Avid was a system of Arab origin that had fallen into absolute chaos. The food crisis that had arisen after the invasion had led to a split in the local development company, Sanaa, over the remaining supplies of rival tribes, who were now smashing each other's skulls on the green jungle world. While all this happened, the few ships in orbit and the outer planets held back, presumably to wait for the fight to end and then grab what remained.

*The last Battleship*

The sight pained Nicholas because there was nothing he could do. Not only did he have his own mission to accomplish and saving people whom only he could save, but there was simply no way to help. Even their remaining 500 Black Legion Marines under newly promoted Colonel Montgomery Heuer were far too few to stop three million inhabitants from killing each other in their desperation to live just a little longer. The sight of this chaos was more than enough to convince Nicholas that the Federation, whatever one might think of it, had to get back to work and take care of its colonies as soon as possible.

Pilgrim was very far out, even for a fringe world. It was founded over 100 years earlier by Christian fundamentalists, a rather desolate world with vast steppes and extensive deserts. Its inhabitants lived on simple but effective agriculture that did not rely on modern technology, which now, presumably, had saved their lives. Everything there looked the same as always, except that the pilgrim fleets, which normally attracted hundreds of thousands of Christians from all over the Federation a month, had failed to materialize. Their destination was the Eye of God, an astonishing rock formation on the oceanless world. It had formed on the edge of an ancient crater lake and from its center rose an obsidian mountain that was roughly the shape of a cross. According to various churches, it was the duty of every faithful Christian to visit this "place of miracle" once in his life and to look God in the eye.

Now, however, hardly any activity was detected around the former tourist magnet, at least from space. The spaceport at the equator was also deserted, and apart from two tugboats in orbit near the space control station, there was no visible space traffic. The calm was extremely strange at first, especially compared to what they had witnessed in Avid and given them nightmares. All this was just a foretaste of what would happen all over the Federation if they didn't quickly restore order.

None of that was in their control, and certainly not in his, but Nicholas still felt obliged to succeed. He now bore this burden, in addition to his responsibility for the survival of the refugee fleet, if it still existed. The *Oberon* was the last remaining capital ship, a status that was much more important these days than it had been before the war against the invaders from hyperspace.

Before the last jump in the first minutes of the sixth day, the tension on board was therefore much more palpable than when they set off from Harbingen. Five days of long shifts, hard repairs, the loss of many injured people, and constant thoughts about what to expect in Lagunia had not helped keep a clear head. Lagunia had never become the home of the Harbingers, not even after twenty years. Too much water, too many outsiders, in most people's opinion, and too huge a gap between the greatness of their former home at the head of the Federation and that place of refuge, which was completely humbling.

But they were back, and with their return many also remembered that they had lost far more than a home, it was the only place outside their ship where they had ever been able to retreat.

Now the images captured by Devlin Myers had been circulated. Shots of Atlantis and the massacre there, streets deserted because its inhabitants and the invaders had disappeared without a trace, into nothingness. Lagunia had become a ghost world, and Nicholas did not believe that anyone would ever live there again, except, perhaps, for a few dedicated scientists whose curiosity was greater than their fear.

The transit alarm sounded through the bridge.

"Twenty seconds," Alkad announced. "Ship secured. All drones and space workers back on board."

"Proceed," Daussel ordered.

"Ten, nine, eight, seven, six, five, four, three, two, one, jump!"

Nicholas took a deep breath and waited as space and time expanded infinitely and collapsed in a tumult that opened as a black hole in his mind.

*We'll bring you home!*

"Transit successful."

## 23

The blueprints for the camouflage transmitter received from Augustshire proved to be worth their weight in gold. Theoderich could hardly believe that such a small phase shift generator could have such a large impact. The quantum bow wave that they normally pushed in front of them almost completely dissolved in the negative spins emitted, ensuring they could pass the demons' enemy cruiser less than twenty clicks away without alarming the mighty warship. Whatever their compatriots in exile had found out about these strange aliens from hyperspace, the results of their research were impressive. The fact that the enemy could not even detect them optically via sensors, even though no light refraction or radar-repellent materials were used, remained a mystery to Theoderich.

If it worked, however, you didn't question it enough to distract yourself. So, he focused on their goal: the refugee fleets of their former compatriots, the ones who many decades ago preferred to submit to an AI rather than remain in the hands of God and His children. They hid behind Lagunia's central star, a red dwarf. As it turned out, they were in much better and much worse condition than he would have expected. Better because over forty-eight ships had managed to escape and only eight of them no longer radiated energy signatures. And worse, since there were only two naval ships among them. Both had extended their radiators and, if you looked at their emissions, could no longer deploy any ammunition and thus had no active weapon systems. Their disguise as TFS *Saratoga* was therefore a completely unnecessary precaution because they could have easily shot all forty active ships to fragments and ended it once and for all.

When Theoderich arrived on the bridge, they had just reached the outermost of the stranded ships, a freighter named *Gloria*, which was already talking to them over the radio.

"... You can't imagine how relieved we are!" said a voice from the loudspeakers, sounding close to an emotional breakdown.

"We're sorry it took so long," Pyrgorates replied, and Theodoric was amazed at how skillfully the captain was able to feign empathy without losing his mischievous grin. "Captain Thurnau sends her best wishes and has instructed us to bring you all home."

"Home?" the man on the other end of the line asked, irritated.

"Harbingen."

He could hear people crying in the background. "W-where is the admiral? Why *Captain* Thurnau?"

"I'm sorry, but Captain Konrad Bradley was killed in the battle for Sol. His XO, Silvea Thurnau, has taken command," Pyrgorates said. "She is currently busy securing our home world."

"That's good news, really good news. We wouldn't have lasted four more days."

Theoderich had considered it a sad necessity to eliminate these few so that they would not stand in the way of a better future for the many. Learning that they would not survive the journey to Harbingen or Sol anyway made the heavy burden a little easier for him.

"Don't worry, we've got plenty of supplies on board, and we're prepared to distribute them quickly," Pyrgorates assured the man with feigned care. "There are two maintenance drones per ship carrying water, food, and repair materials. Tell me, Commander Jakobs, why didn't you jump out of here?"

"Half our ships don't have jumping units and a quarter would have consumed too much energy. We had to make a decision, so we decided to share our resources and stay together. Omega alone knows what was going on in the rest of the Federation."

"I see. A good decision. What about the eight ships that are no longer emitting any energy signatures?"

"We buried our dead there to protect ourselves from the outbreak of epidemic. It's been many weeks, after all." Commander Jakobs suddenly sounded dejected and very tired. His initial euphoria had audibly faded.

"If you agree, we will now start sending out our drones. They will dock at airlocks and hangars marked by us. To do this, we need your docking codes," Pyrgorates explained.

Theoderich was satisfied with his patient wait-and-see manner that did not arouse suspicion. Not that he thought there was any significant danger that these civilians and unarmed sailors would question this help, they were far too desperate for that. But especially in the face of the final victory, the end of their decades of work in the background, it was tempting for inferior spirits to overshoot the goal and stumble in the process, even though there was no one far or wide who could prevent victory.

"Of course. I'll immediately notify the fleet. Thank you, Captain. Thank you from the bottom of my heart!"

"It is an honor for us," Pyrgorates replied. "Juratis Unitatis."

"Juratis Unitatis."

The communications officer, a young man with close-cropped hair, signaled to the captain that the connection had ended. Only now did Pyrgorates seem to notice Theoderich's arrival, and he bowed slightly.

"Chancellor?"

"I have come to witness this historic moment."

He was aware that the last trace of his raison d'être would vanish if the refugee fleet and the *Oberon*, which was to arrive at any moment, were destroyed. A final blow that, in just a matter of minutes, irrevocably ended the oldest internal conflict of the Federation. For Theoderich, there was only one thing left after that: end his life, so as not to offer any opportunity to question him or infiltrate his memory lacunae. The entire conspiracy, which he had built up and carried out in decades of meticulous work, would go with him to the grave, into inexorable oblivion. He would leave a clean slate for his brother and the true Harbingen that would take root anew on fertile soil. Without legacies, without him.

"The last drone will be in position in five minutes," Pyrgorates said and pointed to the screen where the flashing yellow lights of dozens of maintenance robots could be seen, buzzing like a swarm of fireflies, lugging their explosive cargo on their way to the refugee ships gleaming in the red sunlight. Theoderich found that the glowing solar flares of the central star provided an apt backdrop for this memorable day.

"All systems ready? No malfunctions in the ignition transmitters?"

He still considered the incident with the Barracuda, which had damaged their hangar, to be a strange deviation they could not use. But after a brief fluctuation in life support after their transit out of Harbingen, everything had returned to normal. The last thing they needed was a spy on board, but internal sensors had not recorded any decaying biomass as if from a hidden corpse, and life support had since returned to normal operations and recorded the exact number of people on board.

"No. No trace of deviation or malfunction. Nothing stands in our way anymore."

"Captain," the reconnaissance officer reported. "Incoming graviton distortion at S2! It's the *Oberon*."

"Ah," Theoderich exhaled. It felt good when all the pieces in a puzzle fell directly into place, exactly as he planned. He reached into the pocket of his jacket and pulled out the small quantum transmitter that connected him in real time to the quagma charge placed by the courier on the *Oberon*. "Report immediately when the *Oberon* has gone to maximum thrust. Let them know our transponder codes are fake."

∾

Nicholas shook off the transit frost and waited for the situation picture in front of him to assemble once the sensor phalanxes were extended. It felt like coming home, and that surprised him. He had always thought he would be endlessly relieved once he was away

*The last Battleship*

from Lagunia, but instead he felt a wave of nostalgia wash over him as the hologram in front of him resolved into the familiar sight of the system he had, albeit reluctantly, called home for most of his life.

"Contact!" Feugers called from the tier. "Starboard! Twenty clicks!"

As if to underline Feugers's words, the ship shook under a series of violent impacts that made Nicholas grab the command deck.

"Return fire!" he commanded loudly.

Battle alarms and sirens sounded and the bridge was bathed in red light. 500 railguns emerged from their sockets and aligned themselves with the powerful radar ping that was confirmed only seconds later by lidar scan then refined and measured down to the millimeter. The guns pumped their ultra-high-acceleration tungsten cones into space, which hit close to the CQB within the blink of an eye and hammered into the alien ship like a cosmic hailstorm. Amid the cracking armor segments of the invaders' unusually dented battle cruiser, the first Taurus missiles struck, unleashing a whirlwind of harsh radiation. To make the chaos perfect, the volleys of multi-point-defense cannons cut through the bubbling vacuum between the ships where every single molecule of gas boiled. Tracer missiles among the millions of projectiles pulled threads of light into the darkness as they tried to catch the aliens' clunky guided missiles before thundering into the scarred Carbin of the armor.

"I've located the refugee fleet!" Alkad announced excitedly. "They seem to be hiding behind the central star near S1 and—"

"What?" Nicholas shouted when she fell abruptly silent.

"I don't understand, sir. The *Saratoga* is with them. That can't be right."

"Feugers, get on that. Lieutenant Bauer? How are we doing?"

"We are too close for the anti-aircraft shield, but our broadside almost destroyed the enemy."

"Damage?"

"Hull fractures at two sections, rescue teams are on the way. We are losing superfluid helium from four lines."

"The damage that was just repaired," Daussel grumbled. "They were basically predetermined breaking points."

Nicholas just nodded.

"Captain," Feugers said excitedly, "the transponder code is a fake, it's not the *Saratoga*. If I'm not mistaken and the computer isn't malfunctioning, it's the Exile ship *Redemption* that escaped Harbingen before us."

"Oh no," Nicholas breathed, trying to keep his composure. "Full speed ahead! Lieutenant Alkad, overload the reactor as much as you feel it can take!" he ordered. Yet he knew that would take hours. Hours that they did not have when the enemy was a wolf already among the flock of sheep.

∽

"The *Oberon* is at full thrust," the reconnaissance officer reported.

"How long until all the drones are in place?" Pyrgorates asked.

"Twenty seconds."

"Very good." The captain smiled thinly as he realized the finality of their victory. Theoderich did not rebuke him. Now it was really sealed. "Make ready for detonation!"

The fire control officer flipped up the cover of the toggle switch that would seal the traitors' doom and turned to his commander, who was sitting next to Theoderich in the XO's chair.

"Sir? Would you like to have the honor?" There was real anticipation shining in the young man's dark eyes.

Pyrgorates looked at Theoderich, and he gave him a gracious nod. "Go ahead, Captain."

After all, his own pledge was not the downfall of these civilians, he took no joy in that, but the *Oberon*'s destruction, the thorn in the flesh of their cause since his brother Ludwig had left the Federation. He looked at the quantum transmitter and placed his thumb tip on the button. What would it feel like once it was over? Even he could not imagine this kind of redemption.

Pyrgorates stood, smoothed his uniform, and thrust out his chin with satisfaction. He went to the console and suddenly stood still. At first, Theodoric did not understand why he was holding back. The gaunt captain turned around and the fire control officer stood. Long dark blades protruded from his arms, one of which had slashed open Pyrgorates's abdomen from left to right. Beaded intestines spilled out of the wound and slapped the bridge floor like wet fish. Blinking, he stared down at himself. Dark red blood bubbled over his lips and his gaze flickered with disbelief and confusion.

"No one betrays *me*," Sirion said and pulled a ReFace net off his face. Theoderich started to press the button that would seal the *Oberon*'s fate when he looked at the cold-eyed killer's pale, expressionless face. His thumb did not obey him. He looked down and saw a tiny neuro-dart stuck in his hand. Warmth spread through him, like leaden concrete that made him unable to lift even his little finger.

Incredulous and helpless, he could only watch as sheer panic broke out after a few seconds of shock. The five remaining bridge officers jumped up. One attempted to pounce on the Shadowwing, but a casual flick of a monofilament blade split him in half from crotch to neck. Another slipped in the captain's growing pool of blood and broke his neck with an ugly crack on the step leading to the command pedestal. Sirion struck down the remaining three with Pyrgorates's service weapon, the only one on the bridge. He had drawn it with such lightning speed that his movements were blurred.

The door started to open, but closed again after a glance from the killer, as if obeying his mere thoughts.

*That's probably true,* Theoderich thought. He knew everything there was to know about this man, for he had made him what he was. The whispered lies and well-placed memories of his mother and her death at Admiral Bradley's hands had forged a lost boy in the dirt of the Taurus station into a wonderful weapon that knew only one purpose: eliminate the most powerful living enemy of the true Harbingen and Omega's most important agent. Well, that had worked, but it had produced something that Theoderich had not foreseen.

He tried again and again to press the quantum detonator—in vain. There were also no explosions on the sensor screen that formed a frustratingly monotonous background for Sirion. The killer finally pulled the blade out of Pyrgorates's abdomen, and the captain collapsed like a puppet.

"That's for your murder of Konrad Bradley. No one steals a kill from me," Sirion said coldly and then fixed his gaze on Theoderich. The helpless man felt a chill run down his spine. That this man was *his* creature, about whom he knew *everything*, only worsened the fear that rose in him. There was no escape. Not with this man.

"I've always wanted to face you." Sirion took the detonator out of his hand without any apparent haste and looked at it briefly before staring at Theoderich again. "The man in the shadows who pulls all the strings."

"I..." he tried to squeeze words over his lips. It was arduous and exhausting, but feeling began to return to his tongue as his blood filters gradually absorbed the massive onslaught of neurostun and metabolized it through the liver.

"Yes, you. For a long time, I believed you weren't human. Too many strings in one hand, too much of everything to be controlled by just one mind," Sirion continued.

"H-h-how?" Theoderich croaked.

"One courier more, then one courier less. His murder helped me, and Pyrgorates's disposal of the body showed me a way to finally take Lieutenant Fredericks' place." The Shadowwing pointed to the fire control officer's empty seat. He went to the navigation system and entered several quick commands before coming back. On the screen, Theoderich had to watch as the drones turned away and accelerated. Pounding could be heard from the armored bulkhead, followed by the crackle and glitter of a fission cutter burning its way through the carbotanium. "Do you know, *Chancellor*, what I've learned in my life about corrupt men? They are driven by fear. So was the courier."

"Y-you... I-I... "

"I know it was you." Sirion's eyes were still cold as ice, but there was now a faint emotion in them. It was not regret, but something that Theodoric interpreted as a kind of relief. "A life forged of hatred and fear, the true alloys from which murderers are created. I've felt your hammer blow on my neck all my life, a puppet following its predetermined path. That's over now. We've come full circle."

Theoderich looked at the quantum detonator in Sirion's bloody hand. The absurd hope that he might accidentally press the button haunted his still sluggish head. He was able to move his fingers and hands again, but he hadn't done it yet. The Shadowwing was powerful, but he knew *nothing* about *him* and what implants he was equipped with. That was good.

"Si-Siri..." he said, struggling. "M-must... s-say..."

"Say something?" Sirion came closer to hear him.

Theoderich knew he had to be fast because, unlike his counterpart, he did not have reflex boosters. But he had surprise on his side. Carefully, he unfolded the tip of his left index finger and a scalpel knife shot out of it, but that was as far as he got. The killer grabbed his hands, pulled them forward and amputated them with a quick stroke. Screaming, the shadow chancellor stared at the stumps of his arms. Red blood spurted from them and surrounded Sirion like a halo of death, the background noise of his short life of murder and struggle.

"You want to use... this?" He lifted the detonator and placed his thumb over it.

Theoderich did not answer, instead, saliva ran down his lips. He didn't even notice that his body was shaking violently as if he'd been electrocuted.

"I will grant you that wish so the circle closes. For me *and* for you. It's how it always had to be. Redemption." The corners of Sirion's mouth twisted slightly... upward?

He pressed the button.

The bomb was sitting in a small transport box in Lieutenant Fredericks' quarters labeled "P11 palladium." The containers holding the quarks and gluons apart opened and they combined to form the same heat and force of the Big Bang as quagma tore the warship out of the universe.

The flash of light, followed by a ring of frenzied particles racing up and down the electromagnetic spectrum, shone brighter for a moment than the central star right next to it and disappeared a short time later. All that remained was a single reconnaissance satellite, which had already been chased away from the event point and was overtaken by the wave of gamma radiation. It was not destroyed and raced away into the infinity of space.

The fleet of Lagunia refugees, protected by the ecliptic of the red-hot star, could only watch helplessly as their apparent saviors dissolved into dancing atoms just before they received a radio message from the *Oberon*. After several seconds of confusion and disbelief, the first sensor messages spread among the half-starved, dirty women, men, and children who had been holding out for weeks, and their last reserves of strength were discharged in exuberant cheers.

# 24

"Sirion," Nicholas said. "It must have been Sirion."

"What makes you so sure?" Alkad asked. She sounded almost casual, not at all as if he had only made up his mind an hour ago to tell her about his encounter with the Shadowwing.

*Kiya,* he recalled.

They were off-duty and on the observation deck. It rose in semicircular tiers like an ancient amphitheater in front of the huge window at the bow of the *Oberon*. They sat far to the left, away from everyone else. Like curtains as high as houses, the open armored gates limited their view to the sides, but the sight was still awe-inspiring. Lagunia's red central star had about 50 percent of the luminosity of Sol's sun and shone a scarlet hue that shimmered warmly throughout the observation deck and bathed everything in a calm romantic light. The flares, mass ejections of glistening plasma into the darkness of space, looked leisurely despite their proximity and anything but enormous. Yet each of them was a thousand times larger than the *Oberon*.

"He told Jason and me that it would be the last time we saw him. After that, he disappeared. I knew he wanted to kill Pyrgorates, just like me and my brother." Nicholas sighed, trying to figure out his feelings about what had happened in the last few hours before his shift ended. Daussel had almost forced him to leave the bridge, and he had been right. He could no longer think clearly.

"Then he has something to do with the missing Barracuda Hunter? The Shadowwing, I mean?"

"It would suit him. After all, he didn't kill anyone for it this time, it seems."

"Laura Wells." Kiya sounded compassionate.

"Yes," he whispered. "I wanted to kill him for that—put my hands around his neck and squeeze until he stopped breathing. I know that sounds insane, but—"

"No, that's perfectly understandable. This killer murdered someone you loved simply because she was in the way, or because he needed her identity, an insignificant obstacle during his mission. It was so inhuman and unjust that it's hard for me to believe that anyone would *not* think of murder."

"Thank you. I appreciate that. But now that he's dead, I don't feel redeemed, or even relieved. I'm confused. I hated him, really *hated* him, but he brought Omega back to us and saved nearly half a million civilians."

"It doesn't add up."

"Yes. It's hard to accept that he's not the monster I saw him as." Nicholas buried his face in his hands. "And at the same time, it is. This contradiction alone makes me angry with him."

"Now he's dead." Kiya pointed to where Lagunia's star was throwing long threads of bright red plasma that slowly dissolved in space. Even with the darkened screen, the brightness was overwhelming. "A being that, for a cosmic second, had arms and legs and thoughts driven by murderous lust and hatred is now just dust among the stars. A mere memory."

"The real problem is that I don't think I have a right to be angry. What more could I have asked for than for the most dangerous killer of all time to act in our interest? Saving hundreds of thousands of people with his last deed?"

"Maybe that wasn't his intention at all. What if he just wanted to take revenge on Pyrgorates? Recon even considers it possible that the mastermind of the conspirators was on board. That's not improbable given what happened on Lagunia. Devlin Myers also said that the Shadowwing was an instrument of the Exiles for years and was paid by them. Biting dogs tend to bite the hand that feeds them at some point."

"Does that matter at all?" Nicholas asked, looking at the mostly empty seats on the observation deck. Only a few off-duty crew members were there, people who disdained sleep and longed for mental distraction.

Kiya Alkad pondered that a while, and then shook her head. "I don't think so, no. The result is that more people are alive than if he hadn't done what he did."

"There's still this satellite we recovered." He looked down at his forearm display. "It should be on board in three hours, and hopefully we'll know a little more."

"What's it like being the ship's commander?" the navigation officer asked, abruptly changing the subject.

"Unusual, but also confusing. The difference to my tasks as XO is not very big, apart from the greater responsibility that now rests on my shoulders. That's why I never envied Silly—and Dad even less."

"He made the most difficult decision an officer can make, save a few and live with survivor's guilt or save no one and die heroically in battle." Kiya paused. "Both of us and every crewman knows which decision is easier. Nevertheless, Konrad Bradley obeyed his orders and decided to give at least a fraction of the Harbingers a future instead of sacrificing them on the altar of their own heroism. That's true greatness, and everyone on board knows it."

"Omega told me that it was indeed an order. It instructed him to disappear with the colonist ships, cover their departure, and ensure their political survival. Without a Titan at their side, they would have declined into insignificance and probably become pirates or petty criminals in the absence of an alternative."

Kiya took his hand in hers and squeezed it tightly before pulling back. The touch was short—too short?—but some of the warmth of her fingers remained and relieved some of the inner heaviness that weighed on him.

"Children outlive their parents, that's the way things are. You can be proud of yours, both of them. Never forget that not all of us have been so lucky."

Reflex made Nicholas want to ask what was so enviable about a mother blowing herself up on a father's orders, who was in turn executed by a psychopathic conspirator in a dusty valley on Terra after days of cruel torture. But he was able to stop himself from pursuing that impulse.

He knew men and women who had been beaten, imprisoned, or simply neglected and unloved by their parents. The last of those was probably the worst cross a child could carry, and Mom and Dad had not been guilty of that. It was easy to see oneself as the center of all suffering and unhappiness of the universe, but it was simply a misperception that arose from the inevitably narrow view each human being had. His father had tried to explain at some point—at the beginning of his training—that nothing was as it seemed at first glance and that every circumstance was merely at the center of a myriad of chain links that you had to follow to get to this point, and that he in turn would also produce a myriad of links. As an example, he had shown him the holographic representation of a straight line that was slightly rising.

*"What is that?"* Konrad had asked.

*"A linearly rising line,"* Nicholas had replied.

*"Standard progression."*

*"Yes."*

*"Or is it?"* His father had zoomed out several times until Nicholas understood that he had only seen the tiny section of an exponential function. *"If you get close enough, everything looks like a straight line even in an exponential curve. Sometimes slightly rising, sometimes vertical, but none of this is an indication of their true nature in the context of the superordinate whole. Always keep this in mind."*

Well, that's what he had done.

"I'd better get some sleep," he said, rising stiffly. He would have liked to turn away and walk quickly, but instead, he turned back to Kiya. "Thank you, Kiya. That did me some good."

"It gets lonelier the higher you climb on the mountain," she replied ambiguously, nodding with a warm smile on her lips. "See you on the bridge, CO."

"I'm still *Nicholas*," he corrected her with a weary smile. "At least until I go through that door."

"There are many doors."

On the way out, he pondered her last remark, but he could not make sense of her. Or maybe he was just too tired to think clearly. The stray satellite was already on its way back, pulled by an agonizingly slow tugboat drone. Its moderate pace allowed him to close his eyes for at least a few more hours.

∾

The ascending three-tone ring of the telephone set to Free Time next to his bunk was supposed to be gentle, but in Nicholas's sleep-drunk ears, it sounded like the ringing of bells in the sixth circle of Hell.

He had dreamed Jason had come by on a Sunday morning to bake bread with him but had forgotten the salt. So, without further ado, they had replaced the dough with old leather shoes and thickened them with psyllium husks to be healthy enough for Kiya Alkad to eat a slice as well. However, there had been no cold cuts at first, because his house had turned out to be a large satellite standing on an asteroid that was a huge marble orbiting a red sun. This, in turn, only looked like a star but was actually a funnel. Later, Sirion came by, wearing a baker's hat, and brought them some Himalayan salt, but the label said that it had only been dyed pink with the same color that was used to dye salmon meat. Alkad declined, accusing him of never really wanting to call her Kiya.

"Yes?" he murmured in a thick voice. When he felt the cold earpiece on his left ear, the dream receded far enough for him to remember where and who he was.

"Sir, we have recovered the satellite," Daussel reported. "You should see it in person."

"I'm on my way." He cleared his throat and hung the receiver back in his frame. After a few short stretching exercises, which probably achieved more damage than relief to his growing back pain, he went to his wet room, washed himself quickly, and brushed his teeth. He filled a glass with magnesium and took his daily dose of vitamins and trace elements in the form of yellow capsules, which managed to taste like a mixture of tropical fruits and shoes worn too long by an old grandma. As soon as he was clad in his uniform, he grabbed a coffee from the synthesizer next to the desk, put a lid on it, and made his way to the bridge.

Along the way, he made a conscious effort to suppress the unrest rising inside him and instead concentrated on his breathing, the wonderful smell of fake coffee, and the greetings of his crew. He returned salutes, said a few words of encouragement here and there, or reflected the joy and optimism of crew members who had come up with the surprisingly easy rescue of their countrymen in Lagunia.

*Hectic people don't save time, they lose their calm,* his father used to say. Losing his calm was unpleasant enough to appreciate the adage. He had grown up hating his parents' constant sayings but had increasingly made them his own. He had long ago dismissed the inner belief of "I will never become like my parents" as an overzealous pubescent denial of simple truths that one could not escape anyway.

*Whatever you fight, you make only stronger. Acceptance, on the other hand, dissolves resistance and frees the mind to deal with things.* Sometimes Nicholas expected Silly to tell him that she had found a secret notebook somewhere in her quarters that contained his father's scribbled sayings and thoughts.

Only half the staff was on duty on the bridge, and few voices could be heard from the tiers where the constant drone of murmurs reigned. On the other hand, the background hum of the engines was more noticeable and gave the atmosphere the feeling of a midnight watch on an old container ship sailing uneventfully across an ocean at night.

"I'll take over, you can call it a day, Lieutenant Commander," he said to Hellcat. After two shifts, the man looked like the Passion of Christ with thick bags over deep shadows under his eyes.

"Thank you, CO." The pilot saluted wearily and suppressed a yawn before turning and walking out.

"So, XO, what do we have?"

*The last Battleship*

"I'm sorry I woke you, sir," Daussel said and called up a hologram displaying a long code that Nicholas couldn't read.

"What's that?"

"Contents of the data memory we recovered from the satellite."

Nicholas looked down at his forearm display. "It must have come on board only ten minutes ago."

"Omega has deciphered and analyzed everything."

"So fast?" he asked in surprise. "Wow."

**"The encryption was of varying complexity. The 360-degree-dimensional geometric encryption was new to me, but it only affected a single file and was the biggest obstacle,"** the AI reported.

"So, what do we have?" Nicholas was glad that he was still tired enough that even the caffeine rush in his blood struggled to rekindle his excitement.

**"Your guess was correct. It seems Sirion Mantell was the one who killed the captain of the *Redemption* and someone he himself called the 'puppeteer.' It seems that he was referring to the shadow chancellor of the local exiles."**

"Where did you get that from?"

**"A voice recording. Do you want me to play it?"**

"Please." Nicholas straightened and lifted his chin to ready himself to hear a voice he had never wanted to hear again.

"Pyrgorates is about to die, and with him the puppeteer. I can still feel his threads pulling at me. The shadow shies from the light, and it has served me long enough for me to want to illuminate it with a plea for forgiveness. My life will end according to my rules because I want it that way. I don't know if that's good, but it's what I can do and what I've decided. Maybe for the first time in my life," Sirion said. His cool voice overlaid static and scratching noises reminiscent of fingernails over a drawing board. "My blacklinks have extracted several encrypted files from the *Redemption*'s onboard computer that even my software routines cannot decrypt. I loaded them into the satellite's data memory. The bomb was meant for you, but it was my destiny."

That was the end of the recording.

"That's it?" Nicholas frowned.

"Yes."

"A man of few words," Daussel said. "Or emotions, it seems."

"He was a killer."

"One on the right side. At least in the end."

Nicholas made no reply. Instead, he turned to Omega. "Have you been able to reconstruct what happened?"

**"Part of it, because it contained the logbook, among other things. The courier, Lieutenant Commander Jaedong, was an agent of the conspirators and was in the service of the alleged shadow chancellor, who was mentioned several times as the 'chancellor.' Apparently, it was Theoderich von Borningen."**

"Ludwig von Borningen's brother?" Nicholas asked, blinking incredulously.

**"Yes. If that's true, he's dead now,"** the AI explained, without revealing how it arrived at this fact. **"So, the conspirators knew what we knew. But Jaedong was also tasked with smuggling a box of palladium onto the *Oberon*, which he allegedly sold to an engineer. Since I don't miss anything on board, I went through all the sensor recordings again. Such a deal never happened. Jaedong was in the officers' mess once and twice to the toilet, then went to the port hangar and got underway again."**

"The bomb that was meant for us."

**"Yes. Sirion Mantell apparently threatened the courier, took the bomb from him, and hid it on the *Redemption*. For fear of punishment, Lieutenant Commander Jaedong must not have mentioned any of this to von Borningen."**

"Not a bad plan," Daussel said nodding. "At least if you don't expect to survive the whole thing anyway."

"So, he blew himself up along with his former client."

**"Yes, and whether he knew it or not, he saved half a million of my citizens from death because Captain Pyrgorates planned to blow up every ship with the help of some kind of Trojan Horse—maintenance drones carrying mines with remote detonators instead of promised supplies,"** Omega said.

*Did he know that?* Nicholas wanted to ask, but it didn't matter.

*The last Battleship*

Not here and now in his capacity as commander of this ship. Instead, he asked, "What about the files you decrypted?"

"That's where it gets interesting. I could see from them what kind of transmission the local Exiles sent to those out there."

Nicholas froze. "Really?"

"Yes. They also received an answer and sent out six large sleeper ships that were most likely built in Harbingen's Oort Cloud and took on board all the sympathizers who had been brought in from all over the Federation. Among other things, eighty-six Starvans from this system, Lagunia."

"Both events were recorded by the *Quantum Bitch*," Daussel said. "First the Starvans and then the six huge ship signatures in Harbingen at S1 that their onboard computer couldn't identify."

"Yes."

"But what was in the transmission?" Nicholas urged the AI to continue its report.

"An up-to-date political and military assessment of the Federation's situation, including detailed historical treatises over the last three decades, from the point of view of the author, of course, presumably the 'chancellor' who is frequently mentioned," Omega explained. "However, it seems the message was prepared a while ago because it did not contain any of the latest developments, and we must assume that the enemy's network of informants knew about them, such as the peace agreement with the Water People of Warm Depths."

"Or the author has deliberately omitted that part."

"That is possible even if I cannot detect a logical motive for it."

"You spoke of a response from the Exiles. They survived and are really out there," Nicholas swallowed. His neck felt swollen.

"Yes. Their new home planet is called Augustshire. Ludwig von Borningen still bears the title of High Lord and is president for life. Two other colonies have been developed. More political or even military information was not included, only the blueprint for a transmitting apparatus that taps into the local quantum structure. I'm not quite sure about its function yet, but I'm already working on it as we speak. It seems to have something to do with the threat of Species X, about which a lot of information has been sent."

"Then they've done some research on it?" Daussel asked. "That must mean they already knew more than we did back then."

"That's to be assumed. They now know much more than we do, including about hyperspace and how to use it, by the way."

"What kind of information?" Nicholas asked.

"I will tell you, but we should first organize the refugee fleet and send them to Pilgrim, otherwise they won't survive. After that, we must go straight to Attila with full force."

"To Attila?" he and Daussel asked at the same time.

"Yes. It seems our future and that of the Water People of Warm Depths will be decided there. And we must send a courier to Sol."

# 25

The trip to Attila was so uneventful that Jason fell into a deep emotional hole. The hectic activity, the ever-present fear, the constant adrenaline, driven by a Sword of Damocles of a violent death hanging over them, whose thread had worn down to a hair, had forced him into the moment, put blinders on him that he needed to function.

One thing he'd learned during the war. A soldier could get used to anything, fear, sleep deprivation, constant fire. Though the list of things that made life at the front hell was very long, a person seemed able to adapt to everything.

*The Soldier.*

Ironically, it was the silence and uneventfulness that tugged at his nerves during the journey. It was as if he missed the constant onrush of projectiles trying to find their way into his flesh, the roar of engines under full thrust, and the uncertainty of whether he would survive the next few hours, or even minutes.

It might sound absurd to a civilian, but not so for soldiers. So, he repeatedly sought proximity to other officers in the *Saratoga*'s mess, where almost everyone felt the same way he did. Nevertheless, after the end of a shift, when hardly anything happened outside normal Fleet routine under less crazy circumstances, he lay awake in his bunk and stared at the ceiling because he couldn't stand the silence.

The mind had a habit of filling every free space. In his case, it was with memories of the countless moments in the last days and weeks when he had narrowly escaped death. The sweating and his restless tossing were the least of the evils. Worse were the images of his father being executed by Pyrgorates; of his recruits, mangled and chopped up by gangers in the *Novigrad* halo who had attacked his young men and women like barbarians assaulting school children. There were Bakers' butchers doing things that could have come straight out of a horror movie and the pleading crewmen in the infirmary. It felt wrong and wicked that he was unharmed and alive.

During the long days of relative inactivity, a change had come over Silly. She acted calmly and, in his eyes, even level-headed. She retreated to her cabin more often and spent a lot of time on tactical analyses of her battles of the last few weeks. From time to time, she asked him for advice when he was not on duty on the bridge. His skills as a logistics expert had proved valuable in correctly allocating scarce supplies and overseeing repair work. The *Saratoga* had taken a beating in Harbingen and, even days later, was still struggling with system failures and several isolated stations that required prioritized distribution of repair materials, not to mention a demanding service and maintenance schedule for the technicians and drones. There was no point ordering the crew to double shifts only to then spend the next double shifts treating men and repairing machines.

The climax of Silly's transformation occurred on the ninth day. They were in the Zeffo System, a barren vacuum desert consisting of a lonely white giant within a distant asteroid belt. Much farther out was a powerful gas giant with the mass of twenty Jupiters, where the system's S2 was located. Zeffo was only one leap from Attila, a very strange idea. Only two weeks ago it had been the lion's den, the heart of the enemy, and probably the most dangerous place in the universe for a Federation ship.

Jason arrived at the bridge for his shift, his first there after spending a few days at his own request assisting in every section of the guided-missile destroyer to better understand and support procedures. Silly was in her seat on the small platform in front of the semicircle of six specialists from the bridge crew. They functioned as the ship's nervous system via virtual displays. There were

*The last Battleship*

two seats beside her. The one to her right belonged to the XO, Captain Mnuchin, an elderly officer whose serious expression and immaculate hairstyle gave him the appearance of the old school. His own was to her left.

"Captain," he greeted Silly and nodded at Mnuchin. "XO."

The former captain of the *Saratoga* looked humorless, but immediately after Silly announced that she would temporarily take command, he had accepted this order, which was difficult for any ship's captain, and proven unpretentious and dutiful without visible reservation. After more than a week, Jason was able to say with some conviction that Mnuchin had made no effort to make her life difficult. Though there would have been plenty of opportunities to do so. On the contrary, he proved to be cooperative and hardworking, helping Silly and Jason to familiarize themselves with the much more modern systems and new Fleet technology they had never had access to before.

"Ah, Jason." Silly beckoned him over and motioned for him to sit. "In half an hour we'll issue the transit alarm."

"Then it's almost time," he said, nodding thoughtfully. "Attila. I never thought I'd see it for myself."

"The homeworld of the Clicks," Mnuchin agreed, sounding almost moved.

*Not their homeworld,* Jason thought, but didn't correct the XO. Even for him, it still felt like they were visiting the aliens' homeland. *Visiting, what a strange word for a flight to the center of power of a people that until two weeks ago had been our archenemy.*

"Their most powerful world," he said at last. "They are decentralized, have no supreme leadership, and therefore do not know the idea of centralizing power. But Attila is the most fortified and one of the most fertile breeding worlds."

"And we always thought their polar ice caps had melted due to forced climate change, but they love aquatic worlds," Silly snorted. "It's amazing how quickly you misinterpret things because you have your own glasses on."

"Good for the Clicks, anyway," Mnuchin said. "That's why we couldn't see their cities and the like. It's all nicely hidden in the ocean."

"On their moons and in orbit, there was already enough weapon-wielding infrastructure." Silly cleared her throat. "Which brings me to the point I wanted to talk to both of you about. We are a single, half-empty warship with enough damage to be prescribed a month's space dock under normal Fleet regulations. That means we're a symbol and not any type of guarantee. That's clear to all of us, isn't it?"

Mnuchin nodded and Jason couldn't agree more.

"Good. I have therefore decided that we will shut down all weapon systems and place them in their maintenance stations before we jump. The rocket bays will be sealed."

"Excuse me?" Jason was puzzled. Not because he had anything against the order, but out of sheer surprise. The XO didn't say anything and seemed thoughtful.

"It's like this. We're flying a half-loaded pistol into a convention attended by a few thousand machine guns. We might as well eject the magazine and flip the safety catch. We won't fire a shot anyway. If we do, we're finished, and so are the diplomats around Thekarius Angsk. Fleet Admiral Legutke must have had a reason why he wanted us to be present. So, we do that and use the mission not for some senseless powerplay, which would be ridiculous at best, but to provide a clear sign that will support Angsk's mission in the best possible way. We will show that things have changed and that we do not pose any danger or even have any interest in what was in the past. We voluntarily lay down our arms. At worst, they shoot us to pieces and it was all some weird alien plan. But that doesn't make sense, because otherwise they would have crushed Terra when they had the chance."

"I... I don't know what to say," Jason admitted.

"Why? Out with it!"

"I didn't think you would be such a... set such an *extreme* example. In a good way, I mean!" he hastened to add.

"I've never been extreme. It's just that I always thought it was a good strategy to put all your eggs in one basket. If you think of a plan B while forming plan A, you distract yourself from A and build failure into the house before the first stone has been laid."

*The last Battleship*

"I see." He nodded. "In my opinion, this is a very smart move, and it should make the ambassador very happy."

"Under the circumstances, it is the best use of our resources. Sometimes doing nothing is more important than wasting your time pretending to do something," Mnuchin agreed. "A sign of reconciliation and de-escalation, however small it may be, could be a symbol for many others in times like these and set a ball rolling that people will talk about in the future."

"Good. I'm glad you both agree. I have already initiated it. Everything should be complete by the time of transit." Silly turned to the XO. "As soon as we arrive at the Attila system, I will give you back command of your ship, provided Ambassador Angsk grants my request to accept me and Lieutenant Commander Bradley into his legation, at least until we have a chance of returning to the *Oberon*."

Mnuchin tilted his head slightly. "Thank you, Captain."

Half an hour later, the transit was quite uneventful compared to the *Oberon*. The sirens were much quieter and, unlike the Titan's ancient speakers, sounded like the well-tuned sound design of an acoustic advertising logo. Even the red light of the alarm lamps seemed both soft and shiny, as if on the set of a science fiction film. Jason wondered how duty on the *Oberon* would feel to the 80 sailors on board. Previously, he hadn't considered the differences in technology within the Fleet very serious because he had spent most of his time on the *Zarathustra*, which itself had been quite old, although not the museum piece the Titan was.

After the jump—as always, he had the vague feeling that he had lost something in the process—they extended their sensor arrays and navigation started a detailed scan of their surroundings. Two minutes later, there was no doubt that they had arrived in Attila. The hazy ocean world appeared so pale he was not surprised why the first spy footage had led to it being mistaken for a planet similarly poisoned as Terra. Above the long bands of clouds, several hundred habitats floated in orbit like dark birthmarks. The moons, all named with sober Fleet abbreviations, formed an elongated string of pearls that rotated at different intervals around the water-pregnant sphere.

Even before Jason could fully appreciate the astonishing view of the place, which he had never thought he would ever see with his own eyes since Operation Iron Hammer had fizzled out in disaster, the sensors were overflowing with contact warnings. At first, there were numerous reports about ship signatures that the onboard computer assigned to enemy ship types. All the red lights and flashing symbols made Jason feel the beginning of panic. Then there were the numerous defensive platforms, two stations about half the size of Terran space fortresses, and countless weapon systems.

"Uh, Captain," the communications officer called. "I think we're being contacted or something."

"Hold on."

A sequence of clicks emanated from the speakers. They sounded as strange as ever and still made Jason shiver. Although the war was over, the memories and beliefs that had become instincts were so deep that his mind still regarded it as a melody of evil.

"Jason?" Silly asked. "Any ideas?"

"No. I don't know how to establish a telepathic connection, and we haven't yet been able to decipher their clicking signals. They don't follow any logic that we as humans can comprehend."

"You're our Click expert," she replied, pointing forward in a "do something" gesture.

"I have a record of the sequence of clicks that Mother made when we were sitting in the escape pod and she wanted to inform her species that she was one of the occupants and didn't want to be shot down," he said, shrugging. "I have no idea exactly what she was saying, but I could sense her intentions and thoughts at the time."

"'Don't shoot' would be a good start."

"Yes. But not only do we not know what *we* are saying, we will not know what they say in response," he said.

"They'll know that as well as we do." Silly nodded. "Do it."

Jason agreed and sent the corresponding file from his forearm display to the onboard computer, which accepted the transmission request after a brief pause.

"Ah, Ambassador Angsk is already here," Mnuchin said pointing to the sensor screen. Jason saw it too, a long passenger

*The last Battleship*

ferry, a Starliner Explorer 350, sleek, chalk white, and painted with the coat of arms of the Jupiter Parliament. It was docked at one of the space stations in low orbit around Attila, along with two Terran Broadswords, the minimal escort. The sight of her told Jason that Silly had probably been right in assuming that Legutke intended her presence here to be something other than merely providing escort.

The other side reacted to their Click message, which they did not even understand, with another sequence of clicks. Silly just looked at him questioningly.

"It may well be that a large part of it is mere acoustic sensing. At close range, they use something like sonar, which is probably due to their aquatic background."

"But how do the signals get to their planet? There is no medium for sound waves in a vacuum."

"I don't know. They have to conduct scanning in a different way, but Mother and I didn't talk about that. Or rather: didn't think."

"In any case, it's all extremely strange. How can an aquatic culture build spaceships? Or even develop electricity. You can't experiment with electricity underwater, let alone high-voltage research, if you don't want to boil the entire ocean," Mnuchin said as they headed for the same space station where Ambassador Angsk's Starliner and two escort corvettes were docked for lack of better ideas. Silly commented curtly about her order, "They can shoot us if it suits them."

"It's a mystery," Jason agreed. "I hardly thought about it when I communicated with Mother and later with Inseminator. At that moment, other things were going through my head, I admit."

"Maybe they have something like bioelectronics. That also occurs in nature. But never in combination with technology."

"We'll find out," Silly said, shrugging.

She didn't seem eager for their conversation to continue while she used sheer willpower to ensure that they weren't blown out of space. Jumping into a Terran system without transponder queries was like a one-way ticket to hell. Approaching the most-fortified alien world in the known galaxy, not being able to respond to communication requests, and simply flying toward the planet—although at low speed—was a very disturbing prospect. It went against everything Fleet officers had ever known.

Their approach lasted several hours, during which they did not leave their seats, even to relieve themselves. Jason felt like a mouse with amputated paws being carried in a nutshell along a narrow stream, with cats on both banks following them with their eyes. They passed a lot of warships, presumably, the same fleet that Mother had led to Sol, which repeatedly scanned them, but otherwise did not attempt to change flight vectors or attack them.

Jason tried to see a pattern in their flight paths but couldn't find one. A total of 4,311 ships were in the system, which the onboard computer marked as military targets. In addition, there were almost 18,000 others ships that were civilian in nature and frequented the many mining stations in the two asteroid belts and the helium scoops in the uppermost atmospheric layers of the two gas giants of Attila. Most of them were large and bulbous or rings studded with spherical tanks.

He found the radar signatures alone fascinating, as well as the orderly swarm behavior of the many different ships that brought the system to life and seemed to serve as its lifelines. It also helped him remember that the war was over and his knowledge that the Clicks weren't playing a false game because they just didn't think that way. The Admiralty had taken a lot of persuasion and his experience of telepathy for this conviction to prevail, at least in the leadership of the Federation. To look into a foreign mind, to connect with it, and have every twist and turn illuminated because everything is there at the same time, was an experience that left no doubt as to whether someone was honest or not. Therefore, he was not surprised that the Clicks were strange and incomprehensible to the concept of the lie. How could you ever tell an untruth when everyone always *had* to tell the truth, because every thought was conveyed in every conversation?

That realization still amazed him as he thought about it.

The space station where Thekarius Angsk's Starliner was docked turned out to be a transit habitat like Earth's halos. It consisted of two long arms with ten decks—at least by Terran stan-

*The last Battleship*

dards—and a flattened shell that bulged outward and toward the planet. Jason thought she looked like a misshapen gnome trying to hug the celestial body. Ships with fiery exhaust tails frequently went back and forth between the shell and the planet's surface, where they disappeared into the dense clouds covering the area below the station.

The docking process was surprisingly easy. When they were still fifteen minutes away, they received a radio transmission.

"*Saratoga*, this is Lieutenant Hockenberry of the embassy delegation of His Excellency Thekarius Angsk. I have been instructed by our hosts to lead the docking process on the station side."

"Nice to hear a familiar voice, Lieutenant," Silly replied, looking relieved. "I guess it's the airlock that's flashing?"

"That's right, Captain. We've used the past few hours to print a docking adapter that shouldn't have any trouble connecting the two systems. We recommend breathing apparatuses when you come on board."

"Is Mother there?" Jason asked without thinking about it.

"No, Lieutenant Commander, but she has already asked to have you taken to her residence on Attila."

"Residence?"

"Well, that's what we call it. A restricted area in one of their oceans, which is something like their residence." Hockenberry paused. "It's hard to explain; I'm sure you understand."

"I do." And he did. His instinctive depression turned to excitement.

## 26

"This contains a long list of notes on my telepathic bond with Mother," Jason said, handing Silly the small data storage device.

She nodded and accepted it. He held onto the device, so that both their hands clasped it for a moment.

"Also, personal logs on Willy's and my work on the Telepator. Sorry for the name, but he insisted," he added. "Together with the Water People of Warm Depths, Omega should be able to configure it to allow direct communication."

"We could use that," Silly said as he finally let go. She pocketed the device. She sounded nasal through her breathing mask as if she had a cold.

The squat room where they stood was a little too low, even by the *Oberon*'s standards. He always thought of it as a cave system where one could just barely stretch out and walk. The walls gleamed with a soft pearlescence reminiscent of Mother's armor. To his left was the circular airlock to the atmospheric shuttle that would take him to the surface of Attila. In the last few hours, they had met briefly with Ambassador Angsk and his legation of thirty diplomats and officers. Surprisingly, they enjoyed human-sized accommodations that had been prepared for them, complete with their own airlocks and breathable atmosphere. In addition, the pressure in the entire space station had clearly been lowered to cause no discomfort. Jason noticed that only very few aliens could be seen, apart from individual guards, who were posted here and there. But even they were very reserved and did not attract attention.

Spokesman Wisdom of the Singing Geysers, something like the chief diplomat of the Water People of Warm Depths, explained to him that conversations were going well and, so far, were focusing on an exchange of various memories. They wished to sound out the personalities and differences between him and Angsk before communicating specific things to avoid unnecessary misunderstandings. He was glad not to have to rely on a tank anymore, even if it still gave him a severe headache.

Jason would have liked to see both sides build connection and trust and what else could come of it if they engaged in the same exchange that he and Mother did, without a preceding slaughter and the time pressure of an exploding shuttle in the background.

What he and Mother had done had been fascinating, touching and possibly groundbreaking for the future of both their peoples. Yet, how much of that was due to their particular situation? And how much more would Angsk and Wisdom of the Singing Geysers be able to accomplish if they approached it peacefully and with a desire for fruitful exchanges with a future? They could spare themselves the fear and uncertainty that had initially slowed him and Mother and flooded the bond with negative emotions.

"What is it? Do you want to back out?" Silly frowned.

He shook his head. "No. I was just wondering if there isn't a lot more going on here than we're considering right now."

"What do you mean? Because of this Telepator?"

"No. Well, yes, that too, but this is about much more than peace between us and them."

"Yes, it's about a shared blueprint for the future as galactic neighbors, the salvation of our people with their help, and perhaps in the future, flourishing trade that will lift our economy out of the decades-long recession caused by our war-focused industry."

"That's true, but that's not what I mean," Jason said. "If we manage to use telepathy among ourselves, as well as humanity, that will change everything. How many conflicts would become moot? Not just between worlds and political constructs, but even within

*The last Battleship*

families? If everything is open and universal, will we achieve mutual understanding? Will we be freed from the narrow fetters of our constricted individual views of the universe as seen through the glasses of our personal thoughts? That could mean *real* peace within us and between us."

"I always knew you were an idealist. A few weeks ago, I would have dismissed you as naïve for that, but so far, you haven't been wrong." Silly pointed to the airlock. "Whatever you do or see down there, I'm sure you'll find the right voice for all of us."

"Thank you," he said seriously and looked her in the eye. He hadn't thought words like that from her would mean so much to him. "I appreciate that. And please, try not to get mad and smash anything with your fist whenever Angsk does something stupid." He grinned to let her know he was teasing her.

"Dismissed, Lieutenant Commander," she replied with mock seriousness.

He stepped inside the airlock and into the small spherical shuttle with uncomfortable seats that looked more like wall hooks used to impale something. Next to him was a single alien—clad in a pitch-black armored suit, but with no obvious armament—in one of the three other "seats." They launched at once, and after the cabin jerked and shook a bit they descended to Attila. There were no portholes or optical sensors to plug into, which didn't surprise him since the Water People of Warm Depths could only see normally underwater. Their eyes were adapted to the lens effect of water and were useless in space. Everything they saw out here was converted and processed for them by the sensors.

There was nothing he could do but be patient and wait as the shuttle descended. He tried to picture the ship impelled by plasma flames, dropping through bands of clouds toward a great pale ocean that stretched from horizon to horizon with a thin land mass just before the terminator line. He imagined wave crests like streaks of powdered sugar stretching as far as the eye could see, appearing gentle from a distance, yet powerful and filled with the might of nature the closer they came. He imagined small shadows here and there, which he thought he could make out under the tide-laden surface of the ocean. Each of them, he thought, would be the trace of some exotic water creature, with the diverse colors and shapes that would have made any science fiction film pale in comparison.

When a violent thud shook the shuttle, his fantasies burst along with water molecules that resolved into a myriad of tiny oxygen bubbles. The rough descent suddenly became smooth. The material of the sphere began to groan under the growing pressure, punctuated by cracking and sizzling noises. The alien in front of him made clicking sounds, which Jason interpreted as excitement, because he thought he heard it rise in tone, or maybe because he interpreted his own excitement into it.

After what felt like an eternity in the diffusely lit cocoon of uncertainty, they finally stopped and a single jolt shook the cabin. His fellow passenger detached himself from the wall hook that had accommodated him perfectly and stepped in front of a large flap in the floor between them. Jason decided to remain seated until signaled. He watched as the alien withdrew a box and then pulled out a flexible suit that looked like it was made of rubber. The alien thrust it at him, and he assumed it was something for him. A diving suit, perhaps?

He stood, undressed after some initial embarrassment that he knew was silly, and slipped into the cool material. He was glad he wasn't part of a telepathic bond at that moment.

At first, it seemed too big, but as soon as he closed the unusually shaped zipper that ran up to a thick neck brace, the soft fabric tightened until it held him in a comfortable grip. The alien stepped up to him. Jason resisted the impulse to back away as he fingered something on the bulging neck element. Finally, there was a hiss and he smelled a hint of ozone in the air. A transparent sphere formed from the bottom up, trapping his head as if in a jar in Dr. Frankenstein's lab.

"Okay," he said. The only answer was the echo of his voice. That did not shock him, after all, he knew he was going to meet Mother underwater. That changed abruptly as a milky liquid ran into the helmet below his chin, quickly reached his lips and soon rose above his eyes. He kept his mouth and eyes tightly shut as if his life depended on it. The liquid was warm and thick, and a fear of suffocation soon came over him. Soon he began to lash out and stagger, only to realize that someone was holding him in an iron grip. The urge to inhale increased to a primordial demand that left him no room to think. An unpleasant pressure on his chest made him whimper. He felt as if he were being buried under an avalanche.

*Air, air, I'm dying.* The cry shot through his head as all reason fled. Then his body took full control as the last trace of rational thought was overwhelmed by panic, and he tore open his mouth and eyes. The liquid immediately ran down his windpipe like warm syrup, fueling his state of anxiety. His chest rose and fell erratically in convulsive jerks—and then it was over.

*I'm not dead,* was the first thought that arose from his panic. It was a clear, conscious thought, a statement that neither reassured nor exhilarated him. He could not inhale or exhale, and yet he was no longer desperate for oxygen. As his panic subsided, so did the uncontrolled spasms. What remained was the realization that he no longer needed to breathe. The liquid lost its milky white color and became transparent. His eyes stopped burning. There was no movement or floating particles in the liquid, oxygen-saturated mass that filled his lungs like ambrosia.

After a few more minutes—or was it hours?—Jason realized he could see clearly. There was a fisheye effect that took some getting used to, but it was limited. He recognized the Click before him, who slowly let go of him and stepped back, then raised his hands in front of his helmet. The dark gloves bore a strong resemblance to neoprene, although it was probably a programmable nanofiber, otherwise, he would be instantly crushed to the size of a cuddly animal in the depths he assumed he was in.

**Are you comfortable?**

He felt the thought burst in his head. It was as powerful as an entire coffee table album of sound and depth. The question his mind extracted from it was filled with a complex series of feelings and memories that encompassed comforting warmth, sustaining tides full of suspended crackling particles, and the absence of predators. Although almost all of it was foreign and strange, Jason understood the meaning immediately and grasped its emotional core as if it were his own sentiment.

*"Yes,"* he replied with a feeling of approval.

**Good. I am Thousandfold Shimmer of Nourishing Tides, I am honored to bring you here, the breeding grounds of Optimistic Broodmother, Egg-laying Importance, Beautiful Brightness Ray.**

*"The honor is all mine, Thousandfold Shimmer of Nourishing Tides."* Jason was fascinated by the realization that the "nourishing tides" in the "language" of the aliens signified a west–east direction. They did not think in terms of four cardinal directions but in terms of currents of warm- and cold-water masses and those carrying food. That they had learned to apply a sense of orientation lacking almost any element of linear geometry to space travel was even more fascinating. *"What happens now?"*

**Now pressure equalization will occur. Then we will wait for six bubbles twice. After that, you can swim out.**

As if to emphasize his message, bluish water began to flood the cabin and pool around their feet. It rose, first to his knees and then to his waist. This time he didn't panic. He knew what was coming and relaxed in the presence of this friendly alien.

When the entire space was filled, he asked himself one question, which Thousandfold Shimmer of Nourishing Tides naturally "heard": *"How can I swim?"*

**With your fibrils,** was the answer. It consisted of thoughts of him in his—from an alien point of view—strange-looking suit with a glass pimple on his head. From the back of the suite, six long appendages emerged like meter-long tadpole flagella. They waved merrily in the water, rippled in gentle undulations, and carried him gracefully back and forth through deep blue water.

*"How do they work?"*

**Think, then dive.**

*"I will try,"* he promised.

**Fear is not necessary. You will be successful. Six bubbles twice will soon pass. When you dive out of this door, two guards will take you to Optimistic Broodmother, Egg-laying Importance, Beautiful Brightness Ray,** the Click transmitted kindly. **I would like to say goodbye and express my joy that**

**our breeding grounds are no longer in danger from your species.**

*"Peace,"* Jason translated for himself. *"Yes, that makes me very happy too. Thank you, friend."*

The door opened. His first impulse was to walk toward it as his brain followed the processes and reflexes it had known since birth, but this only caused his legs to rise and fall. It cost a lot of effort and barely made any progress. He tried swimming motions, only to find it even more difficult to make progress.

**Steady. Do not use stub extensions. Flagellate. Slow. They are sensitive and full of artificial nerve fibers that are connected to your neural stratum. They will understand and act on their own,** Thousandfold Shimmer of Nourishing Tides assured him.

Jason nodded to himself and tried to *think* that he was flowing toward the open doorway... and suddenly he was floating toward the door, which was slightly wider and lower than on a Terran shuttle. On the other side it was much brighter than he had expected. Thousands of bioluminescent plants lit the water, their long stems bending back and forth in an invisible current like blades of grass in a gentle breeze. At their ends hung spherical capsules of transparent tissue that emitted a turquoise glow that seemed almost solid. They illuminated an ocean floor that resembled a pleasant, hilly landscape with short seagrass. Individual geysers looked like squeezed-out pimples of sand and rock, spewing pitch-black bubbles of smoke upward into the darkness like soot from early industrial smokestacks, as dense and gloomy as a cloudy new moon sky without stars. Jason estimated that, despite their intensity, the luminosity of the plants reached only a few hundred meters, which meant they were several kilometers below the water's surface.

The beauty of the landscape alone was enough to take his breath away and was intensified by a fascinating strangeness that was nevertheless close enough to his diving experience to not overwhelm him. But there was so much more. Fish in the most unimaginable color combinations. The hues were not bright, but rather pale and pastel, as if an artist had painted them. Their shapes were not as strange as he would have thought. They possessed mouths with narrow, bulging lips and expansive and stubby fins that were transparent or dark. They moved gracefully in swarms and singly across the grasslands that swayed back and forth in the invisible currents. Some plucked here and there at the plants, dipped between them, and scurried away excitedly when something startled them.

There were hardly any Clicks down here, except the two guards next to him. They wore no suits—why should they since they were in their natural habitat? Their translucent, chalk-white skin glowed softly as if illuminated by an external light source, and their long legs were bent with claws curving backward. Flagella extended from their backs, whirring around them like halos of fine tentacles in constant motion. Their large, V-shaped heads, whose skin and skull were half transparent, flashed and sparkled dark blue and purple in a firework of igniting neurons.

At first glance they looked frighteningly alien. They had no mouth, but they did have two nostrils, gills that constantly filtered water for nutrients and oxygen, and many moving limbs. At second glance, he saw only ethereal creatures that seemed almost delicate, quite different from the bulky armored suits of their comrades.

The primary difference in their appearance outside of water was not surprising, since for survival in another medium they had to use suits pumped full of water and essential components as soon as they entered the vacuum of space—just like early human space suits. The only difference was that the human medium was air while the Clicks required water. However, Jason wondered why, with their technological advancement that almost equaled the Federation's, they had not come up with a solution that supplied everything they needed in a different form rather than taking part of their habitat with them. Injections, for example, from a supply they could carry with them on their backs.

**Follow us,** one of the two unarmed Clicks transmitted. They pointed with outstretched arms between two hills that had to be close to a hundred meters high. **We will escort you to Optimistic Broodmother, Egg-laying Importance, Beautiful Brightness Ray.**

*"Thank you,"* he thought in reply. *"Are you soldiers?"*

*The last Battleship*

**Yes. You wonder why we do not carry weapons.**

*"Yes."*

**We do not need them down here. The breeding grounds are externally protected, and weapons are prohibited near the eggs.**

*"Eggs? Where are the eggs?"*

**They are everywhere in the sea grasses down here.** The Click waved his delicate arm gracefully to one side as they were carried forward by their teeming flagella like sublime dream figures in the twilight. **They are still small, not much bigger than one of your thumbnails. But soon the time will come for Optimistic Broodmother, Egg-laying Importance, Beautiful Brightness Ray to close their final circle.**

Jason was confused as he received thoughts that showed Mother, shiny and much whiter and purer than he remembered her, floating over a vast underwater landscape, secreting a milky liquid from her abdomen that spread out in the currents in a shower of glitter then sank downward.

*"She nourishes the eggs?"*

**Yes. She laid the eggs last season and will bless them with her remains at the right time before Mighty Warrior, Octopus Devourer, Wise Authority fertilizes them, and their life cycle begins.**

*"She will die?"* Jason was horrified.

**That is correct.** The alien was puzzled by his erupting grief, which flowed into their common bond. **Incomprehension. This day will be the culmination of her life cycle.**

*"I... it's okay."* Jason tried not to think about it anymore.

**She lives there.**

The three of them hovered about ten meters above the seabed, circled a geyser with swelling black bubbles, and passed two hills in a depression that led toward a kind of igloo made of sand. Jason didn't know exactly what he had expected when he had heard he was invited to Mother's residence, but it was certainly more than a pile of sand in the middle of nowhere. Apparently, this was just one of the many cultural misunderstandings he would have to get used to.

**She is waiting for you in there. She is no longer mobile as she gathers strength for the closing of her circle.**

*"Thank you."*

Jason wanted to ask how to get in, but then he saw a dark opening at one side that might be just big enough for him, if his artificial flagella did not decide to wave about crazily in all directions.

He carefully slid into the small dome. It worked much more smoothly than he had thought, he simply imagined himself floating along with slow movements. The dense water, pleasantly warm in his suit, turned out to be extremely easy to navigate with the help of the flagella. Being able to glide in all directions and not just on a two-dimensional plane, as humans usually did, was similar to weightlessness. The difference was that the latter was like being surrounded by nothing, while this was like being surrounded by everything in three-dimensional fullness.

Mother lay inside the strange structure amid a kind of pale green moss lichen with finger-length cones that looked soft. One of the bioluminescent plants outside illuminated the room. Colorful creepers on the walls formed a complex pattern of veins and leaves. Beautiful and yet so strange that he shuddered.

**Fear not, friend Jason,** Mother sent along their bond, which was noticeably firmer than the last time they had met. Also missing was the oppressive headache behind his temples that usually set in after only a short time.

*"I am concerned."*

**An end of cycle is a joy.**

*"But you will die."*

*I* **won't be alive soon. There is a difference. You humans think obsessively in dualities. Man, woman, light, dark, day, night, life, death. Everything seems subject to and reflects dualism. But when does a life ever end and a new one begin? Does the beginning lie in your parents' sperm or egg that joined to eventually become you? Or only in the embryo in your mother's womb, or possibly not until you are born? When you die and your body decays and becomes nutrient** for scavengers and bacteria, is that the end? Or only when your remains have changed into a new form?

*"I am then no longer me."*

**What is an 'I' but repeated 'I' thoughts?** Mother asked.

*"I will mourn you."*

**Thank you. I see that this is considered a compliment among humans. Even if it seems strange to me, I thank you for this gesture and your sadness.** Mother raised one of her lanky arms with its long claws in his direction. The movement seemed weak. Her eyes were almost closed, small slits instead of the palm-sized opals he remembered. **You want to know why I brought you down here.**

*"Yes,"* he thought, ashamed of his impatience in the face of her condition, but his curiosity was just too great, and he could not hide it from her.

**I understand that. The reason is this: I have consulted with Mighty Warrior, Octopus Devourer, Wise Authority, who will become the DNA donor for my eggs. We would like you to become our attaché to the Federation—**

*"An ambassador? But I am a Fleet officer!"* he thought, startled. Yet he also felt a sense of excitement grow within him and joy mixed with pride. Did this mean he could stay in this bond forever? The prospect was overwhelming enough to make tears well in his eyes. He knew he must seem like a junkie offered drugs again after weeks of withdrawal, but that did not bother him.

**We are aware of the special effort the bond demands of you humans and it worries us a bit, but we are interested in solving this problem,** Mother thought, immediately addressing his feelings. **If you agree, we will keep you here for a long time and initiate you into our civilization and our culture, our technology, and our history. Thus, we can build a bridge through you to your species and perhaps send someone from the Water People to join you. Since my next brood will be prepared on Terra, I consider this essential to guarantee peace in the long run.**

*"Of course,"* he thought. *"It will be an honor for me."*

**Keep in mind, before you decide, that this will demand a price.**

*"What price?"* he asked, certain that he would accept anyway, but the telepathic projections he received from her made him less certain.

**You may never see your fellow human beings again because they die. You could become the last human or perish with us down here and die a horrible death. That would be the most unfavorable outcome of what we are facing,** Mother explained with emotional warmth. **Our research on the mirror world is well advanced and we have new findings about the activity of Nightmare Elementals that cause concern. Your fellows up in orbit are being informed of this as we speak, but it may already be too late. If you stay here, you will have no influence on what happens out there. I must use the time I have left to take you on a journey through our history to where we are now. Only then will you understand enough to become our emissary. When this process is complete, which may require intervening in your DNA so you may understand, everything will be decided out there. Are you truly prepared for that?**

*"Yes."* His stomach ached at the thought, but he had no real doubt. Everything he had done had led him here, to this point. Not only was he eager to learn all about Mother and her fascinating people, but the prospect of becoming a central building block of a long peace between their peoples felt like the last piece of a puzzle that would complete the picture of his life. *"I am prepared for that."*

**So be it, Jason Bradley.**

## 27

Silly found the diplomatic mission as boring as she had always imagined. While the habitat was exciting in its own right, she spent most of her time with the envoys in a conference room with a table that had been made for them at the last minute. The top was a bit too low and the seats of the chairs a bit too high, so they looked like children in highchairs waiting to be fed by their parents.

Before they were escorted here about an hour earlier, there had been some misunderstanding. She and the delegation had been brought to a large room with its own airlock but completely empty. Inside, the air was breathable and, according to their forearm displays, corresponded exactly to the optimal mix for humans as found on Federation ships.

At first, they had not understood what they were doing there until their alien companions told them that it was their quarters. The subsequent, rather lengthy, attempts at explanation using graphic representations—the ambassador carried a portable holo-scratchboard with him—produced a somewhat amusing picture. Apparently, the Clicks had assumed that humans felt comfortable in a breathable atmosphere and could live comfortably there. In retrospect, this made sense to Silly, after all, the aliens came from the sea and, like fish, probably slept in the water wherever they happened to be, or somewhere protected from predators.

Humans, Angsk explained with his deft drawings, sought

protection from wind and weather, a kind of cave against the elements and dangerous animals. They also sought privacy. Their species, although it no longer needed these precautions, had not yet evolutionarily detached itself from them.

Their hosts understood quite quickly. The concept of privacy, however, was different. They seemed unable to understand why individuals, especially if they worked closely together and belonged to the same "brood," did not want to see each other during their sleeping and resting phases. It was self-evident there were neither secrets nor shame among their hosts, that nudity was nothing strange, and that when they closed their eyes for hours at a time, they were defenseless. Mutual learning about each other now began in detail, with every word and every drawing.

The ensuing hours were exhausting but had also ensured that at least only two people ever had to share a room. These "rooms" were created by setting up printed partitions in the large chamber pumped full of breathable atmosphere to create the desired privacy. Beds and sanitary facilities—that, too, had been incomprehensible to the Clicks—were to follow later while they deliberated. Silly wondered how much time she would have saved in her life if she had been at home in the water, where everything washed itself.

The friendly but noticeable pressure from the aliens to begin consultations eventually made them nervous. It also induced Ambassador Angsk to abandon the planned protocol, which would have included a lengthy acclimation, a tour of the habitat, and plenty of diplomatic banter, and agree to begin immediately.

Now they sat in their windowless, specially adjusted chamber. On the other side of the table were two tanks filled with a green, viscous-looking liquid. They looked like what Jason had told her about his experiences on the Click shuttle and had eloquently recorded in his report. Four aliens were lined up across from them, sitting on uncomfortable-looking hooks that had extended from the ceiling.

One of the Clicks, however, remained standing and spread his long arms. Robotic arms emerged from the ceiling and lifted him over one of the tanks, which opened. Amazed, Silly and the six members of the delegation watched as the machine stripped the

*The last Battleship*

alien of its armor and long hoses siphoned off fluids. It was not the first time for some of them, and yet the sight of the "naked" alien caused murmurs and whispers that even the most seasoned diplomats could not avoid. The Clicks' armor had always made Silly think they must be squat, powerful robots, optimized for combat, with their four legs and multiple joints. Her second theory had been that they came from extremely massive planets, which was why they were so robust and stout.

The truth couldn't have been further from the truth. They had slender, almost scrawny, legs with two knee joints and claws splayed backward, which were obviously not optimized for walking so they had to have other functions. Their arms were equally thin and long with three fingers, a short, voluminous torso with gills and a rather large V-shaped head. It lacked a mouth but had two nostrils, neck gills that constantly fluttered, and holes about where human ears would be located. The eyes were as big as pears and pitch black, with the glow of whole galaxies in them. But the most fascinating thing was their translucent skin, which was so transparent that a whole palette of bright colors could be seen, constantly changing, beneath it.

"My goodness," she blurted. *I don't know whether to think they're ugly or beautiful.* Realizing that she had spoken aloud, she cleared her throat a bit bashfully, only to find that no one seemed to have noticed.

Everyone stared at the alien as it was gently lowered into the tank by the robotic arms. There it floated in the liquid and closed its eyes as if it felt extremely comfortable.

The Click next to him took out his own holo-board and began drawing on it with a clawed finger. When he was done, he pushed the hologram toward the ambassador.

Thekarius Angsk was a tall man from the core world of Kent. He was fastidiously groomed with shaved-out gray temples, an undercut, and short black curls combed to one side. His glasses were both fashion and statement—no Federation citizen needed visual aids. His chiseled face was that of an eighty-year-old, high-ranking official who had seen a lot, and the esteem of the highest levels of decision-makers was written all over his features. His distant Irish accent, typical of Kent, completed his authoritarian but also sympathetic, almost magnetic aura.

"I think he wants me to get into that tank," Angsk said in extended syllables and with the well-controlled voice of a man who had learned for decades to weigh each word before it left his mouth. There was no indication whether he approved of the proposal or not, but his hesitation was enough for Silly to believe he was not eager to submerge himself in a vat of green alien liquid. She knew for sure, anyway, that she wouldn't even stick her pinky finger in that soup.

"Jason Bradley did it, and he's been hell-bent on jumping back in as fast as he can ever since," she said. "So, it didn't kill him, anyway."

Angsk gave her a sideways glance, then pushed back the hologram and nodded to his Click counterpart. He tightened his tight-fitting pressure suit and stood.

"All right, then. I guess diplomacy requires it." The envoy circled the table and one of the Clicks maneuvered him behind the vacant tank and, with strange gestures, told him to undress—at least that's what Silly believed. When Angsk, surprisingly, undressed without apparent shame, the alien seemed satisfied and ceased his confused arm movements.

While she was still inwardly praising the diplomat for his restraint, he was being lifted by four robotic arms and lowered into the second tank. She wondered how many of these things were hidden in the ceiling. Had the Clicks pushed the tanks into exactly the right position so they could be deployed like this? Or was there something like rails in the ceiling on which the machines moved back and forth? Or maybe it was some kind of morphing nanotechnology, like the Changedust the Federation had been researching for several decades.

Angsk slipped into the green liquid after one of the robo-arms pulled a breathing apparatus over his mouth and he took a few moments to orient himself. At first, he moved back and forth, repeatedly bumping the glass, until he stopped all movement and began to float right in the center as if by magic. He blinked several times, opened his eyes slightly and became still, then he opened them wide.

"What's going on?" one of his emissaries asked, looking around with growing panic. "Is he choking? He's choking!"

"I-I'm fine."

Thekarius Angsk's somewhat scratchy voice echoed from speakers Silly assumed were under the table. It was a little disconcerting because the person speaking was floating in a glass tank. But the Clicks had gone to some lengths to build devices that matched their acoustic frequencies and worked really well. All at once it struck her how complicated the whole situation was. Just a few weeks ago, this would have been the last place in the universe she wanted to be, sitting unarmed across from three rather scary-looking aliens would have made her wet her pants—in the most soldierly fashion, of course. Now, here she was, part of a diplomatic delegation, inwardly congratulating her hosts on having recreated a piece of human technology in such a short time and in such good quality.

"Can you hear us, Ambassador?" one of the emissaries asked with barely concealed concern.

"Yes, I can hear you. This is... I'm rarely at a loss for words, but this is simply incredible." Angsk's eyes wandered to the right, where the Click—he or she?—floated in the neighboring tank. It was clearly smaller and much more delicate than the man. "So much. There's so much."

"So much what?"

Angsk didn't answer and instead shoved a hand at the glass toward the alien, who did the same with one of his—or her?—three-fingered hands.

"Ambassador?" the emissary asked a little louder. "Can you hear me?"

"Yes. Gentle Wave to the Above World, here, is acting as the spokeswoman for this world's Broodmother and a star listener," the ambassador explained.

"A *what*?" Silly gasped in confusion.

"Something like our intelligence service, but without military association. It's hard to explain. In any case, it is responsible for remote reconnaissance and at the same time for linking military, civilian, and research Clicks—the reality assessors. That's the best conceptual equivalent for scientists that I can think of. I wish you could all see what I see, connect with this being and understand it as I understand it, be understood by it as I understand her, and she understands me. All our banter, our words and gestures... How limited. How simple-minded, how *sad*."

Silly exchanged a glance with the brunette emissary.

*Yep, sounds just like Jason in his report and his frenetic stories,* she thought.

"Mr. Ambassador," she said aloud. "I find this very intriguing, and I'm sure your staff will enjoy it as well, but I think we have important issues to discuss that affect both of our species."

"Of course, Captain Thurnau, you're right," he relented and turned back to them. You couldn't see his mouth move as he spoke, since the breathing apparatus obscured most of the lower half of his face. "I'll translate what Gentle Wave is thinking, then we can go from there."

Angsk paused, then continued speaking, "She wishes to welcome you all and thank you for coming here to build and deepen peaceful relations with the Water People of Warm Depths. On behalf of her broodmother, Optimistic Broodmother, Egg-laying Importance, Beautiful Brightness Ray, she desires us to feel comfortable and safe here and asks that you express any wishes you may have so she can respond to them. It is a great challenge for her, and everyone involved in this project to host aliens from another habitat in a species-appropriate manner. Our assistance is therefore greatly appreciated."

"Uh, thanks," Silly said when no one else stirred and sat back a bit in her uncomfortable chair. "I have no idea how this telepathy works, but I've studied Lieutenant Commander Jason Bradley's report on his interaction with the Broodmother in detail and talked to him a lot. Isn't it true that Gentle Wave knows everything you know at this moment anyway, Ambassador? Everything about your mission, your orders, planned tactics, and so on?"

"Yes. That is correct," Angsk stated with surprising lightheartedness. "This will make our mission much easier, and we can have a

*The last Battleship*

long-term peace and cooperation treaty in place in as soon as an hour."

"What, that fast?" a diplomat asked, puzzled. "But Ambassador, we—"

"I know everything that Gentle Wave knows, and she knows everything I know. Our thoughts and memories have merged. It's hard to explain, but it's all there. The Water People would like to trade with us in various fields, exchange technology, and conduct deep space exploration together for the best use of oceanic and rocky planets that best benefit our respective species. They wish to abolish strict borders and are willing to help establish a system of mutual surveillance and security to ensure peace that satisfies both of our hegemonies. They are also willing to help us fight Species X, which to them are something like nightmare creatures or hell elementals."

"That's... that's..." another emissary stammered speechlessly. "That's amazing!"

"Gentle Wave, however, has more information that she would like to share because there is a high-ranking military officer present right now." Angsk fixed Silly with his gaze and his mask moved before his voice came from the speakers. "It is extremely urgent, and we must act immediately."

Silly narrowed her eyes to slits and felt her fingertips begin to tingle as if they were electrified. Even before the ambassador continued, she was typing commands on her forearm display.

"To understand what this is about, I need to explain something I saw in her: The Water People of Warm Depths have been researching the nature of subspace and its inhabitants since they discovered 'Species X,' as we have christened the demons from hyperspace."

"Wait," Silly interrupted him in surprise. "Did you just say, *inhabitants*?"

"Yes. The Water People have come to believe that they are not living beings by our baryonic standards, but entities of another dimension that 'live' in hyperspace, if one can call it that. They only manifest themselves in baryonic mass—material bodies—when they enter our four normal dimensions," Angsk explained.

"Wait a minute. Are you saying we've been fighting phantoms? Been slaughtered by ghosts?" Silly had read Devlin Myers's reports of his alleged experiences aboard the abandoned *Danube* and what the sensor data from Atlantis had shown on Lagunia, but she honestly hadn't been convinced for a second that the pirate was telling the truth. Rather, it seemed as if his imagination had run away with him, or his desire to make a big impression. That nutty criminal couldn't have been right after all.

*Right?*

"I'm afraid it's true. Getting to our space requires a stable hyperspace link, which is a transition of sorts."

"And what if our ships jump through hyperspace?"

"They don't know for sure, but there are indications that the transition is too short to provide a channel through which Species X can manifest among us."

"Wait a minute," one of the emissaries interjected. She looked very pale. "Are these... *monsters* the reason why sleeping transit travelers fall into comas and never wake up?"

"Transit sleep," Silly whispered at Angsk in his tank. "Of course!"

"Yes. The Water People know *that* very well. Unlike us, they are in constant communication with each other when both awake and asleep. When the first cases of transit sleep occurred among them, in the early days of their EITEG technology, the survivors became direct witnesses to the deaths of their comrades. Those who sleep during the jump are *seen* by the hyperspace entities and their soul is killed. There is a brief moment during transit when the 'spirit,' as the Water People call it, touches the realm of hyperspace separated from the body. This happens every night when we sleep, but the jump through their dimension takes the unprotected spirit directly through their territory and they attack any intruder. Always," Angsk said sadly.

Silly tried to forget the tiny pangs of depression and inner emptiness she felt with each jump. It was so brief that she had paid no attention to it, just like every crewman in the Fleet. The thought that she'd had ghosts of another dimension in her head every time she jumped, trying to mentally rape or even kill her, made her shudder. Judging by the sudden silence and consternation of the others on her side of the table, they felt as she did.

"The Water People's research cost many lives, but it has yielded many insights. For example, they have sensors that can measure the phase shifts that emanate from activated hyperspace portals, fluctuations that disturb all of quantum space. It's also how they recorded the first test of an experimental gate on Harbingen's moon Kor, which was, fortunately, short enough that Species X couldn't send ships through."

"*Fortunately*," Silly murmured grimly. "Kor was destroyed anyway."

"I know. But the Water People had to prevent the nightmare elementals from entering our world again at all costs."

Again, a biting retort came to her lips, but she kept it to herself. She was anything but diplomatic, and Nicholas would surely have scolded her for it.

"What I'm getting at is this: four hours ago, a massive quantum fluctuation was detected in the Sagittarius-Carina Arm," Angsk's echoing voice continued from the speakers.

"A hyperspace gate in the adjacent spiral arm?"

"Yes."

"Another alien civilization?" an emissary asked.

"Possibly. Or maybe not," the ambassador refused to commit himself. "Because that's not all. Also, four hours ago, our hosts' long-range reconnaissance recorded an unknown ship signature jumping into the system at S2."

Silly stiffened but said nothing, though a thousand questions were on the tip of her tongue.

"The signature doesn't match any of our known models, even if it roughly resembles a Broadsword. But more worrisome is the fact that the ship didn't jump here from any neighboring system. Every neighboring system to Attila is guarded by at least two listening posts and military installations of the Water People, and none has reported an alien ship, let alone a transit."

"Impossible," Silly finally snapped. "Jumps across multiple systems are impossible."

"And yet it has happened."

"You think it's related to the activation of a hyperspace gate in the Sagittarius-Carina Arm?" she asked, stating the obvious.

"Yes. I believe it, and the Water People believe it."

"But that would mean someone going through a gate to a jump point where there is no exit gate. How is that possible?"

"They don't know. But I took the liberty of looking at the alignment of the phase antenna on the fragment of Kor as seen on the *Quantum Bitch*'s sensor images. It was pointed cosmically very precisely at where the quantum fluctuation was recorded," Angsk said.

"The Exiles," Silly breathed in horror. "But why are they sending a ship here?"

Of course, she already knew the answer to that.

She had jumped up and started screaming into her forearm display even before the pain from her knees slamming into the too-low tabletop had had time to penetrate her consciousness.

# 28

Grand Admiral Gotthold von Borningen stood on the bridge of the HS *Hohenzollern* and shook off his transit frost. The red combat lighting sent an imaginary warmth through the elliptical room. At its center was the large command deck surrounded by three tiers for the specialists of the various ship departments who held the threads of the *Hohenzollern* in their hands.

"Transit successful, Admiral," his XO, Captain Oliver Branson reported on the other side of the hologram that displayed a simple representation of their ship in empty space.

"Deploy sensors, obtain transit reports from the fleet," he ordered automatically, looking to his brother who stood beside him in the rather plain dress uniform of the first high lord of Harbingen. His hands were clasped behind his back and his gaze was fixed intently on the hologram as if he could see something in it that remained hidden from Gotthold. Ludwig von Borningen was nearly 100 years old but possessed the ageless appearance of someone who had been treated early on with the most advanced rejuvenation treatments available in the Federation. The gray temples were therefore more a conscious symbol of his age than a sign of advanced melanin deficiency in his hair roots. His eagle face was focused and controlled in the face of the great moment they had anticipated for over twenty years.

"How long?" Ludwig asked simply.

"Six hours until all ships are through."

"That's a long time."

"Yes," Gotthold agreed with his brother. "But the gates' cloaking devices eat a lot of energy. That not only costs us a lot of ships but also keeps energy away from the event horizon. We simply cannot risk a larger diameter without attracting them."

"I understand."

"We still have the option to change that strategy."

"No!" the First High Lord said immediately. "We are here to do the right thing and to do it with our own hands."

"It wasn't that way when our brothers and sisters prevented the gates from being shut down in the Federation," Gotthold said.

Ludwig waved dismissively. "That was due to necessity and therefore not an offense. The morally reprehensible thing is whatever one could have prevented."

"Admiral, High Lord," his XO spoke up. "We have the first sensor images."

"First the transit reports."

"Of course. Sixty-four ships have reported successful transits, four are currently coming through the event horizon."

"Very good. Now the sensor reports. On screen!" Gotthold ordered. Slowly, the hologram filled with radar contacts in the distance and lidar scans closer to their fleet, which continued to grow every five minutes. They were above the ecliptic behind the gas giant P3X-888 on the inner edge of the outer Attila system, which was separated from the inner system by a wide asteroid belt. The enemy's home world was a pale blue ball, tiny against the brilliant F4 star beyond. It was surrounded, as expected, by military installations and defense platforms that seemed nowhere near as sprawling as those around Terra, but they were still formidable.

Not that it made any difference. They were more than adequately prepared for it.

"The enemy has just over 4,000 warships, mostly concentrated around Attila itself. Here at S2, we destroyed two space stations and forty-two ships with our advance guard, and lost eighty-two ships," Captain Branson reported.

That was slightly fewer losses than Gotthold had projected.

*The last Battleship*

Good. Even with the element of surprise of multiple simultaneous transits, jumping out of an event horizon always placed the arrivals at a disadvantage since they lacked sensor imagery or targeting, while the defenders merely had to shoot at them. "More will probably follow. They've already sent ships through S1."

"What's that?" Gotthold frowned and stuck his index finger into the hologram, directly at a yellow-marked dot that appeared to be stuck directly to a space station above Attila. The lights of the command deck flickered when his finger interrupted the photon stream as if they were complaining.

"A signature that our onboard computer has identified as Terran Federation ship with a ninety-one percent probability, Admiral."

"How is that possible?"

Ludwig also leaned forward and furrowed his eyebrows.

"I don't know, sir, but according to the databases, the radar silhouette resembles a *Trafalgar*-class guided-missile destroyer."

"Resembles?"

"There are variations in the hard points, especially at the bow section," the XO explained. "But the similarities are great enough that it could be a conversion or further development."

"What's a Federation ship doing in the middle of the enemy's hive?" Gotthold murmured, knowing full well none of them would know the answer. "A single one at that."

"Prisoners, perhaps?" Branson suggested. "Perhaps the Clicks have succeeded in taking control of a ship. It would make sense to bring it here and take it apart to wrest its secrets from it."

"Possibly," the high lord said. "I suppose we'll find out soon enough. Have the ships fan out and stand by to destroy anything they encounter in the outer system. I don't want any hidden units posing a threat to our gate."

"Of course." Gotthold inclined his head and waved to his XO to relay the appropriate orders.

The hyperspace gate their brothers and sisters had built and brought here in six self-flying parts was considerably smaller than the one their agents had discovered back in the depths of Lagunia. Camouflage field generators clamped onto the components like the brake shoes of a car and sent out quantum distortion fields that kept hyperspace beings from seeing them and manifesting. Stealth coatings and radar-deflecting surface forms ensured that even their local enemies would have a hard time finding the gate itself. Sooner or later, they would figure it out, but by then it would be far too late. His brother's order was still the right one, he would have done the same. They should not risk anything that put a knife in their backs because they had neglected to guard against it.

"Good, then it is now time to complete the formalities." High Lord Ludwig von Borningen nodded at him, and Gotthold signaled to communications.

"System-wide broadcast, all frequencies!" Lieutenant Jameson reported from the tiers.

Of course, the aliens would not understand them unless there had been a communications breakthrough in the last two decades. Gotthold thought it extremely unlikely, but formalities were formalities and without them they would be nothing more than animals or AI worshippers.

"This is High Lord Ludwig von Borningen speaking on behalf of the Harbinger Exile Command. You are guilty of crimes against humanity and are ordered to lay down your arms. Shut down all reactor cores on your ships and cease all traffic within the system. Any spacecraft that does not comply with these instructions will be destroyed. You have two minutes."

Gotthold nodded and set the timer for 120 seconds. No one expected an answer, but a commitment was a commitment.

Surprisingly, they got a response.

"High Lord, Grand Admiral," Jameson said with unmistakable irritation. "We're receiving an incoming transmission."

"From the Clicks?" Gotthold asked in astonishment.

"No, sir, from the guided-missile destroyer. According to the transponder code, it is the *Saratoga*. It is sending an unknown authentication code, but it has Terran Fleet markers."

"This could be an attempt to attack our databases," Branson warned, scowling.

"Disable jammers," Ludwig ordered.

"Brother, this is a risk. If this is malicious code that is more advanced than we assume, then I can't guarantee that—"

The First High Lord calmly interrupted him. "Our firewalls are multiply redundant, right?"

"Yes, already—"

"Good. If we detect malicious code, we shut down the system and reboot, that should solve all the problems, right?"

"Yes, but—"

"It will be several hours before any significant enemy forces can reach us. How long does a reboot take to get us back to full operational capability? Jameson?"

"About ten minutes, High Lord," the young officer replied from the tier behind them. Ludwig looked at his brother and raised an eyebrow.

"More than enough, I think. We have given them an ultimatum, so we must be able to accept an answer. This risk is necessary and acceptable. But... you are in military command of this operation."

Gotthold nodded and said, "Open the channel."

At first, there was just an ugly scratching sound that made everyone on the bridge flinch. Then came a voice that seemed driven by adrenaline and was repeatedly interrupted by bursts of fire and screams of men.

"This is Captain Silvea Thurnau of the *Saratoga*. I don't know what you devils have done and especially *how*, but we were able to free ourselves and have taken two of the alien bastards hostage. We are now trying to get into their—"

The message was interrupted by static, cracking sounds, followed by silence.

"Silvea Thurnau?" Branson asked with a furrowed brow. "*The* Silvea Thurnau?"

"Voice pattern analysis calculates a ninety-seven percent probability that it's her, based on the old Fleet databases we were able to extract from Harbingen before we left," Lieutenant Usher reported from Cyber Defense.

"What is Admiral Bradley's XO doing on a Terran Fleet ship?" Gotthold asked no one in particular.

"As a ship commander," his own XO added.

"That makes no sense," Ludwig said, staring thoughtfully at the hologram. "Clicks don't usually take prisoners, and every Federation officer is under orders not to fall into enemy hands, and that applies especially to hardware."

"At least it was that way more than two decades ago," Gotthold objected. "A lot of time for things to change."

"But not that much."

Branson chewed thoughtfully on his thin lower lip. "Or maybe she was part of a diplomatic detachment we just blew up. I wouldn't be surprised if our arrival at a bad time led the aliens to suspect a breach of trust or something of that sort."

"Silvea Thurnau as part of a diplomatic mission?" Ludwig didn't snort, but he was quite capable of expressing disbelief without it. "That woman is a sharp axe, and the only hands that know how to wield it, lest she become the proverbial axe in the woods, are Konrad Bradley's—or were."

"Granted, but again, much may have changed, especially with the death of her mentor," Gotthold said, and his XO nodded gratefully. "I'm sure we all expected that after Bradley's death she would have killed herself with either alcohol or a rope instead of moving on. Now she's here."

"That's a lot of unanswered questions and improbabilities," the high lord said.

"Grand Admiral," Jameson called excitedly from his station, "you should see this!"

"On screen."

The holographic situation image changed to show a real-world representation of Attila at a very high zoom level with the space station where the *Saratoga* was docked in the center. It consisted of a thickened spherical center section and two arms to the right and left. The guided-missile destroyer, quite battered and covered with battle damage, detached from the station and fired its thrusters and trailed a glowing plasma tail. After turning about, the plasma sliced into the hull of the Click structure like a circular lava saw. Composite burned to cinders and shredded as the forces holding the structure in orbit split it in two, ruthlessly tearing the rest apart.

Secondary explosions flared, illuminating the darkness in front of the pale planet.

A Click warship—a cruiser, if Gotthold read the designation correctly out of the corner of his eye—opened fire on the Federation destroyer, hitting it in the bow section. Pieces of armor flew into the vacuum under the kinetic force of the harpoons and gases escaped in long fountains that tossed the *Saratoga* about as if in a squall. Thurnau returned fire, but it was imprecise and compromised by the ship's unsteady attitude. Just as he feared the destroyer might be pulverized, another alien ship crossed the first's firing path, preventing it from firing any further.

"What are we seeing here?" Captain Branson asked incredulously.

"The *Saratoga* destroyed the space station it was docked to," Gotthold explained, checking off the facts—a habit he had cultivated since his academy days on Harbingen to put his thoughts in order whenever something completely unplanned happened. "Now she's trying to break out and for some reason not all the Clicks want her destroyed."

"And what do you make of that, Grand Admiral?" his brother asked, looking at him expectantly.

"This could be confirmation that she does have hostages on board and that they are quite high-level."

"*Could.*"

"Yes. *Could.*"

"What course of action do you suggest?" Ludwig asked, but Gotthold could see that his brother already had an idea of his own. Still, he was the commander of this ship and commander-in-chief of the fleet and could insist on providing an overview first before making his final proposal. Yet, he was under no illusions. Even though he was formally in command, everyone, including himself, knew who was really in charge here.

"It will take us about twenty hours to finish bringing all 6,500 ships here. The entire might of our Exile Command Fleet will be enough to shatter the heart of the enemy once and for all and end this war and free humanity, something the weak Federation has never been able to do.

"But Thurnau is an intangible, unforeseen element and I don't like that. At the same time, we are here to lead humanity into a new era, and that will mean acting like an authority that can and does assert a claim of leadership over all citizens of the current Federation, both morally and in fact. Moreover, we are dealing with only one ship, which is not in a good situation. Therefore, I suggest we obtain proof of the Click hostages. Should we get hold of two live specimens, or even dead ones, it would be a great help for our researchers. After all, this strike alone may not end the war. At least not immediately. But we need proof... if the *Saratoga* can make it to us."

## 29

"What a pile of shit!" Dev cursed with a pained expression. "Why is everything here so shitty? And when it isn't completely shitty, someone puts a fucking fan in front of our faces and shits into it until our faces are covered with it."

He saw Willy and Aura give each other rather embarrassed looks, which only made him angrier.

"Now don't act like I'm fucking overreacting!"

"Boss, of course, it's a problem, but all it means is that our plan changes a bit," his energy node specialist said from her seat next to him.

"And we get something on top of it," the flight engineer added.

"Since when did we become the fucking Salvation Army? Is there some memo I haven't seen that says 'Devlin Myers and his pile of despised pirates have earned merit as selfless members of the Human Alliance of Do-Gooders and recommend themselves for whatever dirty job comes to mind for our all-beloved Fleet'? Show it to me!"

"Well, strictly speaking, we saved the Federation's ass," Willy said.

"No, we just told it why it's screwed," Dev corrected him glumly.

"Dunkelheim's obviously not screwed," Aura objected and pointed forward. Outside the cockpit window, they could see the faint glimmer of the fringe world they were approaching from the system's S2. It was strange to come here, to Willy's home, and be met by four "warships." Previously, there had only been a simple listening post with four local space control personnel to interrogate their transponder codes and enter them into the registry, which was required under Federation law.

"Fringe worlds never really belonged to the Federation either," Dev grumbled. "But when more valuable resources than expected were suddenly discovered, then all the damn locust syndicates would come and buy everything up and shit all over it with their credits until no one could breathe."

"Well, that might change."

He looked at Willy with wide eyes. "*You've* become the optimist now?"

"This is my home, Dev." The hunky engineer shrugged his mighty shoulders. For a moment, he looked like a pouting child in the body of a giant. "No matter how crappy it is here—growing up in a tunnel that constantly smells like beer or sewage isn't exactly nice—a part of me is always here. If the courier is right, then this is *the* chance to do something for my world."

"There's no guarantee!" Dev shouted. "It's just the brainchild of a Fleet officer with a stick up his ass and his beloved code monster named Omega. If I may remind you, it's the same guy who got on our nerves and treated us like pirates on our last trip to Lagunia before this new war started."

"He did his job pretty well. That's why you can't stand him," Aura said, and he gave her a nasty look.

"That's true, but it's still a shitty idea."

"Look at it this way," Willy suggested, "we can try to profit now from the demise of the fringe worlds. Without the core worlds, they might last another ten, twenty, or maybe even thirty years without the supplies of protein mash and vitamin cans. Then we die along with them, patting ourselves on the back for having bravely carried on while the rest were annihilated or degenerated into some dystopia under the iron rule of a dictator."

"And that's still the 'good' ending of the story," Aura added. "The more likely one is that the fringe worlds will also be subju-

*The last Battleship*

gated, and then it won't matter that they've upgraded to defend themselves."

"Let's face it, boss," Willy said gratefully following Aura's lead, "it's never happened before that several fringe worlds have set up their own fleet, however improvised and lacking in significant ammunition supplies. These ships are clearly better used as symbols than real weapons to stand up to new rulers."

"Hah!" Dev waved off. "Explain that to the chancellor!"

"I plan to, but in order to do that, I once again have to convince you not to do what we'd really prefer but to do 'the right thing.'"

"I don't know what 'the right thing' is," Dev grumbled, rubbing his temples. "What did it get us last time? We were used and lied to and had the *Bitch* stolen from us."

"Only for a short time," Aura objected.

"Still!" he roared angrily. "She's *my* damned ship!"

"Well," Willy spoke up again, "they also made sure our *Bitch* would still exist in the first place. New reactors—"

"One of which is already gone..."

"—new weapons, complete hull repairs, two kilometers of superconductors, improved onboard systems, nanite mass for the maintenance lacunae, new high-performance radiators, a patched-up drive nacelle—I could go on like this for quite a long time because I supervised the installation of all that wickedly expensive stuff," the Dunkelheimer continued unperturbed. "You don't just ignore a gift like that, no matter how much you despise your benefactor."

"We were supposed to take a bomb to Harbingen for them, and we did," Dev said stubbornly.

"You know their secrecy had a purpose."

"I don't care what 'had a purpose' from their point of view. They used us like a fucking tool—"

"—and then let us escape, knowing full well that it meant their death because they didn't have a return ticket."

"That's why I let you nitwits talk me into evacuating the bastards after all!"

"And look what it got us. We were set free after getting a complete overhaul and are now in decent standing with the Federation's most powerful warship and its crew," Willy chimed in. Aura nodded with increasing vigor.

"Just think about what the Harbingers' offer—the *real* Harbingers, I mean—could mean for us if it works," she said.

"*If* it weren't for *if* I'd be a millionaire by now," Dev quoted with a snort.

"You've always been a gambler. You don't shy away from risk when the reward is high enough." Aura was undeterred. "Why should it be any different now? Why settle for passively watching the fate of the Federation—of humanity—be decided and then living with the outcome when we've been offered a front-row seat? All it'll take is a visit to Willy's dirt ball of a planet and a little diplomatic skill."

"It wasn't that long ago you guys were trying to talk me out of doing the right thing," Dev lamented, "and now look at you."

"Sometimes it takes a little time for us to follow your lead," Jezzy broke in as she floated into the cockpit. "Did I miss anything?"

"No," he grumbled and waved at Aura. "Set course for Dunkelheim."

He didn't need eyes in the back of his head to know that his crew was both relieved and triumphant. He would remind them of it when they were about to be torn apart by missiles under an alien sky.

*Let them have this moment.*

Dev had only visited Dunkelheim once before, to take on a load of gargantua wood. He had sold it at an almost criminal profit in Kent before the core worlds had become taboo for them and half the fleet began looking for them. He had almost no recollection of that day almost ten years ago because he had let Willy talk him into playing a Dunkelheim drinking game the day before, something he would never do again. No matter what kind of flight of nostalgia might seize his flight engineer this time, he was determined to not leave the cockpit. He faintly recalled a spaceport among the huge trees that grew up to two or three kilometers high and looked terrifying. The rest consisted of unreal memories of his breathing mask, itchy rashes, and dark caves.

*The last Battleship*

More interesting were the portrayals of Dunkelheim in the countless movies from New Manhattan's dream factories. They presented its inhabitants as barbaric but chummy sidekicks with nutty quirks, and their planet as a kind of forecourt to hell, where the craziest action sets could be filmed. They were, of course, created entirely on a computer and had almost nothing to do with the real fringe world. At least he had never heard that Willy's compatriots flew on blue flying dinosaurs through shining tree landscapes and fought against green aliens, while below on the forest floor, women and children weaved raffia baskets and ran around in loincloths.

The system was poor because the only asteroid belt was very far out, far from Dunkelheim, and so the first steps toward profitable vacuum mining were subject to a major initial hurdle that had never been cleared. Thus, the space industry was limited to the green-stained rum ball's four moons. They were not enormous satellites that resembled planets, but rather shapeless lumps like Mars's moons Phobos and Deimos, which looked more like large asteroids than real moons. The foreign currency, Dunkelheim's second strongest source of income—after the most popular beer in the Federation—the Spiked Helmet Regiment had brought into the local economy, after their invasion of the fringe world Grande Kahul, had promoted industrial development at that time and supplied the planet with important raw materials like palladium and gold, which did not occur there in large quantities.

In orbit, Dev found things had clearly changed. There was a fleet of 400 ships, mainly transporters for the Spiked Helmet Regiment, officially called MET-3000, although no one used the term. Its escort ships were armed to the teeth and equipped with the maximum—and probably far more—allowed to private ship owners operating under appropriate licenses. But many were also from other worlds: Gotha and Scrapa, as well as Kitami. Judging by their signatures, they did not adhere to any of the Federation's weapons ban laws.

The only space stations belonged to local space control, the king, his parliament, and the mercenary company that organized shipping and rearmament. In addition, there were a few hundred satellites that appeared as small radar contacts but were puny compared to a core world or more developed fringe worlds, like a tidy room with only a handful of toys lying around.

Willy took over communications with space control after Dev gave him the signal, which resulted in a long, coarse gush of Dunkelheimer Masematte, the local language dialect that was a crude mixture of German, Czech, and Dutch. It sounded more like Klingons arguing than a normal request for permission to land, but in the end, Willy was satisfied and gave Dev a thumbs up.

"We're getting an audience with King Gustav," the engineer said, gloating with a broad grin.

"I'm sorry, what?" Dev blinked in confusion. "How did you do that?"

"Well, how do you think? I made big promises!"

"And what kind of promises?"

"Ah... tell you in a minute. What matters is we've got a landing permit and are nearing our goal with rapid strides." Willy waved and slumped back in his seat. "Isn't that nice?"

"What?"

He pointed out the cockpit window. "Dunkelheim!"

Dev thought the hazy brown-green disk could only appeal to a local, but at least it might be fascinatingly beautiful under the thin layer of clouds—although fatally toxic. Before he could ask more questions, he got clearance from space control.

"*Quantum Bitch*, you're clear to land. Follow the two fighters and don't deviate from your course or we'll shoot you down."

"Roger that," Dev sighed and scowled at Willy, who didn't seem to notice and just stared out the cockpit window in satisfaction.

Dev shook his head and followed the two small space fighters with their stubby wings into the atmosphere. The *Bitch* bucked and strained against the resistance of the compacted gas molecules until she dropped toward the clouds, a thin layer that enveloped the entire planet, hazy and beige, but not thick enough to hide the surface.

As soon as they penetrated the cloud cover—it was barely twenty meters thick—the colors virtually exploded. Dense forests as

*The last Battleship*

far as the eye could see painted a fascinating picture of earthy brown and lush green that alternated between branches and the man-sized leaves that merged far up in the sea of flora. There was a mighty mountain massif in the north that pushed out of the landscape and above the vegetation line, reaching twenty-three kilometers in height at its peak with a circular area at its base. Aside from that, everything was covered with the characteristic gargantuas from horizon to horizon. The cleared area, which immediately stood out as unnatural amid a wild world bereft of any outward signs of habitation, was obviously their destination and Dunkelheim's only spaceport, as far as he knew. At 500 meters in diameter, it was not particularly impressive nor large enough to allow aircraft to take off that did not have VTOL capabilities, but it was to the locals' credit that they had managed to wrest any kind of space from the giant trees at all.

As soon as they set down and the two fighters left them—probably due to the four ground-to-air batteries that were trained on them from under cover of the shade at the edge of the forest—he could make out more details in the featureless, granite-colored clearing. There was a small terminal building made of gargantua wood, supposedly harder than steel, built between four trees and surrounded by sharpened stakes like an archaic settlement from pre-civilized times. Red lights were embedded in the leveled stone floor that directed them to the first of four landing pads divided by slots that presumably concealed underground hangars. Security personnel drove up on two cargo sleds as soon as Dev set down the landing gear, followed by a cart with a helium-3 tank and a long filler neck.

"Almost like a normal spaceport," he said and shut down the systems one by one with the toggle switches on his console. The background hum of thrusters and computers gradually died away until it was silent. "Well, let's see what we can accomplish here."

Dev followed an unusually excited Willy into the corridor and waited until everyone had donned their spacesuits and sealed their helmets, except for their Dunkelheimer, who no longer had enough skin to react to any toxin. Then they stepped out onto the extended ramp under the bow into the planet's air. It was moist at nearly 90 percent humidity, as his forearm display told him. In addition, he immediately noticed the unmistakable rustle of the gargantua leaves that stretched up to three kilometers into the air, blowing in the wind in layers of air of varying thickness. It was loud enough that his noise filters had to block out much of it.

Even though a delegation was coming toward them, Dev involuntarily paused to soak up the sheer magnitude of the spaceport's surroundings. Not even during their approach had he realized how enormous the trees were, which the Federation's first prospectors had rightly named *gargantua*. Their trunks were as thick as a Fleet frigate, and even the smallest branches had a girth thicker than an adult. He could have covered himself completely with a single lush, green leaf, and the shiny yellow pollen sheen they gave off was among one of the most beautiful things he had ever seen outside space. You would have thought he had landed in an animated fantasy where everything was a little sharper, glitterier, and softer. The intrusive red warning symbols in his visor that warned him of toxic components in the air he breathed did not fit in at all with his optical impression.

"May I point out that we're only here because an *Oberon* courier told us to be?" Dev grumbled as a dozen huge mercenaries dismounted from the cargo sleds rolling toward them. They were barely distinguishable as men or women, augmented to such an extreme that they rivaled even Dozer. Their eyes were chrome-plated, skin was swapped for dermal armor, gray and colorless, their muscles were full of tubes and valves that poked through the top layer of synthetic covering. They all held powerful weapons of completely differing types that looked equally homemade and rustic. Instead of complete helmet systems, they merely wore breathing tubes in their nostrils or air holes for those who apparently deemed a nose unnecessary.

"Doesn't mean they were wrong," Aura said over the radio.

"From their point of view, they're always right," he grumbled.

"Hello, uh, honored guests," someone greeted them in a loud voice over a speaker. Dev had not seen the short stocky man in a face mask who was struggling past the mercenaries of the Spiked Helmet Regiment with apologetic glances. He looked like a garden

*The last Battleship*

gnome amid bronze statues of Roman gladiators. His accented English was guttural and rumbling, reminiscent of a wooden cart bumping along a dirt road. "Welcome to Dunkelheim. My name is Gisbert Flosbach, and I may guide you today."

"Hi," Dev said simply. "Thank you for inviting me."

"But of course, of course." The spaceport controller began to cluck like a chicken. "King Gustav is already expecting you. Follow me. Ah, one more annoying thing, I'm afraid our security personnel will have to search you for weapons."

Dev shrugged and held his arms away from him. One mercenary, who was so large that Dev seemed an insect in comparison, roughly patted him down, took his Colt revolver from him, and grinned with amusement. He then ran a cyberware scanner over his entire body before nodding calmly in the direction of the officer. Once the procedure was repeated with the others, they were taken into the imposing wooden building. It contained two waiting areas, a security lock, and several unstaffed counters. The ambience of the facility reminded him of a very rustic version of an alpine hut—roughly built, but homey and quaint.

"If you don't mind my asking," he said as they climbed onto an open sled and glided down an elevator shaft past walls cut roughly into the rock, "is it always so easy to get an audience with the king?"

"So *easy?*" Gisbert Flosbach laughed harshly, and his impressive belly bobbed up and down. "He doesn't even receive Federation emissaries."

Dev exchanged a glance with Aura, who merely shook her head, perplexed, and then at Willy, who conspicuously avoided his gaze.

"Willy?" he asked threateningly. "What did you do?"

"I merely mentioned that we had a plan to help him achieve his goal."

"You did *what*? What goal would that be?"

"Well, a seat in the Jupiter Parliament, I guess. The thing all fringe worlds want, especially kings thirsting for prestige." Willy looked at Flosbach, who merely smiled meaningfully. Behind him, every two meters, small yellow lights whizzed past.

"Parliament will never agree to that," Dev said, shaking his head. "What makes you think we can help him do the impossible?"

"Or not get beheaded right now, for crying out loud!" Aura cursed angrily in Willy's direction.

"I said we had an ace up our sleeve that will change the Federation's mind if the presence of the fringe world's fleet at this historic moment weren't enough."

Dev no longer knew whether to be angry, horrified, or confused, and decided to go the route he had the most experience with. "Have you gone completely insane?"

At the same time, he began to puzzle out exactly what Willy could have promised the king. He had no idea what, of all things, they could accomplish in the coming battle.

When the elevator reached the bottom, they traveled several hundred more meters through a musty shaft and turned several times at intersections before arriving in a huge cavern. Two dozen more mercenaries of the Spiked Helmet Regiment were waiting there looking even grimmer and more inhuman than the ones they had already seen.

King Gustav was sitting at the far end of the cavern on an actual throne packed with electronics. A holo-image of the planet hovered in front of him, over which he was discussing and apparently issuing orders to several courtiers. Dev immediately had the impression they had arrived not at some aristocratic court, but at a gathering of mafia clan members who wanted to give the impression of royalty simply because it flattered them.

When the king noticed them, he shooed away his "court." Dev saw the man was anything but a joke and definitely more reminiscent of a sinister underworld boss than a politician and democratic ruler—which he was not.

"Who do we have here? Our ticket into the Federation's game of intrigue!" Gustav III shouted in a rumbling voice and beckoned them to approach. Dev's throat suddenly felt parched. "Come here and tell me why I'm spending my time with you. We don't want to have to hang anyone else in the mines for the Gnaggots." The monarch's uproarious laughter was joined by his mercenaries. Frighteningly expectant savagery emerged on their faces.

"Now we'd better give him something," Willy said. His nostalgia-driven love of home was beginning to fade.

"Have you met this man before?"

"No," the Dunkelheimer admitted. "I only know him from the VRs, but there he always came across as very... well, folksy."

"You don't say. It's not as if this is some damned dictator with a tame 'press'!" Dev hissed between clenched teeth before falling silent as the mercenaries shoved them inexorably toward the throne.

*You'd better think of something,* Dev, he said to himself. *Otherwise, you won't live long enough to hitch Willy to the back of the drive pod!*

## 30

"This is still insanity," Captain Mnuchin insisted as the *Saratoga* limped away from Attila toward the Exile fleet.

"Sometimes, what appears insane is the only basis for action," Silly replied, her eyes glued to the tactical system overview. The bridge crew was extremely calm, which was one more sign among the numerous others of high tension on the ship. No soldier liked to be thrown into a new situation without any mission planning or even a clear objective. It meant an entirely uncertain outcome. But Silly trusted her instincts, and they told her she had to go where the fire was to make a difference. "How far along are the modifications to the reactor?"

"The engineering team estimates three hours of work."

"Good, then we'll cut the power by 0.2 percent every five minutes from now on. That shouldn't be too noticeable and should line up with our upcoming report."

"After firing, you mean?" Mnuchin said with a distinct lack of enthusiasm.

"If you prefer, yes."

Silly felt like a rat running toward a pack of predatory cats in a carnival costume. Oddly enough, it had taken less than ten minutes to convince the Clicks that it was their only chance to buy time until the courier ships she had sent out—including the ambassador's three—could get reinforcements. Fortunately, she had already prepared appropriate instructions for the *Saratoga*'s best pilots by the time Angsk had translated the aliens' revelations. Her sharp nose at that moment had probably also allowed her to present her spontaneous ideas with confidence.

Their new alien allies had warned that it could take days for relief forces to arrive—too long to hold out against the Exiles if they continued pumping ships into the system at the same rate. Her suggestion that the Clicks attack immediately with everything they had to bring the jump point under their control and destroy anything that came through had been rejected. Although they saw the tactical necessity and the chances of victory would have been quite high, they were reluctant to leave their main breeding ground unprotected in case enemy ships also emerged from S1. The inexplicable appearance of humans from the Sagittarius-Carina Arm had unsettled them and raised questions about what else they could pull out of a hat. So, she had switched from rational mode to irrational and suggested that they feign a breakout by the *Saratoga* as if they had been prisoners and now had two hostages on board. The same thing had worked before with the Clicks, and the real thing wouldn't be implausible.

Would it?

In any case, they had agreed to conduct an emergency evacuation and sacrifice the transit station to give their plan a chance, although it wasn't clear what they could accomplish with that other than buy some time.

*If we can just do that, we'll already be a step ahead,* she thought. In any case, no one had been harmed, the diplomatic delegation, except for Angsk himself, had been taken to Attila, and the Click fleet had been informed of their feint. What would it be like for the aliens to fake something? If Jason could be believed, they did not even know the concept of lying. But they understood it—alien or not—and that was what mattered now. If not, it would only be a matter of time until their own allies vaporized them into atoms.

"The ship is moving into position," Mnuchin said. He seemed to have swallowed his annoyance and returned to his mode as a professional Fleet officer.

Silly saw it, too. Two Click cruisers had set out on an intercept course from different directions, according to plan. "The ship" was the one that had flown toward them from one of the docks. It had not joined the contracting mesh of the vast fleet and decided not to let the humans get away with their two hostages. The first projectile would narrowly miss her, a sort of shot across the bow, but the second and third were supposed to hit her drive section and fake irreparable reactor damage. In response, the other Click ship would intervene, warn the first, and then destroy it. The four crew on board had already taken escape pods off the ship.

It was a costly spectacle, even if the alien ship had come back from Sol badly damaged and would have been expensive to repair anyway—if the Clicks had any currency at all. For Silly, it was just more pressure for her impulse to deliver something that produced real results.

"When does it start?" Thekarius Angsk asked. Against her recommendation, the ambassador had uncerimoniously decided to take part in the action because he was convinced that, as a diplomat, he could contribute ideas or even talk to the other side to achieve something in case of doubt. In the end, she had consented and brought him along. Judging by his pale expression, he now doubted whether he had made the right decision, but he hadn't mentioned leaving the ship either—not that that was possible at this point.

"We'll see," she replied, glancing at the radar. "Communication with your new best friends is not exactly easy, as you know. We'll have to trust that our brief conversation in the space station was enough to make it go smoothly. If not, there's nothing we can do about it."

"Normally, to get precision and timing perfect, you would never do something like this without constant radio coordination after each step," Mnuchin added, glancing at Silly, but she pretended not to notice. She felt like arguing, as she usually did, but she didn't want to complicate the situation any further.

"I see," Angsk muttered.

"We're taking fire!" the Defense station in front of them reported.

"Execute evasive pattern," she ordered, and the *Saratoga* headed to port. The alien shot missed them by quite a bit. Two more shots registered, and shortly thereafter two blasts rocked the bridge, shaking them violently in their seats.

"Hull breaches!"

"I see it," Silly grumbled. The reactor area had indeed been hit, and a loss of pressure made it extremely uncomfortable for the technicians working there under high pressure. "Shit!"

"Medics to the reactor room," her XO ordered gruffly, "get repair bots out there!"

"Match speed, switch to drift phase, shut down reactor!" Silly said, joining the general commotion. The two Click ships began their apparent battle with each other and turned away from them. She turned to Mnuchin, "Give me a damage report as soon as it's available, I need to do some calculations!"

"Understood." He nodded and turned away.

Silly stood and walked to the navigation officer at the front left, grabbed the back of his seat, and motioned him to present his virtual display as a hologram above his console. They began to flesh out their plan with clear numbers and data to calculate how they needed to adjust speed and flight vector to get the best result for slowness and believability.

When she finished, Mnuchin was already waiting for her with the damage report. His expression was alarmingly grim.

"We lost four technicians, two of them engineers," he said with a scowl that contained no accusation, for which she gave him credit. "Due to a hull breach. It was probably bad luck. They hit an unrepaired spot between the last two cross-segments of the carbotanium plates and, in addition to the loss of our crewmen, destroyed one of the most important superconductor connections to the secondary combustion chamber in front of the drive nacelle, along with both redundancies."

"A damned fluke shot, of all times?" Silly growled angrily. "You've got to be kidding me!"

Mnuchin merely nodded.

"Send the best people we have left on board."

Her XO pointed to a young woman with shaved hair under her cap. "Lieutenant Cruz from damage control is a graduate of the engineering school." She sat in front of them at one of the consoles, making entries on a virtual display with her fingers. "But that would require her to leave her seat, and we don't currently have a replacement."

"Anyway, make it so. If we need damage control on our way in the next few hours or days, we're done anyway."

Mnuchin nodded again and went to speak with the officer.

"Captain?" Thekarius Angsk said.

She had almost forgotten him. She turned in his direction and raised a brow. It was strange to have seen the tie-wearer, a man she had initially thought to be quite conservative, naked in a tank of green goo, and now hear him speak in an agitated voice. It was as if her mind didn't know how exactly to regard him now—as an enigma in fine threads with undeniable avuncular charisma, or as a telepathy-addicted civilian aboard a warship struggling to maintain outward control as red combat lights flashed and an alarm blared. By now, Silly's mind automatically blanked out such things, or at least pushed them to the edge of her perception.

"Yes, Ambassador?" she asked with barely suppressed reluctance to deal with the civilian.

"I've been thinking about something. If you have time to listen right now?" He made a vague gesture that encompassed both her and the rest of the bridge crew.

As he did so, she was struck once again by how cramped and small it was here compared to *Oberon*, where the bridge was like a theater auditorium, complete with ascending tiers and no less than twenty specialists at the various system interfaces. Her first impulse was to brush him off, but she fought it down as she remembered what Konrad used to say: *Always follow your impulses, but never the first one.*

She took a deep breath and nodded promptly.

The ambassador spread his fingers and took a breath as well.

"We could try a diplomatic... well, feint."

"What exactly are you suggesting?" Silly's impatience grew again.

"A radio transmission. I have been in office long enough, so my name should still be familiar to the Exiles, at least to the senior officers who were involved in politics before they left Federation territory. My prediction is that Admiral Gotthold von Borningen, the high lord's brother, is leading this fleet. I know him personally. In my experience, he is a rational man with good manners." Angsk leaned closer to her. "I could ask them for rescue in exchange for help in the upcoming negotiations with the Federation. I'll play an anxious diplomat caught in the crossfire who only wants to save his skin. My political clout should be known to the von Borningens."

"Why would they even want to negotiate?" Silly asked gruffly.

Now the ambassador frowned and eyed her as if looking for signs of a joke.

"Captain, I thought that was obvious. The fact that the Exiles —apparently in response to a broadcast with up-to-date data from Harbingen on the state of the Federation—have presumably sent their entire fleet into the heart of enemy territory to carry out Operation Iron Hammer can only mean one thing: they want to subjugate the entire human hegemony."

"There are two things I don't understand about this assessment," she said, raising a finger. "First of all, if they have received so much data from the conspirators, they should also know that the war with the Clicks is over." She raised a second finger. "Second, if they want to subjugate the Federation, this is indeed an opportune time for them. But in that case, they could fly straight to Sol and take possession of its beating heart."

Thekarius Angsk shook his head.

"I don't think they know about our agreement with the Clicks, otherwise they wouldn't have come to attack here. Even before I left, our secret service assumed that the conspirators had withdrawn almost all, or maybe all, their agents from their covert positions or that their hired spies had stopped serving them as soon as payments ceased. And don't forget, for them it was their endgame. Moreover, von Borningen would not have chosen this target otherwise, so it is obviously based on outdated information, or at least incomplete information." He shook his head again. "No, I believe the Exiles are pursuing what they consider to be an extremely clever plan: to achieve what the Federation they despise has failed to accomplish in nearly a century, namely, to destroy humanity's archenemy and ensure peace through maximum strength. Let's face it, Captain, if

*The last Battleship*

they succeeded, the core worlds would be more than willing to submit to new leadership under the high lord... as long as the reins aren't too tight."

Silly considered the diplomat's assessment and nodded with increasing emphasis. This man was clearly smarter and more focused than she had given him credit for. Indeed, perhaps he was more than just an intellectual with the right friends in the right positions.

"Why else would he have made that long speech after they arrived, knowing full well that the Clicks could not understand a word of it?" Angsk seemed to believe he had not yet convinced her. "All of that was meant only for the Federation and its citizens, the ruling elites of the core worlds—at least the few that still exist. I bet we'll shortly pick up a public broadcast from them where they casually mention that they have technology that makes them immune to Species X or something like that."

Silly raised an eyebrow, and he raised his hands.

"How else could they jump out of a hyperspace gate without those aliens—those demons—coming out first?"

"We don't even know for sure if there's a hyperspace gate at S2," she said. "Even though I think it's likely, before you remind me that I made that very same argument to promote my plan."

"If there isn't one, we might have a much bigger problem."

"Well, what story do you want to tell the enemy?"

"That's a bit more complex, but basically, it's this: I offer, as I mentioned, to take their side, the winning side, so to speak. Opportunistic behavior is often attributed to career diplomats, so I can play on that unfounded prejudice. Then I inform them that after the *Oberon* jumped from Terra's atmosphere, the Fleet Command was declared outlawed and therefore had to flee. You then fled aboard an escort ship to get to safety, so Harbingen's entire heritage would not be lost should the *Oberon* be captured."

"And why did we attack the conspirators at Harbingen?" she asked. "I'm sure they told von Borningen *that*."

"An old feud, or the knowledge that the Omega access code had to be used quickly. Take your pick." Angsk's expression was pained. "Listen, it's just an attempt to take out as much credit as possible."

"No, that's right." Silly pondered. "We plan to fake a major reactor problem halfway along the route, after we've sent out another message on directional beam. With our last energy reserves, so to speak. Then you will deliver your message. From then on, we'll act like a dead fish in the water. We'll have to rely on von Borningen being curious enough to bring us in. That should buy us a few days, provided they're not in a big hurry and they're interested enough in us."

"But we're not really dead in the water, are we?"

"No."

"How sure are you that the Exiles will wait for days with their primary attack?"

"Well, they're sending four ships through the jump point every two or four minutes, which in itself takes some time. But they need what we would call critical fleet strength for the upcoming battle. The Clicks have over 4,000 ships, plus their formidable defenses. Presumably, the Exiles will first bring the exposed external system under control, so no one ambushes them from behind. Then, as soon as they have brought enough ships through the jump point, they'll launch their main assault. We're expecting three to four days. Still relatively fast, assuming our couriers reach their destinations and then help takes the same amount of time or more to get here."

"So, you're saying that the enemy has practically all the time in the world."

"Yes."

Silly gritted her teeth. *But the worst thing is that they have their own Titan with them.*

The *Excalibur*, von Borningen's flagship, was a slightly larger and beefier version of the *Oberon*, on whose design it was quite obviously based. Those bastards had somehow managed to build a Titan themselves and certainly improve on it. It had stung her when she had seen the first evaluations of the sensor data. The knowledge that the *Oberon* was the mightiest ship of human hegemony had become something of a reassuring certainty that had steadied her since Harbingen's downfall, a final nail of greatness in the cross she had to bear.

Now, even that was turned upside down, and it further fueled her hatred of the Exiles. She hadn't told Angsk, but the *Excalibur* was her biggest problem. It could outweigh 100 ships or even 1,000, depending on how it was equipped. For a battle between two fleets, a Titan was worth far more than its sheer firepower and steadfastness in battle. It provided an incredible number of support tasks, had countless squadrons of fighters or drones at its disposal, and could operate for a very long time with its armies of repair bots and the support of other ships if it was deployed sensibly.

"What do you think could still emerge from the jump point?" Angsk asked, although his gaze seemed to say that he did not want to know.

"I don't know, Ambassador, but nothing good for us, I'm afraid. I don't know where the Exile fleet ended up at the end of their journey, but they managed to build not only a large, modernized fleet, but also a Titan, something the Federation hasn't been able to do for over twenty years due to lack of money and resources. Either their new home system is overflowing with resources and their population has exploded, or they have opted for a robolution."

"A robolution? That's an interesting neologism, but I don't think the religious underpinnings of their culture would allow it."

"Probably not. I also think a general mobilization is more likely. Either way, we should be prepared to experience nasty surprises and adjust our decisions accordingly." She had said the last more to herself than to him, but it didn't matter. She gave him a firm look. "We'll do what you suggest. It can't do any harm."

# 31

"What do we have on the whereabouts of our brothers and sisters?" Ludwig von Borningen wanted to know. Gotthold guessed that he mainly meant their actual brother Theoderich.

"We have heard nothing from the *Redemption*. The last message we received was from Lagunia, just before they planned to destroy the Omegan fleet at S1 there."

"After the arrival of the Omega," Ludwig noted.

"Yes." Gotthold nodded somberly.

"So, something went wrong or they would have sent a message with a quantum buoy long ago."

"Quite possibly. But either way, the *Oberon* is far too far away to be a danger to us here."

The first high lord pursed his mouth in dissatisfaction. "We've been waiting for three days. This has to happen faster."

"No reinforcements from the Clicks have arrived, and the *Oberon*, even if she knew what was happening here, would take at least twelve days to get here from Lagunia by the shortest route." Gotthold shook his head before continuing, "But I think even that's unlikely, they can't know about our cloaked gate technology."

"Unless they hijacked the *Redemption* and stole the plans for building the phase-shifting transmitter. They could draw conclusions from that," Ludwig said.

"Theoderich would never have allowed that."

"No, indeed he would not have. Nevertheless, I refuse to disregard the *Oberon*. I will not do so until the battle here is won."

"I understand."

"What's the status regarding the *Saratoga*?" His brother abruptly changed the subject and pointed to the systems overview hologram buzzing above the modern command deck.

"Our tugs are on their way and will reach her in eight hours. I know that's not very fast, but we need some corvettes to provide protection."

"But the enemy is massing their forces around Attila. It doesn't look to me like they're trying to prevent us from recovering the *Saratoga*."

"Still, I want to rule out the possibility that this is some form of Trojan Horse," Gotthold said. "It's even possible that what we saw wasn't real, or that Thurnau and Angsk are under some kind of mind control."

He thought about his own words and the battered guided-missile cruiser's last transmission. Thekarius Angsk was an old acquaintance of his. He had met him many times at official receptions on Harbingen, in the fleet, and even twice in the Sol System. Angsk had been a smart, conservative diplomat with probably the best network of contacts one could wish for in the Federation. That he had ingratiated himself with them did not surprise Gotthold in the least. The man was an opportunist, typical of politicians without an office that corresponded to their ambition, yet secure in a position from which he was virtually impossible to dismiss because his spider's threads were spun across party lines. This nonpartisanship could only be maintained by people who were not too shy to seize every opportunity to preserve themselves and their careers and to identify such opportunities early on.

Thurnau, on the other hand, was a different matter. He didn't buy that she wanted to make common cause with them, but she had also made it clear that she only did it grudgingly. Her hatred for the Federation was supposedly legendary, if he was to believe Theoderich's account of the last two decades. But was her hatred enough to suddenly join forces with them?

But it didn't matter. Ludwig would lock her up as soon as she was on board, and then they would see how much information she was willing to divulge. The final deciding factor, besides possibly valuable intelligence from Angsk and Thurnau, had been the two Clicks that had been shown to them in the directional beam transmission. Their suits looked different from those they had seen so far on the few records of the war they had obtained. There was a pearly sheen about them and they were larger than the normal ones. This surely supported their theory that they were indeed kidnapped alien VIPs and thus probably the most valuable cargo in the entire galaxy: living Clicks in human hands! Gotthold could not even imagine what could be done with them. Perhaps after a few months or years of research, a real interrogation? Even dissecting one would be a giant leap for xenoscience and possibly their military.

The direct hit on their reactor, however, almost destroyed that hope, and would have if the Clicks had not decided to destroy their own renegades. Gotthold found the situation extremely irritating since he had to weigh the chances against the risks. In the end, however, there were no conceivable risks he could think of that outweighed that great opportunity.

Therefore, he took the safest possible route and had the *Saratoga*, drifting dead in space, towed and boarded her en route to take control and look for hidden surprises. After all, he didn't want to go down in the history books as a naïve King Priam dragging the Trojan Horse behind his walls, no matter how unlikely it was that a single ship could throw a wrench into their plans.

"Bring me the two aliens," Ludwig ordered. "Everything else is secondary. If Angsk is useful, he gets a place in the new order. We'll be careful with Thurnau. We'll keep our word, but we won't promise her anything until we can be absolutely sure, and that won't be until the end of the Federation and all traces of the Omega and its servants."

"Of course," Gotthold replied, a little more humbly than he'd intended. "If everything goes smoothly, they will be here in two days, and then we'll begin our offensive. That would make five days in total, and with 6,000 ships we should be able to destroy Attila and cut the head off the serpent."

"So be it." High Lord Ludwig von Borningen looked at the holodisplay one last time then left the bridge.

"The timing is good," said his XO, Captain Branson, as if to reassure him after seeing the look Gotthold gave his brother. "None of the core worlds are within five days' transit, even if they managed to learn about events immediately. Besides, why would they come here and threaten us? They hate the Clicks even more than we do. And they won't get in our way either, because they'd have to give up their fortress worlds around the jump points here first, leaving many more worlds defenseless."

Gotthold nodded. "The end of our enemies is near, and with it, humanity's freedom from aliens and machines." He pointed to Branson. "Move our fleet to their forward positions. I want us able to strike out as soon as possible."

"Of course, Grand Admiral."

∽

Nicholas entered the workshop, which seemed even more squat than the rest of the ship. As a cadet, he had often been annoyed by the low ceilings of the crew quarters because they worsened his claustrophobia, which was still quite acute at the time. Not that he had talked about it with anyone. A prospective Fleet officer, and of all people, the son of the great Admiral Konrad Bradley feeling insecure on a starship? Impossible, at least that was what he had always told himself before falling asleep so he could find sleep at all. That time seemed extremely distant now, like an alien life.

Chief Engineer Karl Murphy stood in front of one of the many workbenches where technicians in orange coveralls hammered, soldered, welded, and sawed. There were flashes and sparks everywhere and an unpleasant smell of lubricants and ozone lingered in the heavy air, blending into the image of an underground Victorian factory complex that had somehow crammed the contents of three buildings into a single basement.

Murphy's hands were clad in feedback gloves that enabled him to control two robotic arms working delicately on a device that looked like a monolith of metal struts. Inside, a fist-sized heart

*The last Battleship*

glowed and emitted a spherical light. Nicholas thought it looked like luminous dust.

"How far along are we?" Nicholas called as he approached the workbench. The lieutenant commander was smeared and stained from top to bottom. He showed no reaction and continued to stare at the holo-image directly in front of his eyes, which allowed him to see through the structure of the object he was working on and guide the robotic hands with appropriate precision. Nicholas tapped him on the shoulder. "Karl?"

"Hey, kid," the engineer rumbled, blinking a few times in quick succession to make the holodisplay disappear. Then he took his hands out of his feedback gloves and pulled small plugs out of his ears. "What's up?"

"Just checking in to see how far along you are."

"Guess you want to know if we're screwed or not, huh?" Murphy growled a laugh. Not for the first time, Nicholas found that the grumpy officer could well have passed for a dwarf from Tolkien's *Lord of the Rings* had he not been so tall.

"We're flying to Okazaki right now. As Daussel keeps rubbing in my face, it's the only core world besides Kent that's over thirty jumps from Attila. If this doesn't work"—he pointed to the monolith—"then I've traded an improbability for an impossibility and we'll never get there in time."

"We wouldn't make it either way, would we?"

Nicholas didn't answer and instead bit his lower lip. *Silly will figure something out. She* has *to.*

"Well," Murphy continued loudly to drown out the noise of the workshop, "I've got Omega in my ear every time I do something, even though it's working on this Telepator thing on the side, and that's helpful. I think I'll be done soon. Would be a laugh if those conspirator assholes could get it done but I can't. Ha!"

"How long?"

"Phew, hard to say."

"Give me an approximate number of hours so I know how to plan." Nicholas knew he was getting antsy because there were still uncertainties about too many factors in his planning. His entire tactical situation assessment stood on the extremely brittle clay feet of the unknown. It was not a position he was particularly comfortable with. "And remember, I need the same thing again in a very large size."

"That's not the problem." Murphy waved dismissively and casually pointed his thumb at the prototype in front of him, or what would be one someday. It still looked like a skeleton, just barely recognizable as the house it would become. "As soon as this works, we'll build the same thing again on a much larger scale. You guys just have to worry about the power source."

"Got it in the back of my mind once we complete our next jump."

"Let's say twenty-four hours. I should be able to do that."

"I'll give you sixteen," Nicholas replied immediately.

"Okay, I'll do you in twelve, Captain!"

"Really?" he asked in surprise.

"No, man, of course not. But if we're going to do the Kirk-Scotty thing, let's do it right." Murphy laughed loudly, his belly bouncing up and down. "Look, kid, I'm trying as hard as I can. Maybe—and the emphasis is on *maybe*—I can get this thing working in under twenty hours, but I don't want to be guilty of carelessness by rushing it. If I understand you correctly, there's only this one shot and very little margin for error."

"*No* margin," Nicholas corrected, then sighed. "All right. Keep me posted."

"Will do. Just make sure we don't get smashed by our own people after we jump. You never know what people are like when the universe is on fire all around them, haunted by demons and an evil uncle from the past." With that, Murphy restarted the holodisplay in front of his face and slipped on the feedback gloves. "I'd better get on with it now. Nice chat, but bad for our schedule."

Nicholas nodded absently and looked down at his forearm display. Twelve hours until the jump to Okazaki and the next hurdle they had to overcome in their enterprise against all odds. He considered whether their odds had ever been worse and concluded that they certainly had at Terra, probably at Lagunia, too, though without them knowing it. But there had not been as much at stake as there was now.

*The last Battleship*

"I think I'm beginning to understand you better and better, Father," he said to himself, taking a deep breath. "And I don't envy what life threw at you."

With that, he left the workshop and made his way back to the bridge. He probably wouldn't leave it for the next two days. He walked along the corridors, keeping his eyes on passing crewmen, friendly words on his lips, and with time for brief small talk here and there.

Just like his father.

~

"This sucks. Really and truly sucks," Dev cursed.

"You *really* forgot," Willy said.

"Can anyone in this cockpit tell me who in human history has ever liked fucking smartasses?"

"I'm just saying." The Dunkelheimer shrugged his strong shoulders.

"The situation won't change just because we keep freaking out," Jezzy said. She was deploying sensor bundles from their armored nests to determine their position in the XC-44V system and then get them to the next and penultimate jump point. "In thirty-six hours we'll know how good this plan is."

"*You're* telling me not to whine?" Dev ran his fingers through his hair, which had grown far too long. "These must really be bad times for us."

"You're both right," Aura sighed in exasperation. "The plan sucks. It's entirely our risk, and we've got our backs to just about every wall you can think of. But we won't change anything about that now unless someone has a better idea. If you do, then let 'er rip. I really want to hear it."

Before he could say anything rude, Jezzy cut him off.

"Transit successful, position as calculated, all celestial bodies are where they should be."

Dev growled and, now that they were no longer groping in the darkness, accelerated to make way for the fringe fleet ships following them. Under King Gustav's command, and thanks to the prowess of his Spiked Helmet Regiment, they had been able to unite all allied systems—Gotha, Sicilia, New Horizon, Scrapa, Medan, Phu Thien, Kitami, and Jaune—behind an insane plan. Only Wellington hadn't managed to get its ships to Phu Thien, the system closest to Attila, in time.

Well, insane for him and his crew. Gustav was a devious bastard, one had to give him that. Dev almost mistook him for a greedy mobster and completely underestimated him. As a former regimental commander of the MET-3000, the man was shrewd and trained in both diplomacy and tactics.

"What if the Exile bastards are actually attacking Attila like the *Oberon*'s courier said?" he asked no one in particular.

"We assume so, otherwise we wouldn't be here," Willy said.

"Wrong. We're here because we get something for it. Well, we're only here because you insisted that we help out and play do-gooders... again."

"Can't we skip this part?" the Dunkelheimer asked, annoyed. "The child hasn't fallen into the well yet."

"If they're really doing that, then we'll follow our plan as best we can and be showered with riches by two factions at once," Aura said, summing up the rosiest prospects, which were about as realistic as him growing a third leg and learning to play the piano with it.

"Incorrect. If they really are attacking Attila and a mutual wank fest is already underway when we arrive, either the Clicks at S1 will crush us as soon as we emerge from an unauthorized transit, or the Exiles will at S2."

"Assuming that's how they're deployed," Jezzy said.

"It's still better than if there's a hyperspace gate at S1 or S2," Willy chuckled, "otherwise we won't even know we were smashed to smithereens in hyperspace and that our atoms were dissolving into their smallest components."

Dev turned toward the tall engineer. "Really now?"

"I'm just saying it could always be worse."

"Valuable commentary, truly!"

Dev concentrated on the instruments for a while, banishing his crew's babbling to a background hiss somewhere below that of the

*The last Battleship*

engines to clear his head. Sending them and the *Bitch* in advance just because they had the smallest radar cross section in the fleet—thanks to their new stealth coating—was like a horde of flies sending the tiny mosquito to see if it could shoo away a pesky elephant at a watering hole. It was insane, and not at all the treatment he would have expected after saving the Federation's ass, not that the history books would take that fact into account in any way. He was long past such delusions.

Another jump to the next system between them and Attila, the supposedly darkest den of evil in the universe, if one wanted to believe previous Federation propaganda, that was supposed to have changed overnight into the radiant sun of a new ally. He was curious to know how the Fleet propagandists intended to sell *that* to citizens who had been sworn to war and hostility for decades.

Those who were still alive. Well, they probably didn't care as long as they had air to breathe and bread to eat.

From VV-2-Aquila—Dev had read the name from the navigation computer—it was just one more jump. Then it would be a matter of closing their eyes and hoping they weren't immediately burned to cinders by a crossfire of laser fire. Missiles wouldn't need to be wasted on them because they would be blind.

Whining wasn't going to help, at least now that he'd vented his anger at the hopelessness of their situation. So, he unbuckled and went out to the corridor.

"Where are you going?" Aura asked, interrupting a tirade at Jezzy.

"I'm going to the fucking mess and spending the next thirty-six hours playing through simulations, each involving a lost little *Bitch* and a pack of horny fucking assholes just waiting to gangbang her at Attila's S2. Maybe in the 1,000 scenarios that make us look like a Jackson Pollock painting I'll find the one with a jar of lube lying around." With that, he stomped off and, without turning back, called out, "Take over."

## 32

"It's really working!" Silly exclaimed with relief and slapped Angsk on the shoulder so hard that the ambassador almost fell from his seat. "By Omega, man, you really do have a knack for a proper speech. I almost bought that all myself, even though I knew it was a lie."

"Uh, thanks." The diplomat avoided her gaze and adjusted his jacket.

On the main screen, they watched as the two Harbinger cruisers towed them toward the waiting fleet—a direction their guts felt was wrong. But sometimes you didn't have a choice, especially as a warship commander.

"Actually," Angsk said, "I think it was the live footage of our two guests that made the difference."

Silly thought of the two Clicks who had come on board to give their delay tactic as large a chance of success as possible.

"You could be right about that," she said, nodding. "After all, no officer in history would turn down a chance, however small, of getting his hands on an extraterrestrial, let alone two, after more than seventy years of unsuccessful attempts. After all, there were more than a few in the Admiralty who believed the war had only raged for so long because we knew so little about each other. How are you supposed to spot the weak point of something you've never taken apart?"

"That's a valid argument."

"Yes, one that von Borningen apparently shares."

"Ma'am?" Mnuchin piped up. The undertone in his voice made her sit up and burst her sense of optimism and relief like a soap bubble.

"What is it?"

"The tug escort," said her XO. The holoscreen materialized out of colored photons in front of their command podium. On it was the escort that provided cover for the two tugs. Small glittering dots detached themselves from some of them. "They've launched boarding shuttles. Four of them in all."

*Four!* she repeated in her head. *One for each airlock. Damn!*

The burst bubble was no more than a fading memory as she puckered her mouth and zoomed in. They were boarding ferries, little different from those in the Fleet except that the contact rings on their bows were square, not round, as was common in the Federation.

Part of her wondered for what reason the Exiles had decided this change to the plan, and another part filled in the blank by explaining that von Borningen had always been about doing things differently than the Federation. So, it might be just a sign of contrariness, a desire to do things on his own terms.

"This is not good. Not good at all," she growled, leaning forward in her chair. "We can't let them on board!"

"No, we can't," Mnuchin agreed with her. The neutral expression on his face just about drove her crazy, whether out of envy or pure situational frustration, she didn't care.

"I don't need a parrot, I need solutions. If we open fire and destroy them, they'll make mincemeat of us, and we won't get close enough to the jump point to figure out what's going on."

"There's not much we can do except barricade the areas in front of the airlocks and arm our crewmen."

"If those bastards have even a handful of Marines with powered armor with them, they'll grind our soldiers into hamburger."

"Yeah." Mnuchin's face grew a touch more tense. The screen showed fourteen minutes until the boarding shuttles would arrive. He quickly followed up with, "How about airlock control prob-

*The last Battleship*

lems? After all, we don't have a working reactor and everything is on emergency power... officially."

Silly nodded. "We should definitely do that." She opened the tactical map on her forearm display and projected it in front of the close-range display. "Eight more hours until we reach the Exiles' formation. That's way too long."

"If the airlocks don't work, they'll use fission cutters to gain access," their XO said. "That would take about an hour with the Fleet's latest equipment—for the heavily armored outer airlock, at least. The inner one will take half that time. So, at best, we have two hours before they're on board and see through our plan."

"They wouldn't get onto the bridge that easily," she mused. "The Carbin walls continue through the two access bulkheads." She pointed to the two faintly outlined entrances to the right and left of her podium, dull and dark as blackened granite.

Mnuchin looked at her and frowned.

"We could say that the ship's computer, under its emergency protocol, detected a hostile takeover of the ship after the reactor failure and therefore sealed off the control center to prevent a total loss," she said, thinking aloud. She didn't like it herself, but she didn't see too many alternatives. "By the time they cut their way in here, it's bound to take a lot longer. Half a meter of mono-bonded Carbin is not exactly a sheet of plywood."

"That could work," Mnuchin agreed. "I don't know how long it will hold them off, but it will buy us some time. What about the crew?"

"I want them to cooperate. There's no point in people throwing their lives away. They should submit but make no effort to actually help the enemy."

Her XO was obviously as uncomfortable with this as she was. But since he didn't object, he probably didn't see any other way out of their predicament, if it was a way out at all, or just delaying the failure of their plan without getting them anywhere.

Two hours later, almost to the minute, Marines in black powered armor were in the corridors of the *Saratoga* and taking her crew into custody. No one was forcibly taken away or restrained, but they were not armed either and thus no more dangerous to the armored soldiers than ants. The intruders turned the ship upside down in search of the two Clicks, but Silly had brought them to the bridge earlier. They were now standing behind her like two powered-down robots. Whatever was going on in their telepathic bond was beyond her perception, and that was probably just as well since her thoughts were already sufficiently occupied.

While Angsk talked over the radio with the intruders—a major who sounded like a chain smoker—she studied the data from the molecular bond generators that were buried under the bridge floor and made up the Carbin sphere they were currently standing in. It would be a hard nut to crack. The ambassador once again proved to be a skilled orator, although fear-sweat stood on his forehead and formed fine droplets that shone in the red ceiling light like morning dew. He managed to keep the major busy for nearly an hour with queries to his authority and reassurances, asking for quick solutions as he feigned panic. After all, an AI taking control was something the Exiles had to regard as the sixth circle of hell.

Five hours remained before they reached the enemy fleet. To Silly, it seemed an endless, unmanageably long time that stretched on forever. The bridge suddenly seemed half the size it had before, the breathable air thicker and less oxygenated, even though she knew that was not true. Autonomous life support could sustain the *Saratoga*'s command center for days before they had to start worrying about real problems.

At some point, however, even Angsk's powder was spent—either that or the marine major had been instructed to stop looking for other solutions and forcibly gain access to the bridge. Their crew still gained half an hour doing what they could by inventing minor delays, before being "evacuated" to the boarding shuttles, which immediately began the return trip to their mother ships. Apparently, the Marines were not planning on returning and were set on taking control. Angsk did his best to mask his fear even now, assuring the major that they were doing everything they could from their side of the security bulkheads to ensure rapid progress as well, fighting the AI's firewalls and trying reboots.

But the longer the verbal show went on, the more monosyllabic the marine's answers became, and the clearer it became that he either had no more patience or had seen through the farce and was not happy about being led around by the nose. Either way, Silly didn't think it would turn out particularly well for them when the last fission flame went out and Carbin half a meter thick crashed to the bridge floor.

"Now all we can do is wait," Mnuchin said, stating what everyone was thinking, except the two Clicks, perhaps. Who knew what was going through their minds?

∼

Okazaki had turned out to be an absolute disappointment—militarily as well as politically. Once the *Oberon* jumped into the core system, he had at first been relieved to see that there was still a world unaffected by the war against Species X. But it quickly became clear that "business as usual" meant that the simplicity of battle had been replaced by the complexity of politics.

At the jump point, elaborate scans and questions from space control cost them a precious half hour before their new transponder code, issued by the Admiralty at the Sky Fortress itself, was accepted and they were allowed to move freely. This was followed by dozens of invitations from various politicians and key officers who hoped to improve their positions in Sol—as if there was nothing more important before the imminent fall of their civilization. Nicholas had the feeling Okazaki was playing a game called "if you carry on as always, then all the madness can't be true."

He turned down all invitations and explained that they had received orders to dismantle the local faulty hyperspace gate. The local fleet raised no objections once he assured them that the dismantled components would be handed over to Okazaki authorities. Every kilo of valuable resources counted twice these days. Nicholas let them know that the Admiralty simply wanted to ensure that the work was carried out and completed by skilled personnel. Such a form of external control by the Fleet was something pretty much every system was used to, so no one asked any serious questions.

It was a bitter realization that he could not even attempt to address his real goal: to enlist the help of the Okazaki fleet in the liberation of Attila. If one thing had become clear in the first hours after their arrival, it was that there was no interest here, whatsoever, in participating in the Federation's efforts to hold together a human hegemony that only really existed on paper. It was "every tribe for itself" again, and that saddened him as he watched the shuttles flit around the giant ring where the flames of welding torches flashed in hundreds of places.

"How much longer?" he asked his XO without taking his eyes off the holodisplay.

"Chief Engie says four hours. The phase transmitters are already installed, but repairing the gate is proving difficult," Daussel said.

"But Omega is helping them."

**"That is correct, CO,"** the AI said over the speakers in the command deck. **"The problem was not easy to solve. It involved errors in the power control system."**

"In the *software*?" he asked, irritated.

**"Yes."**

"I have to admit that surprises me. The control software for all the gates was uniformly programmed on New Texas. Why would there be any software error?"

**"The probability of this is vanishingly small, close to an impossibility. Also, there were exactly 328 bugs in the code that caused minor failures and false sensor signals. By themselves, they are very inconspicuous, but they add up to a complete failure of the gate."**

"That sounds like sabotage."

**"Yes."**

Nicholas shook his head. "So, the Okazakis themselves disabled their gate? But why?"

"To avoid participating in Iron Hammer," Daussel said. "Okazaki is one of the few worlds that had a completely separate strike group, and still do. They probably thought they wouldn't be needed to attack the Click home world since our numbers would have been overwhelming anyway. This way they would have avoided any casualties and gained more influence in the Jupiter

*The last Battleship*

Parliament with their increased military power without firing a single shot."

**"I basically agree with that assessment,"** Omega said.

Nicholas pursed his mouth in disgust. "And now they're doing it again."

"Well, we didn't ask them, but I guess that's just as well," Hellcat said with a somber expression. "Otherwise, they'd have put us down like so many rabid dogs."

"Is there any way to speed up the repairs?" Nicholas asked, looking up as if speaking to God.

**"Unfortunately, no. I have to work with several autonomous subroutines that are currently digging through the code in order not to provoke a reaction from the installed security measures. The software is well protected, which the saboteurs knew and countered by taking their time and being stealthy. I need to reverse the same process they had months to do in a matter of hours without setting off the digital alarm bells,"** Omega said. **"But it is working, and we will be able to jump soon—with the hope that this phaser transmitter works based on the plans Sirion Mantell sent us."**

"If not, we'll have other problems," Daussel grumbled. Nicholas wished his XO could have enjoyed his brief period of optimism a little longer before refocusing on playing officer sourpuss.

"Chief Engie Murphy has successfully tested the small prototype," he said as much to himself as to Daussel and Omega. "So, I don't see any reason why the larger version won't work."

**"It has merely been scaled up and is not otherwise different,"** the AI agreed. **"There is no rational reason to assume a malfunction as long as the power supply remains stable."**

Nicholas gave Daussel a look that said "See?" and connected with Murphy.

The engineer was out on the ring with his technicians, directing the countless drones that were pretending to dismantle the ring, when in fact they were setting up power supplies as well as placing charges in case their plan did go awry. They could not allow another Species X fleet to enter Federation territory.

"Yeah?" Murphy growled. The air supply to his helmet crackled in the background.

Nicholas tried to imagine what it must be like for him, out there so close to that huge structure. Compared to it, the *Oberon* was merely a glittering cigar against the darkness of the stars. There was a constant flicker and flash of corrective thrusters from drones and space workers along the structure. Keeping track of it all was daunting. Not only did the engineer have to direct a complex repair and preparation operation that would have been challenging under normal circumstances, but he also had to make it look like they were doing the opposite of what was really going on.

"How's it going?"

"We haven't been blasted yet, so I guess pretty good."

"I've set the approach pattern we'll use to collect you," he said and sent the corresponding data to Murphy's forearm display, just under five clicks away on the ring. Once the gate was activated, there would be little time. There were two listening posts at Okazaki's S2, one old and the other new, both still operational. In addition, there were two dozen heavily armed defensive platforms with short- and medium-range weapons. These were not currently on full alert but were built to respond immediately to any unauthorized transit into the system with swift destruction. Thus, the gate, planted directly at the jump point, was always within range of the missiles and railguns. Once activated, they would barely have time to jump before Okazaki's military pressed their red buttons.

That was why he had to make sure to quickly get his people back on board once they were done and, if possible, all the drones as well. In these times, man and machine were equally valuable and hard to quantify in terms of money.

"Pretty sick shit, Captain," Murphy said after a long pause. "It could work, though. Just make sure we're not picked off in the process. I promised my people this wouldn't be a suicide mission."

"It will work. CO out."

Nicholas cut the connection and began discussing the plan with Daussel and Hellcat. The latter's grin grew wider and wider while his XO's face darkened noticeably.

Almost four hours later, the moment arrived. Murphy trans-

*The last Battleship*

mitted the long-awaited message that the charade was over, and his drones were running out of power. Nicholas ordered the *Oberon* to maneuver closer to the ring and alerted the hangar crew to stand by for combat landings. He didn't expect the defense crews at S2 to attack them directly, but he didn't think they would hesitate a second to destroy the hyperspace gate once he activated it. If that happened before they were through, there would be a lot of questions that he didn't have answers for.

The *Oberon* flew sideways in a leisurely arc and presented her port side to the empty gate. The technicians, clad in their space suits with thick mobility units, swarmed like moths that could not escape the almost magnetic pull of the open port hangar. This move saved time because the drones were still doing their fake work of laying superconductor cables. They were linked to six mobile antimatter annihilators, small cylinders scarcely larger than a terrestrial elephant and thus mere motes of dust compared to the ring structure. They would have to work until the end to keep up appearances, severing connections and laying explosive wires.

When Omega signaled that everything was working, including the phase-cloaking generators, whose quantum effect was of course not visible, Nicholas ordered the drones to return and had the *Oberon* turn her bow toward the center of the gate. The maneuver made it obvious they were attempting a transit, along with the energy buildup in the ring itself.

"Incoming call from Listening Post Alpha," Lieutenant Jung reported.

"Patch it through to the XO," he ordered, and Daussel dutifully picked up the receiver in front of his seat.

"No, Lieutenant... Yes. We're collecting our bots... No, the power surge in the pattern cells is due in preparation for synchro blasting the six links... Of course." Daussel hung up and nodded to him. "We might have a minute."

Nicholas didn't believe it. "Open observation deck armored gates!"

At the front of the ship, the massive bulkheads parted, revealing the curved seating tiers of the bridge amphitheater. Prepared demolition charges ruptured the vast window as the event horizon built up within the ring. It created an unreal darkness, impenetrable and crumbling at the edges like water slopping over a riverbank. The drones engaged full thrust toward the *Oberon*'s open maw like tiny yellow bees and were swallowed up in ever-increasing numbers.

"Incoming transmission from—"

"Refuse it!" Nicholas shouted, staring at the holoscreen. "Transit alert!"

Amber lights illuminated and the signature whine of the jump alarm rang through the bridge and throughout the ship.

"Ten seconds!" Alkad announced.

"Defense platforms are firing at the gate!" Lieutenant Bonjarewski reported from Defense.

"Full acceleration!"

Nicholas watched as the *Oberon* made its way into the event horizon, first at a leisurely pace, then like an oversized rocket, while space behind them was flooded with hundreds of tiny radar contacts. It was a shame they were forced into such secrecy, had Okazaki joined them, they could have prevented a possible Exile hyperspace gate in Attila for as long as they wished.

He swallowed and tried to focus on the moment. It would be close. Very close.

## 33

Fission cutters had nearly cut a circle into the right access bulkhead to the *Saratoga*'s bridge when the *Oberon* came through Attila's S2.

Like a giant space whale, the Titan pushed through the event horizon that now, at such close range, almost certainly had to come from a gate. The blackness was circular and huge and its edges strangely blurred. She had no doubt now that the Exiles somehow managed to not only be invisible to Species X but also make a hyperspace gate disappear on radar and telescope images.

"I'll be damned!" Silly murmured as she alternately glanced at the radar screen and at the virtual window in front of the bridge crew's specialists. At multiple zoom, the window showed the ship's leisurely jump into the system. By now the *Saratoga* had reached the enemy lines in a large open area below the formation of von Borningen's fleet, a kind of quarantine area where they could not harm anyone. She had to hand it to them, the bastards had been really careful.

"Fire up the reactor!" she ordered, "full acceleration toward the *Oberon*!"

"It would seem that we bought enough time," Mnuchin said with a fair amount of satisfaction in his voice. Even the hiss of the fission cutters ceased.

"Is that so wise?" Angsk's voice was tense.

"What?"

"Giving up our cover. They'll open fire now, won't they?"

"Maybe, but maybe not. After all, they've got other problems now." Silly smiled grimly as she watched the reactor reach full power before thrusting the ultra-high-heat propellant from the drive pod to accelerate forward. Her prayers were now for her crew on the *Oberon*, not herself.

The Exile fleet went into a kind of shocked paralysis for a few dozen seconds before opening fire on the *Oberon*. Hundreds of ships sent out their long-range weapons to destroy the newcomer. Only the advanced position of the thousands of ships prevented the Titan from being pulverized to dust. Against the power of so many railguns even the *Oberon*'s massive Carbin armor would have been ineffective.

As the *Saratoga* headed for the S2 at full thrust, Silly hoped that the Marines would retreat, but they did not. On the contrary, they resumed their attempts to gain access to the bridge. Their fission cutters crackled and added to the rising temperature on the small bridge. The only good thing was that no one was shooting at them. Everything was focused on the *Oberon*, which was already raising its anti-aircraft screen to deal with the barrage of enemy guided missiles racing toward her.

"Pass out the weapons," she instructed Mnuchin and took manual control of the *Saratoga* as everyone present rose from their seats and received the assault rifles her XO retrieved and distributed from the weapons locker embedded in the wall.

Over the next few minutes, she watched as the first projectiles in the flak field of short explosions and dense clouds of shrapnel were destroyed. Like a behemoth, the *Oberon* surged toward the superior enemy. Pride filled her heart, even though she knew there was no chance her Titan would win this battle. If the Click fleet had set out on an intercept course, then perhaps, but left completely on her own, Silly saw no outcome that would not end with *Oberon* vaporized into a cloud of highly excited particles.

"Captain! Contact at S2!" the reconnaissance officer shouted from his station in front of her.

"On screen!" she shouted. Her eyes widened as she watched another ship push through the event horizon. The *Oberon* was only ten clicks away, beginning to engage in battle with her own fire. For a moment, she thought she saw another Titan in the fleet, and her heart skipped a beat, only to remember that there had been only one remaining battleship in the entire Federation, but that didn't apply to the Exiles.

"Holy shit!" Angsk blurted next to her. He was not carrying an assault rifle. "That's a Titan!"

"Yeah, I can see that too," Silly breathed. The behemoth's bow looked very much like the *Oberon*'s, albeit slightly wider and shallower, with the characteristic slit of the observation deck that looked like a mouth. "If this one gets through, my ship is history!"

She took to the navigation computer again and tapped into the *Saratoga*'s last bit of acceleration capacity. Then she entered a course correction.

"*Oberon*, this is Captain Silvea Thurnau," she said as she tried to contact Nicholas over the radio but got only ugly static. "Our signal's being jammed, but if you can hear me, it seems that there is a cloaked hyperspace gate at S2 along the edge of the event horizon. Ships can only get through it very slowly, although four can come at a time. We must destroy it."

She waited for a response, then tried again, then finally slapped her armrests in frustration.

"We're about to have company!" Mnuchin called. He had taken cover with other bridge crew personnel, assault rifles trained where the enemy Marines would shortly cut through the bulkhead.

She looked down at her navigation data. Sixty seconds to go. The enemy Titan, which was emerging directly behind the *Oberon*, was already fifteen percent through the event horizon. It would be close, but it could work. Silly fired the *Saratoga*'s few remaining guided missiles. As they impacted, a tiny area along the smooth darkness of the hyperspace access briefly flared, turned a sickly brown, and then disappeared again.

The newcomer began to open fire on them and especially on the *Oberon*. The *Oberon* seemed to understand their move and also aimed for the invisible ring. But the few missiles were intercepted, and the railguns could not find anything without automatic targeting.

Silly checked their course one last time, nodded with satisfaction and ran to Mnuchin to get her own rifle.

"What do we do?" the XO asked.

"The right thing. It's been an honor."

Mnuchin looked sidelong at her. Then the ruined bridge bulkhead crashed to the ground and the rattle of fully automatic weapons erupted.

∼

"*Saratoga*, this is Commander Nicholas Bradley of the *Oberon*, come in," Nicholas called into his phone. "Silly?"

Frustrated, he slammed down the phone and shook his head at Daussel's questioning look.

"The signal's still being jammed."

"Jamming is the least of our problems," Hellcat remarked glumly, pointing at the tactical holomap between them. It was updating by the second and painting a more pessimistic picture each time. The Exiles had indeed come, as Omega had predicted, with thousands of ships, at least three strike groups, if not four. They had brought not only a huge fleet, but also Titans.

*Titans!* he thought tensely.

The ship—obviously von Borningen's flagship—hovered in the middle of the enemy formation like a behemoth swarming with insects. It was slightly larger than the *Oberon* and certainly much more modern, considering the advances the Exiles had probably achieved in twenty years. As if that wasn't bad enough, a second Titan was coming into the system behind them and would fully arrive in a few minutes. At first, he had considered firing at it with everything he had, but that would have weakened their defensive screen against the myriad projectiles that were hitting them from the opposite direction. In addition to the flak and PDCs, all the railguns had to be used to support the defensive fire and weave as dense a net of projectiles as possible.

So, they were trapped, squeezed between two opponents they could not defeat. The *Oberon* was not in her best condition, and even if she was, she would not have had an easy time against even one of the newer battleships. But now there were two, and not to mention a whole fleet of fanatics.

"We need the Clicks," Daussel said.

"Even if we could communicate with them by radio—which we can't—they'd get here way too late."

"They're already on their way," Hellcat said, pointing to the screen near Attila. Sure enough, over 4,000 of the long-range radar's contact points were on an intercept course. Based on the distance, the current image was more than an hour old, so they would be well past that by now.

"But it doesn't change the fact that it's going to take them at least twelve hours to get here," Nicholas gritted his teeth, fighting back the hopelessness that was trying to take hold of him. "How long until the Titan is through the event horizon behind us?"

**"Twenty-two seconds at its current speed,"** Omega said, **"but I don't think it will come to that."**

"What do you mean?" he asked, confused.

**"Captain Thurnau is creating facts."**

Nicholas called up an optical image from the aft cameras and immediately saw what Omega was talking about. The *Saratoga* had stopped firing and was being harassed by the Titan, which was also firing at the *Oberon*. Four boarding shuttles, which had been clinging to her hull like greedy ticks, disengaged and accelerated away with impulse engines burning.

"Silly!" he breathed in horror as the guided-missile destroyer crashed into the edge of the hyperspace field and dissipated in a lurid explosion. A glimmer began along the edge, became a flicker, and then vanished. Left behind was a steel-gray ring structure of six constituent components. Two of them were completely shredded by the *Saratoga*'s impact. A cascade of colliding debris destroyed the once cloaked hyperspace gate. The event horizon disappeared at the same time as the last glowing pieces of the cruiser's hull, slicing into the Titan's aft third like a precision laser cutting butter, right where the *Oberon*'s reactor section began. The same seemed to be true of the Exiles' successor model because, with the disappearance of the passage into subspace and with it that part of the battleship, it lost all power.

"Silly," he repeated, torn between the need to scream over their loss and to sigh in relief because she had lifted a dangerous burden from his shoulders. *Not now,* he reminded himself and swallowed. *Your crew is counting on you.*

Magnified images showed hundreds of crewmen being sucked out of the exposed decks, arms and legs flailing, and gradually freezing in a vacuum. Nicholas thought of the thousands of men and women on board who would die a horrible death without any life support.

"XO, gather all the respirators you can and pack them into the shuttles. I want our medics to take them to that ship."

"Sir?" Daussel was confused.

"You heard me."

"Would they have done the same for us?" the lieutenant commander asked with a scowl.

Nicholas did not answer and instead picked up his telephone receiver. "Lieutenant Jung? Put me on system wide. We may have a chance to get through now."

"You may speak, sir."

"This is Commander Nicholas Bradley of the *Oberon*. To all Harbingers: The Clicks, who call themselves the Water People of Warm Depths, are no longer our enemies. I understand that you want to liberate humanity and that we have different ideas about exactly how that should be done, but you are making a mistake. These aliens are as fascinating as they are intelligent, and they spared Terra when it was at their mercy. There is an alternative to a fight in which many of us, if not all of us, would lose our lives. The Federation will be reorganized after this day, one way or another. We are willing to negotiate with you about it rather than you senselessly throwing away lives. Come to your senses and sit down at the table with us!" He hung up and took a deep breath.

"The signal was jammed with directional pulses, CO," Jung reported with regret. "They're coming from the *Hohenzollern*, the enemy Titan, and they're covering our entire forward communications array."

"It figures von Borningen wouldn't want his people to hear that," Hellcat grumbled.

*The last Battleship*

"What do we do now?" Daussel pointed to their bow section. In front of it, a hurricane of explosions and shrapnel was raging just five clicks away, joined by hundreds of bursting guided missiles per minute, straining the *Oberon*'s ammunition supply.

"We attack," Nicholas decided and zoomed in on the *Hohenzollern*. "Here."

"We're not going to make it. They've got a whole fleet of reinforcements and we're all alone."

"Maybe it'll be enough if we destroy their jamming equipment."

"I don't think the Exiles are going to stop combat operations just because we ask them nicely," Daussel said. "Especially not with their flagship and von Borningen in their midst."

"A small chance, but a chance." Nicholas stiffened. "Realign all railguns, prepare long-range torpedoes, all launch bays. Reactor to full power, overload thrusters!"

∼

Dev squinted as they jumped, expecting... what, actually? Not opening his eyes again? Feeling an invisible wall slam into him and ending up as a bloodstain on the two-dimensional subspace transition?

"Transit successful!" Aura reported. The surprise in her voice resonated in his soul.

"Somebody fry me a stork!" he sighed and powered up the secondary systems again. The forward and dorsal sensor phalanxes extended and scanned the space surrounding them at Attila's S2. Dev didn't wait, however, but immediately steered the *Bitch* into a sharp turn to the left in anticipation of an immediate attack.

"There's a lot going on here," Willy said as the first sensor images came in.

Close-range scanners showed more than 300 misshapen fragments floating erratically in space, colliding and rebounding again in different directions. Some of them radiated an astonishing amount of energy, so they could not be very old. In addition, there was a gigantic piece of dead matter that radiated some heat, but otherwise betrayed hardly any energy potential.

"What the hell is that?" he growled.

"Looks like a shipwreck. The stern's been cut clean off, but other than that, I don't see any impact craters or anything like that," Aura said. "I have the *Oberon* on screen. She's only fifty clicks away and accelerating toward a fleet of—oh shit!"

"What is it?" Dev frantically called up the full sensor image to the main screen and his mouth suddenly went dry. The Exiles' fleet was huge, and they had a freaking Titan. "Wait a minute. They actually had two Titans?"

"The fleet is coming through. The *Estrella* and the *Calista* have arrived," Aura said, ignoring his rant.

Dev signaled the *Oberon* and waited for Lieutenant Alkad to report. To his surprise, she put him through to Commander Bradley.

"Captain Myers," Nicholas said. "I must confess I'm surprised to see you here."

"Did you think we weren't coming?"

"Yes."

"Well, you'd have been damned right too, if I'd had my way. I see it was as much of a suicide mission as I feared," he growled and glanced at the scanner image. The problem was that they couldn't even run away because the fringe world fleet behind them was pushing through the jump point, one ship after another. They were agonizingly slow, but fast enough to effectively block the conjunction zone... and their only way out, except for the S1 between Attila and its central star. That seemed endlessly far away and was blocked by two fleets. He was not sure which one he should find worse, fanatical Harbingers or creepy aliens.

"We'll do what we can do."

"And what is that?" Dev sounded resigned.

"We'll try to destroy their flagship and cut the head off the snake," Nicholas said.

*Is this guy completely insane or just tired of living?*

"They'll shoot you to pieces, man!"

*The last Battleship*

"Maybe, but the *Hohenzollern* is jamming our radio signals. If we're going down, I want to at least try to give sanity a chance."

"Shit!" Dev thought of King Gustav's plan and had to admit that it wasn't much better, but it could work in the current situation. "I know you don't like to take suggestions from *free* people like me, Commander, but I have an idea how we could increase our chances of survival to at least one percent if everything goes well, which it probably won't."

"Go ahead, I'm open to any suggestion at this point."

*Miracles happen every day.* "Good, you won't like it, so I need you to promise that you won't punish me or my crew in case the plan succeeds."

There was a brief pause in the radio communication.

"Fine. What exactly do you propose?"

Dev explained, and with every word he got out, it struck him just how utterly insane it sounded.

"*That's* your plan?" Aura asked in horror when he finished.

"And that Bradley guy's 'improvements' just made it worse," Jezzy whined.

"When I fly by the seat of my pants, you guys complain." Dev threw his arms up then quickly lowered them again and typed in the appropriate navigation commands. "Now I have a fucking plan and you guys complain because you don't like it!"

"Because it's not a plan, it's suicide!" Aura's eyes sparked with anger.

"Only if it doesn't work."

"How do you expect it to work?"

"With a bit of luck."

She stared at him for a moment, then rolled her eyes in resignation.

"Uh, boss?" Willy said. "I'm right there with you, for whatever that's worth. Better to try to cut off the snake's head than to run away from it because it'll just bite you in the ass."

"See?" Dev smiled. "Someone understands me and has some perspective. We have no choice anyway. The fringe fleet is pushing us from behind and a fucking fleet of Exiles is pushing us from the front. So, unless we want to end up as ketchup in a sandwich, we'd better make sure there's no more bread."

"That analogy sucks," Aura said. She was probably right about that.

"If it works, the name of this ship will become immortal," he said, accelerating the *Quantum Bitch* at maximum power.

"I knew that was your ultimate goal in life," Jezzy murmured.

Willy smiled. "Look on the bright side, we could be the one thing that tips the scales."

"Or the fly that gets swatted first." Aura glowered at the engineer.

"Yeah, or that."

# 34

Lieutenant Commander Richard "Hellcat" Bales snatched the C-3 helmet sporting a fierce looking wildcat from a technician and slipped it on without slowing his stride. The CO's orders made him nearly burst with relief when he really should have been shitting his pants. What he was supposed to do with his Barracuda squadrons was completely insane, even by his standards.

*But it's better than being stuck on the bridge staring at holograms instead of sitting in my cockpit pushing buttons where I can see what's happening,* he thought.

"Hey, CAG," Alphastar called to him. His wingman trotted to his side and stayed beside him as they made their way to their fighter access points. Their footsteps joined the hollow thump of the other pilots' boots as they ran along the aisles of the dorsal launch bays, frantically adjusting their G-suits and donning their helmets. "It's good to have you back."

"You sure? I took your job back."

"Ah," Alphastar waved dismissively. "Didn't like it anyway. I had to justify myself all the time. You can do the job much better, you old dog."

"If we pull this off, I'll quit the force and retire, man," Hellcat assured him with a grin. "Because there's no way we can top this in this lifetime, guaranteed."

"First we have to survive it," his oldest friend pointed out. "Seems like the most difficult task in the universe right now."

"More difficult than a controlled atmospheric crash into the *Oberon*'s hangar while she's spinning and just before she jumps?"

"You win!" Alphastar laughed as they reached the tubes to their cockpits. They slammed their fists together and then slipped through.

Hellcat slid into his seat and activated the nanonic harnesses that flowed like mercury over his shoulders and crept along his legs before joining and tightening in front of his sternum. Using three toggle switches, he started his Barracuda's primary, secondary, and tertiary systems and took a deep breath.

"All right, boys and girls," he addressed his squadron leaders over the radio, "you have your orders, and no, they're not a joke. Stick extremely close to the vector instructions. This time they'll be issued directly from the bridge. Everyone must be exactly in their designated position. Any deviation from the target course, no matter how small, will result in friendly fire."

He waited for his squadron leaders to confirm, and then for the green light above his head to signal launch clearance. A jolt went through his cockpit, followed by two more short shudders—impacts on the *Oberon*, he knew. The battle shifted from long-range to mid-range.

The green light flashed on, and he hit the ready button for the mass catapult and shouted "Good hunting!" into the radio, then accelerated at downright gentle 4 Gs and shot out of the launch shaft.

∼

Dev licked his parched lips as he slowly slid the *Quantum Bitch* right onto the edge of the *Oberon*'s huge drive nacelle. It was big enough to hold several apartment blocks side by side. The composite, several meters thick, glowed cherry red under the heat of the ultra-hot plasma flame that extended several hundred kilometers. The onboard computer instantly complained with flashing warnings and appeals for immediate cooling or disconnection of the

*The last Battleship*

landing struts, but he shut them all off. Instead, he double-checked the magnetization to make sure they were firmly seated. In his mind, he saw the four "feet" of his ship glowing like blanks pulled from a forge and banished his pain at the thought.

This was the part of the plan he liked least because his ship's suffering was passive and not a consequence of anything he was doing, but it had to be done. This close to the exhaust tail it would be impossible for enemy infrared sensors to pick them up, and optical sensors were useless amid the flak screen and all the muzzle flashes. Any spy drones that came in behind them would be blinded by the drive pod's photon corona, so this was the best place for them to be—at least for the next few minutes.

"Would you look at that!" Willy gushed.

Dev saw it, too. The *Oberon*'s fighters—there must have been hundreds of them—shot out of the giant battleship's flanks like tiny arrows, little more than flashing lights amid a storm of explosions and projectiles. From this distance, it was hard to believe that each of the Barracudas was as big as a small truck. Many of the agile stub-winged spacecraft went into perfectly synchronized turns, some ascending to the top of their mother ship while the others disappeared beneath it. Then they raced forward, past the many guns keeping up a continuous fire in all directions. It looked like a mass slalom as the fighters tried to remain close to the hull to avoid colliding with a cannon or being shredded by the impact of a railgun bolt.

"Boss, it's getting warm," Jezzy said accusingly.

"I can tell," was all he said.

In fact, the temperature was rising sharply as the heat from the landing struts spread throughout the *Bitch*'s hull and into the interior. He began to sweat and opened his jacket. He considered extending the radiators, but it was too early for that. Their total area was larger than that of the ship itself and would give them away. With the current plan, the tiniest mistake would be enough to cause everything to fail.

Dev made a few quick inputs and screwed up his face. They had ten minutes until they reached the critical temperature of 42 degrees Celsius. Their body proteins would begin to denature if they didn't cool down quickly. Not a lot of time for the *Oberon* and her fighters to set things up, especially since they would be far from finished by then.

"We'll get into our spacesuits," he decided on the spur of the moment.

"Already?" Aura asked.

"Yes, that's what I just said."

"But if the power goes out before we—"

"I know that," he interrupted gruffly. "But if we die first, it won't matter anyway, will it? The damned temperature is rising much faster than expected and we won't last long. If we get too hot our suits will use too much energy to cool us down."

~

Nicholas looked at the tactical screen and tried to compensate for another port impact by shifting his weight to his left foot. The hits were becoming more frequent now that over 1,000 enemy ships had begun firing on them after establishing a direct line of fire. The rest were already positioning themselves to attack the jump point where more ships from the fringe worlds were emerging, painfully slowly but growing in number all the same.

He felt like a magnet in the middle of a minefield attracting everything that could explode. The shocks were violent, tearing mighty craters in the armored hull. The next few minutes would pose the ultimate test of their aged Titan's endurance.

"Shouldn't we start concentrating fire?" Daussel said anxiously, grabbing the command console as the deck shook again.

"No. We'll spread out our fire as best we can to keep them all a little busy and not let them suspect what we're up to."

"They'd never guess anyway."

"Never say never," Nicholas said frowning. "Especially in a battle like this, you can't say anything with certainty. What about our guys out there?"

"Ten percent casualties so far. Most of them are random enemy hits. There have been a handful of hull collisions, but they haven't resulted in much damage."

*The last Battleship*

"Every pilot gone is a bitter loss," he objected through gritted teeth. Ten more minutes until they were inside the critical distance to the *Hohenzollern*. The enemy Titan was already retreating using its maneuvering thrusters, but so slowly that it wouldn't make much difference. Turning back was not an option for the enemy commander or they would lose half their firepower and jeopardize their launch bays. So, they did just what Nicholas would have done, massed their fire on the *Oberon* and hoped they could destroy them before they crashed into the *Hohenzollern* like a battering ram, because what they were doing had to look like suicide.

"Distance is shrinking," Daussel said. "Five thousand clicks to go."

"Stand by torpedo salvos. Ring pattern, full acceleration!" Nicholas ordered. Torpedoes were long-range weapons, and rightly so because they had to be catapulted far from their launch bays before they could ignite their powerful engines. To do otherwise would cause serious damage to their mother ship's hull. Yet that also left them vulnerable to defensive fire for about twenty seconds after ejection, and that could happen very quickly in close combat.

However, that was exactly what they meant to do.

The gap continued to melt away as the *Oberon* was pelted with railgun bolts and missiles from virtually all sides. The onslaught was so massive that the flak shield only managed a 90 percent interception rate, which meant the hull was flashing with impacts the entire time, and in several places at once.

"Signal Captain Myers," he ordered and then called, "All torpedo bays open fire! Reduce thrust! Initiate turning maneuvers!"

~

Hellcat kept his Barracuda right on the *Oberon*'s nose, wingtip-to-wingtip with Alphastar to his right and Firestarter to his left. They were a small section of the two double circles of fighters strung around the battleship's bow like pale rosettes. When the torpedoes emerged from their forward launch bays, he did not see them through the cockpit window at first because they were too small, but he did see them on the radar. More visible were the tracer projectiles of the *Hohenzollern*'s PDCs being fired from the enemy Titan's tiny bow cannons. They destroyed most of the torpedoes before they could ignite their engines. Those that did shot toward their targets. Some of them smashed into the observation deck's armored doors like flaming fists. Of course, they didn't breach them, it would take a lot more than that.

Another volley followed. Some were intercepted, others hit their target, then came the third wave. As soon as defensive fire began, Hellcat gave the order, *"Now!"*

He disengaged the magnetic retaining bolts from *Oberon*'s hull and let the onboard computer take care of his fighter's attitude before arming the first two missiles.

"Mark 1 and 2, fire!" he shouted and fired his. Together with 400 other guided missiles the rising rings of fighters fired, they raced away and covered the remaining 500 kilometers in thirty seconds. By that time, the *Oberon* had initiated its turning maneuver and her bow was slowly turning down and to the left as if in slow motion.

The *Hohenzollern*'s point defense, busy intercepting the torpedoes, did not switch to the new targets fast enough. A total of 270 missiles found their target, crashed into the armored doors already littered with craters, and tore holes in them. The force field behind them glowed under the individual explosions.

The armored doors of the *Oberon*'s observation deck opened as well, and hundreds of yellow maintenance bots flew from their burrow like a swarm of bees. They arranged themselves into a cloud between the rings of his fighter squadrons so as not to block their field of fire.

"Now it's your turn," he radioed to Devlin Myers on the *Quantum Bitch*, then to his pilots, "Attack!"

∼

Dev deactivated the magnetized retaining bolts on his landing struts, only to find that two of them had already melted. So, he jettisoned the struts entirely and thanked his spacesuit for keeping

*The last Battleship*

his body temperature at a stable 36 degrees Celsius while the air in the cockpit was more than 46 degrees.

He accelerated the *Bitch* to the maximum he thought he and his crew could tolerate, and raced close along the *Oberon*'s dorsal surface, dodging explosions as railgun bolts slammed into the hull, spraying fire and debris. He circled turrets spewing their ammunition at opponents and lifted away when approaching missiles thundered into the abused Titan.

Even out of the corner of the eye, it was obvious the aged battleship's hull had been badly scarred by the bombardment. Deep craters overlapped in places, and soot fields the size of soccer stadiums disfigured entire sections. In several places, flames licked out of holes where conduits had been hit. Escaping air hurled crewmen, furniture, and equipment into the vacuum like a geyser.

But an astonishing number of her guns still fired from the relative protection of their recesses.

When he reached the forward third of the ship and the bow was leaning down to the left, three missiles crashed into an already deep crater in quick succession and breached the Carbin armor directly above a row of railguns. Judging from the secondary explosions that followed, they must have hit a magazine. A hull area of twenty or thirty square meters reared up like plastic blistering from heat, then burst in a cloud of debris and roiling gases.

"Shit!" he cursed and jerked the Bitch to port. The evaporating particle cloud flung her violently to one side. It would have hurled her into a sensor bundle and shredded her to pieces if Dev hadn't been able to steer her away at the last moment.

Then, finally, they passed the bow and shot forward.

The squadrons of Barracudas were already closing the short gap between the Titans. They fired all their guns at the disintegrating armored doors of the *Hohenzollern*'s observation deck and lined up their Vulcan U2 cannons at the inferno to overload and collapse the force field behind the doors.

"The drones!" Aura shouted excitedly.

"I see them," Dev said absently and came in directly behind the close-flying swarm of spherical bots that, like a single creature, immediately accelerated when the *Bitch* rocketed over the bow.

It took the enemy several precious seconds to finally identify them as a threat, but instead of the *Hohenzollern*'s PDCs, which were reaping a bloody harvest among the brave Barracuda pilots, it was the other Exiles' cruisers and frigates that reduced their fire on the *Oberon* and redirected it toward the drones. Controlled from the bridge of their mother ship, the drones quickly arranged themselves into a cocoon that surrounded the *Bitch* like flying ablative armor.

The impacts came in dozens... per second. One drone after another exploded or vaporized under the kinetic energy of railgun bolts or the heat of exploding missiles.

"Fuck, fuck, fuck," Dev shouted and increased acceleration. They had just covered over half the distance to the *Hohenzollern* when he brutally jerked his beloved ship around, mentally excusing himself in the process, and was jerked around in his seat so hard that even the nanonic seatbelts couldn't prevent his left shoulder from popping out of its socket. There was no time to scream because he had to wait for the right moment to start up the engines again, which he had just shut down.

Racing backward, they followed their cocoon of maintenance bots, their numbers dwindling in lurid explosions, toward the glowing, cherry-red force field of the *Hohenzollern*'s observation deck. A violent thud shook the cockpit as if struck by an invisible fist.

"Hit in the stern! Hull breach in the reactor room!" Aura shouted over the din of the yelping alarm.

*"Shit!"* he cursed as he watched the reactor power on his screen rapidly plummet. The pain in his shoulder seemed to increase in exact proportion.

∼

"The *Bitch* has been hit!" Alphastar radioed.

"I see it," Hellcat replied. From his cockpit window, he saw the converted corvette lurching and having difficulty using its maneuvering thrusters to steady its murderously fast flight. If Myers didn't stabilize soon, they would miss their target and crash into the *Hohenzollern*'s hull.

"They're not going to make it."

"No, enemy fire is too dense," he agreed with his wingman, mouth agape. Then he came alive and shouted over the general channel to all Barracudas, "Maintain continuous fire on the force field. Take up position around the *Quantum Bitch*. We need to be her shield now or the *Oberon* won't survive this."

"That's suicide!"

"Yes, but it's the only way." Hellcat jerked the control stick aside to comply with his own order and noted with pride that the remaining 77 pilots followed him without hesitation. "Let's show these bastards! Juratis Unitatis!"

The radio resounded with shouts of Juratis Unitatis! as they abandoned their evasive maneuvers and created a static tube formation around the *Quantum Bitch* as she struggled to stabilize her course. Within seconds, they lost a dozen fighters in a hail of Exile projectiles, then another, forcing them to form up closer and closer as the improvised shield became increasingly smaller.

"It's been an honor," he said, holding down the fire button for his twin Vulcan U2 rapid-fire cannons. The force field, covered by the hundreds of thousands of finger-thick projectiles from his fighters, now glowed darker than a red dwarf at the end of its life cycle and flickered off in several places.

～

"Get rid of the damned thing!" Dev's shriek was almost hysterical.

"But then we can't—" Aura started to object, but he didn't let her finish.

*"Do it, or we'll die!"* he shouted at her, then confirmed the release of the reactor core lock. Moments later, his energy node specialist engaged the ejection mechanism and hurled the reactor out of the hatch below the stern. Less than 50 meters from them, the neutron chamber melted into lava so hot that it was slow to lose heat even in the cold of the vacuum.

Dev sank his hands into the neural cushions of his armrests and plugged into the virtual control network. He used the remaining cold gas supplies to get the *Bitch* stabilized again.

*You motherfuckers,* he thought in rage fueled by shame and horror at the *Oberon*'s fighter pilots who were plunging to their deaths for his survival. *You fucking motherfuckers, you can't do this!*

"Are you crying, boss?" Aura asked in shock.

"Shut up and go with Willy!" he commanded. The engineer had left the cockpit. He had no clue why and he didn't care. All that mattered now was to get through that force field and not crash into the *Hohenzollern* like a bug on a windshield because the sacrifice of those damned men and women would be in vain otherwise.

*Now I'm thinking like those Fleet bastards,* he thought, and directed the maneuvering jets with rapid finger movements to turn their uncontrolled tumble forward at thousands of kilometers per hour into a reasonably stable flight. However, the cold gas supplies were emptying at an unpleasant rate.

Just before they hit, the last remnants of the force field disappeared along with most, if not all, of the Barracudas. He yanked the *Bitch* to the right as hard as all her port-side jets would allow. That impulse cost them their left stub wing, along with their weapons ports, and the ship rotated about her central axis as she crashed like a meteorite into the observation deck seating tiers. There were twenty hull breaches and about twice as many failures of primary and secondary routines as the result of the impacts. The damage ended just short of the entrance door, which was pierced by their aft sensor phalanx like a spear.

As the *Bitch*—or the wreckage she now was—stopped surrounded by smoke and debris pulled into the vacuum of space, he saw a ball of explosions through his window that had to be the *Oberon*.

But he did not think about that. He unbuckled his seatbelt and hurried into the mess hall, knelt in front of the holotable, and transmitted a sequence of short signals via shortwave radio on his secret frequency. A small input panel on the side opened and requested a DNA sample. He removed his glove and pressed his index finger against it. Taking the sample took thirty seconds, enough time to lose his pinky to a nasty frostbite along with any

*The last Battleship*

feeling in his other digits. He barely got the glove back on and groaned in pain.

The *Danube*'s antimatter bomb still lay peacefully in its hiding place. He grabbed it by its front to pull it out, but with only one hand he was only able to move the forty-kilogram monstrosity a few centimeters.

"I'll help you," said a monotone metal voice behind him. Dozer gently pushed him aside to reach into the compartment and take out the bomb like a baby. "You help Willy and Aura."

Dev shook his head. "There's no point. We don't have a reactor, so we don't have a thruster. We're not going anywhere."

"Go to Willy and Aura. I'll finish this."

"What?" he asked, puzzled, but the augment zombie was already rolling toward the newly created aft opening. The wall where the passage to the cargo module had once been was completely wrecked. He could see past frayed steel panels to the top two tiers of the observation deck and the impaled access door from which he heard the thump of boots.

Dozer was incredibly fast and was already turning left past the door before he could call him back.

*"Shit!"* He scrambled to his feet and staggered out of the mess hall. He glanced around and found Willy and Aura fiddling with the two missile bays under the intact right wing. The flaps were open, and cables were hanging out of them. Willy's head was inside one of them and circuit boards and components were pouring out of it.

"What are you doing?" Dev asked in irritation as he heard *Hohenzollern* Marines getting closer.

"Something crazy. You'll love it," Aura replied, plucking the Dunkelheim engineer from the pile of destroyed chairs he had used as a ladder. "Now get out of here!"

∽

Nicholas paid no attention to the fluorescent tubes that had fallen from the ceiling, nor to the flickering red light, or the dust that trickled down from above with every heavy hit and disturbed the hologram.

"Barracuda squadrons ninety-eight percent destroyed!" Feugers reported.

"Hull breaches at sections 1 to 30. Atmospheric losses on decks 2, 3, 5, 6, 8 and 9," Alkad continued the bad news.

"Failure of all port railguns," Lieutenant Bauer added, but Nicholas had seen for himself that one of the central superconductor nodes had been hit, taking a whole series of systems with it. His ship was turning into a flying wreck.

"It has been an honor, sir," Daussel said the words that millions of soldiers in human history had spoken before their demise.

"Not yet." Nicholas insisted grimly and stared at the *Hohenzollern* on his tactical display.

∼

When the containment chamber's magnetic coils shut down in the antimatter bomb Dozer carried as he sprinted through the hail of fire from the Exile Marines, the 50 grams of trapped antimatter reacted with the nearest 50 grams of matter to create an annihilation followed by a flash of bright white light.

The 1.7 trillion kilojoules of pure energy left no trace of the *Hohenzollern* other than a storm of hard gamma radiation that bathed the surrounding space in sheer energetic chaos. The sphere of heat and oscillating neutrinos that followed the mass beta decay of atomic nuclei at the epicenter of this orgy of destruction spread out. Several dozen of the surrounding ships in the Exiles' fleet were swept up in the hurricane of destruction and were either instantly shredded or were cooked by the heat along with their trapped crews.

∼

The scale of the destruction stole the voice of everyone on the bridge of the *Oberon* and showed once again why antimatter weapons had been outlawed in the Federation and never used, even though everyone knew there must have been some hoarded in secret laboratories somewhere.

"We have a contact, Commander!" Lieutenant Alkad was the first to break the silence. She sounded triumphant.

"On screen!" he ordered. He saw the image of a spy probe they had dropped at the jump point, which, unlike the *Oberon*'s sensors, were not immediately burned out by gamma rays because of its distance from the annihilation. He saw the *Quantum Bitch*, if the shot up and dented skeleton of a spaceship, hardly identifiable as such, still deserved the name. She was riding the shock wave. Two exhaust flares glowed beneath its sole remaining wing. "Are those rockets?"

"Looks like it," Daussel sounded dazed.

"Get those people inside and get the medics ready." Nicholas reached for his phone receiver. "Jung, what about the jamming field?"

"It's offline, sir," the communications officer replied into his ear. His voice sounded busy.

"Then put me through on all frequencies."

"There won't be enough power, I'm afraid."

"Then take all weapons systems offline."

"Sir?"

"You heard me."

"You are online, Commander."

The tremors and jolts immediately increased. He had minutes, if that, before the end.

"This is Commander Nicholas Bradley, acting commander of the *Oberon*. Von Borningen is dead and his flagship with him. He prevented you from hearing me before.

"I urge you to end this senseless bloodshed. Your motives for this invasion may be honorable, intended as it was for the liberation of humanity, but the war with the Water People of Warm Depths came to an end over Terra when the aliens spared us. We were here on a diplomatic mission to establish the cornerstones of a lasting peace treaty. The Federation you hate so much is practically no more. Now it's your choice what to do about it. Will you assume the legacy of humanity that oppressed you before and do the same?

Or will you free yourself from it and use your position of strength for genuine acceptance of your beliefs through insight and deliberation? The Water People of Warm Depths were able to see past seventy years of enmity and make contact with us.

"I am sure humans can do the same among ourselves. To do our part, we are willing to go into exile with Omega so as not to stand in the way of human reunification. Decide how you want history to remember you." Although he was repeatedly interrupted by shocks and tossed back and forth, he had no trouble hearing the astonished murmurs from the bridge tiers.

"Bradley out."

# EPILOGUE: THE WARM DEPTHS

The Water People of Warm Depths underwent their birth of intelligent consciousness after a long journey as invertebrate medusae along invisible currents at the bottom of the endless ocean. There, hot vents spewed black gases enriched with a wide range of minerals and trace elements that spread with the currents as a boon to local life. They provided valuable nutrients for deep-sea corals, which even this far down retained a memory of colors.

The only limit imposed on the Water People of Warm Depths was their world, where the water ended in the form of massive, impenetrable cold. Their habitat was enclosed, manageable and fertile, and contained everything they needed. Generation after generation they laid eggs, fertilized them, and reproduced beautifully in the complex currents between the geysers.

Many thousands of sextillions—analogous to a human's thousands of years but based on their six instead humans' ten fingers—had to pass before the Water People of Warm Depths made the greatest leap in their development when the first of them learned to communicate without relying on pheromones. This lifted them above all other denizens of the warm depths, for the currents made all chemical communication enormously difficult, and imposed relentless evolutionary disadvantages.

How the non-material exchange of thoughts first occurred was not part of their collective memory and had faded with history. But

## Epilogue: The Warm Depths

at some point, some form of cognitive emergence must have developed that turned clans of usually no more than two sextillions that competed for breeding grounds and food into a common society of individuals, individuals who recognized their place in the puzzle of the whole and consciously left behind their dualistic boundaries without losing their sense of individuality.

For countless generations, their telepathic gift and ability to share thoughts and memories was an evolutionary advantage. First, this enabled them to protect as many eggs as possible in fertile or protected areas away from predators. Later it allowed them to explore and develop complex relationships. The highly developed moral construct adapted to them was extended by philosophy and mathematics and a science based on shared observations according to the standard of the Water People, who passed their progress from generation to generation.

It was at this time that they drilled their first hole into the top of the world. A beam of light so glaring that it caused members of the people who were too close to flee fearfully into the dark depths shone down into the floodwaters teeming with life and abundance and brought an abrupt end to the age of knowledge. There, where the world stopped at a hard wall, there was something else.

The moment of contact—the Water People did not count in days, having never experienced periodic cycles—with the wise Sky People ushered in an historical epoch as drastic as the emergence of telepathy. The aliens, delicate and peaceful in their habit and nature, proved to be a highly educated, exploratory species. An exchange began between their peoples that lasted many sextillions. Fascinated by the Water People's telepathic gift, the Sky People explored the function of their neural microtubes and were able to use them to establish a connection with the wave network of quantum entanglement and complex thinking organs inherent in every higher-evolved creature. Thus, the Water People of Warm Depths also stimulated a new stage of evolution for the wise Sky People.

The Sky People thanked the Water People with nothing less than the stars. Had it not been for the hole in their sky, it would never have occurred to them that they lived in an ocean under

*Epilogue: The Warm Depths*

several kilometers of ice on a cold moon on the edge of Orion's arm in the Milky Way. Stars! Planets! Moons! A great sea of nothingness, terrifying and fascinating at the same time.

The Sky People opened doors everywhere for them—to wherever the Water People's new dreams and joys of discovery led. In the restless, autonomous workshops in their massive mothership, they produced the first robotic water suits that allowed them to take their habitat with them, leave the water, and wander on planetary surfaces. The Sky People left them the Sky Forge, a factory of wonders with electronic brains full of plans for spaceships and stations, a compass for exploring the Great Nothing through which they ventured, tentatively at first, then ever more boldly.

After the wise Sky People left to take their discovery of telepathy back to their own breeding grounds in the distant Andromeda Nebula, the Water People of Warm Depths had already inhabited two more planets and were learning to survive in space with their new aids.

~

*"You got all that technology from other aliens?"* Jason asked, fascinated, as the last of Mother's thoughts flooded into his mind. Whether it had taken days, weeks, or months, he didn't know, but plenty of time had passed. *So much information!* Fascination was a totally inappropriate word, he realized. No expression was sufficient to *experience* the touching fullness of the entire evolution of a species. Nothing had a comparable force and power to make one kneel humbly before life and its wisdom.

**Yes. The wise Sky People were the impetus for our second great evolutionary leap, similar to your discovery of fire or your capability for cognitive fiction, which could form complex civilizations from clans, as telepathy did for us,** Mother answered.

Her condition was now much worse than when he arrived, and he didn't have any tubes stuck in his stomach. He wasn't bothered by them now, he was too fascinated by the long journey she had taken him on.

*Epilogue: The Warm Depths*

*"They gave you the stars."*

**And for this we still revere them today, after all the millennia of your era.**

*"It's been that long since they left the Milky Way?"*

**Yes. Our people do not develop as fast as yours, if you want to regard technological development as progress.**

*"You are developing much more important things."*

**I can't presume to judge that. But we are always learning as a people, as we did during the first invasion of the Nightmare Elementals.**

*"Over Lagunia,"* Jason thought and shuddered.

**Yes. We managed to discover hyperspace much earlier because we found corresponding files in the Sky Forge that our alien friends had left us. But we were not prepared for the existence of the Nightmare Elementals,** she answered. **Only our near annihilation made us ask ourselves questions about the limits of our telepathic abilities.**

She sent him the image of a hideous monster with black skin and rigid tentacles under a narrow torso. The whole creature looked like the terrifying perversion of a Click yet without translucence—It was only dull and sinister.

*"Wait a minute,"* he thought. *"That's not Species X."*

**Yes, it is. Species X exists only in the mirror world.**

*"This is hyperspace."*

**Yes. Many of us recognized the monsters of our nightmares in the Nightmare Elementals, beings whom we feared greatly.** She paused so that he could realize the full significance of her thoughts. Then she continued. **Species X does not exist, Jason Bradley.** Tentatively, weakly, she moved an outstretched claw to where a human's temple would be. In her large brain behind the translucent skin, the colors wound around each other in fluctuating cyclones. **They are a manifestation of our thoughts that accumulate on a higher dimensional plane of existence and somehow live on. Maybe there they take on a form of expression beyond that quantum space that you have discovered and that fascinates us very much.**

*Epilogue: The Warm Depths*

*"But how did these thoughts come to us and how could they... attack us?"* he asked, confused.

**We do not know that. Our reality assessors believe that it is against nature for our dimensions and those of non-material manifestations to interact, which is why we have prohibited hyperspace gate technology. There were even thoughts of banning transit jumps as a means of interstellar travel, but too many of our breeding grounds would have perished.**

*"I have seen people disappear who were killed by these demons. Where do they go?"*

**We don't know. Theories range from a complete erasure from the space-time fabric as some sort of corrective effect of the universe to a transition to the mirror world because of their thoughts.**

*"Because they believed they were being killed?"*

**Yes. We don't know and our reality assessors won't know anytime soon. But we have discovered one thing: how to stop them.**

*"How?"*

**Because they are Nightmare Elementals, we have intertwined our dreams and resolved them in that way.**

*"Dreams intertwined? Resolved?"* Jason felt like a child reading an encyclopedia for professors.

**Our telepathic connection as a species was not always as unrestricted as it is now. We have come to realize that fears are greatly diminished by a shared openness between individuals. All our thoughts, and especially sensations, have since been shared and are always available. This embedding and the complex mental field of our existence have ensured that we no longer feed the mirror world with new life.**

*"But why should only our fears manifest entities in another dimension?"*

**Perhaps that is not so. We are convinced that there is also a dimension of good manifestations, or perhaps nothing like that exists, and we only retrieve what we think.** Mother moved her head slightly as if it pained her to think about it. **Our**

*Epilogue: The Warm Depths*

**interest in this is no greater than our desire to leave untouched that which nature wishes to withhold from us.**

*"I understand."*

**You brought us plans for a technical telepathy solution. It came from you?**

*"Actually, it comes from a clever engineer and our most powerful AI, the Omega."*

**Our reality assessors have spent the past few weeks—**

He interrupted her. *"Weeks?"*

**Yes. The battle has been won and peace now reigns. Our reality assessors have used this time to combine your approach with our genetic manipulation capabilities and develop a way to give you humans biological, long-term, and heritable access to shared thought space. It will take time, but we hope you can help us with it if you want to take a place alongside us.**

*"I wouldn't miss the next evolutionary step of humanity for anything,"* he thought excitedly. *"You are bringing us a new age, just as the wise Sky People brought one to you."*

**Yes. This prospect makes us joyful and humble at the same time. When you are ready, we can bring you to your people to help them integrate the mind nodes,** Mother suggested.

*"I have another question: If the Nightmare Elementals don't really exist, can we undo their manifestation?"*

**We are not sure, but we think it is possible. It will be worth a try once you are in a protective telepathic bond that no longer... pollutes hyperspace, as we once did as well.**

*"That's good news,"* Jason thought gratefully and closed his eyes.

**Would you do me the honor of witnessing my transition into the next cycle?**

Her question was wide-ranging and surprised him. Emotions attached to it washed over him like a wave, but none of them were burdened by sadness or even regret, and he knew it was much more than a friendly gesture, it was a chance for a deeper understanding, for himself and for humanity, that an end to existence could be regarded in another way.

# EPILOGUE: EXODUS

"If I have to sit through one more reception, I'll shoot myself," Nicholas said, mostly to himself, as he stared out the huge panoramic window of the open observation deck at the sun. Mighty flares shot out, formed ribbons, and flung their deadly beautiful plasma at the canvas of space like cosmic painters who had found a three-dimensional form of expression.

"There were only four," Kiya Alkad said. She was the only one present and she sat nestled against him, her head resting on his shoulder. "The reception on Attila was impressive, you have to admit. I've never experienced anything like it."

"The one on Dunkelheim for the founding of the Coalition of Fringe Worlds was... well, actually, I don't have the words for it."

"Merry?" she suggested.

"It takes getting used to. I felt like I was witnessing a pagan ritual more than a political ceremony, complete with barrels of mead."

"Or were you jealous because the *Quantum Bitch* crew was being honored and not you for a change?" He could almost hear her sly smile.

"That was, frankly, the best part of it."

"What about the reception with Harbingen's new First High Lord? That one was hopeful, at least."

"Yes." Nicholas nodded thoughtfully. "All the pomp was

*Epilogue: Exodus*

disconcerting, yet it was probably the only important meeting besides the big species meeting on Attila."

"A peace treaty between Harbingen and the Exiles, who would have thought?"

"Strictly speaking, we were never at war with each other, and they only showed a willingness to compromise because we're going into exile instead of them. It's like we've switched roles."

"Not quite. We may be withdrawing because we're keeping Omega and the Federation is afraid of it, but there is another difference: we are leaving because we choose to and have long been estranged from the Federation anyway. Some wounds heal best with time, and we've been doing our thing for twenty years."

"We're leaving in friendship. I think that's the most important thing." Again, he nodded. "I'm almost a little wistful now that everything has turned out so well. Peace with the Clicks, political integration and recognition of the Fringe Worlds as such, the creation of a Council of Human Hegemony, and free trade between the Clicks, the Core and Fringe Worlds, and the new Harbingen. Something so unthinkable not long ago that only a brutal war could accomplish it. That's kind of sad.

"Hopefully they'll achieve some good from it after we're gone. I don't want our sacrifices to have been in vain. Silly, Hellcat, Father, and so many others who were friends and family to our comrades."

"Here we are, sitting in the *Oberon*'s observation deck after two months of dry dock, waiting for our colonist fleet of over ten million Harbingers to leave with us for new shores," Kiya summarized, gently taking his hand in hers. "We saved Omega, which, incidentally, helped decide this war, and thanks to Jason we are able to banish Species X and liberate all the core worlds. We owe that to them, those who made the greatest sacrifices. I'm sure they don't want us to drown in survivor's guilt, but instead gratefully accept and enjoy this gift they've given us."

"You're right," he said, smiling away a lone tear that ran down his cheek and left a wet trail. As it dried, he knew instinctively that it was an important tear and would last for a long time. "My mother used to say 'If someone took two pieces of candy from you,

*Epilogue: Exodus*

the best way to make peace is to take one piece of candy from them.' Today, I think I understand what she meant."

"That's wise. I think in our case, everyone has taken enough candy away from everyone to create a balanced starting point that is acceptable to everyone, a basis for building something good together."

"I hope so, too. But it's not our concern now. How liberating."

"What about the reception on Terra?" Kiya changed the subject. "You didn't complain about *that* one."

She tugged at the ostentatious medal on his chest.

"If I hadn't been allowed to give my speech on the fallen and on peace, I would have killed myself with that thing," he laughed, then shuddered as he thought of the thousands of soldiers, civilians, and journalists, all the cameras in the great hall of the Fleet under the Himalayas. The thunderous applause still rang in his ears, even though it was nearly a month since he had stood there on stage.

"What about Jason? You're going to miss him, aren't you?"

"Yes, but it will be a good feeling. He's found his place among the stars. What more can you wish your brother?"

**"Captain,"** Omega's voice came over the speakers.

"Yes?" Nicholas and Kiya intuitively lifted their eyes toward the ceiling high above them, knowing full well that the AI's voice wasn't coming from there at all.

**"The fleet is ready to depart. Carcassonne has given permission for departure and Admiral Rosenberg sends his warmest greetings. He has asked for a 'postcard.'"**

Nicholas grinned.

"Thank you, Omega. Have you set our destination?"

**"Yes. I have analyzed all the star charts from the Federation databases, and the best location for our jump to Andromeda is at—"**

"Wait," he interrupted the AI, raising a hand, "If you've calculated the appropriate conjunction zones at the edge of the Milky Way and Andromeda galaxies, then you already know where we're going to come out, right?"

**"That's right. I was just going to give you—"**

*Epilogue: Exodus*

"No. I just want to know one thing about our destination: is it nice there?"

**"By any human standard, yes."**

"Good. As for the rest, let's be surprised. Not making plans for once will be almost like a vacation." He looked at Kiya, who nodded with a smile and pressed a gentle kiss to his lips.

# EPILOGUE: FREEDOM

"It looks good," Dev said as they stood on the observation deck of the Rotterdam Spaceport in orbit around Ruhr, looking through the large panoramic window and down on bay A23-B. Willy, Aura, and Jezzy simultaneously turned their gazes from the completely renovated *Quantum Bitch* and looked at him.

"What was that?" Aura asked first.

"Well, at least it isn't complete *shit*," he said.

"I was beginning to think you had a brain injury," she chortled.

"Did you just laugh?"

"No, I would never do that."

"Maybe the time has finally come when we don't have to swear or argue anymore," Willy said in good humor. All of them looked at the husky Dunkelheimer before they all burst out in derisive laughter.

Willy raised his hands defensively. "Okay, okay. Little joke."

"Here comes Dozer!" Jezzy said excitedly, extending her right index finger, which left a grease mark on the armored glass.

Dev saw it, too, the brand-new orbital shuttle with "Dozer" painted on it. They watched as four shipyard drones that looked like moths with folded wings, attached the shuttle under the cargo bay. It was not the newest model, but one of the best available under the current circumstances, he had no doubt.

Fleet leadership had been extremely generous, especially after he

*Epilogue: Freedom*

had answered Legutke's question about the reward he and his crew desired in front of running cameras after their personal reception and their award of the highest civilian order the Federation and Fleet could bestow on them. "We want to have our *Bitch* back in shape, a clean slate, and some spending money."

The media had interpreted that as modesty, even though any bit of space technology was currently priceless while rebuilding a rudimentary interstellar network. The name of his ship also went viral, and his request for a clean slate was seen as something like a romanticized case of honor among thieves.

They were living in a crazy universe, that much was certain.

"So, what do we do now?" Aura asked and put an arm around his shoulders. He hesitated for a moment and did the same to her and Willy next to him until they were standing in a row, shoulder to shoulder.

"I don't know, but every remaining world pretty much needs everything from everywhere. If that doesn't turn up some good smuggling routes, I don't know what to do," he replied.

"We could try legal trade," Willy said in a rumbling voice.

Silence fell again for a moment before they chuckled.

Jezzy rolled her eyes. "You really ate a clown's breakfast today."

"I don't give a shit what we do as long as you're with me and I don't lose anyone else." Dev nodded slowly as if verifying his own words. "I love you guys, you know that."

"We love you, too," Willy said.

"When you're not trying to kill us," Aura said with a grin.

"Then you should stop busting my balls." he laughed and patted them on the back. "Now come on, we have, once again, a refurbished ship to fly out of dock."

"Where do you want to go first?" Jezzy asked.

"I don't care, but we're not going with the *Oberon*, so don't get any ideas. Trouble sticks to her like shit."

"They practically single-handedly saved humanity."

"That's what I'm saying."

"How about Augustshire? Now that we have cloaked jump gates, it only takes a few days to fly there," Aura suggested. "We've never been there before."

*Epilogue: Freedom*

"Or we can pick up the mind nodes on Attila first, then we won't need a transit alarm and can go through hyper."

"We'll just do both," Dev decided. He couldn't wait to get back into the cockpit.

"We also have another invitation from King Gustav to Dunkelheim—"

"Which we will by no means accept."

"He's promised us as much Dunkel beer as we can load," Willy pointed out.

"I couldn't drink enough of it to be senseless enough to set foot on your home planet again."

"Off-worlders," the engineer snorted.

"Besides, it's good to have another outstanding favor. The list is pretty long already."

"Why do I get the feeling we'll all have to cash these in very soon?" Aura asked.

"Because you know your family well," Dev said with a grin. "So, off to new adventures, and don't you dare put another scratch on the *Bitch*!"

# AFTERWORD

Dear Reader,

So, this is the end of the *Oberon*'s journey. I haven't had this much fun writing in a long time, and I hope you had just as much fun reading this volume. If you liked it, I would be very happy if you could give it a star rating at the end of this e-book or write a short review on Amazon. That's the best way to help authors like me keep writing exciting books in the future. If you want to get in touch with me directly, you can do that. Just write to: Joshua@joshuatcalvert.com—I answer every email!

If you subscribe to my newsletter, I'll regularly tell you a bit about myself and my writing and discuss the great themes of science fiction. Plus, as a thank you, you'll receive my e-book *Rift: The Transition* exclusively and for free: www.joshuatcalvert.com.

Warm regards,
  *Joshua T. Calvert*

Printed in Great Britain
by Amazon